Beatrice Aird O'Hanlon has a (BA Mod) fr(in French and Classical Civilization. She trair in 1976 and has worked in clinical researc years. Beatrice self-published a novel several y(*Coolavella*.

Beatrice is a true francophile and she and her husband spend long summers in the Vienne where they have a farmhouse in a quiet hamlet. Beatrice lives in Delgany, Co. Wicklow with her husband Michael and their Burmese and Siamese cats. This is her second novel.

CROSS CURRENTS

BEATRICE AIRD O'HANLON

Published by the author in 2013
using SilverWood Books Empowered Publishing®

SilverWood Books
30 Queen Charlotte Street, Bristol, BS1 4HJ
www.silverwoodbooks.co.uk

Copyright © Beatrice Aird O'Hanlon 2013

The right of Beatrice Aird O'Hanlon to be identified as the author of this work
has been asserted by her in accordance with the Copyright,
Designs and Patents Act 1988.

All rights reserved. No part of this publication may be reproduced,
stored in a retrieval system, or transmitted in any form or by any means,
electronic, mechanical, photocopying, recording or otherwise,
without prior permission of the copyright holder.

This is a work of fiction. Names, characters, places and incidents either are products of
the author's imagination or are used fictitiously. Any resemblance to actual events or
locales or persons, living or dead, is entirely coincidental.

ISBN 978-1-78132-091-4 (paperback)
ISBN 978-1-78132-092-1 (ebook)

British Library Cataloguing in Publication Data
A CIP catalogue record for this book is available from the British Library

Set in Sabon by SilverWood Books
Printed on responsibly sourced paper

This book is dedicated to all those who strive to make this world a better place for all living creatures, human kind and animals, through their dedication, hard work, integrity and compassion

Chapter 1

In the oncology ward on the second floor of the Dublin City Hospital, Nurse Rose-Ellen Power stood by Dr Pierre O'Hegarty as he examined a patient. She wondered why the young woman languishing in the bed in front of her had not responded to any of the therapies he had prescribed: the latest combinations of chemotherapy, clinical trials with silver bullet drugs, radiation. He had told her that the cancer had spread too far when the patient had come to see him with the initial symptoms.

She noticed the patient's tiny fragile chest struggling to expand as she gasped for air, and her tired eyes had that faraway stare as if her spirit had already departed her body. Interlaced through her bony fingers curled a set of ruby-red rosary beads and beside her lay a well marked missal with holy pictures falling out from between its parchment leaves. Tiny pearls of sweat settled on her forehead. Rose-Ellen wondered about the young woman and feared that her future would be short and bleak. She thought of the haphazard way nature's dice can fall on those least deserving, like this young mother. Rose-Ellen observed Pierre's concern for the patient and the tender and sensitive way he spoke to her as he sat on the bed and examined her.

'Dr O'Hegarty, will you write up more sedation for her?' a nurse whispered at his side. He left the bedside to prescribe a drug that would ease the woman's suffering and make her parting from this life less painful.

Rose-Ellen had heard that Pierre was held in high esteem in the hospital and noticed the respect afforded to him by the nurses. She hoped that she would be able to live up to his expectations and that her work as a clinical research nurse would contribute to alleviate the suffering of patients with cancer, such as this young woman.

They walked back to the office together. Rose-Ellen had only started in her new role as research nurse a week ago and already she had myriads of questions, but Pierre seemed preoccupied with the endless demands made on his own time.

'Is there no hope at all for that young woman?' she asked as they descended the stairs to the ground floor.

'Unfortunately, we have tried everything and some cancers have a sinister way of creeping up without any specific symptoms, so by the time we saw her, it was too late,' he said. She detected a slight twinge of regret in his voice.

'It is important that patients come to the clinic in time, and then we can select the appropriate trial for them. Sometimes going into a clinical trial is the only way patients have access to the latest drugs so it is imperative that we attract the major players in the pharmaceutical industry, and get involved in trials with the latest therapies.'

He spoke confidently and enthusiastically about the various research programs he had in the pipeline and continued to discuss the latest drugs and strategies in combating cancer as they walked down the long spiral stairs. When they had reached the bottom he turned to her and said, 'Now you can see why clinical research is crucial in the area of oncology.'

'Absolutely,' she mumbled.

As they walked back along the corridor to the office, Rose-Ellen could barely keep up with him. Pierre walked on down the corridor with a purposeful air, while Rose-Ellen kept pace with him. When they arrived at the office, he pushed open the door and made his way through Rose-Ellen's office to his own at the back. He sat down and lifted the phone. She felt drained from listening to him and wondered if her life from now on would be spent keeping up with his sharp, zappy mind as she tried to retain all the information he had fired at her.

They both shared an office on the ground floor of the hospital, a drab functional room wide enough for two parked cars, divided in two by a glass door. On the wall over Rose-Ellen's desk were two large shelves which groaned from the weight of research protocols and heavy medical text books, which had been gathering dust over time. Any free space was taken up with files and documents.

After about half an hour, she was about to broach the issue of discussing her role as research nurse with Pierre, but balked as his phone rang again.

His mobile phone went off several times and at one stage he walked round the office and seemed to be trying to allay somebody's fears; probably a relative of somebody who was gravely ill. After about an hour all seemed to be quiet, and Rose-Ellen got up to knock on the door to his office when a young lady doctor poked her head round the main door.

Rose-Ellen turned to face her. 'Can I help you?'

'I want to have a word with Dr O'Hegarty about a patient on the third floor,' the young doctor said with a look of concern.

'Sure! Go in through the door. He's free at the moment, but for how long is anybody's guess!'

'Thanks.' She smiled gratefully and made her way into Pierre's office.

Rose-Ellen wondered if she would be happy working so close to Pierre with all of the activity that seemed to pivot around him. He was at the beck and call of doctors and patients alike. She had drawn up a long list of questions, and while she could find some answers on the internet there was nothing like the hand of experience. After a while the young doctor made her way out and Pierre stuck his head into Rose-Ellen's office.

'Oh, I'm sorry, I realise that we must sit down and have a serious chat about your role and responsibilities here at some stage,' he said.

'What about now?' she asked.

Then his mobile went off. After about ten minutes, when he had finished the conversation, he snapped it shut. 'Sorry about that. It's been just one of those days. Good idea, no time like the present! I just need to write up a report on a patient from the clinic and then I'll be with you,' he said, moving some files aside.

But time dragged on and Rose-Ellen wondered if he had forgotten her. She looked into his office and caught his gaze from behind his fine gold-rimmed glasses. She decided that now was a good time. 'Pierre, are you free now for our chat?'

'Sounds good to me,' he said moving a bundle of files over to one side on his desk. 'If you bring your chair in here we can discuss the trials that are up and running, and those not quite ready,' he said.

Rose-Ellen got herself a cup of coffee and put the milk back in the small fridge near the main door, then carried her chair into Pierre's office. She sat down opposite him with some protocols on her knee and opened up her notebook.

'Now, about the department here. I select the various clinical trials and research projects deciding what we can undertake. This depends on many things such as funding, suitability of patients and whether we are in a position to take on the work,' he said.

'So there would be slack periods and hectic ones, depending on what trials are going on, right?' she asked.

'Correct. Shay McAdam, the Registrar, as well as tending to the regular patients in the hospital, looks after the clinical trial patients, takes their consents, does the physical examination etcetera. However, the overall responsibility for all trials lies with me, and please don't be afraid to ask me anything at any time. Clarity is very important in the world of clinical research; there is no room for any ambiguity.'

Pierre then got up, stepping over a pile of research periodicals on the floor, to fetch some documents out of the large green filing cabinet in Rose-Ellen's office. She looked round his office and then let her gaze follow him next door. She thought that it seemed bare and ugly, and wondered if a few pictures might liven up the dull taupe-coloured wall. As he flicked through the various files in the cabinet in her adjoining office, he continued to speak to her.

'As research co-ordinator, you will mainly be concerned with the management of the clinical trials, preparing the protocols for submission to the various authorities, entering the data and seeing the patients at their trial visits, but of course the overall welfare of the patients will be under my care, and that of Dr McAdam.'

She noticed how his beige cords hugged his finely honed figure, and a soft beige jumper lay nonchalantly around his shoulders giving him a strangely boyish demeanour.

'Don't worry, I'll offer you as much support as possible. I'm concerned to not only ensure that the trials are set up in a timely manner, but also anxious that you're content in your new role,' he said, returning and standing in front of her. She noticed how tall he was with that almost military bearing which some men possess.

'So how many clinical trials are awaiting review by the Ethics Committee in the hospital at present?' Rose-Ellen asked flicking through the pages of her notebook.

'At the moment four clinical trials have just been approved by the

Ethics Committee, so these are the ones I want you to concentrate on. They are mainly in the area of breast and ovarian cancer using different pharmaceutical agents. Four others are awaiting approval. I'll get the post-doc student to go over everything with you. However, the breast cancer trial is of paramount importance and this will need to be submitted to the Ethics Committee next week. Remember the deadline for submission is the last Thursday of every month,' he said, sitting down opposite her.

She realised that she had about four days to prepare the submission for this long and difficult trial, and for a brief moment panic seized her.

'Look, in order for me to do the submission in this short space of time, I am going to have to clear out the office. I am sorry, Pierre, but I simply cannot work in chaos.'

'What do you mean chaos?' he asked.

'I'm going to have to shred and discard stuff wherever necessary. I presume that you're OK with this?' she asked casting her eye into her own office.

Rose-Ellen had spent most of her first week wading through bundles of clinical trial protocols. Stacks of old journals and periodicals had been allowed to accumulate to dizzying heights and scattered sheets settled wherever they had fallen. She had started to organise the room and make some changes.

'Of course I understand, but please check with me first. I'm afraid that I'm a bit of a magpie; par for the course really as a researcher, one tends to hoard. I also like to have medical papers at my disposal for reference. No doubt some day I'll organise a small library for these research papers, but until such time they will remain here,' he said, emitting a sigh.

She got up and went through the door to her office, picked up a letter at random from the shelf and examined it. 'Take this letter here. It's nearly five years old,' she said, glancing at the date. She looked at him and he did not appear to understand her frustrations. 'I'm sorry, but I simply can't work in chaos.'

'Before you chuck anything out, please consult with me!'

'Don't worry, anything important, I'll check with you,' she said reassuringly.

'I admit things have been allowed get a little out of hand here. I've just, well, been very busy.'

'I understand.'

'Don't worry. It'll get sorted out in time. Now, any more questions?' he asked.

'Yes, just a few. I am wondering what phases these trials are at. I just want to organise my time over the next few weeks,' she said.

'Of course. Most of them are in Phase 3 stage, assessing safety and efficacy of the drugs over two years. We do however have one short Phase 2 trial involving only about fifty patients. It is quite an intense clinical trial, and of course the patients will be sicker, so that will be time-consuming. Finally, we have one Phase 4 trial which is post-marketing surveillance mainly looking at safety. That won't be too difficult or taxing, but we can go over each one at a later date and in more depth.'

'Sure. There's a lot happening at the moment,' she said, folding her arms and staring at the stack of protocols in front of her.

'Indeed, and every month more clinical trials will need to be submitted to the Ethics Committee for their review and approval. You will be completely responsible for the Ethics Committee submission of all clinical trials in the department. Is that understood?'

'And what would happen if for some reason we miss the breast cancer trial submission for this month?' she asked nervously.

'I trust that won't happen,' he said with a smile.

Then his mobile rang. After a few moments he spoke. 'I thought that she would last another few days until her husband came to see her with the children. That's a shame. I'll be up shortly,' he said, moving around the office. Rose-Ellen got up and went to her office and started to arrange the documents on her desk into bundles.

Pierre snapped shut his mobile and said to nobody in particular, 'It's sad when a young woman dies leaving a family. Something I'll never get used to. I'm just heading up to the second floor to pronounce death on the young mother we saw today.'

Rose-Ellen remembered the patient. 'How old was she?'

'Twenty-eight, and leaves three children all under the age of seven.'

She felt a lump in her throat as she could not imagine what her own life would be like without her mother. She wondered how those poor little mites would fare without the loving tender hand of a mother to guide them through their hazardous journey into adulthood. At twenty-five years of age, Rose-Ellen imagined herself in a few years time becoming a mother too, with all the protective instincts that it entailed and now pondered on how bereft this family would be.

Pierre grabbed his stethoscope and left the office. Rose-Ellen did not envy him as he made his way out and wondered how he coped with such crises on a daily basis. He would have the task of breaking the news to a heartbroken husband and father. She wondered how people like Pierre remained calm and professional while at the same time were probably affected by such sadness. She was determined to give of her best in her new role and to support him as much as possible.

Chapter 2

Rose-Ellen loved nothing more than working alongside her father in the family emporium in the town of Loughbow, in County Wexford, about two hours from Dublin. 'Power's Finest Emporium' was an established delicatessen and grocery business, purveyors of fine food and wines, and had been in the family since 1885. Rose-Ellen liked to get away from Dublin every other weekend and spend it in County Wexford with her family and her boyfriend, farmer, Danny Redmond. Maurice and Kitty Power were proud of their two daughters, Rose-Ellen and Olivia. Rose-Ellen, the elder, could turn heads with her grace and charm.

'You're a natural beauty, like the pear blossoms out yonder, fragile yet strong,' her father remarked to her one cold day, looking out at the enormous pear tree in their garden, its clumps of white frothy petals withstanding the buffeting wind. He loved to think back to the time when she was a little girl with an abandoned gaiety, her winsome smile charming all whom she met.

'Now, beauty is no good without a touch of sparkle. Your independent spirit might seem intransigent to some, but that's the way with us Powers. We never compromise on matters of importance,' he had said resolutely. But she knew only too well that she had inherited the wilful spirit of her father's family. Why her aunt, Dotty Power, was still arguing with the council after all these years over a bramble choked lane at the back of her house was beyond comprehension.

One Saturday morning shortly after starting her new job at Dublin City Hospital, or DCH as most people referred to it, at the end of July, Rose-Ellen was helping her father in the shop. Only recently having returned from America and living in Dublin, she still liked to go home most weekends. Rose-Ellen was arranging Kitty Power's home-made jams for labelling when a commotion started up outside. Curious to find out what was happening she went to the door and saw her boyfriend, Danny Redmond, arguing with somebody in the street. Danny had parked his tractor outside the shop causing a line of cars to build up, their exasperated drivers impatient to move on. Typical! she thought. She could hear him now, roaring at a man honking his horn.

'I'm not movin' and that's that!'

Rose-Ellen made a hasty retreat inside. Her father was delicately removing the paper from a round of perfectly matured Irish blue cheese. 'What's going on? There's no peace on a Saturday. I don't know where all these cars come from at all,' he murmured.

'It's Danny, he's holding up everything with that tractor!' she said.

She remembered the first time Danny talked to her about the huge machine with its massive tyres carrying enormous bales of hay. She had been impressed as he told her that each bale weighed nearly one thousand pounds.

Suddenly with a loud curse, Danny burst through the front door of the emporium. Peeping through the rows of jams, Rose-Ellen watched him as he greeted her father.

'Mornin', Mr Power, how are ye?'

'Oh hello, Danny,' her father said, looking furtively in his daughter's direction.

Making his way over to her, Danny whispered, 'Listen, love, I'd better not stay long. Will I see ye tonight? Maybe we'd go for somethin' to eat in that new fancy place in Wexford? I was passin' so I thought I'd drop by.'

Without looking at him, she said casually, 'What was all the commotion about outside?'

'Ah, nothin' really. Just some eejit who has no tolerance for farmers or their ways.'

'Which means blocking up the whole street!' but he was not listening to her.

'Well, what do you say? Tonight at half-seven? Look I'd better go,' cause I think that fecker has called the guards.'

Picking bits of grass from his collar, she gave him a quick kiss on the cheek.

'You'd better go. Pick me up at seven-thirty. But not in the tractor!'

He left to face the mayhem outside. She looked at her father who stood there with a slightly bemused expression and said, 'You know, Dad, sometimes I feel that Danny and his brothers think that they're immune to the laws of the country.'

'Well, he's thought highly of around here, despite his ways. It's the likes of Danny that has stood up to these bloody moguls in the EU for the rights of Irish farmers. They would be nowhere today only for farmers like him. You couldn't find a more decent man. You can come across plenty of glib talkers, but usually there's nothing to them, like some of those politicians who never achieve anything; only looking after themselves,' her father said.

The Redmonds were farmers who lived in a large solid farmhouse below the Blackstairs Mountains, surrounded by hay barns, machinery and a state-of-the-art milking parlour for Danny's three hundred dairy cows in County Wexford. Danny and Rose-Ellen had known each other since they could barely reach a cow's udder and had attended the same school. Rose-Ellen had always fancied Danny in a light-hearted way but there was never anybody else for Danny, only the beauty from out by Loughbow. He told Rose-Ellen that he had fallen in love with her the day he saw her playing camogie for Loughbow at an inter-county match, and he knew that she was the one for him.

Maurice Power was delighted that Rose-Ellen and Danny Redmond were an item. Two old Wexford families would soon be joined together. There was nothing that his sharp merchant mind would welcome more. 'Now, my pet, don't be cross with Danny. It's just his way; he's his own man.'

'I know, Dad, but everywhere he goes there's commotion.'

He came over and placed his hands firmly on her shoulders. 'I'm pleased that you're going out with him. Did you know that the Redmonds and the Powers are two of the oldest families here in the south-east? Their ancestors sailed up the Suir with Henry the second in 1171 to hunt out that traitor Richard Fitzgilbert de Claire, better known as "Strongbow". And according to the ancient annals, the king was accompanied by a knight by the name of de Paor when he knocked on the gates of Waterford city resplendent in green and red with ermine, his golden sword glittering out of his fur-lined scabbard.'

Her father's blue eyes lit up excitedly as he recalled this little gem from history. 'Now you can't get older than that. I know he's not that sophisticated and you've got used to some smart men, but he's down-to-earth and sensible and well, he's the best in the world and I'd be very happy to see both of you together,' he said proudly, moving away to savour the excellently matured odour from the famous blue cheese as it rested regally on a silver plate.

Rose-Ellen knew how her father loved to be part of an older order, associated with the history of chieftains and kings, but at times she found his meanderings into the family tree a trifle boring and irrelevant.

'Dad will you stop pairing us off. We're only going out,' she said exasperatedly. But in her father's mind, she and Danny would make the perfect couple. Still, she had missed Danny when she was away – his spontaneous charm and easy laid-back style. Although not as cultured as some of the men whom she had met abroad, he was a down-to-earth, solid, no-frills type of man. Like many women, who think that they can fine-tune a man's ways, Rose-Ellen was hoping that she could do this with Danny.

That evening Rose-Ellen put on her finest dress – a silver shimmering, body-hugging one which she had recently bought. At seven pm sharp, she heard the sound of a large honk and looked out.

'Jesus, Mary and Joseph! What is that?'

Her father came over to the window. 'It's a bailer. An awful dangerous looking thing too.'

Danny jumped down and came to the door. He was dressed in a brown suit. Rose-Ellen opened the front door and looked out at the huge machine parked outside on the driveway.

'Danny, if you think I'm getting up on that yoke in this dress to go to dinner then you have another thing coming.'

'Look! I don't have the car. Conor was supposed to come back from the races with the car and he's got delayed. I'll park the bailer away from the main street in Wexford and we can walk the rest of the way.'

'What! Are you joking? No way am I getting in to that! The smell alone is enough I can get it from here. I dread to think what it would be like inside the bailer. Why didn't you get a taxi?'

Her father who had retreated back to watch the TV heard the commotion at the door and came out. 'Hello, Danny.'

'Evenin', Mr Power. I hope that the weather stays good.'

'Indeed. So you're going into Wexford?'

'Not in that,' Rose-Ellen said sharply.

'Don't worry, I'll give you both a lift to Wexford, and you can leave the bailer here and get a taxi back. Now how's that?'

'I don't want to put you to any trouble now, Mr Power. It was just one of those days when all the cars are gone and I didn't want to keep herself waiting,' Danny said, winking sideways at Rose-Ellen.

'No problem, I'll get my coat,' her father said, retreating to the hall.

Rose-Ellen sat in the front of the car while her father drove, and said nothing. Danny had booked a table at the flashiest restaurant in Wexford. Rose-Ellen noticed the fake zebra covered seats in the cocktail lounge where they waited while their orders were taken, and the golden banisters leading upstairs to the dining room, adorned with huge red and gold Chinese vases. Mouthwatering smells of charcoal suffused the air and whetted her appetite. Most of the men turned casually to steal a sneaky glance at Rose-Ellen as the waiter escorted them to their table. Danny pulled out the turquoise button-backed velvet chair for Rose-Ellen who took off her jacket and laid it on the back.

She glanced round the dining room which buzzed with weekend *bonhomie*, the chatter and clinking of glasses enhancing the lively atmosphere of the place. This was where one wanted to be seen in Wexford. The owner was a slick business type who had recently returned from the building trade in London. The rich decor, bordering on vulgar, smacked of someone with lots of cash and little taste.

Halfway through the main course, Danny put down his knife and fork and leaned back on his chair. Casting his eye around the restaurant he waved to somebody a few tables away, took a drink of wine and cleared his throat.

'So tell us about the new job.'

She put down her knife and fork. 'Well, it's a research job and involves understanding the whole concept of clinical trials, cancer ones mainly. It's demanding, requiring certain skills: meticulous attention to detail, understanding how trials are run, dealing with the corporate world and of course caring for patients. My boss is a Dr Pierre O'Hegarty and he seems nice, but doesn't say much. They say he is a brilliant doctor in the hospital and that's all I can say for the moment. Well, it's early days. I've only been there a couple of weeks.'

'Sounds very interesting. Ah, I'd say ye'd be well able for it though. Now I've been thinkin', Rose, I mean about you and me.'

'Go on,' she said matter-of-factly, as if he had suggested some sort of business plan. 'Well, I seen this ring, and I think it'd suit you. It's a beauty, not too flashy, just lovely, just like you pet, and a good, decent carat too.'

She wondered what Danny Redmond knew about carats, other than the huge field of carrots growing in the field beyond his house and eyed him suspiciously. 'Danny, what would you know of diamonds and their quality?'

His drooped head almost hit the plate. He was dismayed. Looking up, he fixed her with a stare.

'You don't give me credit for anythin'. Didn't I spend ages in Lacy's jewellers discussin' diamonds and rings a few months ago?' He glanced down at his plate, and moved his hand nervously across his fair hair swept neatly back from his shiny round face. This was a gesture she had come to recognise, and indicated to her that he was uncertain and tense.

Rose-Ellen reached out across the table and squeezed his hand. 'Danny, I'm sorry. I didn't mean to question you. Well, it's just that this is so…so unexpected.'

But he seemed to have lost his nerve. Rose-Ellen sensed a sudden tense atmosphere between them, but she was curious to find out more.

He called the waiter. 'We have a little celebration; can I see the wine list again, please?' The waiter bowed.

Rose-Ellen was impatient. 'Ah, love. I'm dying to see the ring.'

'Calm down, all in good time.'

Danny carefully perused the wine list. 'Let's see. Somethin' special to celebrate this auspicious occasion, our engagement,' he said, articulating every word.

He looked up at the waiter, 'A bottle of *Taittinger* please.'

'*Taittinger*, sir, is very expensive. Perhaps I could suggest –'

'No! *Taittinger* it is and that's it,' he said, handing back the wine list.

Rose-Ellen wondered how Danny knew about good champagne. 'You've learnt a thing or two from the horse racing over the years, even if you never made anything on the gee gees!'

'Oh, it's not only the races that I learnt about the good things of life, Rose-Ellen,' he said, wiping his lips with his napkin.

Rose-Ellen looked down at her plate where some grilled salmon and a small, rather lonely looking cherry tomato stared back up at her. In the last few minutes she had lost her appetite and was embarrassed now at her impatience, like a child wanting what was not hers yet.

He reached out and touched her hand. 'Sure, darlin', I'd do anything for ye, you know that,' and taking her hand, he lifted it to his cheek.

The waiter returned with the champagne in a cooling bucket. He turned the bottle several times before removing it from its nest of ice, and with great aplomb, but with a barely audible 'pop', opened it. Rose-Ellen delighted in watching the pale straw-coloured liquid with its winking bubbles and shimmering highlights fill her glass, topped with its frothy layer. She had inherited a taste for the finer things in life from her father, as Mr Power liked to think of them both as true Epicureans.

By the time the desserts arrived, Rose-Ellen was light-headed and satiated and left most of her big, boozy apricot and Armagnac soufflé.

As they got up to leave, Danny helped her on with her jacket. 'I'll show you the ring back at your place,' he whispered.

They took a taxi to Rose-Ellen's home, *Uisce Gaire* – Laughing Water, named after the sound of the stream that flowed through the reeds at the back of the house. It stood near an old medieval cemetery overlooking the Slaney River. *Uisce Gaire* was over a hundred and fifty years old, a fine solid building covered in ivy, with a gnarled, pale lavender wisteria hanging languidly over the front door. Danny's bailer had taken up the entire front of the drive way. Her parents were in bed as it was after midnight.

Rose-Ellen made a pot of tea and brought it to him on a tray in the drawing room. Danny was silent. Sometimes, after a few drinks and without the company of his friends, he withdrew into himself. Rose-Ellen sipped her tea. She got up, pulled back the curtains and looked out at the garden where all was quiet. A nail of moon swung in the sky, still bright enough to sprinkle a dapple of moonlight, which filtered through the tall Scots pines and monkey puzzle.

Laying the cup back on the saucer, Danny hauled himself up from the low chair. His huge frame bent down and Rose-Ellen watched as he carefully lifted her left foot and tenderly removed her silver sandal. He then produced a dark blue velvet box from his jacket pocket in which lay the most beautiful ring, and placed it on her fourth toe.

Rose-Ellen sat back on the sofa and was amazed at the sparkle of the ring, an exquisite, marmalade-coloured marquise diamond. She reached down to touch it as it glittered in the glow of the dimmed lamp. The stone dazzled with its mixture of brown, burnt orange and canary yellow and, due to its shape and cut, caught the light continuously. Its beauty captivated her. 'Oh God, Danny, it's fabulous! I can see so many colours: yellow, brown and orange, and they all seem to change like a rainbow!' She got up and threw her arms around him, kissing him.

'Here, let me put it on your finger,' he said. Bending down, he removed the ring, and slid it on to her elegant fourth finger. 'Now, there. It matches your colouring.'

She held her hand at all angles towards the light to enhance the ring's sparkle. 'I can't wait to show everybody. Oh my beautiful, bold ring!'

'Ah, no little delicate solitaries for you, my pet. No, no. I decided on gettin' the best and the boldest. Now, pet, I must be off. It's been a long night, so the next thing is to set the day and I'll leave that to you.'

Her expression changed. 'Danny, we've all the time in the world for wedding plans.'

He watched her moving around the floor, dancing and humming gently to herself, her ring finger held aloft. She was like a wild thing, giggling to herself. He pulled her to him. 'I love ye, Rose, I always will, you're part and parcel of me. I feel it here inside,' he said, touching his chest.

'We go back a long way, Danny, you and I, and you've always been there for me, even when I was far away, and that means a lot.'

'Indeed we do. I still have all your letters you sent me when you were away trainin' in London and then Boston. Indeed yes. I learnt a lot from those letters –' He sat down again. 'The long hours of night duty, the wonders of medical research and this I've never forgotten.' He looked down at his folded hands on his lap. 'The night you had to lay out the body of a dead child after a fire.' He fell silent. 'I've kept those letters all these years.'

She sat down beside him. 'Yes, it all seems such a long time ago, and yet, it is not even five years, if even that. How time flies. You know I had this urge to travel after qualifying as a nurse in London, and knew that if I didn't I would regret it all my life. Oh, while life was hard nursing people and doing those odd shifts in hospitals aren't easy, I'm glad I travelled and saw a bit of the world.'

He took her hand in his and kissed it. 'I missed you so much during those years when you were away in those big cities in England and America. I used to wonder if you were all right and whether you were happy. Sometimes I had this urge to get on a plane and go and see you, such was the loneliness I felt for you. But then when you came back last year, well I just had to ask you to marry me now, 'cause surely to God, you would be snapped up. I'll make you the happiest woman alive. I've wanted you from the first time I saw you play on the camogie team many moons ago.'

She put her hand through his hair and kissed him on the forehead. 'Danny, I'm honoured to be asked to be your wife.' But she felt light-headed and giggly and got up. 'Oh, it must be the champagne, I feel so giddy.'

He hauled his big frame from the soft sofa. 'OK, my pet, I must be off. I can't keep the taxi man out there any longer.'

Clutching Danny's hand, she reached up and kissed him once more. 'Thank you so much, love. This probably sounds ridiculous, but when I look at this fabulous ring it reminds me of those sunsets I saw in Africa; the way the light changes so quickly, it's hard to describe, something magical…' she murmured, her voice trailing off.

Danny gave her a great big bear hug and retreated into the cold night air.

Chapter 3

Rose-Ellen's friend Siobhan Matthews worked as a theatre nurse in the endoscopy unit at the DCH. They had trained together in London. Siobhan had chosen an eight-to-four job so that her evenings were free to spend with her lover of many years, a happily married bank manager, who was quite content to tag her along with all sorts of romantic talk and plans for their future.

'I think you should ditch him,' Rose-Ellen said to her over lunch in the hospital canteen in a fit of anger at how feckless her friend appeared to be. 'You never look to the future or plan for the day he'll dump you. All you seem to care about is the here and now. Some day you will be old and tired and will have nothing to show for all this gallivanting.'

Rose-Ellen chided her friend, as she recalled the hours Siobhan spent on dolling herself up, preparing the most exotic meals for their romantic weekends together.

'His children will soon be teenagers and the weekends will become fewer and fewer. Don't be a fool Siobhan! You deserve better!'

'What! And end up with the likes of Danny Redmond. Never! Every one knows that you could do so much better than that *culchie*.'

'Well at least he's available and I'm number one in Danny's eyes.' Now she had touched a raw nerve with Siobhan.

'True, but there's plenty of time.'

'But it won't last forever. Don't be so naive Siobhan.'

They say that the truth always hurts and so Siobhan inevitably changed the subject rather than face up to the state of her romantic life, a silly dalliance with a married man by which she held such store.

'So how are things in the research department?'

'I feel under constant pressure of being the research clinical trial co-ordinator, having to do everything, manage and run the clinical trials, as well as see to patients, take all of the bloods and get bogged down with Ethics Committee bureaucracy as well.'

But Siobhan showed little sympathy. 'Now, isn't that the job you applied for! The alternative is being up on the wards and listening to all the moaning and groaning and doing night duty and the rest of the bullshit you'd have to put up with. Did you speak to Pierre about your workload, or is it too early yet?'

'Sometimes I feel very isolated down there in that office on my own; it's kind of creepy at times. I miss the company. In the States we had a huge research department in the hospital in Boston, but here it's like as if I'm a mouse tucked away in my little dark room.'

'I wouldn't carry on like that as it will be expected all the time, and you'll get no thanks for that kind of loyalty. Cop on to yourself, girl. So, how do you like working with Dr O'H? I gather he's not given much to small talk.'

Rose-Ellen wiped her lips with her paper napkin. 'Some say in the hospital that Pierre is aloof and tends to keep to himself, but others praise him for his fine brain, calm nature in a crisis and discerning judgement. He's the sort who would prefer not to waste time and energy on superfluous banter, even though at times his reserve makes me feel uneasy. I never know what he's thinking. He says only what he has to. Sometimes we can spend hours working together saying little. You know, Siobhan there are times when I feel the urge to poke my head inside his door and break the silence, and just say something, anything at all. Other times I want to scream and jolt him out of his silent world of clinical trial abstracts and statistics.'

'I hear he's a bit of a shite to the junior doctors. In fact some of them can't stand him! Oh, they tell us things because they know it won't leave the theatre.'

'I'm sure that things will improve once I'm more organised.'

'That's always the way when you start a new job; taking over from whoever's gone before you, and the mess they've left. Now don't complain. Wouldn't it be worse if he were always wanting you to be at his beck and call. It's not easy dealing with the terminally ill and old Doolan gives him no help at all'.

'I gather he's only waiting to retire.'

'He's been retiring for years. The bloody fellow should go and let somebody young and dynamic take over and help Pierre. Then you wouldn't have to be saddled with a lot of his work.'

'I'm very fond of Dr Doolan, he's a real pet, one of the old school,' Rose-Ellen said, crumpling up her sandwich paper into a ball.

'So! I'd prefer someone who was a bit of a gobshite and got the work done instead of a smooth charmer who did feck all. He only became a consultant because somebody died years ago and they couldn't fill the position.'

'Still, he's not the worst.'

'I get the picture. So tell us, what's new down in Wexford?'

'Oh, since I've got engaged life's been hectic; people inviting me out all the time to look at the ring, wish us the very best. I suppose it's a type of curiosity.'

'Still, an engagement is a great talking point. A new life together, and they mean well.'

'I suppose so.'

'And tell us how are you getting along with the future in-laws?'

'So far so good, but it's early days yet. I can't see my parents ever becoming bosom pals with the Redmonds; just different types.'

'To be perfectly honest, Rose-Ellen, I never thought you'd end up with Danny, just seems a bit odd. I don't know, don't get me wrong, I'm sure you love him, but he's…well, he's not exactly sophisticated or refined,' Siobhan said, putting down her knife and fork carefully on her plate.

Rose-Ellen knew what her friend was hinting at. 'He's uncomplicated and in a strange way too I find him funny and natural. I suppose that's his life. The simple way of the land and his animals; constant, and at least then you know where you stand.'

'God, I thrive on the unpredictable!' Siobhan said, nodding to somebody at another table.

Rose-Ellen sensed her friend's misgivings, but still she had to show loyalty towards her future husband. 'Ah, it'll work out with time; it's amazing how a woman can influence a man.'

But Siobhan stared out the window and Rose-Ellen felt that in that look there were many unsaid thoughts.

Chapter 4

A meeting on the Cytu AB trial for ovarian cancer was scheduled to take place in Vienna at the end of September shortly after the trial had been approved by the Ethics Committee in the hospital. By accompanying Pierre to the meeting, Rose-Ellen would miss the Annual Ploughing Championships which was to take place outside Enniscorthy. Danny was very disappointed that she would miss the most important day in the farming calendar.

'Mammy and Mairead wanted you to give them a hand with their stall. Ah, ye know, helpin' with the jams and the honey and stuff like that,' his tone betraying the disappointment he felt. The Redmond ladies, Josie and her only daughter, Mairead, had run a successful stall for years at the Ploughing Championships.

'I'm so sorry, love. I'd love to be there, but you know how these meetings always seem to clash with something else,' Rose-Ellen said, feeling a trifle disingenuous, as there was nothing that she would dread more than being at the beck and call of Josie Redmond and that bossy daughter of hers.

'I feel terribly let down, that's all,' and he hung his head. After all, they had recently become engaged and Danny was very proud of his beautiful fiancée and wanted her to accompany him to the most important meeting of the year in the farming calendar. 'Could ye not have arranged this bloody meetin' for another time? Ye know the Ploughin' Championships is the highlight of the year!' Danny exclaimed exasperatedly.

Rose-Ellen was seated in the Redmond kitchen. Danny, dressed in his dungarees, cleaned his greasy hands with a dirty rag, his fair curls tumbling down his face. He really did not understand anything outside of farming; it was his whole life.

'Look, love, it's a terrible pity that this meeting has clashed with the

Ploughing Championships and you know I'd give anything to be there with you, but I have to go to Vienna and that's all there is to it. These meetings are always held after the summer recess, that's just the way it is.'

He beamed a broad smile and stole an arm around her narrow waist. 'I suppose so. It'll only be like this for another few years anyway, 'cause when we've the house built and are together, that'll be that! No more feckin' meetings away, just the two of us and you can concentrate on things local.'

Whilst Rose-Ellen preferred solitude, Danny was gregarious and sociable as well as being a great sportsman. He had won several Wexford County Championship medals in hurling in the famous Wexford colours, yellow and purple. Rose-Ellen got up to fetch her mobile from her coat pocket in the hall. On her way back to the kitchen she noticed all the silver cups proudly displayed on the sideboard in the midst of Josie's heirlooms.

'A lot of silver, Danny.'

'And I hope to add another cup to that by winnin' at the ploughin'.'

Danny was grinning at her now. She shied away from his gaze and noticed his mother cleaning with what looked like an old pair of knickers. Nothing would surprise her about Josie Redmond, who had caught the strange expression on Rose-Ellen's face. Josie looked down at the cloth she vigorously moved over the floral plastic table cover removing stains and breadcrumbs.

'Purcell's! The best of cotton; couldn't be bothered to tell ye the truth with all those fancy cleaning cloths not strong enough for the chores I need to do around here,' she muttered as she moved away and started to furiously shine the kitchen sink and draining boards with the article of clothing that had seen better days.

Rose-Ellen glanced out the window at Mr Johnnie Redmond, Danny's father, easing himself into the car towing a trailer full of sheep with the sly, beady-eyed Mattie panting in the front seat. The sheepdog had no paw, act or part in rounding up this lot of sheep for the mart. Poor Mattie had no earthly idea how to herd sheep despite having had endless training with whistles, sticks, food and finally deprivation, but it had made no difference whatsoever. To Mattie sheep were for frightening and rustling rather than herding. He would be more inclined to make off with one of Josie's prize pullets or take a bite at a passing leg. Rose-Ellen felt a sudden frisson as she thought of the earthiness of farming and how tied she would be once the fine bungalow was built on one of the Redmond's fields.

She recalled her father's words to her soon after the engagement: 'Look, darling, he's a fine catch, is Danny Redmond, one of the biggest farmers around for miles and a good man too; hurler extraordinaire, and sure you're not getting any younger. In a few year's time you'll be approaching Becher's Brook.'

Her mother was horrified. 'Maurice, leave the girl be! Let her make up her own mind. She's a smart girl and no man's fool.'

Shortly after their engagement, Danny and Rose-Ellen went down to the local pub for a drink before going bowling. They went in Rose-Ellen's car because Danny would only start drinking and they would end up having to get a taxi if they had taken his. Inside, Danny's friends Declan and Christy were waiting for them.

'I promised I'd meet them. We won't stay long,' he said reassuringly to her. But she knew better. Once Danny set foot inside the pub there would be no moving him.

'Hello, Rose-Ellen,' Christy greeted her.

'Hi, Christy,' Rose-Ellen smiled at him as he offered her his seat. Danny went to the bar to order the drinks.

'I hear you won't be at the Ploughing Championships. Himself says you don't care for that sort of thing any more,' Christy said, taking a long gulp from his pint.

'Oh, I quite enjoy them, but I can't go unfortunately this time due to work.' Rose-Ellen wondered what Danny had been saying to Christy.

'Let's see the ring then for luck,' Declan said, glancing down at her hand. She held her finger up for them to admire the ring and out of the corner of her eye she spied Danny coming down with the drinks; a gin and tonic for her and a pint for him. He sat beside her and they all raised their glasses to the newly-engaged couple.

Rose-Ellen turned to Danny. 'Danny, I never said that I didn't want to go to the Ploughing Championships. You know that's not true. I can't go because of work.'

'Relax, Rose, just relax.'

'No I won't. That's what you told Christy.'

'Well if ye really wanted to go with me you'd have cancelled that trip to Prague or wherever the hell it was.'

'Vienna. I can't and that's it. But why did you make up that story to Christy about me not wanting to go to the Ploughing Championships?'

Danny leaned forward and said to the two lads who were staring at them now with a slightly bewildered air. 'Listen to this. We're only just engaged and already she's accusing me of lyin'.' He turned to her. 'Woman, what'll ye be like after a few years?'

Rose-Ellen got up and took her bag. 'Right. That's it. You can go ahead with your bowling tonight because I'm going home.' She headed for the door.

A man at the bar turned around to see what the commotion was. Danny brushed by him and followed Rose-Ellen out to her car. He caught up with her just as she pulled open the car door and he closed it just as quick.

'Listen, I was only blackguardin' in there with the lads. Sure ye know I wouldn't tell a lie about you, Rose. Christy is inclined to let his imagination run away with him.'

She was seething with rage as she glared at him. 'He's not the only one whose imagination runs wild. Listen here to me, Danny Redmond. Let's get something straight. If I marry you, you'll promise me that you will not attribute things to me that aren't true. Is that clear? I can't be going around the place defending myself against whatever it is your imagination conjures up.'

'I'm sorry, love. It won't happen again, I promise. Now will you come back in and have a drink? Let's celebrate our engagement and then we'll go bowling.'

She went back into the pub and was determined more than ever to enjoy herself in Vienna and not let Danny's interests interfere with hers.

Rose-Ellen could have had anybody in the county, and it just seemed the right thing to get engaged at the time, like most of her friends. She had mulled over the idea of marriage to Danny and at times the prospect chilled her to the bone. He would look after her, was reliable and trustworthy and would make a good husband. Above all he loved her, loved her completely and unconditionally. But sometimes her misgivings would not go away easily and often they hounded her, so much so that she became distracted.

Chapter 5

It was the end of September when Rose-Ellen and Pierre spent a week preparing for the three- day conference in Vienna hosted by IQI Pharma Corporation, a large US pharmaceutical company, which was launching the Cytu AB trial for the treatment of ovarian cancer. They finalised last minute documentation and organised coverage of duties at DCH. They notified patients and put clinic appointments on hold except for any emergencies, which would be dealt with by Dr Doolan .Sitting in the departure lounge at Dublin airport waiting to board the flight to Vienna for the conference, Rose-Ellen cast her eye around while saying abstractedly to Pierre, 'Are we the only ones going out at this time? There are no more flights to Vienna today and the conference dinner is tonight.' She noticed how much more relaxed Pierre appeared to be in his leather jacket and open-necked shirt.

He examined his boarding card and then glanced up at the screen. 'Well, there are five investigators in Ireland for this trial and I expect that they'll be on this flight with their co-ordinators. Oh, did I mention that Shay will join us too? He's coming later via Frankfurt.'

Rose-Ellen thought of Shay McAdam, Pierre's research Registrar and the few brief encounters she had had with him. Pierre cast his eye around and spied Dr Sam Casey making his way towards them and waved at him. 'Hi, Sam!'

'Ah hello, Pierre. I was wondering if you'd be on this flight,' Sam said, placing his bag on a vacant chair and sitting beside Pierre, who turned to introduce Rose-Ellen.

'This is Rose-Ellen Power, research nurse at DCH.'

Sam smiled and reached out a welcoming hand to Rose-Ellen, who then listened quietly as they both caught up on news.

They were soon joined by other attendees including two from the

Eastern Infirmary on the other side of the city. Pierre introduced them as Dr Dennis Dunne and Aine Kelly. Rose-Ellen knew that Dennis and Pierre were rivals, having worked together in Canada.

Aine sat down beside Rose-Ellen. 'Hi, I suppose I'm your counterpart at the Eastern.'

'Hi, Aine,' Rose-Ellen said, putting her briefcase on the floor.

'Have you ever been to Vienna?' Aine asked as she fumbled in her briefcase. 'I believe it's beautiful. I'm sure we'll be taken on a tour of the city.' Rose-Ellen had not even considered touring as part of the itinerary.

'Oh, that would be wonderful,' Rose-Ellen said. 'There's such a lot to get through at these meetings, but it would be a shame if we couldn't get a glimpse of such a beautiful city away from learning about blood sample timings, eligibility criteria and safety reporting.'

On the flight out Rose-Ellen sat beside Aine, but said little during the flight as Aine discussed the various trials they were undertaking, how frantic their unit was and how she had not a spare minute between investigator meetings, research presentations in the hospital and co-ordinating clinical trials.

The dinner on the first night in Vienna was a convivial affair and afterwards Rose-Ellen had a chance to chat casually to Pierre in the bar. She noticed that his cold politeness mellowed after a few drinks. He leaned back in his chair and twirled his liquor in the glass as Rose-Ellen talked about growing up in Loughbow. 'It must have been a wonderful experience to have grown up surrounded by such fantastic grub when such things weren't that commonplace in Ireland.'

'My Dad loves his food more than anything else. We'd all be in fits watching him tasting some perfectly mature cheese or smelling his adored prize hams. Mam used to say he handled them like newborn babies.'

Pierre smiled at her. 'Sounds like a wonderful man whose priorities are right,' he said.

'So why nursing and not the food business if that was in the family? Did you always have a caring streak in you?'

'Yes, ever since I got a first aid kit from my auntie one Christmas when I was a little girl. I don't know why, but I spent my time bandaging everyone and everything: injured crows, badgers caught in snares and the odd hen with a broken wing.'

As Rose-Ellen painted a picture of her childhood in rural Ireland, Pierre appeared to be taken with the happy, carefree time she was describing – a child's world, full of innocence and spontaneous gaiety. Gradually his guarded expression gave way to something softer.

'You've a big heart, Rose-Ellen. I mean it. I've seen the way you deal with the sick and the vulnerable; lots of patience and kindness.' She blushed as people rarely commented on these characteristics.

At times throughout the conference, Rose-Ellen's mind wandered from the pie charts, statistical analyses and bar graphs to Danny and the Ploughing Championships. For long periods while sitting in at the various presentations and meetings she found it difficult to concentrate and wondered how much was pure 'research' and how much was simply marketing. Pharmaceutical company representatives spoke buoyantly and confidently about the superiority of Cytu AB over all of the other tried and tested drugs on the market, at times basing their arguments on what seemed to be the flimsiest of statistical analyses.

On the second day there was a round table discussion on Cytu AB for delegates from various countries and it was chaired by Myra Stephenson, Project Manager for the Cytu AB clinical trial from IQI Pharma Corp in the US. Myra was responsible for co-ordinating the trial globally. The patients would be selected in the various hospitals from different countries. Research nurses, such as Rose-Ellen, were responsible for co-ordinating the trial at their particular centre.

Myra tried to reassure everyone at the table that the trial was not as difficult as it appeared initially. 'These patients are out there, but you really must find them,' she said, in her strident, American tones.

'We know they're out there, but do we have the time and facilities to identify them? That's the dilemma. We're so overwhelmed with huge clinics and massive underfunding that undertaking research over and above our daily clinical work will be the big challenge,' Dr Roisin Broderick said matter-of-factly to the self-assured American.

'Employ a dedicated specialist nurse. One who is familiar with the disease and who will assiduously look through your database and identify suitable patients for this trial. It's worth it, given the high percentage of patients who'll have a recurrence of their disease at some point in time,'

Pierre said confidently. They all turned their attention to him as he continued, 'Also, most ovarian cancer patients present with disease that has already metastasized and the yearly mortality is reckoned to be in the order of sixty-five per cent of the incidence rate, so the onus is on us to try and help these patients as best we can.'

Dennis Dunne from the Eastern Infirmary eyeballed Pierre. 'We can't justify the full-time efforts of someone doing a database trawl for these patients. Be realistic!'

'I tell you it can be done. Be optimistic. Think broadly. The patients are there and could well and truly benefit from this trial. It's a life and death situation so it's important to search for them. As physicians we owe it to them,' Pierre said calmly and deliberately.

'I don't think it's that easy,' Dunne said with exasperation.

There was a hushed silence in the room.

'OK, OK, we get the message. Just see how you get on after the first few patients are enrolled and we can maybe fund a part-time research nurse. But first, let's get a few patients rolling in. OK everybody?' Myra's decisive voice boomed around the table.

That evening Danny phoned Rose-Ellen at the hotel just as she was getting ready to leave for the gala dinner, which was to take place in a glittering hotel adjoining one of the famous palaces of Marie-Theresa off the Ring Boulevard which circles Vienna. His familiar voice at the other end was a welcome change from the confident, smooth patter of the pharmaceutical types. 'Well, how's it goin'? Are ye enjoying yourself in Vienna?'

He hummed a few bars from the Blue Danube Waltz.

'Vienna is wonderful and so much more beautiful than I expected,' she said. She remembered the Ploughing Championships and asked, 'How was the ploughing today?'

'Ah, great, great. Ireland won again. A fellow from down Urlingford way beat the big German on the stubble reversible.'

Rose-Ellen presumed that this had something to do with the straightness of the line furrowed by the plough but decided not to ask for fear of getting a complete lecture on the joys and pitfalls of ploughing backwards.

'Ah, ye missed a great event!' Danny continued. 'Massive. The best ever with TDs, politicians and some celebrities too. And ye know what?

Mammy and Mairead's stall went down mighty well! Sold out they were of everything! And with plenty of orders for more too!'

Rose-Ellen could visualise the two Redmond women mobbed at their stall by marauding gangs of cushion-loving, home-spun earthy types clamouring for the last of the Redmond jars of jam, which disappeared like sacks of rice from a convoy relief truck in famine-stricken lands.

'And you? Did you see any new tractors you fancied?'

'No, no, nothin' in the tractor line, but I seen a fabulous new bailer. Jesus, mighty it was too.' He sounded as if the Grand National jackpot had eluded him by a noseband.

Then there was silence. Rose-Ellen had run out of conversation. She simply could not share his enthusiasm for farm machinery.

He continued, 'But I miss you. Surely do. It wasn't the same, I mean, without you.'

'Ah, love. I know. I'll make it up to you at the weekend. Sorry, Danny, but I must dash – we're off tonight to the gala dinner and the bus is waiting downstairs.'

'Oh, God, don't be late! Well, enjoy the night and see you at the weekend.'

Rose-Ellen grabbed her stole, dashed out the door and went down to the waiting bus. She was the last to arrive and got the only seat available beside Dr Shay McAdam.

'Well, how's it going?' he said, as he looked out at the magnificent St. Stephen's Cathedral in Vienna built in 1147 with its gigantic Gothic tower.

'There's a lot to take in initially but so far so good,' Rose-Ellen said, as she settled herself into the comfortable seat.

'I've been to so many of these types of meetings. Follow the protocol and these trials are all the bloody same,' he said languidly. She turned to him and wondered how he could appear so miserable in such a beautiful city.

'I reckon the same PhDs write up the studies and send them around the world with a few changes, variations on a theme,' he said wearily as he folded his arms in front of him – a gesture she felt reflected how disenchanted he had probably become with conducting clinical trials. She wondered what he meant by this remark, as each protocol was designed for a specific compound by different companies and research organisations. In the end she felt that the comment reflected an inner smugness.

She looked outside and noticed the modern Haas House opposite St. Stephen's Cathedral. She did not particularly want to get embroiled in discussing clinical research with McAdam on this whistle-stop tour of Vienna before the gala dinner.

'It's amazing how the glass facade reflects the beauty of the cathedral and opens it up.'

'I believe it was, and some say still is one of the most disputed buildings in Vienna,' he vouched knowledgeably.

She turned to admire the beautiful River Danube with its needle-like tower in the distance. The Danube Island was electric with bars and shops and restaurants, giving the place a characteristic Caribbean air.

McAdam's small, pinched, mottled face, stub nose and sandy hair, together with his slightly rounded shoulders, reminded her of a hyena. Shay McAdam was both sexy and repellent. His neat hands with perfectly groomed fingernails rested on his lap. A bad sign in a man, according to her father, indicating someone who was inclined to laxity and arrogance. A most unsavoury combination.

The bus journey took them through some of the most beautiful parts of this glittering city heaving with grand buildings and statues in Baroque and Rococo styles, which in their day outshone Versailles in magnificence and grandeur. As the bus briefly stopped outside the Burgtheatre, Rose-Ellen caught glimpses of the statuesque marble figures of Goethe and Schiller. 'I could spend weeks here in this glorious city just walking around, taking in the architecture. It's so, so beautiful,' she murmured.

Ignoring Rose-Ellen's various comments on the wonders of this great European city, as well as deliberately talking during the guide's brief introduction on the sites, McAdam boasted to her about the various trials he was involved in, as well as the grants he had received from large multi-national corporations to carry out his own research projects. Pierre believed that everyone on his team should be allowed to develop their skills and ideas in a research setting. He was unusual in this sphere as many consultants preferred to retain the grants for their own pet projects. He also realised that obtaining research grants and their funding was largely dependant on the number of articles published in scientific journals. Without publications, the chances of obtaining a grant were virtually nil.

The world of clinical research was cutthroat and Shay McAdam, like most co-investigators, was anxious to have his name acknowledged in as many research projects as possible for career building purposes.

Finally, having toured the famous Ring Boulevard, which circles the city built during the reign of the Emperor Franz Joseph in 1857, the bus came to a halt and parked outside the State Opera House, Wiener Staatsoper. This wonderful Renaissance building, which attracts the best artists and performers from all over the world, stood majestically in front of them, and Rose-Ellen found it so captivating that she took a photo of it on her mobile. She quickly gathered her things and scampered off in her high-heeled sling-back sandals, following the others across the busy street to the hotel, anxious to get away from the arrogant McAdam.

Once inside, she waved at Aine who was wearing a chocolate-coloured linen outfit that had probably cost a small fortune, but simply made her look prim and old maidish. Rose-Ellen chatted with the other research nurses and then she noticed Pierre. He was leaning against a pillar in the stately courtyard of the building talking to another delegate and smiled over at her. Rose-Ellen caught Pierre's attractive French accent as she daintily crossed the marble floor to approach them. She could barely discern what they were saying but snatched brief snippets of the pros and cons of high dose chemotherapy.

The other oncologist, whom she had met earlier at a poster meeting, greeted her politely then discreetly made his excuses to mingle amongst the delegates.

'I see you had the pleasure of getting to know Shay a bit better,' Pierre remarked.

'Yes, he's certainly proud of everything he's doing,' she said, sounding a tad insincere, even to herself.

'He's exceptionally clever, a quick thinker and very decisive,' Pierre said. Rose-Ellen was not sure whether to believe him or not, but then he added wryly, 'At least he thinks he is.'

They soon moved inside to the dining hall. Rose-Ellen was aware of Pierre's guiding touch at her elbow. Feeling hot under the bright chandelier, she slipped off her stole.

'Remember, if there's anything you don't understand, please ask me. It's a difficult therapeutic area,' he whispered.

There were research teams from seven other countries; delegates mingling and catching up on the latest research projects and Pierre and Rose-Ellen parted as they each looked for their place names at the various tables. Rose-Ellen found herself placed between Dennis Dunne and Shay McAdam at dinner. They were seated under a splendid domed ceiling painted in opulent yellow and gold and twinkling with magnificent chandeliers. A small quartet played Viennese waltzes and mazurkas gently in the background and the waiters, dressed in period attire, moved stiffly and formally between guests. As one waiter approached her with a plate of tenderly cooked slices of beef, he courteously bowed to her. She could not help but admire his outfit. He wore a scarlet and black waistcoat with gold buttons, white stockings and the daintiest black and white spat shoes. He smiled at her and moved to serve McAdam on her left. Briefly she imaged herself waltzing with this young handsome man under the glittering lights, but then Dennis Dunne's smooth patter to her right took her out of the brief reverie and reminded her of the present.

'I hear things are busy enough at DCH,' Dunne said casually, leaning back in his chair and glancing over at McAdam.

'Can't complain. Got to keep the pharma giants happy,' McAdam said, dicing the meat on his plate into tiny pieces with his fork which he held like a pencil.

'So how many trials are you involved in now? Last time we met I think it was nearly ten, which is a hell of a lot.' Dunne drank some wine and continued. 'Jesus, that wine's bloody great. But come to think of it, O'Hegarty was always quietly ambitious.'

'Fifteen, including some difficult investigational trials which I'm heading up.'

Dennis Dunne let out a short sharp whistle. 'Christ, that's a lot! These investigational trials I presume are Pierre's babies?'

'Now, why does Mr Nice Guy always get the kudos for anything that happens in clinical research in oncology in DCH? Damn it, these trials are mine!' McAdam said coldly.

'I'm impressed. I didn't imagine that you were the pioneering type.' Dunne smiled malevolently at McAdam.

'Lay off, Dunne! They're my own concepts for which I've received funding. You know fuck all about me.'

'I know enough to recognise a bullshitter when I meet one. DCH has come a long way from when I was a junior there,' Dunne said cynically.

'And you're still only an effing Registrar.'

Dunne was very sensitive about the fact that despite being the same age as Pierre, he had not made it to consultant level.

Rose-Ellen felt the atmosphere around these two positively toxic and tried to reduce the tension. Turning to Dennis Dunne, she remarked, 'So do you think that you'll be able to get plenty of patients for the Cytu AB trial?' Rose-Ellen felt slighted by his vapid and curt reply and despite the beautiful surrounds wished she could be anywhere else but between these two vipers.

The tender succulent beef and its delicious Béarnaise sauce were wasted on her and she left most of it. She longed for the evening to finish so that she could wander around this magnificent hotel. After the dessert, McAdam got up from the table.

'Time for a breath of fresh air, a smoke and a change of scene,' he said, glancing maliciously at Dennis Dunne and strode outside.

Sam leaned across the table to Rose-Ellen. 'Everything OK? You look deathly pale.'

'Yes, fine, thank you, but I think I'll go to the ladies' room and then take a walk around this building.'

'Good idea.'

Sam got up and came round and gently pulled Rose-Ellen's chair out from behind her. She stood and immediately felt as if the ground were coming up to meet her. Panic seized her as she fumbled in her bag for her handkerchief. The room began to sway. She realised that she should not have drunk those two schnapps. Tomorrow she would have the mother of all hangovers. Then a series of hiccups seized her. She took a quick gulp of water and some deep breaths but they continued relentlessly. Her only concern now was how to get to the ladies in one piece. As Rose-Ellen left the room, Myra Stephenson lifted her glass to her lips and sent her a dart of disapproval through narrowed eyes.

Chapter 6

When she returned from the conference, Rose-Ellen was overwhelmed with work. To add to her woes, Ms Horne, the Director of Nursing, wanted to see her urgently.

Rose-Ellen thought that the name Horne suited her: cold, hard and unyielding, like an old shoe horn. Seated in her office Ms Horne sized up Rose-Ellen, who was dressed in a smart, well-cut navy trouser suit. 'Ms Power, I believe in being frank with people. In these tenuous times, research jobs as yours are not secure. Many of these positions come with only a yearly contract basis and, worse still, they don't provide for a pension.'

Rose-Ellen listened to Ms Horne and thought that her life must have been mapped out and as predictable as a Swiss railway timetable. She looked at the woman sitting opposite her imagining that she went through life armed and buttressed with insurance policies, pensions, indemnities against all calamities and with a good, secure government job. She resented that smug, self-satisfied look the Ms Hornes of this world manifested. Glancing down she noticed the small number of flimsy sheets of paper perched neatly on the Director of Nursing's tidy desk and remembered the mounds of paperwork and files in the research department which awaited her, with no help from a clerical assistant or girl Friday.

Ms Horne did not waste any time in coming to the point. 'Nurse Power, we're very short-staffed in many of the major wards in the hospital and you are highly qualified, so I would appreciate some help. I was wondering if you might take on the role of night sister relief around the hospital for the odd weekend, or help out in ICU during the week. Of course you would get the time back in lieu. It would mean also that you would be on the hospital's pay roll, rather than relying for your income solely on the funding for research from the pharmaceutical giants.'

For a brief moment Rose-Ellen thought she was going deaf, so bizarre appeared this request. She cleared her throat. 'Ms Horne, I was employed solely to work for Dr O'Hegarty. That is what my contract states. There is no mention in it of me working outside of normal hours for the hospital. I'm very sorry and I appreciate how understaffed you are, but I really think that this is a most unusual and inappropriate request.'

Ms Horne fiddled with her pieces of paper while she thought out her next move. She clasped her hands neatly together, placing her chin firmly on them and looked sternly at Rose-Ellen. 'Nurse Power, I have to run a tight ship in this hospital. I see someone like you working five days a week, nine-to-five, no nights and no unsociable evening shifts, whilst we have others doing one week in six on night duty. So I don't think that it's too much to expect that you, as a nurse, share the burden of patient care.'

Rose-Ellen chose her words carefully. 'But you are not comparing like with like and I do work late in the evening as I don't have anyone to help me with administrative tasks. I'm the only person in the research department and my terms of contract have already been agreed with Dr O'Hegarty. As I said, I am employed solely as a research nurse.'

Ms Horne fixed Rose-Ellen with a piercing gaze. 'Dr O'Hegarty. Ha! Well, Dr O'Hegarty will take orders from me when it comes to my nurses' duties for patient care in this hospital. Is that understood? I'll have a word with him and we can sort something out, but you must take your share of burden in this hospital like everybody else.'

'No, I'm sorry but it doesn't work like that. You see, as I've said, I have nothing to do with you and your rosters.' She stopped to allow her words sink in. 'I work directly for Dr O'Hegarty and the research department.'

Ms Horne seemed shocked at this reaction. 'I have never encountered such forthright insolence and insubordination in my life.' Her ample bosom heaved with indignation.

Rose-Ellen got up and stormed down the corridor and banged the door of her office after her. She marched into Pierre's office. She was seething following her encounter with the Director of Nursing. 'Excuse me, Pierre, but I was wondering if I could speak with you about something that's cropped up.'

He looked up from the patient's chart he was reviewing and pulled a chair over for her. 'Of course. What's up?'

She told him about her meeting with Ms Horne. 'Maybe you could have a word with her, if you don't mind. She is an impossible woman and is determined to get me up on to a ward by hook or by crook. I really couldn't bear the prospect. I get the impression that she resents me and will do anything to make life as difficult as possible for me.'

His expression changed. 'That's possible. It's also the case that she doesn't understand what you are doing and so has no control over you. The Hornes of this world like to be in control. But don't beat yourself up over it. Leave this to me. This is preposterous! What that woman expects and gets are very different matters. Don't worry. I'll have a word with her,' he said reassuringly.

When Pierre had gone, Rose-Ellen wondered what would happen to her. She could not bear the idea of going back to the wards. It simply did not interest her any more.

Chapter 7

Pierre was involved in several other clinical projects as well as undertaking his own research work in the specialised scientific laboratory in DCH. IQI Pharma Corp was becoming increasingly anxious regarding the recruitment of patients to the Cytu AB trial globally. So management at IQ Pharma Corp. organised a last minute meeting in November in London to resolve any difficulties and to attempt to boost recruitment of patients to the trial amongst the European centres. As DCH had enrolled the greatest number of patients to the trial to date, Pierre was invited to give a presentation on his recruitment strategies. With twenty-six patients enrolled in three months, he was way ahead of the European investigators.

Neither Pierre nor Rose-Ellen could afford to be away from their hospital duties in the run-up to Christmas but they had little choice.

'It'll be just another PR exercise – nothing new, I'm afraid,' Pierre said tiredly one Thursday evening as he sat down to tackle the myriad of research papers and correspondence awaiting his review. Rose-Ellen looked at him and wondered where he got his vast reserves of energy; nothing seemed to faze him. With his fierce work ethic and fathomless memory, he could quote from papers written years ago, statistics and trial results tripped off his lips like general conversation and his knowledge of medicine was as prodigious as any text book.

On the following Tuesday morning, Pierre and Rose-Ellen flew from a packed Dublin airport to London City and took a cab to the Hilton Docklands. The biting wind almost seared their faces as they climbed from the cab and entered the hotel's glass fronted entrance. After a quick strong coffee they moved to the designated suite in the hotel, and within three quarters of an hour Pierre took centre-stage and stood in front of the vast audience providing an in-depth presentation on the various recruitment drives and strategies that he and Rose-Ellen had undertaken to enrol suitable patients to the Cytu AB trial. He elaborated painstakingly on all of the avenues they had explored to identify and recruit these patients with ovarian cancer, who were eligible for inclusion in the trial. Rose-Ellen sat in the back row, watching and admiring Pierre.

It was a long day and they still had to fly back to Dublin that evening. At six o'clock Pierre and Rose-Ellen were sitting in the airport lounge when Rose-Ellen glancing at the screen discovered that their flight was delayed. She looked at Pierre and pointed to the screen. He read the information, sighed and got up. He was restless.

Rose-Ellen watched him as he made his way back to the duty free shops. An elderly lady passed him and dropped her stick. She was burdened with various bags and a large heavy coat. Pierre stopped and picked up her stick and offered to help her with her baggage. Her face lit up immediately and she smiled and chatted to him. She soon linked him and he sat her down and bought her a coffee. No wonder he rarely had any difficulty in persuading patients to consent for clinical trials as they held great store by what he told them, with his assured and confident manner as well as his subtle understated charm, Rose-Ellen thought.

Rose-Ellen found him attractive, stimulating and inspirational, but there was a sombre side to him too. His world of clinical research was much like hers, which made their partnership logical. She stared back at the screen. There was still no move on their delayed plane. Trying to settle into the seat and make herself as comfortable as possible, she must have fallen asleep. Suddenly she felt a nudge at her elbow and noticed Pierre at her side.

He carried a tray on which lay a roll wrapped in a napkin and a small bottle of red wine. 'I thought you'd like something to eat as it's anybody's guess when we'll get away.'

Rose-Ellen sat up and muttered her thanks. She felt strange – that same hung-over feeling she had experienced on night duty when she had slept during the day. Now quite ravenous, she settled the tray on her lap and proceeded to open the wine and tuck into the delicious spicy chicken roll. After a while, Pierre produced a small packet from his jacket pocket.

'I thought this might suit your colouring,' he said shyly. 'After all, it's coming up to Christmas. But it's also to thank you for all the work you've done for the trial. You needn't open it now if you don't want to.'

Somewhat embarrassed, she stared at the package and then smiled at him. 'Oh, Pierre, thank you – of course I'll open it now.'

She cleaned her sticky fingers with a tissue to unwrap the packet. As she unravelled the crisp silver and red Christmas wrapping paper and an inner layer of soft white tissue, a beautiful cashmere and silk pashmina revealed itself. It felt so soft to touch. It was jade-coloured with interwoven gold flecks, creating an exquisite shimmering effect. Rose-Ellen put it up to her face, feeling the soft fabric and then draped it around her shoulders.

'Oh, it's beautiful, absolutely gorgeous, and I love the colour. Thank you so much, Pierre.'

He smiled at her. 'You deserve it,' he said, and drank his wine whilst glancing at the TV screen overhead.

She re-wrapped the pashmina carefully in its package and put it away in her briefcase. On the way home on the plane, she thought about Pierre and how thoughtful and insightful he was. The pashmina suited her colouring perfectly and she had told him once that she adored such items of clothing and could not get enough of them. She watched him now, two rows in front of her on the plane, engrossed in completing *The Times* cryptic crossword when most of the other passengers were asleep at this hour. She knew that tomorrow would herald another busy day for him with a staff meeting in the morning and a huge clinic for the rest of the day. She reflected on her role in DCH and was heartened that as long as she was working with him, she would feel fulfilled and driven in her capacity as research nurse/co-ordinator.

Chapter 8

It was three weeks before Christmas when the hospital annual dinner dance was taking place. Danny had agreed to accompany Rose-Ellen to it. However, he was anxious to return to Wexford immediately after the dance in order to milk his cows the following morning.

'Can't you stay overnight and relax and go down first thing in the morning?' Rose-Ellen asked him, standing away from a flicking tail of a cow in his milking parlour.

'You don't understand. It's all in a day's work and I like to plan my day and be on top of things,' he said to her as he fixed a teat to one of the teat cups on the milking machine. She could barely hear Danny's voice over the swish of the milking machines as she watched the white frothy liquid jump and splash as it filled the glass container. The cows stood there passively, each content to be milked from great bulging udders. She reached out and touched one; its warm coat felt good and wholesome. She moved her hand along to the bony prominence of its hips and it turned and gave her a mistrustful look. The milking in Danny's parlour all seemed so mechanised and yet so perfectly natural.

'Look, love, we might even stay up the whole night and have early breakfast the next morning somewhere in Dublin after the dinner,' she muttered.

He was bent low, busily removing a piece of hardened dirt from a muddy udder. She could barely see him from underneath the huge milking sack. 'We could indeed. But I'll be leavin' early the next morning to be down in Wexford to do the milkin'.'

'Very well then.' She walked away, and as she did he called out to her.

'I might get Conor to milk them. But remember, Rose-Ellen, you'll be marrying a dairy farmer and so the milkin' will always come first.'

'I understand.' She got into her car and drove over to *Uisce Gaire.*

Rose-Ellen wondered whether Pierre would go to the hospital dance or be too busy with the demands of work. She did not know very much about him socially except what people said around the hospital. The day before the dinner dance, Dr Doolan's nurse, Eleanor, met Rose-Ellen in Dr Doolan's office. They were trying to sort out the data for a number of patients of Dr Doolan's who were enrolled to the Cytu AB trial. Rose-Ellen asked her about Pierre.

'I'll put it this way; he's not the sort of man you'd warm to. I mean he's just a bit aloof, unapproachable, I suppose, except of course to patients and he's marvellous with them, especially the really sick ones. There isn't a thing he wouldn't do for them. Dr Doolan would be lost without him too; thinks the world of him.' She stopped briefly and thought. 'In fact he told me only the other day that Dr O'Hegarty is one of the most gifted men he has ever come across,' she said, arranging sheets of paper neatly in order, clipping them together with a paper trombone, placing them inside a plastic folder and handing the folder to Rose-Ellen.

Rose-Ellen had nodded in agreement, recalling Pierre's prodigious memory and knowledge.

'Yes, I see what you mean. But what about the man himself?'

She reflected on the question for a moment. 'As I said, I don't know very much about him, he sort of keeps to himself, but I do know that he lives on his own in an apartment in Monkstown and that he is a great sailor. He has a classic cruiser in Dun Laoghaire. I heard that he often sails over to Wales and the North of France, so I'd imagine he's pretty competitive. He's supposed to have a wicked sense of humour too, but I haven't seen much of that in evidence. Mind you, that doesn't mean anything,' and she resumed her paperwork.

The dinner dance was held on the second Friday in December. As Rose-Ellen was leaving to collect her dress from the dry cleaners, she popped her head into Pierre's office.

'Are you going to the dinner dance tonight?' she asked.

He looked up at her and said, 'Indeed, and you?'

'I wouldn't miss something like this for anything. I managed to persuade Danny to drag himself away from the "far-im" and his prize cows for one night.'

He smiled as she mimicked Danny's Wexford accent. 'I'm really looking forward to meeting Danny. I feel as if know him already.'

'See you later then,' she added, and with that she made her way out into the icy air.

Rose-Ellen wore a pale orange halter-neck dress and gold brocade jacket as she strolled in to the foyer of the magnificent glass fronted hotel twinkling with chandeliers in the city centre on Danny's arm. She was excited and looked around to see who was here. She quickly glanced in the mirror to check on her hair, which was coiled up in ringlets emphasising her fine sculpted features. A simple row of pearls sat snugly on her neck.

Rose-Ellen and Danny sat at a table with the nurses from the oncology ward, some junior doctors and their partners. As it was a formal do, Rose-Ellen had asked Danny to hire a dress suit, but he was having none of this suggestion. He said that he had never owned one and was damned if he were going to hire one of those 'panda suits' when he had perfectly good suits hanging in his wardrobe, barely worn. He arrived in a black suit and looked as if he were attending a funeral instead. They would go down to Wexford after the dance as Danny was anxious to milk his cows early the next morning.

At the dinner, Ms Logan, Clinical Manager, sat beside Danny who was soon in animated conversation with her about lambing, calving and the various breeds of hens. Ms Logan was on her own and was delighted to have someone to pay her attention.

'I love the farming. It's a great job. You watch the seasons change from the birth of spring lambs to the quietness of the winter,' Danny said, in-between slurping his vegetable soup.

'Although I have delivered many babies, I've never seen a lamb being born. I'm sure it's wonderful,' Ms Logan , chuckled animatedly.

'Tis indeed wonderful. I suppose I'm a sort of a midwife too. I haven't called a vet now for a long time; myself and Mammy are great with the sheep. After all these years, she understands them well. Mind you they can be difficult too at lambin' time, contrary like.'

Rose-Ellen gazed around the dining room as she sipped her white wine. Briefly her mind wandered off as she did not particularly want to hear about the joys and pitfalls of lambing. Besides, she had witnessed it all before when she had helped Danny out at lambing time last year.

Then she spied Pierre out of the corner of her eye. He arrived when most of the guests were seated. His discreet arrival into the main dining room, with quite the most elegant lady on his arm, caused heads to turn and a slight hush to fall. He was in full evening dress – white bow tie – and his partner wore a stunning black silk moiré evening gown. Rose-Ellen wondered who she was, as Pierre guided the lady towards the consultants' table.

Ms Logan leaned across Danny and whispered to Rose-Ellen, 'Isn't Dr O' Hegarty a fine-looking man and such a gentleman! So calm and rarely gets flustered. Our lives would be so much easier if the others could take a leaf from his book. You're very lucky to be working with him. I gather she's a physio from the Eastern Infirmary. Oh, I hear she's very well-connected. Comes from a long established family in the hotel business.'

Ms. Logan then looked over in the couple's direction and murmured to no one in particular, 'A handsome couple; indeed they are.'

Rose-Ellen watched as Pierre helped his beautiful escort remove her jacket.

Throughout the meal, Rose-Ellen stole a glance at Pierre and his lady friend from time to time. Initially he spoke to his lady friend, but during dessert, he mostly ignored her, talking mainly to Mr O'Neill, the consultant on his left.

People became more animated throughout the meal. Ms Logan spoke to Rose-Ellen while Danny just seemed to retreat into himself. 'What sort of research are you doing? We on the wards don't know very much about research. It's a bit of an enigma to us.'

'Mainly oncology clinical trials. Dr O'Hegarty takes on a lot of challenging projects, and of course I have my own clinic work to do as well.'

'It sounds interesting but I daresay you are very busy between the research work and the clinics,' Ms Logan said, almost chopping the creamed meringue on her plate in two with a heavy thrust of the spoon. Pierre briefly stopped at Rose-Ellen's table to say hello to her and some of his colleagues. Rose-Ellen introduced him to Danny who clasped Pierre's hand with a vice-like grip.

'I hear great things about you, doctor, from herself here,' he said, smiling at Rose-Ellen. 'She loves her job. I seen how happy she is and she tells me she's gettin' on great.'

Rose-Ellen flinched when she heard 'I seen'!

'I'd be lost without her. She's done wonders with our research department,' Pierre said, winking at Rose-Ellen.

Rose-Ellen hoped that Pierre did not notice Danny's occasional bad grammar – it became particularly shocking when he was nervous.

'Love will you try for my sake to say "I have seen" and not "I seen",' she said, when Pierre had moved away.

'Look, it doesn't matter about these things. They're not important. It's the way we all talk at home. Sure I don't see anythin' wrong with "I seen". Everybody says it.'

'But that doesn't mean it's OK.'

She had tried over the years to improve things on the grammar front, but it was impossible, as grammatical abuse seemed to be ingrained into him. He dropped past participles where he should have left them in and put them in when they were not required. Still, she presumed that Pierre was far too much of a gentleman to allow his expression to betray any awareness of Danny's syntactical blunders.

Then it was time for the dancing. After much persuading, Rose-Ellen coaxed Danny up on to the floor and they danced and jived. As Danny lifted her up in the air during a tango, she spied Pierre's lady friend sitting at an empty table with the wife of one of the consultants, – a portly, middle-aged woman, bejewelled and bedecked, as would befit someone in her position. They seemed to be in deep conversation, chatting and nodding like old friends.

Exhausted from dancing, Rose-Ellen went to the ladies room and on the way noticed Pierre at the bar with two of the consultants. She shyly glanced in his direction and he called out to her. 'Rose-Ellen, come and join us!'

He quickly drew up a high stool for her at the bar. With a slight rustle of her evening dress, she manoeuvred herself on to the high seat. As she sat there, Ms Horne glided by with one of the consultants and gave Rose-Ellen an insipid smile. Pierre noticed Ms Horne as he picked up Rose-Ellen's jacket, which had slipped on to the carpet.

'That infernal woman! At least she won't be bothering you any more with requests for a part-time nurse. Now, Rose-Ellen, you know Dr Davies and Mr Geraghty,' he said, introducing her to the two consultants, and she smiled at them.

'Can I get you something to drink?'

Oh, what the hell, she thought. Danny had just bought her a liqueur, but what was the harm in another.

'I'll have a glass of white wine, thanks.' She wondered if Danny would notice that she was gone to the ladies for a long time and how he would take her absence.

Pierre got the attention of the barman and ordered her a glass of wine and when it arrived he raised his own glass in a toast. 'Here's to your health and recruitment to the Cytu AB trial!'

'I'll drink to that!' she beamed.

Dr Davies took a sip from his brandy glass. 'Trials! I gave them up a long time ago. Too much difficulty with the Ethics Committee in the hospital. I remember a time when they'd turn down trials for the least little thing. I was waiting nearly eighteen months once for a trial to get approval and they just kept rejecting it with one flimsy excuse after another.' Twirling the glass, he seemed to address nobody in particular. 'There was a clergyman on the Ethics Committee and I believe the bloody man questioned everything. They say it's all different now – much slicker. And a good thing too!'

Pierre swirled the contents of his glass. 'Oh, there are many reasons why a trial can be turned down. A lot of them are written by PhDs, clever people, yes, but oftentimes very removed in their thinking from a clinical setting, and that can make recruiting difficult.'

'We don't seem to have a problem with recruiting,' Rose-Ellen said, as she looked around and returned her glance in Pierre's direction. He certainly looked more relaxed and at ease than she had ever seen him. He was observing her now as he leaned against the bar, nursing a brandy.

Suddenly Pierre's mobile went off and he moved away to answer it. 'I'm sorry but there seems to be a problem at the hospital with a patient, so I'll have to go. Please excuse me,' he said, returning to the group. He turned to Rose-Ellen. 'It's a patient on the new breast cancer trial.'

'Do you need a hand?' Rose-Ellen asked.

'No, no, not at all. You stay here and enjoy the evening.' Before Pierre left altogether, he returned to the ballroom.

Rose-Ellen knew that the breast cancer trial was tricky and if there were problems or any deterioration in the patient's condition, the data would need to be recorded into special research forms. Company policy dictated that all serious adverse events had to be recorded within twenty-four hours. This task would ultimately be her responsibility.

She replaced the wine glass on the table and went to look for Danny. She found him roaring laughing with two of the nurses' boyfriends at their table. They were discussing GAA Inter-Hurling championships. Danny's voice rose above the murmurings of the guests. 'Hurling is more than a sport. It's nearly an art, like the way you move. Think of the great illustrious hurlers of the past, how they moved like cougars on the field, and their swings were grace itself. They were like Gods on the field!'

Glancing around the room, Rose-Ellen saw Pierre whisper something to his lady friend who had stood up. They kissed and he said goodbye to her. Siobhan bumped into Rose-Ellen as she was gathering up her things to leave.

'Are you coming over to me later on? Ah, just a few drinks and a bit of *craic*.'

Rose-Ellen envisaged Siobhan entertaining until eight am.

'Thanks Siobhan. I'll see, but I won't promise anything. I'm going to stay up in Dublin.'

'Great see you later,' and then Siobhan was whisked off to dance by a rather drunk young man.

Rose-Ellen went over to Danny. 'Love, I'm going into the hospital with Pierre.'

'What? I thought ye were comin' home with me!'

She sat down beside him. 'I'm sorry, Danny. But there's a problem with one of the patients and I need to be there to record the data and to help out.'

He took a gulp of his coke. 'Oh, then don't let me interfere with your work. After all, you know best.'

She bit back a reply and reminded herself to be professional. 'Danny, you could drop me at the hospital now and then head on home down to Wexford.'

'Work's more important than being with me. I get it.'

'You're being unfair, Danny.'

'What's unfair about it?'

'I have responsibilities, that's all, and you should be more understanding.'

'So do I have responsibilities. Cows don't milk themselves. Jaysus, I'd be a millionaire if I could invent a way of makin' them milk themselves. Christ, we'd all be in clover now if that were the case, wouldn't we?'

'Don't be so sarcastic. I didn't plan that this would happen.'

'Nobody is sayin' you planned it. Only don't be too quick in future to be tellin' the rest of us how to lead our lives, OK? And sure, why do you have to go? Are there not people in the hospital who cover the night shift? I don't get it!'

'Danny, it's too difficult to explain and I am not even going to try.'

Danny dropped Rose-Ellen off half an hour later at the hospital.

'Bye love, I'll drive down tomorrow morning and see you later on in the day,' she said, leaning over to kiss him goodnight.

'Take care now. I presume you'll get a taxi to take you to your flat,' he said, leaning over to her as she stepped out.

'Don't worry about me, I'll be fine. Now safe driving and no falling asleep,' she said, banging the door and watched him as he drove off in his estate car. She quickly changed out of her evening attire and put on something more practical.

The young patient was receiving treatment in the three-bed unit, a type of step-down ward just off the intensive care unit. She was in an isolation ward due to her susceptibility to infection. The central line was blocked and as a result, she would not have been able to receive her continuing treatment, but more importantly would have been prone to a serious hospital acquired infection.

This was a difficult time for the young woman because she urgently needed to complete her treatment. The patient had a central line through which all intravenous therapy was fed. It consisted of a large silastic tube which had been inserted into her right internal jugular vein in her neck, the entrance site, through which a catheter led to another vein, the superior vena cava and then into the right atrium of the heart. The exit site was on the skin on the chest wall. The young woman was feverish with a high temperature of nearly 104F and Rose-Ellen realised that Pierre would have to act quickly to bring her status under control.

A young doctor was already there. 'So tell me what the problem is,' Pierre said.

'The central line might be blocked, or worse infected', the doctor said. Rose-Ellen discerned the tiredness in his voice. She stood there gowned in a sterile outfit, her hair in ringlets and face glowing with make-up. Pierre looked at her and then turned to the doctor.

'Did you call Dr McAdam?'

'I did, but he's busy and told me to call you.'

Pierre went over and examined the patient. 'Did you rinse the line?'

'I tried to but I didn't want to force it, so I thought it best to call you.'

'The site looks infected. We'll need to take a blood culture and see what grows,' Pierre said, lifting up the gauze dressing holding the catheter in place on the patient's chest wall. Rose-Ellen moved over and noticed that blood was seeping through the gauze dressing which attached the catheter to the chest wall.

'It's important that she gets her treatment. Can you stay?' Pierre asked.

'I've six other patients to see around the hospital,' the young man said, putting his hands in his pockets.

'That's fine. We'll manage,' he said, turning back to Rose-Ellen. Pierre put on sterile gloves, tweaked and rinsed the catheter until it was patent. He then took a sample of blood which would be sent to the laboratory for culture.

Rose-Ellen could see that the patient was very weak and the mucous membrane of her mouth was laced with tiny crusted ulcers. She looked through the patient's chart. The patient was in the advanced stage of her disease. Pierre reviewed the blood results in the patient chart. 'Her blood count is way down,' he murmured. 'Can you draw up two grams of this please?' he asked a nurse who had just cleaned the infected area. He motioned to the two vials of antibiotics on the trolley with the rest of the sterile equipment. Rose-Ellen was standing beside him making her own notes. The nurse drew up the antibiotics into a syringe and handed them to him.

Pierre gave the IV antibiotics to the patient.

Rose-Ellen concentrated on the case books for the trial as the patient was part of a clinical trial with a new drug for advanced breast cancer.

Pierre came over to where Rose-Ellen was busily writing up her notes.

'That central line will need to be changed. I'll arrange for that to be done as soon as possible,' he said, while removing his gown and gloves and discarding the used phials and syringes. 'Did your fiancé not mind you leaving him?' he asked casually.

'Yes, he was very disappointed as we had planned to have an early breakfast together on the way down to Wexford,' Rose-Ellen said. Now she was regretting that she had left Danny to travel on his own. 'I'll make it up to him at the weekend,' she said, and resumed her paper work.

For the next couple of hours Rose-Ellen sat with the patient, whose condition remained stable. The hospital was quiet and ghost-like except for the passing shadows of nurses going on their break, the odd cry from a patient's fretful sleep, or the night sister creeping through the wards on her soft rubber soles.

Rose-Ellen felt the crepuscular world of night duty was another world, waiting for the first spears of light that herald dawn. 'If you don't need me anymore, I'll go now,' she said to Pierre, while yawning.

'Yes of course. The patient is stable now. Thanks for coming in, but it was a shame you missed the rest of the dance.'

Rose-Ellen suddenly felt herself overwhelmed with embarrassment, but could not have said why. She supposed it was to do with the almost surreal situation with a sick patient in which both she and Pierre had found themselves.

She muttered, 'Goodnight,' and headed to the main reception where a taxi awaited her. Within minutes it arrived and she flopped into it barely able to stay awake. On the way over to Siobhan's, she pondered on the scene which had just passed and felt saddened by the fact that Danny had to make his own way down to Wexford. After all, they had arranged to have breakfast together. Then she thought of Pierre and how deftly he had managed to sort out a potentially dangerous situation with the patient, and her spirits lifted.

Chapter 9

Rose-Ellen enjoyed Christmas spent at home. As she worked in a research capacity at DCH, she was able to take a huge chunk of her holidays together as the department closed as did most of the main pharmaceutical companies. Although busy helping her younger sister Olivia at the emporium, she was relieved to be away from the hospital. Olivia had recently become engaged to Brendan Carragher, a young man with lots of ambition. He was a County Councillor, primary school teacher, small farmer and part-owner of a pub.

'Brendan Carragher is a mighty hard worker and he'll be a good provider too,' Maurice said, shortly after the engagement was announced.

'But, Dad that's not why I'm marrying him,' Olivia protested.

'Being a good provider is very important, believe you me! He's got a pleasant manner about him and I like the way he looks you in the eye too,' Maurice said confidently.

'Ah, Dad. I'm glad you approve of Brendan. He's one in a million,' she said, going over to her father and putting her arms around him.

'Darling, you deserve the best,' he said, and turned away as there were tears in his eyes.

Loughbow, on the River Slaney, was bathed in the soft gentle climate of the south-east of Ireland, where summer brought sweetness in the air from the green pastures further inland. Out of the town on the Wexford road, the Slaney meandered through fields of corn and barley where plump cattle grazed. Rose-Ellen had grown up not far from this town, steeped in history, founded in the sixth century. The town had seen many battles, including those of the 1798 rebellion. Maurice Power maintained that the rebellion still held a strong grip on the local population.

The family members were frantically busy with orders in the run-up to Christmas; there were dressed turkeys, Kitty's famous plum pudding from a secret recipe handed down for generations, glorious golden-honeyed hams hanging and maturing for months, and the most luxurious hampers for the true Epicureans. Nobody could rival 'Power's Emporium' for gourmet food.

Rose-Ellen relished helping her mother put the final trimmings to these splendid containers of the best gourmet food, for which they were famous throughout the county. Each hamper consisted of a willow basket made by a weaver in Ballyedmond, the insides of which were laid with a special filling; fine, soft and spongy, yet strong enough to support the weight of the produce. The hamper display was Kitty's responsibility. She carefully filled each one with an assortment of jars of her own home produce: delicious home-made plum jam, slightly tart cranberry sauce, rich brandy butter, hand-made chocolates packaged in a golden bell, various liquors, coffee almond fingers, jars of mincemeat each with red and white gingham cap, a pink and green box containing after dinner mints, and a tin of her own delicious mince pies with an old photo of the premises taken at the turn of the century embossed in gold with the name, 'Power's Emporium'. Each hamper was enveloped in fine cellophane paper, which was then sprayed lightly in frost and wrapped with a large gold and white bow.

On Christmas night, the whole family went to midnight mass in the town as they had always done. Maurice was tired and irritable having worked non-stop for most of December and was now looking forward to putting his feet up, gorging and drinking for the rest of the week. The shop would be closed until the end of December. Maurice's sister Mona joined them. Mona was the principal of a primary school. She had never married and lived on her own in an old-fashioned pebble-dashed bungalow on the outskirts of Enniscorthy with her three West Highland terriers.

'I wonder what we'll get this year for a Christmas present. I could open a boutique with the beautiful silk scarves and shawls she has given me. I don't know if it's because she doesn't really know us or she can't be bothered or else has no imagination,' Olivia said casually as she prepared a hot whiskey one evening.

'It's the thought that counts.' Rose-Ellen looked at her sister and wondered where she had got such notions.

Maurice gave the traditional toast with the champagne around the fire for people who arrived on Christmas morning; friends and neighbours. Danny called with a Christmas present for Rose-Ellen and a bottle of port for Kitty and Maurice. 'I hope you like it, love,' he said, giving Rose-Ellen a big hug. The smell of roast turkey in the oven suffused the air and mingled with the rich aroma of the Christmas fir tree in the hall.

'I love Christmas. I really do,' he said, inhaling deeply.

Rose-Ellen gave him a kiss. 'Thanks, love. Will you have a drink?'

'I will surely,' and he followed her into the drawing room where the beautifully laid out Christmas table covered with a snow-white crisp linen cloth decorated with golden crackers and silver candelabra awaited the Christmas dinner.

'Hello, Danny and a Happy Christmas to you,' Kitty said, coming over and giving him a big hug. Cindy, the little Pomeranian dog, was running round and barking excitedly.

Rose-Ellen clasped his present to her bosom. 'Before I open mine, here's your present, Danny and Happy Christmas.'

'Ah thanks, love.'

They sat down in front of the blazing fire and Kitty brought in a bottle of port and some glasses and handed a glass each to Danny and Rose-Ellen.

'Here's to both of you,' Kitty said, raising her port in a toast. They toasted the occasion that was. Danny turned and looked at Rose-Ellen. 'Here's to you, darlin,' and he bent down and gave her a kiss.

They started to open their presents. 'Oh, Danny, it's only gorgeous,' Rose-Ellen said, holding up a magnificent woollen three quarter length camel coat with ivory-like buttons. 'I must try it on for size,' and she got up and put on the coat over her flame red dress. 'It fits perfectly too and feels so soft,' she said, rubbing the wool surface. 'Thanks, love,' she said, giving him a hug. 'Are you not going to open yours?' she asked eagerly, looking at Danny with his unopened present still on his lap.

He tore open the wrapping paper which revealed two smart pure cotton shirts and a history of hurling in Wexford down through the years. He kissed the book and the shirts slid off the sofa. 'Oh, baby, I'm going to enjoy readin' this,' he said, winking at her.

'I thought you'd like it.'

'Like it! I feckin' love it!'

The Christmas dinner was a splendid fare when the whole family sat around the table in the late afternoon for a sumptuous feast. A warm fire glowed and a plump turkey was placed majestically in the centre of the table where long vines of natural ivy wove their way through the tall stately crystal and bone-handled cutlery. Maurice ceremoniously carved the turkey. He stood poised with the carving knife and fork in his hand and looked in Kitty's direction.

'I think we're all here now and you can go ahead and carve Maurice. Everything is on the table so just help yourselves,' Kitty said, reassuringly. When the food was passed around Maurice said grace. Kitty blessed herself quickly after grace and got up to take the turkey back into the kitchen followed by Cindy. On her way back she placed a log on the fire. Mona got a bit merry and started to reminisce about Maurice when he was a baby and they roared with laughter, much to his embarrassment, while Kitty spoke of the lean Christmases when she was growing up.

On St. Stephen's Day, they all donned wellingtons and hats and went for a long walk.

'Maybe we'll see the hunt,' said Kitty, tying her scarf tightly as there was a mighty wind outside.

They set off by the river and made their way over the fields. Kitty and Olivia went ahead and Rose-Ellen tagged behind with Maurice who was having difficulty clambering over the ditches. She wondered about her father and his fitness. She felt he drank too much, but she suspected that many men did at this stage.

'Dad, you'll have to take more exercise.'

'That's enough. At my age there's no point in changing habits,' he said, grappling with a bunch of reeds to steady himself as he manoeuvred across a trout stream.

Then they saw them in the distance in the black coats with the odd scarlet one. 'Oh look, the hunt, here they come. Watch out!' Rose-Ellen shouted, as horses galloped after the barking hounds to the sound of the bugle. There in the front thundering by, past the bank and over a double ditch, was Mairead Redmond, Danny's only sister, her head down as she scalped the poor beast with her whip.

The Powers stopped for a drink in the local pub on their way back. The Redmond`s car was parked here with a horsebox in tow with Mairead's hunter who whinnied every time he saw another horse. Josie was leaning against the car and tending to Mairead's face, which was bleeding. Rose-Ellen went over to greet her future mother-in-law.

'Hello, Josie and Happy New Year to you.' She turned to Mairead and greeted her too. Josie was carefully cleaning Mairead's face with a cotton ball from a large tin labelled 'Josie's Medicine Box' on the ground nearby.

'There, there, that should do it now,' Josie said, dabbing the wound under Mairead's swollen eye. 'Happy New Year to you, Rose-Ellen.'

'Can I help?'

'Ah, no thanks, we'll be grand.' Josie seemed to be in control.

'What's in the tin?' Rose-Ellen asked.

Josie put the cotton wool away, closed the bottle of antiseptic and looked at her beloved tin. 'That's special. There's anythin' and everythin' in there, for all ailments under the sun for beasts and humans, from sore throats and backache to mastitis in cows.'

Rose-Ellen was intrigued. 'Can I have a look?'

'Course ye can, love,' and she kicked the tin gently over to Rose-Ellen who peered inside. Inside the tin was an Aladdin's cave containing everything required to treat minor ailments: udder cream, scouring liquid, anti-inflammatory drugs expired by nearly two years, nettle juice and tincture of camphor oil, flea powder, and factor fifty sun block for pig's ears, worming pellets, oxytocin for slow farrowing, needles, syringes, latex gloves and a big jar of cider vinegar. Josie had read about cider vinegar and its many benefits and gave it regularly to all the family and beasts.

'I see you like to use the cider vinegar,' Rose-Ellen said.

'Mam, hurry up. I don't want to be here all night,' Mairead said impatiently to her mother, while giving Rose-Ellen a filthy look.

'OK, love, nearly there.'

Josie looked at Rose-Ellen. 'The cider vinegar is great. They don't know I put it into everything; nothin' much, just a drop here and there. It works wonders and keeps coughs and colds away. I put a bit in the calves' and sheep feed; gives them a lovely shiny coat before the Enniscorthy Cattle and Sheep Fair,' she said, firmly putting a sticking plaster on Mairead's cut. 'There, love. Ye'll be as right as rain.'

Mairead got up, brushed her jacket down and without looking at either woman sauntered into the pub.

'So did you have a nice Christmas, Rose?' Josie turned to Rose-Ellen.

'Yes lovely, thanks. And you?'

'Ah, ye know, busy, busy. That's the way when you've a big family. Are you comin' in for a Christmas drink?'

'Of course. I think Mam and Dad have gone in already.'

'See ye inside so. I just need to put things away first.'

The place was packed and Rose-Ellen could see Danny in the distance and waved to him. He waved back at her, but had his head down and ear cocked and seemed to be listening attentively to Mairead who looked in her direction and turned away again, while monopolising Danny's attention.

'Happy New Year, Rose-Ellen,' someone shouted and she felt a hand on her shoulder. Turning round she saw Conor, Danny's handsome younger brother. 'My future sister-in-law. Here let me get you a drink for the Christmas,' and before she could protest Conor came back from the bar with doubles. After what seemed like hours, Danny strolled down and put his arm around Rose-Ellen who, at this stage, was sitting with her parents.

'Well, did you have a good Christmas?' he said, pulling up a stool beside Rose-Ellen.

'We did thanks,' Rose-Ellen said, and drank her wine. She was annoyed with him that he had spent so much time with Mairead. 'What happened to Mairead's face?' she asked after a while.

'A thorn or something scraped her as she was riding through the woods; at least that's what she says. Mind you, it wouldn't surprise me if someone had taken a whip to her.'

'What do you mean?'

'Ye know she's keen on Declan's brother.'

'The butcher in Fethard? So?'

'Big problem. He's married. He says he's gettin' a separation, but the wife isn't that keen.'

Mairead Redmond was the talk of the place and was as stubborn and headstrong as the horses she rode. 'I think your sister should come with a warning sign for danger.'

'I know you don't like her, but at the end of the day she's family.'

'She's trouble, Danny, and you know that as well as I.'

'If it's any consolation, Rose, the feelin' is mutual.'

'So why is that? I've never done anything to Mairead.'

'It's jealousy.'

'Not on my part!'

'Sure I know that. Mairead is not exactly a ravin' beauty, if ye get my drift, and she hasn't come either with buckets o' charm. Naturally, she sees a lassie like you, beautiful, good job, intelligent and finally, here's the main reason. You're marryin' me, her favourite brother, and she feels threatened.'

Rose-Ellen laid her glass firmly on the counter. 'It's time that Mairead grew up and started to get a life of her own. The way your mother was cleaning up her few cuts and bruises a while ago, you'd think she was a two-year-old.'

'Don't forget she is my Ma's only daughter, so there!'

Rose-Ellen realised that there was no talking to Danny when it came to Mairead and so she turned and talked to Kitty for the rest of the evening. That night before she went to bed, Rose-Ellen sat with Kitty to have a quiet cup of tea before retiring. 'Mam, I don't know what it is about Danny's family, but I have come to the conclusion that few in that family really like me.'

'Oh, I don't know. Why do you say that? Don't you come from a good family and are young and intelligent. My God, what more do they want?'

'I don't know, it's just a feeling I get. I have the impression that Danny's father would have liked him to marry one of the two Brennan sisters who run the family farm outside of Bunclody.'

'And an uglier pair of women I have yet to meet. Those two are married to the land and their memories and would never make anyone happy; self-contained tight bitches, too mean with their emotions and their money,' Kitty said, as she passed the biscuit tin to Rose-Ellen.

Chapter 10

Josie Redmond had her boys and husband ruined with kindness and indulgence from picking up their wet towels and sports gear to providing each with individual daily menus.

'They deserve it, and they work hard all day long and you've got to keep a man happy, Rose dear. It's all ahead of you,' she said calmly as she lovingly ironed their shirts, boxer shorts, pyjamas and jeans.

Rose-Ellen hated being called Rose, but Josie Redmond never called her by her full name. She said that there was just simply too much movement of the tongue required and this was difficult with her false teeth.

Then there was the wanton cruelty of the unwanted kittens in the Redmond household. Conor invariably had a gun and quarry in tow. A few days after Christmas, he was making off down to the river with a sack that seemed to be both moving and whimpering at the same time. Rose-Ellen was busy making turkey sandwiches for Josie to take to the Irish Country Women's Association that night and watched as he headed off out the yard with the poor innocent victims awaiting their watery grave. The poor little things had no chance of any kind of a life once they were born on the Redmond farm. She could not bear to look and turned to Danny.

'Danny, any chance I could take those kittens and give them a home? It's not right; it's just so cruel. Will you get the sack from him?'

He continued to read the racing results in the paper, ignoring her pleas. Rose-Ellen went over and pulled the newspaper down in front of him. 'Did you hear me? I'm talking to you about the kittens. I'll take them home; Mam and Olivia will look after them until they're old enough for homing.'

He looked at her sternly. 'They're only vermin.'

Rose-Ellen left her mound of buttered bread and went out and caught up with Conor as he made his way down the field to the river. He was walking fast as if he could not wait to finish the cursed deed.

'Conor, wait! Listen to me for a minute. I know what you have in the sack.'

He continued walking with a steady determined pace. 'So?'

She was trying desperately to keep up with him. 'Please give me the kittens. Look, I'll get homes for them. You shouldn't drown them, the poor little things. They don't deserve this.' She could hear them and their pathetic mewling inside the sack.

He stopped, turned and looked at her. 'There'll be more in a few months' time. We've enough cats on the place as it is. We're nearly over-run with them.'

'Then why don't you get the female spayed? It's not fair to take it out on the poor kittens. Drowning is slow and painful for them and can take two or three minutes. I know because I remember Daddy's brother doing it and as kids we hated it. I still can't bear to think of it.' The weak little cries of the kittens continued as Rose-Ellen watched the outline of one trying to climb up inside the sack.

'This is life in the country, girl. If you marry my brother you'd better get used to it.'

He turned on his big, muddy wellington boots with the task at hand, but as he did Rose-Ellen reached out and grabbed the sack from him. He seemed to offer little resistance.

'I won't get used to wanton cruelty even if I do marry your brother.'

He stood there laughing at her. 'You're such an ould softie, Rose. Dublin and the city life would suit you better and anyway those kittens will only have a few days, 'cause without their mother's milk they won't survive.'

Rose-Ellen knew this to be true and that without the mother cat their fate would indeed be grim. Turning back towards the house she called after him, 'I'll take a chance with them.'

Returning to the house she looked inside the sack and saw five beautiful little kittens, all colours, their tiny eyes still closed, meowing. Without the mothers' milk they would be dead in a week, she reckoned.

Danny was still at the table, his eyes glued to the racing results on the paper. He looked up when she came in with the sack. 'What have ye there?'

'You know damn well what I have and I'm taking the mother cat home with me to nurse those kittens until we can get homes for them,' she said, laying the sack down gently on the floor.

'Are you crazy or something? Who's goin' to look after them over at your place?' He moved his big frame back from the table and stretched out his long legs in front of him. Rose-Ellen felt that there was no point in talking to him. When it came to cats Danny was made from the same hard mould as Conor. Cats were not like cattle or sheep; they did not generate an income, so they were treated with the contempt that the Redmond family felt they deserved.

Rose-Ellen went out to the yard calling for the mother. After a few minutes a tortoiseshell cat emerged from under a tractor and brushed against Rose-Ellen's legs with swollen wet teats, crying out pathetically. Rose-Ellen picked her up and stroked her under her chin. 'You poor thing; looking for your little darlings.'

Wrapping the cat in her coat and placing her with the kittens in the back seat of her car, Rose-Ellen knew that Olivia and her mother would look after the kittens until they got good homes and the mother cat could be spayed.

Olivia fell in love with the mother cat as soon as she saw her. 'Oh, you beautiful thing. I'm going to call you Tiger Lily because of your fabulous coat,' she said, almost squeezing the mother cat with kisses.

Rose-Ellen never spoke to Danny again about the kitten episode, nor did any of the Redmonds ever allude to the disappearance of the beautiful tortoiseshell cat from the yard. Tiger Lily was probably just considered one of the many 'yard' cats in the Redmond household; tolerated to fend off rodents. Days later Rose-Ellen was still upset about the episode.

'That's the way with all of them, darling,' her mother said matter-of-factly as she placed her hat on her head to go down to the bridge club. 'They don't look at things the same way as we do, and particularly not farmers. They're hard and cruel just like nature.'

'I'll never get used to cruelty, never mind the other things,' Rose-Ellen said casually.

Her mother looked at her quizzically. 'What other things?'

'The deep-frying. It goes on morning, noon and night. I swear to God they have chips with their breakfast down at the Redmonds. It's chips with everything. Huge big wedges piled high on their plates like pyramids with lashings of red sauce on top and then soaked in vinegar. The whole house smells of the chip-pan!'

Her mother stared at her in disbelief. 'My God! They're digging an early grave with their teeth down there.'

Chapter 11

The research department at DCH reopened in early January. Pierre was reviewing a patient's chart and looked up when Rose-Ellen breezed into his office.

'Hi there, welcome back. How did Christmas go?'

She sat down and removed her scarf. 'Great! Of course like half the country I ate far too much. And you? Did you have a nice rest?'

'Lovely thanks. I went sailing over to the Isle of Man and up around Strangford Lough with a few mates.'

'Sounds terrific. I'd love to be able to sail. I've only ever been on a boat once.'

'Then I insist you come with me one day and you can experience the joys of the sea.'

'Oh, I'd love that,' she said excitedly.

At the end of January, Pierre and his friends had arranged to go sailing one weekend. The Tuesday before the trip, while reviewing some patient charts in his office, Pierre called out casually to Rose-Ellen in the adjoining room. 'If you're not doing anything on Saturday maybe you would like to come sailing with me and some friends? We won't be going far.'

She was just returning a large file to a shelf. Surprised, she turned to face him. 'Why not? I'd like that. As it just happens I'm not going down home this weekend as Danny is away on some course on crop rotation and the parents are in Killarney for the week. They need the break after the Christmas.'

'We'll set off in the morning, but probably only go over as far as Howth and maybe a bit beyond. The weather is likely to be a bit unpredictable for the weekend. I'll fill you in on the finer details later.' He glanced at her with that look she had become used to – the half smile that could be interpreted as anything one chose. 'You'll enjoy it. It'll be fun!' he said.

'Thanks, Pierre, that's something to look forward to, she said, turning to fill up the *cafetière*.

'Now, as you haven't done any sailing before, I suggest you bring plenty of warm woollen clothes, a windcheater or something to keep out the cold. It can get very, very chilly out at sea and it's still winter,' Pierre said, tapping his pen lightly on the desk.

'What do you want me to do? If you like I could prepare the food in the galley. It's what I'm good at as I don't think I'd be much good on deck. It's only a suggestion,' Rose-Ellen said enthusiastically.

'Let me tell you about these guys; they are a mixed bag. French lecturer, barrister and GP. They are pretty easy-going and like to do a lot of talking and a certain amount of drinking.'

She smiled at him. 'I'm getting the picture.'

'So just come along at about ten am. I'll text you with precise directions on the morning as to where we are moored.'

'I'll look forward to it,' she said.

On Saturday morning Rose-Ellen rose early and baked a pineapple pavlova to bring with her. After all they would be out at sea all day and this would be nice and light. At ten o'clock sharp she made her way to Dun Laoghaire, following Pierre's precise instructions. She carried the pavlova gingerly fearing that it might fall.

Pierre was already at the pier, and spying her in the distance he called, 'Rose-Ellen, over here. Here let me help you,' and with that he jumped on to the quay and helped her with her rucksack and the pavlova which was wrapped in tin foil.

He introduced her to his friends: Peter, fellow doctor; Ivan, university lecturer in French and barrister, Joe. They all shook hands with her.

'Now, Rose-Ellen, if you remember nothing else today, remember this. On board everybody is equal. The sea makes no distinctions. Here we are all exposed and powerless.'

She felt the soft breeze on her face. Looking out, she saw the jade-green sea glimmering with dappled sunshine. According to the forecast it would remain so for another few hours before squalls were expected.

Peter stayed on the pier and jumped on at the last minute once the boat was ready. Ivan was at the boom and Pierre was checking the tension in the halyards. Joe was wandering around the deck with his binoculars.

Once out at sea Rose-Ellen noticed the camaraderie amongst the men and wondered exactly how long they had known each other. It had quickly become apparent that they were long time friends.

'When are you getting rid of the old lady, Pierre? She's seen too many gales; time to give her a rest,' Peter said, moving his fingers over the flaking paint on the side.

Pierre was absorbed in uncoiling rings of rope. 'Some day. But not just yet. I have to concentrate on the Circle of Ireland first and that's my priority.' Peter looked over at Rose-Ellen.

'Ah yes, the competitive element. And where do you come into all of this, Rose-Ellen? I mean the sailing.'

Rose-Ellen was looking out to the horizon. 'Pierre and I work together, and he asked me to come along. As it happens, I had nothing planned for the weekend.' She turned and looked at Pierre. 'And besides, it's a refreshing way to spend a fine day.'

'A refreshing way to spend a fine day! I like the way you put that, Rose-Ellen,' piped up Joe. Joe was tall and angular in a well-cut pair of jeans and tennis shoes and had a tired look about him. He finished his cigarette and stubbed it out, placing the butt carefully into an antique silver cigarette case. Looking out to sea and watching the wheeling gulls overhead, he reached for the binoculars and seemed to speak to no one in particular. '*I would that we were, my beloved, white birds on the foam of the sea. We tire of the flame of the meteor, before it can fade and flee…*Look at them – scavengers, parasites, feeding off the waste of animals and us humans, and yet they are so perfectly formed, so beautifully white, but with the eye of a hawk.'

'I didn't know you were such a bird enthusiast,' Ivan muttered.

Joe continued looking at the squawking gulls. 'I'm not, but it's just, well, I see how free and unburdened they are.'

'But would you like to be a seagull, like rats scavenging from life's wastes with a lifespan of probably only five years?' asked Peter.

'No, I don't suppose so, but I could do with being a bit more unburdened by the parasites and wasters of life.'

Pierre was sitting on his haunches going through a box containing bits of string, screws and tools. He looked up at Rose-Ellen. 'Joe is involved in family court cases, so knows a thing or two about strife.' He then turned to Joe and asked casually, 'So why did you choose to become a barrister?'

'I sometimes wonder that. Perhaps I like the dark side of life too – something quirky in my make-up,' Joe said, smiling over at Rose-Ellen.

She listened to them with amusement and then glanced out at the horizon. The boat was well out of the harbour which was now a distant speck as the boat picked up speed, driven by a brisk south-easterly wind. The sea was dotted with other boats and a long flat merchant ship could be seen out on the horizon. Peter carried a large basket and some rolls and headed below to the galley.

After a while she wondered where Pierre was and hearing his voice went down to the galley. There she found him trying to sort out all of the food that they had brought. Pierre looked up at her as he brushed a stray lock of hair out of his face. 'I had no idea they were going to bring so much food. It'll be some feast.'

'I got a present of this fabulous salmon from a patient yesterday. The kids hate fish and so I thought it such a shame to waste it so here it is, and my wife made up a few salads to go with it, so we won't be hungry that's for sure,' Peter said, taking the various items from the basket.

'Thanks, Peter, that's wonderful. What else have we here? Pizza and some cold meats,' Pierre said, searching through the packages which lay on the small galley table.

Rose-Ellen piped up. 'Can I suggest that I prepare lunch? You see, sailing is new to me. I could let you guys get on with things on deck.'

They both looked at her. 'It'll only be for a while and after lunch you can have a chance to go on deck. How about that?' Pierre said.

'Seems fine,' she said, pulling back the parchment paper on the huge cold salmon.

Pierre looked slightly out of place in the small confined space with his tall angular frame. 'Cooking is second nature to me,' she said, washing her hands at the tiny sink.

'Are you sure you don't mind? That would be marvellous. The cooking facilities are very straightforward, nothing too complicated, though the galley's a bit tight,' Pierre said.

'Of course I don't mind. OK. I'll fire ahead so,' she said, and before they went up, she called out, 'So, gentlemen, let's say one-ish for lunch.'

Joe shouted down. 'Aye, Aye, *Capitaine.*'

On the table were several bottles of red and white wine, crusty bread and salads. Rose-Ellen sat down, unsure where to begin. She rolled up her sleeves and pulled open the first drawer which was full of penknives. She quickly closed it and opened another which was full of odd corks wrapped in elastic bands. Finally the third drawer had a selection of neatly arranged knives and forks with purple and yellow handles. Pots were stacked away carefully and dark green mugs with sailing emblems of yachts and anchors hung from little red hooks.

She smiled as she thought of Pierre and how tidy he was. 'A master in miniature packing,' she mused to herself. She could hear the banter of the men upstairs.

Joe was pontificating again. 'I don't know why people always feel that they have to be remembered when they die. Why is it so important?'

'I suppose they like to feel that their lives had some meaning; that they hadn't lived in vain,' Peter said vaguely.

'Does it really matter when one is dead whether or how one is remembered? It doesn't to the deceased. I don't think it should alter how we lead our lives,' Pierre said.

Joe said, 'But that's why we have all the laws we have, and probably religion, too, to ensure that there's some order to the world. Otherwise there would simply be anarchy. I believe that this is partly why religion was invented – to frighten people with the afterlife.'

'You don't know that. You're only presuming, and that's dangerous. Surely it's looking forward to the happiness of a future life that is the object of all religion,' said Ivan.

'I see the clouds are beginning to accumulate. I'd better let out the sails,' Pierre shouted over the wind.

Rose-Ellen chopped, seasoned and mixed. She found a large yellow cracked dish for the tiger prawns which she drizzled with some olive oil, and mixed in some herbs for the starter. She arranged the salmon on a large battered looking tin foil platter that had seen better days and an accompanying assortment of salads – crispy leaves of lettuce, tomato and cucumber salad, a crumble of pine nut and feta and wild rice mixed with French beans were placed in different places on the table. She removed the pizzas from their boxes and popped them in the oven hoping that they would fit, and they just about did. She barely managed to squeeze the white wine bottles into the tiny fridge when she spied three rather lonely looking eggs and a dried up lemon.

'Oh great, now I can make some sauce for the fish,' she delighted in the discovery.

Rose-Ellen placed the whole cooked salmon in the middle of the table like a trophy. She whipped up fresh hollandaise at the last minute with the eggs and lemon juice, taking care not to scramble it. The table was indeed a fisherman's banquet. Time had seemed to fly. She looked at her watch. It was already a little after one. Then she heard some movement on deck and Pierre was the first to clamber down the stairs, followed by the others.

Smiling at him, she turned back to get the paper towels but they were high up on the top shelf and out of her reach. Pierre came behind her, reached up and retrieved the towels for her. He was close to her now and she could smell the salt sea breeze from his untidy hair. He stood there smiling down at her with his perfectly symmetrical white teeth and moist hair tousled from the spume.

'Rose-Ellen, *vous êtes merveilleuse*!' Then he took her hand and guided her to the top of the table. She slid in beside Joe.

'Jesus, what a spread! You're wonderful! Would you like to come and cook for an old bachelor sometime?' He had a twinkle in his eye.

Ivan went upstairs and hauled up a bottle of white wine which hung over the side of the boat to chill in the cool seawater. 'It should be nice and crisp now,' he said returning, and opened up the bottle of Chablis and served everybody with a glass. Peter remained above steering the boat.

'Cheers!' Joe said, and they all raised their glasses to Rose-Ellen. Ivan passed around the prawns and salad.

'I can't believe that we are being treated to hollandaise sauce. I must say that the *haute cuisine* in this little galley has improved immensely. Do you know Rose-Ellen one couldn't even find a sprig of parsley on this boat before?' Pierre said, as he cut the salmon.

'One can only accommodate what is necessary on a boat; one learns to live with the minimum,' he said, ceremoniously handing around the salmon.

'Anyway, as I was saying,' Joe resumed while helping himself to a large slice of pizza and almost a plateful of salad. 'Why are we here? It's starting to preoccupy me more and more. I suppose it's middle age and of course "ego," wondering if my life has any meaning; if I'll be missed when I leave this wonderful earth.' He looked around the galley and raised his glass.

Pierre passed him a piece of salmon. 'Oh, Joe. Speculation and worry. You'll never be any wiser and of course speculation is the enemy of calm.'

Joe sat back and twirled his glass. 'Calm, well I was never that. I could never be calm. I tried everything, yoga, spiritualism, but my fizzy mind couldn't sit still for longer than two minutes. I've always been a bit of a fidgeter. However, strange though it may seem, I can sit for hours in the law library, ploughing through tomes of old cases, trawling through years of case histories and the time just seems to pass and I get lost in my legal world.'

Pierre was a little more resigned about the afterlife. 'Just enjoy this wonderful life and accept what comes your way and deal with it as best. When one thinks of the tens of millions of years when one will no longer inhabit this wonderful earth, it makes me savour each second as if it were my last.'

They all looked at Pierre but remained silent. After some time, Pierre got up from the table and uncorked a bottle of red wine. 'Is there anything after life? Or shall we ever be held accountable for our actions on this earth? Who knows? Nobody has really come back to tell us what it's like out there in the big blue void. Now, who's for more wine?'

Joe raised his empty glass. 'Yes, what's it all about? We go on reproducing ourselves on this earth making the same mistakes over and over again, and those who should be having children aren't and those who shouldn't are.'

Pierre looked at Joe, his confirmed bachelor friend. 'You know, my friend, few could argue with someone who could pick up information like a vacuum cleaner and retain it like you. You have the facility of recall; useful when the minutest detail could ultimately decide the outcome of a legal case. But the problem with you is that you've been working with the dangerous and the misfits of society in the courts too long and you've become a cynic.'

'But it's true. You see it everywhere; lumbering the planet with children who can't be fed or educated.'

'It's simply ridiculous to look at the world like that,' Pierre said, with a hint of annoyance. 'We should all be grateful for being here in the first place, just being alive. After all, being born is a bit like winning the lotto. For every one of us here, there were millions of other potential beings at the time of our conception.'

'Life comes in all forms and shapes and this is what makes it so interesting,' Rose-Ellen said, passing around the salad.

'I'm entitled to my own views,' Joe said, twirling his wine glass.

'Yes, but they're dangerous too,' Pierre replied.

'I limit my views to a few close friends such as you,' Joe said, looking around the galley.

'I hope so,' Pierre said.

There was an awkward silence while Pierre continued pouring the wine. When he came to Rose-Ellen she placed her hand over her wine glass. She did not want to drink too much during the day. 'No more wine, thanks, Pierre.'

'Sure?'

She turned to Ivan. 'So you lecture in French. I keep meaning to go to the Alliance Francaise and take it up again. My dream is to open a little coffee shop in France some day. Oh, it's only a pipe dream.'

'Dreams are the fabric of life. Go for it, girl. Don't talk about it, just do it. If you've learnt French at school, it will help. But if you want to work in France, then without French, forget it,' he said, breaking some bread and mopping up the sauce from his plate. He then got up from the table.

'I'd better relieve Peter.'

'Good idea,' Joe shouted.

Ivan clambered up the stairs and Peter soon joined them.

'The salmon was delicious,' Rose-Ellen said, setting a place for him.

'Good, I'm delighted.'

Pierre got up from the table, looked out of the galley window.

'I wonder about the weather,' he said.

'So let's drink to the present,' Joe said, and raised his glass.

'To the present!' they shouted, and touched their glasses.

After about an hour, the sea became rougher and the boat was heaving a bit.

Pierre looked out in front of the boat. 'We seem to be only ones out sailing. All the other boats have retired.' He went up on deck.

'Now, to more immediate matters. Anyone for coffee?' Joe said, moving around the galley.

'Oh, but what about sweet?' Rose-Ellen asked.

'Did somebody say sweet?' Peter beamed at the prospect of something sugary and sticky.

'Well, I baked a pineapple pavlova this morning, so it will be nice and light after the rich meal,' Rose-Ellen said, getting up from the table to clear things away.

'A girl of many splendid talents,' Joe smiled, patting her on the hand.

'I'll put on the coffee,' Peter said, as he removed the end of the salmon and the bread basket.

A little after four pm, Rose-Ellen went up on deck. Pierre was at the wheel steering home. He called out to Ivan who was loosening halyards. 'Give it full sail, the wind is very rough and we need to get back home.'

When the boat returned back to Dun Laoghaire late in the evening Rose-Ellen gathered up her rucksack and got ready to leave. Pierre was doing some last minute navigational checks. 'Thanks so much, Pierre for today. I really enjoyed it,' she said.

He looked up from his log book. 'I'm so glad you came, Rose-Ellen and thanks for all your help. Did you take some of the wine with you? Please take a bottle or two; they brought far too much as usual. Sometimes these sailing trips can turn into big drinking sessions, especially when there's no wind.'

'I can imagine. Thank you.'

'Here let me help me with some of your gear,' and with that he went to the galley and selected a good bottle of red wine, wrapped it in some newspaper and put it in her rucksack.

'Come out again with us. Maybe you'd like to learn a little more about sailing.'

'Yes, I'd like that. Thank you.' And with that she gathered up her things and said goodbye to the lads who were putting away the equipment.

On the way home she wondered what Danny would think of her going off with Pierre and his friends for the day. She suspected he would not mind. In the end, she decided that she would say nothing to him about it. This would be one thing that he did not really need to know.

Chapter 12

Rose-Ellen did not particularly want to go down to Wexford each weekend to see Danny as she also had a hectic social life in Dublin. So one weekend at the end of February she decided to stay up in Dublin and, as it happened, Pierre asked her to sail to Howth with him on the Saturday. It was their second sailing together.

'I would have liked to have accompanied my girlfriend, Moira, to some horse trials in the UK, but it was not possible time-wise, as I have to work late tonight to finish an urgent report. We'll just sail over to Howth and back. Peter will come with us, he's doing some locum work on the Friday night, so I expect he'll hardly be able to stay awake.'

'That sounds perfect, Pierre. It'll be nice not to be dashing down to Wexford again.'

'I know what you mean. So shall we say the usual time on the quays in Dun Laoghaire?'

'Ten o'clock. That's great,' and she headed towards the door but stopped and looked back at him as if she had forgotten something. 'Oh, is it OK if I take a canvas with me and do some painting?'

'Painting? I didn't know that you were an artist as well. How many more talents are you hiding?'

She blushed. 'It's nothing much, but I have this seascape that I want to finish for Mam's birthday and I was hoping to finish it this weekend.'

'Of course you can take your canvas on board.'

She smiled at him.

On Saturday, Rose-Ellen took the DART and arrived promptly at the harbour in Dun Laoghaire. It was a nice, soft day with a calm breeze. On deck Pierre's long, loose brown hair blew across his features, giving him a romantic aura. She watched him as he moved around the boat, his lithe figure with the springy gait of a youth absorbed in the riggings and the ropes.

Towards afternoon all was quiet except for the gentle movement of the boat on a relatively calm swell. After a hearty meal, Peter wrapped himself in a sleeping bag and lay down in the galley snoring loudly. Pierre glanced at Rose-Ellen as she completed a gentle scene of a boat moored in a bay bathed in the lavender light of evening. Her hair with its golden flecks cascaded down her face whilst a curl nestled in the hollow of her neck.

'Not bad at all,' he whispered behind her while examining the canvas.

She looked up and caught his soft smile as a shaft of sunlight broke through the dreary clouds. 'I love when the painting surprises me. That's what makes it all worthwhile,' she said, adding one or two touches to the sky on canvas.

'Your hair is nice like that. I'm used to seeing it up on your head.'

It was at quiet moments like these that Rose-Ellen wondered if they would ever talk about themselves, and this time Pierre did, as if the gentle lilting of the boat and thrum of the sails evoked memories of another time, a more distant but happier past. He leaned against the mast, savouring the brief interlude of sunshine before it disappeared.

'This reminds me of sailing in Brittany when I was growing up.'

'So tell me about your childhood in France?' she asked, taking down the canvas and putting it away.

'Oh, it was idyllic. Those summers spent in Brittany are what one could only dream of now. I know everyone's childhood is rosy but going out on my uncle's boat so young, two, three, four times a week was sheer bliss.' Out on the horizon leaden clouds were blanketing the brief glimpse of sunlight. 'People in Brittany have the sea in their hearts. Their folk tales are all about sailors being lost at sea, and St. Malo, where I used to stay, was the cradle of Breton folk songs.' He turned to Rose-Ellen and she caught his momentary expression of nostalgia. 'Then summer was over and the inevitable would happen.'

'What was that?' she asked.

'I would kick and roar at my mother when I had to return to boarding school and my poor uncle would just look on helplessly.'

Rose-Ellen put away the remainder of the painting materials into her canvas bag. The wind had whipped up and Rose-Ellen put her hand through her slightly damp hair. The sun had emerged briefly again, glinting low in the western sky. She felt a little awkward as he came over and smoothed a curl from her face. She could feel the light and gentle touch of his hand on her skin and felt a slight frisson, but then shyly looked out at the horizon. He turned away and busied himself with the immediate demands of sailing. She felt confused by this touch of tenderness and found the situation slightly awkward now in the confines of the boat.

'I forgot I have my Aunt Grace calling this evening for dinner. I hadn't realised how late it was,' Pierre said, standing over her. 'I need to call to my apartment, so I can run you to the DART on the way.'

'That's fine, Pierre.'

He parked the car on the road outside his apartment.

'I won't be a sec', he said, getting out of the car. She watched him as he made his way up the steps to the apartment. After a few minutes, Pierre rushed back to Rose-Ellen who was listening to the radio in the car. 'I don't suppose you'd fancy a bite to eat?' he said, opening the driver's seat.

She looked at him a bit sceptically. 'What do you mean?'

'Well, my aunt left a message on my phone to say that she is unwell and can't see me today, so I could muster something up for us if you like.'

'Why not,' Rose-Ellen said, smiling at him while reaching for her jacket and bag.

Pierre's apartment was on the first floor in a large three-storey Georgian building in an end position on a well known terrace in Monkstown. Rose-Ellen climbed the fifteen steps up to the bright red door and turned around to gaze at the sea.

'What a fabulous panoramic view across Dublin Bay.'

'The elevated site maximises the superb views of the coast. That's why I bought it,' he said, putting all of the sailing gear in the hallway.

The apartment consisted of one large room and another small room, together with a kitchen and a bedroom. It had beautiful classic pieces of furniture but the kitchen was sparse and small. Several oil paintings of ships and seascapes hung on the walls of the main room and hallway. There were few ornaments and no family photos.

'Who did the paintings?' she enquired.

'My uncle painted them – he's an avid sailor,' Pierre said, as he prepared a light meal.

'Would you like a hand?' she called to him.

'No thanks. Won't be a minute.'

Rose-Ellen scanned his bookcases. There were books in French by Sartre and Camus, rows of classics and leather-bound books by Pascal and Montaigne embossed in gold. Next to these were books on medicine and sailing and, most bizarrely, an entire shelf devoted to children's books: the adventures of Tin-Tin, Asterix, Jules Verne and Antoine de Saint-Exupéry.

Pierre was humming to himself and Rose-Ellen was enthralled by the unique sound of Reinhardt's 'LimeHouse Blues' which filled the air. Moments later, carrying a large tray into the main room, he noticed her peering at the bookcase.

She turned and smiled at him. 'What a wide selection of books! Have you read them all?'

'Pretty much. I re-read the classics, and of course one never tires of the great philosophers.'

They sat by a table overlooking the sea view and had a delicious salad of dressed crab with asparagus, crunchy bread and a bottle of crisp Savoy wine. Rose-Ellen felt relaxed and at ease. 'So what does it feel like to be a Frenchman living in Ireland?'

'I'm not totally French, only half, biologically speaking. My father was Irish and my mother was French but I was brought up in France and stayed there until I was eighteen; when I came to study here. So yes, I do feel more French.' He leaned back on the chair and thought for a minute. 'What does it feel like? I don't know, really. Strange, I suppose, but once you leave your birthplace nothing is ever the same. It's a schizophrenic feeling, for want of a better word, and of course I do love it here now. I didn't always, though.'

'So how does Ireland compare with France?'

He cut some of the crusty bread, offering her a slice. 'Very favourably. I like the laid-back lifestyle here, how natural people are and the freshness of everything.' He reached for the bottle of wine. There was still a quarter left. 'More wine?' he asked, and she nodded. 'I love both countries, but the French are…how shall I say? More formal and more reserved, so at times I feel as if I'm pulled and dragged between two quite different cultures.'

She took some wine. 'A bit like being at cross-currents, I suppose.'

'Yes, you could put it like that, and a sailing metaphor too!' he said, and smiled.

'And so where do you think you'll end up? I mean, which country will you settle down in?'

'Oh, that will depend on many things. I couldn't really say,' he answered vaguely, getting up and starting to clear away the plates.

Rose-Ellen drank her wine and watched the huge white ferry, *The Ulysses*, as it made its way out towards the horizon to the east and across the Irish Sea. 'What a great monster of a ship. I suppose it's a lot safer than being on a small boat. I mean if there was a storm.' As she twirled her glass, she thought of the sea and its portentous ways. 'You must have had some pretty scary moments at sea.'

'Indeed.'

'Tell me about the most terrifying time you ever had.'

'Oh…you don't really want to hear about it,' he called from the small annexed kitchen.

'Why not? This is real life drama!'

He came out with some crystal glasses which he put in the small cabinet on the wall and sat down at the table. 'Well I do recall a pretty horrendous scene last year off the south-west coast near Mizen Head. Are you sure you want to hear about it?'

'Sure!'

'It was one of those times one never forgets. I suppose it's etched in my mind forever.'

Rose-Ellen settled herself into the chair and listened attentively. He pulled a chair and sat beside her. 'It was about a year ago when I had volunteered to be doctor on call for the Shannon coastguard rescue service one weekend, and was called out to a scene where a Portuguese fishing vessel went aground off the coast of Mizen Head. The forecast had been bad, and I had great misgivings about a rescue at the time. You see, the weather was dreadful, the worst I had ever seen. The sea had a five to six metre swell.'

'Were you on a helicopter?'

'Yes. I remember vividly the pilot trying to keep the helicopter steady over the rolling ship. Looking down I could see white-tipped peaks dancing as the sea flattened in a wide circle underneath due to the downdraught from the rotor blades. I became nervous as he struggled for position to hover over the deck before the winch man lowered me on the cable for the search and rescue.'

'I bet you were scared!'

He nodded.

'Apprehensive certainly! You see, this sort of manoeuvre takes split-second timing. Crosswinds create tremendous vibrations as a pilot tries to steady a helicopter, and remember, the light was fading. The boat continued to roll back and forth in the churning sea. It's funny how the imagination can take a hold of one under these circumstances.'

'I can't even begin to imagine what you must have been thinking as you waited to be lowered down by winch,' Rose-Ellen said, looking out the window at some gulls hovering overhead.

'I thought at one stage that the moving mast of the ship was pointing its rolling finger of metal at me, as if it were warning me to stay away.' He leaned over on the chair and dusted away some breadcrumbs from the table. 'The tricks the mind plays on one at such times! But once the 'copter was steady, and with pinpoint accuracy, the pilot gave the "go" over the headsets. The winchman lowered me on to the deck.'

'I bet you were terrified to look down.'

'I tried not to while making my descent as the roar of the six ton helicopter overhead obliterated all other sound with the whirr of its blades.'

'I couldn't do that; I can't stand heights.'

He smiled at her. 'I could see waves breaking over the deck of the ship, but dangling at the end of the cable; there was little time to think of myself.' Pierre became quite animated as he recalled this frightening time. Rose-Ellen listened excitedly to his every word. He took a gulp of water from his glass. 'A man waving a red flag suddenly disappeared as a crashing wave lashed the deck and washed him overboard. Several lifejackets floated in the water and for a brief second I wondered about the men that were lost. There was debris everywhere; fish boxes and bits of rope and nets all floating around the sloppy sea. It was a mess. I braced myself for the landing jolt. I could feel the boat coming up to meet me. And then it came. Thud!' he exclaimed as he clapped both fists together to simulate the noise of his landing.

Rose-Ellen let out a gasp.

'My legs buckled as I hit the slippery deck. I quickly unlocked the winch hook. With the downdraught from the rotors and the rising dense spray, I could barely make out any shapes. Everything seemed to be a blur and I couldn't catch my voice.'

'Oh my God! Scary,' she said, placing her glass gently on the table.

'Then a hand grabbed me, pulling me into shelter, down two corridors and into a small cabin.'

'I can't even begin to think of how frightened you must have felt!'

'But the different sounds are something I'll never forget.'

'What do you mean?'

'Well, it's hard to explain, but in a crisis like this so many things are happening together, but I do recall that when the whirr of the helicopter's turbines faded, they were replaced by the thunder of the storm.' He stopped and went into the kitchen and came back with a full jug of water. He sat down and resumed his story. 'Now, where was I. Oh yes, two men lay on the ship. I examined both but they were already dead.'

He stopped. Rose-Ellen saw that he was visibly moved. She moved her hand towards him, slightly touching his. He composed himself and continued. 'Fortunately three of the other crew members were located by the skipper. Two were seriously injured, one with head and spinal injuries, the other with fractures.' He stopped as if remembering something.

'And the two who died; were they young? With families?'

'Yes, one of them was only nineteen and I think the other was a man in his forties. Such a loss of life, but that's the sea, the cruel merciless sea.'

Rose-Ellen shuddered at the thought of dying at sea. Pierre looked at her and then out to sea as if distracted. She got up and stretched herself.

'I must be off. Thank you for a wonderful day.'

'Glad you could come. Poor Peter was so exhausted after being on call; he wouldn't have been much company.'

He came over and helped her on with her jacket. She saw his perfectly chiselled features outlined in the evening light and wondered what he was thinking. He turned to her and attempted a smile. Her eyes caught his and she felt her lips quiver with longing, longing for closeness and intimacy. With that ardent yearning still in her heart, Rose-Ellen turned and gazed at the sea and briefly thought of Danny.

They said goodbye and Pierre watched as Rose-Ellen made her way down the steps to the DART across the way. As she looked out of the train on her way back to her apartment she reflected on their time together on board. She thought of Pierre standing over her in the fading light with that focussed gaze and wondered what he had been thinking about at the time. She felt a tinge of excitement as she recalled his touch on her face; a thrill almost. As she looked out the window at the passing rocks and sea she was aware of his silent presence, as he swung out of the mast laughing animatedly as a young boy would, like a shadow weaving in and out of her thoughts. Then her phone went off. She fumbled and got it out of her handbag. It was Siobhan. The train was almost at her station.

'Hi, Siobhan.' She held the phone to her ear.

'Where are you?'

'I've spent a very nice day at sea with Pierre.'

'Good for you. Are you interested in going out tonight?' Siobhan asked eagerly. But Rose-Ellen was not in the least enthused. Her day had been filled with happiness that she now just wanted to savour.

'Ah, I don't think so, Siobhan. I had a wonderful time. Pierre's so different on board, almost another person.' She could hear her voice change as she described him to her friend.

'Now, Rose-Ellen, be careful. Don't get at all involved. You have to work with the guy for God's sake. And besides, what about Danny? After all, you're an engaged woman!'

'I know, but I did feel something, a slight awkwardness out on board and I think he did too.'

'Of course he did! He knows you're bloody well engaged and he has a girlfriend. It's called intrigue, love, nothing else!'

'I suppose so,' Rose-Ellen lamely said, not wanting to hear any more of Siobhan's clinical view on what had been a lovely afternoon.

Chapter 13

It was March and the Cytu AB trial had been in progress for six months.

'The Project Manager from IQI Pharma phoned today and is very pleased with the rate of recruitment here,' Pierre said to Rose-Ellen who had just walked into the office laden down with bottles of bloods which needed to be spun in the centrifuge.

'That's terrific.'

'How many have we now in the trial?'

'Fifty enrolled and ten in screening,' she said, after she thought for a while on the status of the study.

'Shay has been instrumental in enrolling many of these patients,' he said.

'Sorry, but I'd better get these bloods ready for the courier.' After she had placed all of the blood tubes in the centrifuge and slapped its lid down firmly, she phoned the courier to come and collect the bloods. They would be sent to Switzerland for analysis for the trial. She folded her arms and looked at Pierre.

'That's terrific! she said enthusiastically.

Study drugs were missing and consent forms were not signed properly, but Rose-Ellen realised that sometimes these items got overlooked with all that clinical research entailed.

A week later, she could not find the informed consent for a woman from Galway and sought McAdam out in his office. She stood in his doorway with folded arms and said, 'Do you have a minute to discuss a patient for the Cytu AB trial, because I can't find any consent for her?'

Busily writing up a patient's report, he ignored her. Going over to the shelf she took down the Master Trial File, which contained all of the Cytu AB trial information. Opening up the file at the consent section, she said to Shay, 'Do you have a minute?'

He nodded.

'The patient in question is number thirty-two and I can't find any corresponding consent for her. I know that you took bloods from her because they went off to the lab in Switzerland a few days ago and I have the results here.'

He looked up from the documentation. 'What's this all about?'

She repeated the patient's number.

'Oh well, she'll be in next week for her second visit and I can get her to sign the consent form then,' he said vaguely.

Rose-Ellen felt her heartbeat race and she wondered if she had heard correctly. Putting a patient into a trial with out consent was one of the greatest crimes in clinical trials. 'You can't enrol a patient to a trial without first taking their consent.'

'So what! She was due to have her bloods done as part of her routine management.' With clinical trials, transparency was essential and there was no room for any kind of shoddiness. 'That won't do. Her bloods were sent to Switzerland, so therefore she's in the trial.'

'I explained everything about the trial to her. I just forgot to get her to sign the damn consent form.'

Rose-Ellen was shocked at the blithe insouciance he was manifesting. 'Sorry, Shay. That won't do. No consent – no procedures! Remember, GCP.' Good Clinical Practice was the mantra that Rose-Ellen lived by and she guessed that he could not be bothered with the tedious, pernickety adherence to GCP.

'Consents and the rest of the bloody paperwork for these trials are your responsibility as trial co-ordinator. I have more important things to do,' he said dismissively.

She was disgusted at what was unravelling in front of her. She could not believe what she was hearing. 'If it's not written down in this game, then it's not done. Is that clear? While I could explain everything to the patient about what is involved as study nurse and trial co-ordinator, ultimately it's you, the doctor and co-investigator, who must take the consent from the patient and countersign their signature.'

Without looking up he muttered, 'I'll get her to backdate the consent form.'

'That's not how things are done. Everything must be completely transparent for the auditors. We can't afford to be flippant, not with clinical trials. It's just too damn serious and the repercussions could be enormous for all of us.' The atmosphere in the room was electric but Rose-Ellen would not give up. She sat down and continued looking in his direction. He finished writing and replaced the top of his pen, then stood up.

'Look, the last thing I want is a lecture from you wittering on about clinical trial rules and codes of practice designed to please auditors and no one else.'

He grabbed his coat and left. Rose-Ellen was shocked and concerned.

Chapter 14

'Courier companies! They'll be the bane of my life,' Rose-Ellen said, to nobody in particular, pressing the start button on her laptop.

Pierre came out and sat on her desk. 'How would you like a trip to Singapore?'

She gasped. 'Singapore?' What do you mean?'

'Well, you know that I'm going to Sydney in two weeks time for the Non-Hodgkin's study. I'm stopping off at Singapore *en route* for an oncology conference and I would like you to attend it. I think it would be of benefit for you for the type of work we do here. The conference is aimed at specific oncological trials.'

So Rose-Ellen accompanied Pierre to the oncology conference in Singapore in March. During the week-long conference in Singapore, she wondered about the authenticity of the data presented by the pharmaceutical companies, how statisticians could 'crunch the numbers', how even the most marginal beneficial effects of a drug were teased out to enhance its profile and therapeutic effects. While listening to the sessions, she reflected on her own life as research nurse: were her valiant efforts going towards the betterment of humanity? Or were they merely helping to swell the coffers of the pharmaceutical company or their shareholders? Still, she consoled herself that without drugs and the pharmaceutical companies who supported the research, healthcare globally would probably be in a poorer state.

On the last night Pierre phoned Rose-Ellen in her room. 'Hi, it's me. Fancy a non-corporate night?'

She knew exactly what he meant, having had enough of listening to presentations on block-busting research, and reading dry statistical abstracts on trials and their clinical and statistical merits.

'What are you suggesting?'

'I was wondering if you would like to go to Geylang, where the locals eat. It's not far from here and I hear the food's wonderful.'

'Sounds good to me.'

'I'll meet you in the lobby in an hour. How does that sound?'

'Perfect.'

Not having to dress to impress she could just be herself with Pierre. He was waiting for her in the foyer of the hotel. Coming down the stairs, she noticed him casually browsing through one of the many brochures extolling the virtues of Singapore. He stood up when she arrived and she smiled as they were wearing almost identical outfits – crisp white shirts and pale blue jeans.

'We're like twins; same outfits!' she giggled.

'Or it could be just telepathy!'

They took a taxi to Geylang in the Eastern part of Singapore. 'How did you manage to extricate yourself from the corporate dos?'

'One just has to be firm and say no,' he said, snapping shut his Apple iPad after checking his message box. 'You get no thanks for always being available. I can't tell you how relaxing it is to be away from it all for one night.'

On the way there, Rose-Ellen stared at the grandiose nineteenth-century architecture that contrasted with the huge, Lego-like concrete blocks rising from the countless roads that led from the airport. Here was the flavour of the East: hot, spicy and teeming with life and colour, with some of the best food on the island and pulsating with the smells and sounds of the Orient.

When they got out of the taxi, Pierre took her hand in his. She could feel her heart race a little. His hand felt warm and firm to touch and yet there was gentleness too about the way he held it. 'Just keep with me. It's noisy and frenetic. One could easily get lost. These streets are virtual souks.'

She saw men standing on every corner and harassed-looking women dressed in local styles weaving their way through the crowds, weighed down with heavy shopping bags. They walked on and came to a street full of colourful restaurants where blue, green and bright red neon lights flashed, giving the place a surreal atmosphere. He turned to her. 'What do you fancy? Chinese, Indian or European? Remember, this is Singapore and they have everything.'

'I think I'd like Chinese.'

'Good choice!'

They passed a Chinese restaurant which seemed animated and full of *bonhomie*. Inside people talked, drank beer and ate heartily. A tiny Chinaman with a long beard and dressed in a cream, silk tunic smiled a broad smile at them, and bowing, swept them inside and guided them to the only vacant table in the restaurant. After perusing several menus, they decided on the coconut rice and chicken curry, noodles with roast pork and prawns and peppered crab. Rose-Ellen could feel her stomach churn while reading some of the dishes on the menu, particularly frog's leg porridge.

Pierre saw her grimace. 'I can see that your European sanitised tastes are being given a jolt here. It's not any different to snails in garlic or oysters in champagne.'

She peered at him over the large menu card and whispered, 'Pierre, just because you've grown up eating frogs and snails doesn't mean the rest of us have to get used to such things,' then added, 'I'm afraid to look around at any of the tables here in case I see something still squirming or swimming.'

'Not here in Singapore,' he said, 'though in other parts of Asia that's possible.' They ordered beers. The waiter hovered over them briskly preparing their table and cutlery. She noticed how Pierre was careful with food, rarely touching the crackers or sauces which arrived, and barely sipping his beer. Then the hot, steaming dishes arrived. Rose-Ellen had never seen such an array of spicy, mouthwatering fare. The delicious aromas of charcoal and caramelised scents suffused the air around their small table. Pierre thanked the waiter and inhaled the wonderful aromas.

'Now please, what can I tempt you with? Some of this delicious chicken in coconut? Or the pork? God, this is good!' he exclaimed.

'I think I'll start with the chicken,' Rose-Ellen said cautiously, and then helped herself to a bowl of the steaming, jasmine-scented rice.

Pierre used chopsticks. 'I couldn't handle the chopsticks at all. You see, I don't eat a lot of oriental food. Wexford isn't exactly a Mecca for Asian cuisine.'

He smiled. 'Let me help you. It's fun and once you've mastered the art, you won't ever eat Chinese food with a knife and fork again.' He opened up her package of chopsticks and placed a chopstick in each of her hands. She felt his warm hand on hers, guiding her through the process of using the chopsticks, picking up a small ball of rice and gently putting it with a piece of chicken to her mouth. She could feel her heart fluttering inside her chest and wondered if she had lost a beat, while feeling hot under the strong lights. She thought that she was going to faint and then the delicious chicken touched her tongue and awakened her senses to its delightful taste. Pierre took his hand away and helped himself to some food.

'So tell me how are you enjoying the conference and have you managed to catch any of the delights of Singapore?'

'Yes indeed, I have. The conference is very good; there are so many interesting abstracts and posters. I have the time to absorb the information, as most of the time at work there's simply no opportunity to read.'

Pierre served himself the crab and then offered some to her. 'I understand. The demands of the job. Try this, it's delicious.'

She demurred as her plate was heaving with food.

'Have you managed to get away at all; do any shopping in the evening after the meetings?' he asked.

'The hotel has a lovely mall with some fabulous silks so I'm afraid that I did some serious shopping there. I visited the Botanic Gardens one afternoon which was free. I would have liked to have gone up on the Flyer, but well, there just isn't time for everything.'

'The Flyer would be wonderful to see the harbour, but that's it. One of those blasted things is the same as any other, but then I'm a sailor!'

At the mention of sailing, she asked, 'What about the race around Ireland you're planning? When does it start and what will it involve?'

'The Circle of Ireland? If I started talking about the race I'd never finish. It's in June so I'm already planning to make sure we have everything ready, and of course selecting a crew. I'm still undecided about a few; can't make up my mind. What does it involve? Basically sailing around Ireland, competing against other boats and winning in my class.'

'You lead a very busy and demanding life.'

'Busy enough, between medicine, research and sailing. I must say I do like research. If I had my way I'd get into it full-time.'

Then the dishes were cleared away and it was time for dessert. Pierre did not even look at the menu. 'I don't do sweet,' he said succinctly.

But Rose-Ellen ordered a dessert from the copious menu and soon a long glass of multi-coloured ice cream arrived; pink, mint and vanilla, slathered in Chantilly cream and chocolate sauce, topped with a bright red cherry and impaled with a twirling umbrella with sparks flying madly around the colourful mound. She felt a tad childish having ordered this huge dessert after such a banquet.

'You never know from the menu what guises desserts come in,' Pierre whispered, detecting her slight unease at the contents of the ornate glass.

'This ice cream is not as good as the ice cream in Downe's Ice Cream Parlour in Loughbow. Ireland is the only place for decent ice cream,' she said, daintily picking at the contents with a long spoon.

They left the restaurant and wandered out into the brightly lit streets. The air felt humid and lights dazzled everywhere. People ambled peacefully in the balmy night air, bicycles and cabs streamed up and down the road and life teemed after hours, unlike home. As they turned a corner Rose-Ellen nearly lost her footing on the pavement, but Pierre's steady hand moved to the gentle curve of her back and steadied her. She could feel his firm hand through her thin cotton blouse and this sent a quiver through her very being.

'I don't know about you, but I couldn't possibly go to bed after all this food. I'll have to walk it off.'

Pierre looked at his watch. Smiling at her, he said, 'Good idea.'

They seemed to stroll forever in the warm, equatorial, balmy evening. Rose-Ellen felt relaxed and chatty after the food. Pierre was attentive and engaging. At one stage, she became quite giggly and found herself flirting with him.

'I feel full of energy. There must be something in those Chinese herbs.' She had no idea how long they had walked, but it seemed an aeon. Pierre's long strides reflected his great stamina. He insisted on stopping in a local coffee house.

'Why not,' she concurred.

'I can't go to bed without one,' he said.

Inside, she ordered a green tea and sipped it demurely. Pierre asked for a short espresso.

It was after one in the morning when they got back to the hotel having walked for over an hour in the sticky heat of the Singaporean night. In the lift on the way up, they stood in silence. Then, as the lift door opened on her floor, he turned to her and said, 'Rose-Ellen…'

'Yes?'

'I…nothing'

'What is it?'

'Nothing. Goodnight.'

'Goodnight, Pierre.'

The lift doors closed. Rose-Ellen walked down the long corridor to her bedroom. As she removed her make-up in front of the mirror in the bathroom, she wondered what Pierre was about to say. Maybe he was going to invite her for a nightcap! Then she thought of Danny. She had not spoken to him for several days. She wondered what time it was at home and whether she should ring him, and then decided not to. That night she fretted in her troubled sleep.

Chapter 15

Rose-Ellen bought silks for her mother and Olivia, and a smoking jacket in dark racing-green, emblazoned with scarlet and fire-spewing dragons for her Dad.

Kitty Power could not conceal her excitement as she opened up the bags out of which tumbled packets of tissue paper revealing rolls of exquisite silks, satins and the best of jersey/cashmere mixes. 'My God, these are gorgeous!' Holding a length of rich lavender silk up to her face, Kitty gazed at herself in the mirror.

'Oh, darling, it's only beautiful! The real thing! I can't wait to get a three-piece suit made up. Maybe something nice for the wedding.' Then she stopped and gasped as she spied a folded rectangle of silk fabric with a pale apricot and lemon design peeping out from another piece of tissue. 'Isn't this divine?' Taking it out of its tissue and wrapping it around her waist Kitty danced around the bedroom, humming to herself. Olivia and Rose-Ellen were in stitches laughing at their mother.

'Mam, you'd want to see yourself, you're hilarious!' Olivia gasped.

But their mother was not listening to them and their sniggers of derision. 'Why not? It's not often I get to parade around the floor in pure silk.'

Maurice was delighted with his smoking jacket. He tried it on and stood in front of the mirror, but it was difficult to hide his corpulent belly. 'This is fabulous. I'd never dream of buying anything so luxurious and it fits perfectly too.'

Kitty tightened the belt around his waist. 'Daddy, you look like an emperor in it.' She winked over at Rose-Ellen and Olivia as they watched their father prancing around in his new silk smoking jacket.

'God knows what he'll expect now when he wears that gorgeous jacket. We'll all be pandering to his every whim,' Kitty said.

Rose-Ellen bought smart jeans for Danny. She was determined to get him out of those dungarees once and for all. Holding them up, he looked at them somewhat sceptically. 'They're lovely, pet, but I dunno. Will I get into them at all? They look a bit tight on me.'

'Now, Danny, you won't know until you try them. Put them on and let's have a look at you.'

'You know what you have to do, Danny Redmond, and that is to cut down on some of the food. You're too fat and that's all there is to it. What you eat in a day would sink a liner! Here, give me a belt and that will do the trick. Now, the cut of those jeans is excellent!'

She looked at him, but it was hard to hide years of abuse when it came to food. 'Do you know that I scoured the shops for a pair that'd fit you; it was nearly impossible to get something in your size 'cause you'd be a giant compared to the people in the Far East,' Rose-Ellen said matter-of-factly as she adjusted the belt around his ample girth.

He gazed at himself in the mirror; front, back and side and could not decide whether he liked the jeans or not. 'They're not the sort that Mammy would have bought for me; too tight down there,' he said, motioning to his crotch. Rose-Ellen watched him turn and move in front of the mirror and supposed that Josie Redmond would have bought something that would give a man plenty of leeway in that area.

'But tight jeans are much smarter than those big baggy things you wear around the place with pockets and zips all up the leg. And besides, these are smart jeans to wear when you go out, not for mucking around the place with Mattie.'

'Thanks, love, they're grand, I needed a new pair anyway,' he said, quickly taking them off.

Chapter 16

A patient had complained of chest pain whilst taking the trial drug Cytu AB and had subsequently suffered a myocardial infarction – a heart attack – following which, Shay McAdam did an electrocardiogram – ECG, tracing of the heart's conduction. In the medical notes, McAdam had stated that he had performed a second ECG some days later. Pierre came into the room and saw Rose-Ellen scrutinising the strips of paper which recorded the heart tracings.

'Is everything OK?'

'I'm just wondering that myself,' she said, letting her head fall into her cupped hand. He came over and took the strips out of her hand and examined them. 'Something's odd here.'

'I wonder if you're thinking what I am.'

'Well the paper manufacturer's name is running repeatedly along the bottom, "Electro Cardiac Technology", but the cut has sliced through the word "Cardiac". It would seem that the same ECG tracing has been cut in two.'

She got up.

'The first tracing ends with "Car" while the second tracing starts with the word "diac", which only means one thing.'

She grabbed the tracings out of his hand. 'I'm going to get to the bottom of this.'

She strode into McAdam's office across the corridor without knocking. Inside she found McAdam on the floor doing press-ups, 'forty-five, forty-six, forty-seven…' he said mechanically. He leaned back on his right arm when she walked in and she noticed how his left sleeve was rolled up past his elbow, and a small ball of cotton wool was anchored to his skin with non-allergic tape at the elbow joint of his left arm. Moving over to his desk she slid her fingers across the still warm glass tubes of blood upright in the rack there.

'What's this? Are you testing your own blood?'

'Now why would I do that? I'm extremely fit,' he said tartly. She shuddered at the malign way he stared at her, his cold grey eyes full of contempt.

'I thought…'

'I don't care what you thought,' he snapped.

'So whose blood is this then?' she asked. She had a strange sense of unease.

'For a patient on the breast cancer trial who came in early to have her bloods taken on her way to work.'

'OK then, I can spin these for you. I've a batch of bloods going to Switzerland today.'

'No, that won't be necessary. I'll do it myself in a minute.'

'But it's no problem. I can then send all the bloods together by courier before noon today.'

'No, I said. Now leave it at that. What did you want anyway?'

She could sense by the tone the ire in his voice. She thrust the paper strips at him.

'What can you tell me about this?' she said.

He examined the ECG tracings and said nothing. 'I'm wondering as to why the same strip of paper has been cut in two, giving the impression that two ECGs were done.'

'I have no idea,' he said, pushing the ECG strip of paper back to her.

She then pointed out the break in the word 'Cardiac'. 'How do you explain that? I can't send this document to the company; it looks as if you only took one ECG and cut it in two. This is serious. An ECG is crucial as part of the diagnosis of myocardial infarction.'

He threw his hands in the air and shouted at her. 'A second ECG was bloody well done!'

She stood there implacably, her arms folded. 'So where is the second strip then?'

'In your hand.'

'I have one ECG recording in my hand, cut in two. Not two!'

He remained silent.

'If you say that you did a second ECG then so be it, I can't argue with you. But you'll have to document in the patient's hospital chart that you actually took two ECGs and one is missing. At the end of the day, you have to come clean.'

He looked at her with a slightly malevolent grin. 'Come clean? So that's it. What are you implying? Some underhand stuff? You should watch your tongue. You're far too free and easy with your choice of words. Some day it will land you in serious trouble! I checked the patient and she is fine.'

She was unhappy with his explanation about the ECG. She was livid and frustrated by his complete indifference. She hoped that her misgivings had not gone unheeded, but she had her doubts as he insouciantly resumed his press-ups: 'fifty-one, fifty-two, fifty-three...' etc.

Later that afternoon she sat with Pierre. He looked worried. 'Putting patients onto a new chemo agent without proper cardiac assessment is potentially serious, and particularly one who had chest pain.'

Rose-Ellen knew that safety was always of the utmost priority in Pierre's mind. She had seen patients whose side effects were so awful that they had to discontinue the chemotherapy.

He examined the ECG tracings again.

'Looking at the readings they're exactly the same tracing, and it does show some heart changes, which need to be treated. I'll have a word with Shay. How is the patient?'

'As far I know she's all right.'

Rose-Ellen knew that in order to ensure that she was not blamed for another's carelessness and ineptitude she was going to have to keep Pierre up-to-date on all of the activities in the research department, and particularly anything to do with Shay McAdam.

'Pierre, there's something about Shay I just don't get. There's his constant preoccupation; as if his mind is thousands of miles away when I'm trying to tell him about a patient's medical history, or a serious adverse event.'

Pierre got up to leave. 'I'll speak to Shay about the ECG,' he said, and walked out the door and down the corridor to the large oncology outpatients clinic. Her eyes followed him. The burden of patients' treatment and subsequent outcome – the length of time they had left on this earth – weighed heavily on his stooped shoulders.

Rose-Ellen wondered why McAdam's part-time nurse, Helen, was not involved in the trial and supposed that McAdam preferred to have complete control over the trial data himself, without the involvement of others. Later that day she bumped into Helen up in the X-ray department and asked her about her role.

'He won't let me near his precious Cytu AB trial notes; says it's too complicated and besides, he doesn't want me interviewing the patients. He maintains I would need to be trained on the protocol. "But so what?" I said to him. "I'm willing to learn".'

'Did he now? Well, Helen, I'd be happy to train you. After all, a lot of the procedures can be done by a nurse – it'd make more sense,' Rose -Ellen said, her eyes wide with disbelief. Rose-Ellen sat down on a bench in the corridor and wondered if this were all part of McAdam's own skullduggery; wanting exclusive control over the trial data.

The following week McAdam was away for two days at an oncology meeting in Germany. Rose-Ellen tiptoed across to his office and took down some of the Cytu AB files. As she probed through the files, she discovered blood pressure and pulse readings had been crossed out and re-written. So he had changed his mind, the scoundrel, she muttered to herself. But most worrying of all, was the fact that all of the patient consents had been signed with the same pen, and upon close scrutiny, they all looked as if they had been written by the same person, bearing a distinct likeness to McAdam's own signature with that same light, feathery scrawl she knew only too well.

'This patient data looks made up – and to think that this company is paying big bucks for this!' she murmured to herself, as she closed the last folder. She wondered why the patients' medical notes looked as if they had been put together on an *ad hoc* basis, and were so flimsy when they should have been bulging with information and medical history for this type of patient who presented with advanced cancer.

Later Pierre called into Shay's office. He could see by Rose-Ellen's expression that she was visibly upset. 'Is anything the matter?' he asked.

'I don't know where to start. Of those patients who have been recently enrolled to the trial, some are actually ineligible for various reasons. Others have thin hospital medical files with no hospital number, no previous medical history and it appeared as if Shay McAdam has made up his own file and not bothered with a proper hospital chart with its own specific bar code. I just wonder who these patients are, as I have never come across their names in any of the clinics.'

He sat down.

'There's a sinister thread here, which we shall need to unravel before the whole fraudulent mess gets into the public domain. And another thing! The Director of Laboratory Services in Switzerland rang me this morning and asked if there could be some mistake with the bloods sent for the Cytu AB trial as the results were all within normal limits, which is odd coming from this cohort of very ill patients. He also said that the test tube bar codes did not always match the specific corresponding accession number on the requisition form.'

Rose-Ellen thought back to her strange encounter with McAdam when he was doing press-ups in his office. 'Maybe he's sending in his own blood for these patients he's invented.'

'Why do you say that?'

'I don't know, it's just a strange feeling I have. I came into his office last week to confront him about the ECG and there was fresh blood in test tubes on a rack in his office which he said he had just taken from a patient for the breast cancer trial, but here is the sinister thing. He had a cotton ball attached to his arm. Besides, there are no bloods due for the breast cancer trial, as I know all of these patients and when their visits are due.' She stopped and looked at Pierre allowing what she had said sink in.

'Look, maybe it's nothing, who knows, but it did strike me as odd and the blood was still warm in the test tubes.'

'So what are you implying?' That he could have used his own blood and sent it away for analysis for a patient whom he had concocted for the Cytu AB trial, but pretended that the blood was for a patient in the breast cancer trial to throw you off the scent.'

'Something along those lines,' she sighed.

'Leave no stone unturned. I would like you to make a list of all anomalies and Shay will have to be confronted. I've organised an audit to be done on the Cytu AB trial next week,' he said.

'Rightly so,' she muttered. Her blood ran cold at the mention of the word audit.

The next day she sat in Shay's office and pondered the provenance of these patients. There was a knock on the door. She ventured a glance outside and saw a small grey-haired man standing there. He seemed somewhat perturbed.

'Hello, what can I do for you? Please come in and sit down over there,' she said, motioning him towards the chair by the window.

He let out a weary sigh.

'I was hopin' to meet with the other doctor, a Dr McAdam, I think he calls himself.'

'Dr McAdam is away for a few days, can I help? I'm the research nurse here.'

'Well, it's like this. The wife was takin' some pills he prescribed for some research they were doin' at the hospital, and she wasn't well all day yesterday, and when I took her to her GP he didn't know what the pills were for and asked her and she didn't know either. I wanted to find out more, so that's why I came in here. I have them here with me,' he said, producing a large packet of pills from his pocket.

Rose-Ellen saw that they were the pale blue Cytu AB capsules. She looked at the man, tired and harassed, as he sat down. Her worst fears were realised. His wife was taking the Cytu AB trial drug and McAdam had not bothered to tell her that she was taking part in a clinical trial. Had McAdam sat down and discussed what was involved in participating in a trial with a drug unknown and untried in terms of its risks and benefits? She wondered if the patient was even eligible to go into the trial with its strict entry criteria. What would happen if the woman had become seriously ill on this untried drug, or worse had died and was not even supposed to be in the trial in the first place? She shivered with the prospect.

'Did your wife know that she was in a clinical trial?'

'She didn't mention anything to me about a trial, and if I had known this I wouldn't have allowed her to be used like a guinea pig.'

He was very upset and dried his eyes with a large white handkerchief.

Rose-Ellen began, 'She's in the trial for her cancer. It's a good drug, but I'm sure that Dr McAdam would have explained all of this to her beforehand.' She sat down and waited a minute for him to compose himself and then resumed. 'I mean, did she get a leaflet or information sheet explaining what was involved?'

He looked up at her. 'Information sheet?'

'Information about the trial. Because, if so, she would have had to sign a form, a consent form saying that she agreed to take part in the trial.'

'Look, Nurse, the way it is with my wife, she's not with it half the time. She's very down in herself and worried about this and that; between me and her own health and then the grandchildren, ah, she's a terrible worrier.'

He looked down at the floor.

Rose-Ellen sighed. This was so typical of McAdam; half-heartedly explaining the trial to a patient. Looking at this man, anxious, frightened, and unnecessarily so. She moved her chair a bit closer to him. 'You said that your wife was not well; what sort of things is she complaining about? Because she's in the trial we'll need to see her ourselves just to ensure that it's nothing too serious and report it to the authorities, you understand.'

'I understand all right. Well, she was getting pains in her stomach, feelin' sick all the time, kind of gone off her food, and she normally has a great appetite, nurse.'

After taking a history from the man about his wife, Rose-Ellen thanked him and then made an appointment to have his wife seen as soon as possible by Pierre.

He dried a tear.

Rose-Ellen got up. 'Don't worry now; everything is going to be OK. I'll see your wife tomorrow and afterwards Dr O'Hegarty will take a look at her. He's wonderful with the patients so you need have no worries.'

'Ah, Nurse, you're a star. Thanks very much.'

The man thanked her profusely again and again and finally let himself out closing the door gently behind him. Rose-Ellen immediately searched for a possible consent form for the man's wife and there it was – signed and dated, but only by Shay McAdam. There was no signature from the patient. It appeared as if McAdam could not be bothered to explain the trial fully to her and obtain her consent. It seemed as if there was an air of sloppy disregard about this patient. McAdam was becoming slick, careless and potentially fraudulent.

The following week, a three-day audit took place at DCH on the Cytu AB trial.

Chapter 17

Rose-Ellen and Pierre were in her office. It was late in the evening and the auditors were still there and probing through the data for the Cytu AB trial.

'I think he is forging the names on the consent forms. Maybe I could be wrong, but it looks suspicious to me. The writing appears to be all the same; same pen, same scrawl and you don't need to be an expert on handwriting to see this. Basically it stinks!' Now she had said it. Rose-Ellen settled herself into a chair.

She could see that he was troubled. 'Careful, now. That is a fraudulent charge, Rose-Ellen.'

'I think that you need to look at them yourself.'

'He could have given his own biro to the patients.'

She knew that doctors had a tendency to stick up for each other, but she was determined to follow her own hunches. 'Pierre, when you look at as many signatures on consent forms as I do, you know that they are all very different; random, some child-like, others are like a scrawl and then there are those signatures that are almost printed, but these, well, they just all look a bit similar.'

He sat down, leaned back on his chair, let out a deep sigh and put his hands through his hair in a gesture of mild irritation. 'Please show me some consent forms and I'll look at the signatures. This catalogue is an auditor's nightmare – ineligible patients! Frankly, that's all we need. If he is falsifying the data, it'll have repercussions for us all: you, me, Dr Doolan, this place and it will haunt us for the rest of our days.' She felt unnerved at the way he was speaking to her.

'Pierre, I don't mind taking bloods from any patient that I know about, but if Shay is inventing patients…'

Pierre rose again from his seat. 'What a nightmare! Look, I've been invited to Paris to speak about our situation at DCH re: Cytu AB at an international conference on oncology. I want you to provide me with the latest figures for the trial; the usual things: numbers recruited, screen failures, withdrawals and adverse events. I need to firm up on this issue and our suspicions before going over there. Because if these patients don't exist, well then, all this data is meaningless!'

Rose-Ellen bent down to pick up her biro which had fallen on the floor as she flicked through the large folder on her desk. As she did Pierre got there first, and their hands briefly brushed, a moment of fleeting intimacy so human and yet so fraught with expectant desire. She blushed and looked away to hide her confusion.

'When is Paris?'

'In two weeks time.'

He sat back in his chair. He had both arms in the air; hands clasped. He turned and looked at her. 'You know, getting into trouble with the authorities is serious business, and potentially McAdam could be getting himself into very deep waters. Fraud in clinical research is a crime here. But this here is too big to let go; it could have monumental ripples in the clinical world of research at large. If we disregard this, people could spend years and a lot of money basing their research on this drug. Can you imagine the situation down the road? If the science is flawed then it means that all those years of research have been in vain and the results will be meaningless,' he said leaning forward and tapping his fingers on the desk in frustration.

Rose-Ellen realised that Pierre was right. She had begun to see the bigger picture, the enormous repercussions of clinical research fraud – because other researchers could use a trial, a concept, a theory on which to base more science. That in turn could become flawed and the cycle would be repeated. All because of someone's ego, a callous disregard for one's fellow men, an insatiable yearning for one's hospital to be the best recruiter in a trial and to have one's name on as many research papers published as possible.

Rose-Ellen got up and moved over to the tiny window which looked out on to the back of the hospital and watched the raindrops as they splattered against the windowpane. She thought of how selfish types like Shay McAdam did not see the wider sphere, but only the short-term glory:

their name on some research paper, another addition to their CV. She turned and faced Pierre. 'I don't know if this is just a hunch or what.'

'Out with it! Hunches or gut feelings can be crucial.'

'Even with those patients who do actually exist, some of them for sure shouldn't be in the trial at all,' she said.

Normally it took a lot to ruffle Pierre. 'My worst fears confirmed. No wonder the recruitment rate is so high,' he announced with an exasperated tone. He got up and leaned against a filing cabinet. He turned and gave her one of his piercing gazes. 'Are you quite sure about this? I mean, have you checked everything thoroughly against the medical history to ensure that they are eligible?'

'Yes, yes, I have. They don't fulfil the entry criteria. I'll get their medical charts and you can see for yourself.'

'OK, we'll see what the audit finds. Now about those other patients. Was it ten or fifteen whom you had doubts about whether they actually exist? Have you checked out all correspondence? Letters from GPs, referral letters? Can you check who these patients are, maybe by contacting them?'

She sat down. 'That's just it. There's no hospital number on these files and I've written to some but have had no reply. That's after I tried to contact them by phone. It's as if they don't exist.'

Pierre looked concerned. 'Is it possible that he could be manufacturing patients for the trial?'

She took a deep breath. 'As I said, it's only a hunch, and I'm trying to follow up with the Medical Records Department to see if these patients exist. They probably do, it's just, oh, I don't know, the files don't look genuine.'

'What has McAdam got to say about these patients? Have you spoken to him about them, where they came from, who referred them?'

'He says they exist all right. Apparently they were admitted through casualty via a large GP practice, but according to Medical Records they would still need a hospital medical file with the five digit hospital number and the special hospital patient bar code.' She yawned. 'I need a coffee,' she said. 'Would you like one?'

His expression softened. 'I could do with some strong coffee. Thanks.'

She got up and filled the *cafetière* with three good mounted tablespoons of ground coffee, poured fresh water into the machine and pressed the button. Soon it was gurgling and wafts of percolated coffee filled the small room.

From the intense way Pierre was perusing the files Rose-Ellen could see the strain he was under. She brought him over a mug of hot coffee. 'Thanks,' he said. He went silent, wrapping his hands around the warm mug of coffee and smelling its aroma. Then he turned to her. She could see how tired and drained he looked; his eyes buried deep into his sockets from worry and lack of sleep. It was well known in the hospital that Pierre shouldered a lot of responsibility for Dr Doolan and now it would appear that McAdam was also a concern.

'Suspecting something is one thing, but accusing somebody of professional misconduct is quite another matter. What does McAdam think he is doing! If he is found to be in breach of the law, I'll do all in my power to get to the truth even if it means crossing him off the medical register.'

'If he is cooking the books then why do you think he is doing it? I mean, what is his motive?' said Rose-Ellen.

Pierre looked at the mounds of paperwork on his desk. 'Who knows what goes on inside that skull of his. Prestige, kudos for being the investigator at the centre of the highest recruiting hospital in the world for a ground-breaking drug, some strange kicks at power?'

'What about money? After all, this research department gets well paid by IQI Pharma for each patient enrolled. There are at least ten visits per patient in the trial and so we're talking serious money here.'

'And it's not a paltry sum per visit either. IQI are one of the best payers of any pharma company. But the funds don't go to him. They go to the Hospital Research Fund, so that's no reason why he'd pocket the money.'

All payments received from pharmaceutical companies for clinical research go to a research fund in the hospital. This is very strictly controlled and how funds are spent is carefully scrutinised by auditors and by the Ethics Committee in the hospital.

'But what if he were helping himself to funds?'

'Oh, come off it, Rose-Ellen. We are answerable to the Ethics Committee for every penny we make on a clinical trial. We'd have the hospital accountant breathing down our necks for any irregularity.'

'Well, there are other ways he could be making money from the trial.'

'Such as?'

'There are trial drugs that have gone missing.'

'How come? They should go directly to the pharmacy when they arrive.'

'A whole boxful that arrived several weeks ago still can't be found anywhere and apparently Shay McAdam signed for them. With great difficulty and a lot of paperwork, I managed to get replacement drugs for those patients who needed them.'

'Is it possible that he could be selling them on to patients who are desperate for a drug for their cancer? Patients and their relative can look up anything now on the internet and they will pay huge amounts of money for a ground-breaking drug such as Cytu AB.'

'I don't trust him one bit. For all we know he could be selling the drugs to desperate women whose families would pay anything just to give them another year or two of life at the most. Have you not seen his clothes, his new car, the latest gear? You can bet that he's not getting that on his hospital salary.'

He thought for a while. 'When I am in Paris would you please try and locate these missing trial drugs, and then I want you to check all of the patient charts with Medical Records. If we are found to be a fraudulent institution the whole place will be closed down, and our names tainted forever with this scandal. I also have looked at the bloods for those patients whose bloods seem to be too healthy and they would be more likely to come from a healthy rugby forward than an ill cancer patient, so that is scary to say the least.'

She shuddered at this prospect. Her name and Pierre's dragged through the newspapers; this stain on her otherwise impeccable CV.

'He must be stopped!' he exclaimed bristling with indignation.

She was barely listening to him now, exhausted from having worked late the previous night. She thought of the next day and how busy she would be with more patient visits, a monitoring visit from another company's Clinical Research Associate for a different trial and endless paperwork, a sign of what her life was becoming, not to mention the ongoing audit.

Rose-Ellen looked at her watch. It was after eight pm. She got up to leave, picked up her bag, tied her belt firmly on her coat and dropped the keys of the office in front of him. 'Now, don't work too late.'

He was sitting at his desk going through his e-mails and looked up at her. 'Goodnight, Rose-Ellen.'

She could see that he was tired; tired from endlessly giving of himself and trying to be all things to all people. As she opened the door to leave, she called back to him. 'See you tomorrow.'

Rose-Ellen held her head high and she could feel Pierre's eyes follow her as she strode confidently out of the door. As she drove home that night, she began for the first time to fear for the outcome of the Cytu AB trial.

Chapter 18

It remained cold and dreary outside. The weather had been relentlessly wet and it appeared as if there would be no let-up.

'Love, of course I'll go to the Open Field Day. It's been in my diary since January.' Rose-Ellen leaned into her mobile to catch what Danny was saying to her.

'Good girl. 'Cause I'm on the committee, and there'll be a lot of preparin' and organisin' and no better woman than yourself to get stuck in.'

She had managed to persuade Pierre to let her have some extra days for the May Bank Holiday. 'Of course! But please try and get things sorted out beforehand so there won't be such a deluge of work when you return,' Pierre had cautioned her.

'Of course I will.'

Rose-Ellen called down to the Redmond farm on the Sunday. Two neglected lambs were being bottle-fed in the kitchen when she arrived. One tiny one who was taking short, shallow breaths was still wrapped in newspaper by the Aga.

'Hello, Rose. How are ye at all? Here take these eggs; we painted them at the I.C.A. meeting,' (Irish Countrywomen's Association) Josie said, presenting her with a basket. Rose-Ellen looked inside at a multitude of coloured eggs – green, red and blue, all with cheeky expressions.

'Ah, Josie, they're gorgeous. Thanks so much. How are you?'

'Tired. Up the whole night with this lot,' she said, turning to look at the lambs.

'Right we'll go so! Put on a pair of wellingtons 'cause the fields will be mighty dirty and mucky,' Danny called to her from the hallway.

She tried several pairs of wellington boots which Josie presented and finally settled on a pair of Mairead's riding boots. 'She won't mind and I won't tell her,' Josie said, taking the paper out of the boots.

Rose-Ellen walked up the fields with Danny who was anxious to check on the status of various animals, in particular the lambs, after the relentless rain. Mattie ran after the sheep scattering and frightening them hither and yonder, until Danny whistled at him. The dog then wheeled around and followed them with head lowered.

Sadly, they found that one lamb had died from hypothermia during the night. Rose-Ellen bent down. 'You poor little thing; you didn't make it,' she said, almost choking on her tears. Danny removed the carcass.

The ewes were inquisitive. 'I'd better check on them,' he said, going to each one and examining her.

'They think I have nuts for them,' he called back to Rose-Ellen who kept a good hold on Mattie.

'Poor Mattie,' she said, stroking the dog. He looked at her through sad eyes. 'No, darling, I'm not going to hit you. God knows, Mattie what goes on in that head of yours!'

Mattie's fur felt long and oily to touch. 'Mattie could do with a cut now that summer's coming,' she shouted, as she caught up with him.

'I've enough to be doing with shearing the sheep,' he said curtly.

She watched Mattie rush on ahead of them.

Over in the next field stood the Friesian stock bull; a splendid animal nearly four years old. Rose-Ellen noticed how Danny watched him out of the side of his eye as they kept walking. Just then the bull looked up, his massive head fixed on them. 'Pay no attention. Just keep walkin'. That fellah is dangerous; not to be trusted. As long as Mattie is with us he won't come any nearer.' Rose-Ellen could hear her heart racing and kept striding briskly with Danny until they passed into the next field.

'Should he not be in a shed?' she asked looking back to see the bull standing in the same position, his eyes fixed on them.

'Him in a shed! Jaysus! He wrecked yards of fencing inside when we tried to house him. Electric wires had no bloody effect on him either. He kept climbin' up on the other bull and kickin' everything in sight. Bulls hate sheds. But his calves are the best, so that's why I keep him.'

Then Rose-Ellen saw two more unusual animals. She remembered

Danny speaking lovingly of his new arrivals some months back.

'Herbie and Mynagh, me two alpacas, all the way from Peru.'

'They don't seem frightened of us,' she said.

He opened the gate into the field, and the alpacas approached them. 'They're lovely animals. Come on! Let's go over and take a look. They say if you've alpacas they keep the damn foxes away.' He turned to the dog. 'Get behind me, ye blackguard.'

He grabbed the dog by the scruff of the neck. Mattie did not resist; this treatment just seemed normal for him.

'He hates the male, Herbie, 'cause he gave him a mighty kick some time ago, and they don't forget things like that.' Mattie lurked behind Danny's boot as if he were trying to make himself invisible. Rose-Ellen suspected that cowering was second nature to the dog as a result of side kicks, blows from hurling sticks and other forms of indignity.

Meanwhile, Herbie, the grey alpaca, had seen the dog and started to hiss, but then he seemed to calm down as Danny talked sweetly and reassuringly to him. The smaller alpaca came over to Rose-Ellen. 'Is this the female?' she asked Danny.

'That's Mynagh.'

'Oh, you're a beauty,' she said, stroking Mynagh's beautiful fine coat of deepest colour black with tinges of blue.

She turned to Danny, 'What on earth possessed you to get involved in alpacas?'

'Don't know. I might get into it full-time. Mynagh's expecting in July, and I'll sell the lambs, and Herbie'll be used as stud.'

'Are they expensive to keep?'

'Not really. Apart from special pellets and hay, there's little else. But ye wouldn't make anything on them for a few years. I'd have to build up a herd. There's big money in their wool.'

'Wool?' she gasped.

'Yeah, I'm now a wool merchant too with everything else I do. But sure, Rose-Ellen, you've got too busy with that big job of yours up in Dublin to be bothered listenin' to me half of the time. I tried to tell you one day, but I might as well have been talkin' to the cabbages.'

'Danny, this is the first I've ever heard of you and wool.'

'Did you know that their wool is as soft as cashmere and warmer, as well as being lighter and stronger. I send the wool to the spinner and you can have as much of Mynagh's wool as ye want. Now what do you say to that proposal?' he said, stealing an arm around Rose-Ellen.

'Her wool feels gorgeous to touch. If I could have some wool, Danny, I'd definitely take up knitting again,' she said, continuing to stroke Mynagh.

'I believe it's great for knittin' baby clothes.'

Rose-Ellen walked on and said nothing.

On the way back to the house they passed Danny's beloved cows. He turned and looked at her, while pointing his stick in the ground.

'I'm pure broke with the milkin'; sure there's no money in it at all.'

She knew the difficulties dairy farmers were having. 'Danny, you've been dairying all your life, you'd be lost without your cows, and people need milk and dairy products.'

'Maybe so,' but he had moved on and walked back up to the farm.

The Open Field Day was held annually in a large field outside of Loughbow in mid-May. She knew what would be expected. Like the other wives, sisters and girlfriends, she would be assigned to the background, serving soft drinks, tea and sandwiches, humouring everyone and being charming to all. Danny was host for the day and everybody wanted to talk to him about all kinds of things – how to raise funds, how to get loans for machinery, what were the best of breeds – and he had to be all things to all people. Danny Redmond had the common touch. He made all feel welcome and at ease no matter who they were or where they came from. And most importantly, he remembered everybody's name. Danny was also shrewd and had a sharp mind and farming had now become technical, so this attribute was very advantageous.

The Mammy, Josie Redmond, buzzed around in the background. Rose-Ellen could hear her thick accent a mile away. Josie was surrounded by a small group discussing the best way to cook game. 'Ah, my boys are great shots. We have game at least once a week in season, all organic, no antibiotics, and sure, look at them; never sick, as healthy as anythin'.'

'I wouldn't fancy removing the entrails and gizzards,' one rather sensitive lady in the group muttered meekly, but Josie had an earthy, practical side to her.

'There's nothin' to it. Once you've removed the innards, just wash the insides with bakin' soda and water and rinse well. I keep the neck and giblets for makin' stock and freeze it, and the feet make lovely *consommé*,' she said, emphasising the last syllable. Rose-Ellen moved away, not being particularly interested in hearing about Josie Redmond's ways of skinning, cooking and freezing game.

She looked over and Danny was standing in the centre of a group and holding forth for all his worth. He was attempting to speak over the chucking sound of an old steam engine powering a 'Ransome' heavy threshing machine in the background. Its name, 'Ransome', was engraved in big bold capital letters at the side. It was one of the few in the whole of Leinster. Its black fumes billowed in the air in the direction of the small crowd. The intense expressions on the faces of those listening followed his gestures as he demonstrated a point. She presumed that they were discussing the latest range of muck spreaders, buck rakes, silage wagons, slurry pumps, straw blowers and dancing diggers, one of Danny's favourite subjects. The land was everything to him, and these people were his life's blood, and Rose-Ellen understood this perfectly well. Towering over all the others in the group, Danny knew how to engage their interest. They all listened spellbound to this fiercely proud man who stood up to Brussels and those moguls in the agri-business. Christy Coughlin stood next to Danny. Christy was a delicate type with a waxy pallor giving him the aura of something that had been exhumed. He had been friends with Danny all his life and ran the only funeral parlour in the neighbourhood with his uncle.

Danny was for the most part, uncomplicated. Rose-Ellen remembered him sheep-shearing last year, how he could shear almost two hundred sheep in a day, his powerful hands lifting the passive beasts, dealing deftly with each as they lay limp in his strong arms with hardly a nick or a scratch. She recalled him pulling calves, up to his elbows, never losing one.

Danny waved in her direction.

The crowds were milling around a huge pig spit. Children dragged their fathers over to the puppet show and young girls giggled and tittered at nothing at all. Spying Geraldine Peacock sidling up to her Rose-Ellen was about to retrieve the sandwich plates and make a hasty retreat, but it was too late. Geraldine's saccharine sweetness and thinly veiled slyness were finely honed to manipulate and outmanoeuvre even the most discerning of types. Geraldine was married to Des who owned the local amusement arcade.

'Hi there, Rose-Ellen, how's it goin'? I haven't seen you for ages. Working hard?'

'Ah hello, Geraldine. Just thought I'd help Breda out with the sandwiches.'

Geraldine's beady little eyes were like jumping beans, fishing for more news. She was always so neat and trim, not a hair out of place, in her latest boutique outfit, a coffee-coloured satin dress showing just a nice respectable bit of *décolletage*. An orange ostrich bag with white feathery bits emerging from the clasp was slung casually over her bony shoulders. Geraldine's brain moved in a trajectory ungoverned by any of the laws of logic, and conceptual thought was virtually unknown to her as all her views were based on whim and personal experiences. Everything was tagged and labelled like the boutique clothes which hung on her so elegantly. Danny's voice could be heard over the microphone as he called out the rules before the tug of war got under way.

'There's no stopping Danny when he gets goin', has them all spellbound,' she said, looking up at Danny who was standing up on a platform with a microphone. Turning to Rose-Ellen, she enquired, 'So tell us, have ye decided on a day, I mean for the weddin'?'

'No, to tell you the truth, Geraldine, I haven't even thought of it. I've had so much on my mind these days,' she said, recalling recent events at DCH.

'Oh, well don't leave it too late. It's lovely to have your children young and then you can grow up with them and enjoy being a nana to their children,' she said confidently, taking a sip from her tea. She looked pathetically at Rose-Ellen with that look reserved for those who do not have children and are never likely to know the joys of motherhood. Rose-Ellen felt like upending the remainder of the sandwiches over her head as she recalled how Geraldine had walked up the aisle although barely out of a school uniform. Feeling only truly comfortable with people who were clones of her, Geraldine Peacock was always ready to take a swipe at others.

'I simply can't understand how you're living alone in a rented flat in Dublin, while being engaged to an eligible bachelor and fine farmer in County Wexford.'

Rose-Ellen stood up, the tray of sandwiches poised in the air. 'Well, duty and hungry mouths call, as they say, so if you'll excuse me I had better continue with the sandwich round.' She moved through the crowd chatting to everybody, and then she saw Mick Kiersey standing in the doorway of the Guinness tent, a large bottle of the black stuff in his hand, his eyes lingering over her movements. He had a twinkle in his eye as he gave her the look-over, and raised the bottle to her.

'Kiersey with the suit', Danny had called him.

'Here's to you, Rose-Ellen.'

'Hello, Mick! Long time no see.' She had once been crazy about Mick, but he was always a hard man to pin down with his hectic lifestyle.

Mick Kiersey was at one time a pig dealer and now had his own pig farm and pork plant. He was dangerous when it came to women and had gone out with Rose-Ellen a few years ago before she and Danny were serious about each other. Mick had never forgotten her. However, like all driven men, he was ultimately in love with power and its trappings. Business came first with Mick and after a high rollercoaster ride of pleasure and enjoyment, Rose-Ellen realised that she would always play second fiddle to his business interests. Mick had dallied with a few women since then, but nothing serious. In his late thirties, he was at his prime.

They said he was a womaniser, charming, but tiring easily of his women, discarding them like faded flowers on a graveyard dump. Mick could be a difficult adversary, and ran a hard bargain, being smart, cool and very tough. Carrying himself well with a whiff of confidence, he had that romantic Spanish Armada aura, his sleek black hair carefully combed back to give him the smouldering looks that made him irresistible to women. His pale silk tie, crisp white shirt and fine, grey jersey wool suit lent him a dapper and debonair air, and set him apart from the rest. However, Rose-Ellen supposed that he was there to make some contacts for his pork business, recalling how Danny supplied him directly with feed and straw.

While women wondered what made men tick, most men desired women, and particularly those as charming as Rose-Ellen. 'Rose-Ellen, you look as lovely as ever. I should never have let you go. I might as well be honest with you, but there's never been anyone else since you. I mean that.'

'Ah, Mick, what's done is done.'

'I hear you're engaged to big Danny.'

'That's right.'

'Plenty of time for tying the knot, so to speak. Haven't you your whole life ahead of you?' he said, looking at her in that old familiar way. He was smiling at her with that knave-like grin she could not easily forget.

She could feel the air charged with that indefinable old black magic, as he exuded charm and confidence sprinkled with a whiff of lustful roguery that many women found intoxicating. However, any kind of involvement with Kiersey was at one's peril.

'I hear you're doing very well with the pigs.'

'Ah yes, business is brisk, can't complain, and I'm going to open another factory outside Waterford soon.'

'God, Mick, that's great. You always had a good business head.'

'True, true, a bit like cards. You've got to know when to hold them, and when to fold them. Ye take your chance.'

But she knew better. It was not by chance that Mick Kiersey was one of the slickest businessmen around. He had an astute eye when sizing people up, a good business brain and took risks and gambled when things were tough. She recalled the times they went racing together; the mad betting, his sports car with the gleaming hub caps, the money he made and flung round just as quickly at the card tables afterwards. Wild unstoppable moments, like a crazy dream.

'Champagne loses its magic if it's not served at the correct temperature. It's a bit like a woman, sensitive and temperamental,' he used to say.

'It's nice to see you again, Mick,' she said, 'but I'd better give round the sandwiches.'

He quickly drew out a card from his breast pocket and handed it to her with a mischievous look. 'If you ever feel like a good time, maybe a day at the races, get in touch. I mean that, Rose-Ellen!' The card was smartly typed and embossed; clearly only the best for Mick. Raising the bottle to her, he said, 'Like old times.'

Rose-Ellen smiled and turned on her heels with the tray. Crossing the field, she looked back at the doorway and found that Mick had gone, and in that instant she felt as if a flame from her past had been briefly re-kindled.

A Ceili took place that night over in the large marquee near the entrance. Rose-Ellen was sitting outside after dancing with Danny for nearly an hour in the tent listening to one of the local bands. Then an arm crept around her waist.

'Hello, gorgeous! Where've you been hidin'?'

'Fingers!'

'How about a dance?'

Fingers O'Loinsigh gently pulled her up to dance, and they made their way on to the floor when the chief guitarist played some sixties music. She had always looked up to Fingers supposing that he had earned this name from playing the piano. He once told her that he could play all Chopin's waltzes to concert standard. But Kitty put her right about Fingers.

'Darling, Fingers is no Liberace. He got that name because, well, he's a bit…light fingered, ye know, would help himself to the contents of a lady's handbag when she wasn't looking, cigarettes and small change. He used to nick things for people.'

Rose-Ellen was shocked. 'What sort of things?'

'Well the odd piece of silver, such as an old Irish Georgian candlestick, a rare whiskey and sometimes even perfume. Sure, why do you think he always wears that big black coat with the long pockets?'

She looked at Fingers now as he twirled and jived with her, and not a care in the world. His fair, unbrushed hair shooting in all directions from his head defying gravity, and his wild, mad blue eyes. She was gently released from Fingers' grip by Danny.

'Now, Fingers, I'll have this one, if ye don't mind,' Danny said, taking Rose-Ellen off into the centre of the floor for a slow dance. She could feel Danny's powerful arms around her waist and lifted her lips to his, and gave him a kiss and thought of their life together.

'Oh, Rose. You're drivin' me crazy,' he said, squeezing her. They then lined up for An Laisair's Reel. They did square chains and the Irish Knot. Everybody cheered them on, tapping their feet and clapping their hands in time with the music, until she fell into Danny's arms and he had to carry her off the floor. He gave her a big kiss before letting her down and gazing at her in the bright lights of the dance floor.

'You're the most beautiful girl here today, and I'm so looking forward to our wedding. We should set a date soon,' he said, clasping her around the waist and hugging her to him.

But she looked at him, smiled and said nothing.

Chapter 19

It was the beginning of June and Rose-Ellen needed to pay the taxi fare to Walkinstown for one of the Cytu AB patients out of the research funds. She looked up the latest bank statement for the Cytu AB account on the computer and discovered that there was hardly any credit in it. The research account in the hospital was funded by the pharmaceutical companies who pay for setting up a clinical trial in the hospital and for all trial patient visits and procedures.

'There's something not quite right here,' she murmured to herself. IQI Pharma Corp paid the clinical research department at DCH for each patient visit for the trial out of which a certain amount was allocated for patient travel expenses. After lunch Rose-Ellen rang the bank. She asked to speak to a manager. 'Good day, Ms Power. I believe that you wanted to speak to me about an urgent matter.'

'Hello. Yes that is correct,' Rose-Ellen said.

'So, what seems to be the problem, Ms Power?'

'Well, I know that we received payment recently from IQI Parma Corp. for patient recruitment for the end of the last quarter for the Cytu AB trial to the research account, and with over seventy patients in the trial, that is a lot of money, but there would appear to have been several transactions made and there's very little credit there, so I would like some more details of these transactions please.'

'Ah yes. I see here that several large credits were made to this account in the last quarter, but there have been quite a few withdrawals,' he remarked.

Her pulse quickened. 'Withdrawals? I don't understand. Only I, Dr O'Hegarty and the hospital accountant have access to this account.'

'That may well be, but it would appear that somebody has been withdrawing funds on a regular basis.'

Rose-Ellen moved uneasily in her chair. 'But who?'

'Any of the four signatories – either yourself, Dr O'Hegarty, the hospital accountant or a Dr McAdam. I'm sorry but I cannot tell you who has been making these transactions as they have been made by bank transfer.'

'I didn't know that Dr McAdam had signatory rights.'

'Yes. It would appear so.'

She took a deep breath. It was quiet in the hospital and for once nobody seemed to be looking for Pierre. This meeting would have to take place, and the sooner the better, Rose-Ellen thought.

'Pierre, there's something I need to speak to you about.'

He was studying a patient's chart. He spoke without interest. 'Unless it's very urgent, I'd prefer to concentrate on something else. I have to write an extremely urgent report on a patient. Oh, by the way, I've had a word with McAdam and he's not to enrol any more patients to the Cytu AB trial without first discussing their eligibility with me. No bloods either are to be taken or sent to Switzerland by him. Either you or Helen, his research nurse, can take the bloods.'

'Oh!' Rose-Ellen said, surprised.

'I've looked at the notes of those ineligible patients you identified and in some instances the patients can remain in the trial, but in the others they must come out. McAdam is contacting these patients to withdraw them from the trial without any further delay.'

'Well at least that's something.' Rose-Ellen moved away, busying herself suddenly with more filing. She had to mention the funds. She was damned if she were going to let it slip by. She turned and faced him.

'I phoned the bank today.'

'Why so?' he seemed surprised.

'Well there is precious little in the research account, despite the fact that over seventy patients have been enrolled to the Cytu AB trial.'

'What point are you making?' he said, without looking at her.

'The point I'm making is that, first, Shay McAdam is signatory to this account, something I didn't know about and, second, if he is then there is a huge possibility that he is helping himself liberally to the account because there was hardly anything in it when I went to withdraw some money this afternoon for patient taxis. Unless of course it is you or the hospital accountant who is making these withdrawals, but it sure ain't me!'

He put down his pen. 'I made him a signatory as well as he needed money for expenses for attendance at meetings.'

'I should have been informed. After all I am study co-ordinator and need money for patient expenses.'

'I'm sorry. I ought to have told you.'

'But where's all that money gone to? As soon as it goes in, it's siphoned off.'

'That can't be. I certainly have not taken a cent from this account and I'm sure that the hospital accountant hasn't and neither have you, so that leaves only one suspect. McAdam was only to have taken enough for his expenses for the conference in Germany, and before that the one in London. And besides, he would need to have the sanction of the accountant to withdraw funds. The accountant would need to sign off on any transactions made by him.'

She moved her chair over and sat beside him. 'So how did he just take money out like that? We're talking about a lot of money here.'

He leaned back on the chair. 'God only knows how he managed to do it without the accountant's knowledge or sanction. Now on another note! The audit report will be out soon and that will dictate the outcome of this trial. We cannot be whistleblowers; any findings or accusations must come from an objective party.'

Chapter 20

Several hours passed and Rose-Ellen could barely concentrate on her work as the tension in the air was volatile. Finally Pierre came over to where she was working on her computer.

'The audit report is here and the findings are shocking. I'm meeting Shay now to get to the root of this and want you to be present as well. So, shall we go over?'

'Sure,' she said, closing her computer and following him across the corridor to Shay's office. McAdam was waiting for them. Pierre and Rose-Ellen sat opposite McAdam.

'There are serious anomalies in the data for the Cytu AB trial. This is something I can gladly do without at this stage in my career. Now the FDA will probably be on top of us. They'll want to see everything; everything we have ever done. They will probe and probe. After all, Dr Doolan and I are the principal investigators. Anything done is done in our names, not in either of yours, much as you may think it is, and the reputation of this hospital is at stake,' Pierre said sternly.

McAdam leaned back on his chair and threw his biro casually back onto his desk. 'The FDA's relationship with IQI Pharma Corp and the rest of the pharmaceutical conglomerates is cosy to say the least, and besides, in the last few years they've only inspected three per cent of sites, so I wouldn't worry about them. I don't know why you all think that I manufactured the patient data. Now why would I want to do that? Jeopardise my career? No I am not that naive!'

'I wonder,' Pierre said crisply. 'A trial's data can hinge on minor issues, minor anomalies, irregularities, discrepancies, call it what you want, and these can dictate if a centre is fit to run trials or not. Auditors decide what a minor issue is. Not you, a co-investigator,' Pierre continued beginning to feel his temper rise.

'I just haven't had time to complete everything in the hospital medical files,' McAdam said. 'That's why there are only small notes on pieces of paper for some patients. But don't worry, I'll get round to it.'

'You have been allocated a part-time research nurse from the oncology ward, and if you had used her for the task she is paid to do, none of this would be happening. What does she do as a matter of interest? That is her job, a medic like you doesn't have time for all of the nuts and bolts involved in the clinical research, and you should know that. If you delegated some responsibility to her then the damn trial work would be done properly and not sloppily.'

'Well, I like to keep on top of things and manage the trial myself; the less people involved the better,' McAdam said, and gave Rose-Ellen a thunderous look.

'There's too much at stake here. There's suspicious data, contrived files for patients who probably don't exist, trial drugs gone missing, dodgy signatures on consent forms and blood reports so healthy that frankly they look as if they came from a selection of healthy sports stars. Is there any more that we need to know? There was so much going on that I had to have the site audited.'

'Look, they were small factors, nothing serious, and besides, that protocol is badly designed. The entry criteria are ridiculous,' McAdam added lamely.

'That's not for you to decide. No wonder we have so many protocol violations in this trial when you continually enrol patients who simply aren't suitable. You either stick rigidly to the protocol or you step down as a co-investigator in the trial. What about the bloods? You still haven't provided any reason why the bloods are so healthy from this cohort of patients. Of course if the patients are unsuitable for the study, well then, that will explain it, but if you have been fabricating patients to swell the numbers for this trial, selling the trial drug or whatever, think of the ramifications this could have for the trial and research that's based on half-truths; data that is perhaps useless but more importantly fraudulent!' Pierre shouted.

'I'll have to go. I'm wanted up in ICU,' McAdam said.

'I have not finished yet. The audit findings have been critical and you will have some explaining to do about the many issues which have arisen over the course of the last few months. This is too serious for flippancy. Do I make myself clear?' Pierre shouted.

'OK, I get the picture.' And with that McAdam left.

He did not even look at Rose-Ellen on his way out. Pierre leaned back on his chair and looked at Rose-Ellen, then fixed his eyes on the ceiling.

'A drug like Cytu AB fetches a high price on the internet in the international market. People will pay anything for another year or two of life.' A recent financial audit in the hospital had revealed fraudulent activity, funds disappearing, and the sale of the trial drugs to unknown parties over the internet.

Pierre then looked gravely at Rose-Ellen.

'My God, to think that he is using the trial drug to flog on to unsuspecting women who have exhausted all avenues; who have tried everything, vulnerable, frail women who want just another few months at the most. This makes me sick to the core.' He turned away and looked out the window. She could see that he was visibly upset.

'What do you think will be the outcome of this?'

'I'll have to discuss this with management in the hospital, the Fitness to Practice Committee. Of course the Medical Council will be notified too. This is extremely serious. Clinical trials in Ireland are subject to law and failure to abide by the rules, thereby jeopardising patient safety, is dealt with harshly here by the courts.'

The next morning, before rounds, Pierre crossed the corridor and confronted McAdam in his office. He calmly walked into McAdam's office and found him sitting at his desk typing on his laptop. He did not close the door. Rose-Ellen was just about to head up to the laboratory with some specimens and noticed Pierre in McAdam's office. She laid down the specimens and moved closer to the door to witness the scene in McAdam's office. Pierre stood while waving the sheets of printed e-mails at McAdam. 'Now we know why you need money!'

McAdam stood up and tried to snatch the pages from Pierre's hand. 'What the hell do you think you're doing?' but Pierre, being taller and more agile, held it aloft.

'No you don't. You have some explaining to do first. Here are some damning e-mails printed off showing that you have been flogging the drug Cytu AB on the international market through the internet.'

'How the fuck did you get hold of these?'

'A hospital audit picked them up. The findings arrived on my desk first thing this morning from the accounts department. Also the Fraud Squad have been alerted.'

'So what? If I can help women with this drug, then they will benefit.'

'Don't be so naïve. You weren't helping these women; in fact you couldn't give a damn about them. You were doing it for the money and nothing else; to pay your gambling debts or feed your newly found penchant for the finer things in life. And you were pocketing the money. It's all here in the audit! Trial drugs sent from this place and e-mails about payments to you from people as far away as Canada. The financial audit is delving deeper into this. Why was payment not made into the research account if you are so concerned about these patients? I am suspending you completely from anything to do with research in this hospital. You'll have to face the Fitness to Practice Committee as well as the Medical Council, because as far as I'm concerned you shouldn't be let near patients, never mind sick and vulnerable ones in this trial. How you ever chose medicine is beyond me! To think of you flogging a drug that is unmarketed, a drug that is yet untested, on to frail, vulnerable women desperate to do anything to claw back one or two years of life at the most truly sickens me. You were also stealing from the hospital and the company. Only the lowliest of beings could stoop to this.'

McAdam had had enough. 'What I do in my spare time is my business and you have no right to go snooping through my private affairs. These women are going to die anyway, and so why not help them? It's their only hope.'

'What about the patients in the trial who were due to get this drug? And who has examined these patients who have received the drug unethically on the internet from you? What you do in your spare time does concern me if it is criminal and involves the trial. Have you any idea of how serious this is? My God, you could be facing a long custodial sentence.'

McAdam laughed out loud. 'I doubt it. No government agency is interested in chasing anything less than a hundred thousand euros over the internet. It's simply not worth it. Far too costly! So back off!'

He eyeballed Pierre.

'I'll get my solicitor after you for slander and defamation of character. You and that bitch Power are too quick to assume and speculate. I have worked tirelessly for you and this trial. I've gone on meetings covering for you, doing all of the statistics for trials, because you are too damn thick to do them yourself.'

Pierre threw back his head in a mock laugh. 'Oh, come now. Stats are not a doctor's preserve. Stats are a meaningless mathematical language of odds and probabilities and chance which few can do or even understand. You've been consistently lax in your work, and frankly there are just too many strange and odd coincidences that have been happening here of late.'

'Without my efforts, you'd only have a few patients in this trial.'

'It's a pity you didn't put fewer patients into the trial and concentrated on their eligibility and wellbeing. You would have saved us all a lot of embarrassment and heartache. The trouble with people like you who use fraudulent means is that you start off at the beginning with small amounts of money, and then when you can get away with it you continue until the stakes are huge. The same with the data; carelessness at first becomes outright fraud after a while. An odd signature copied here and there; who is to know or to check up on you? Oh yes, you get high on what you've got away with – the deceit and not being caught. I could go on, but what's the point. You are so far into dishonesty and trickery now that I expect there is no turning back for you.'

'Who trawled through charts into the dead of night looking to assess if patients were eligible while you were swanning off around the world giving presentations on how great the recruitment was here? I bloody well did! Certainly not you!'

'That's enough. I have taken the decision with Dr Doolan, and with the CEO of the hospital, to have you suspended from your research job in this hospital. There is simply too much at stake. There is the reputation of this hospital, and this clinical research department. We are going to organise another audit, this time an international audit, to comb through all of the trial documentation. You will have to accept the findings of the Fitness to Practice Committee when they review your case.'

McAdam watched while Pierre made his exit.

He shouted menacingly at him. 'Go to Hell! You'll pay for this. I won't take this lying down!'

Pierre turned to face him. 'And I want every cent paid back that you owe,' and walked out the door. Pierre heard the strong thud of a boot as McAdam kicked its frame.

Chapter 21

It was mid-June, the season when fairs and shows were in full swing around the country. The vivid yellow of wild buttercup and rich vermilion of flimsy poppies dazzled the countryside, and sheaves of wheat and barley swayed in the soft summer Wexford breeze. Danny and Rose-Ellen were in the kitchen of the Redmond home. Danny stood by the window and Rose-Ellen sat at the table.

'And what's wrong with good Irish beef?' his mother said defensively, furiously knitting a mauve jumper. A rose-patterned knitting bag stuffed with balls of wool lay at her feet.

'Oh, nothin' at all. It's just that I'd like to give it a go and breed some of these fellahs. They're fine lookin' cattle.' Danny wanted to get into breeding Angus beef.

'It's not their looks that matter. Ye won't be showin' them or an'thin' like that. They'll be bred for the table,' Josie said, without looking up as she poked for more wool inside the bag.

'And what's wrong with a bit of adventure anyway! I'm going to Scotland and that's all there is to it.'

She sighed as she looked out of the window. 'You're as stubborn as the mules my father used to keep. There's no point in talkin' to you.'

Danny looked at both his parents who had worked hard all their lives and lived through lean and tough times.

'When I think of all the care and attention I've lavished on them cows, and yet I'm workin' at a loss. I'm thinkin' of gettin' out of milk,' Danny said, pulling out a chair from the table and sitting down.

'There's no money in it any more. We're paid a pittance for a litre of milk. By the time I pay for the feed for my cows, fertiliser, fuel, not to mention the bloody machinery, I've nothin' left at the end of the month.

I'm borrowin' every year from the bank to keep me head above water. It's all goin' to the suppliers and the shopkeepers. It's a joke bein' a dairy farmer. I'll get some of these cattle, start off small with a good bull and some heifers, and do everything myself; castratin' and taggin', go from calf to beef.'

His father was sitting over by the window reading the newspaper. 'So you're thinkin' of gettin' into beef instead and that's why you're going to Scotland. You're crazy to be thinkin' of buyin' more cattle. The price for what we get and what they sell is only scandalous and it's costin' more and more each year to feed these beasts.' He took his head out of the paper and eyeballed his son.

'Listen will ye! Last week heifers weighin' five hundred and fifty kilos were sellin' at the mart for near eight hundred euros, and when ye break everythin' down after they've been processed, the butcher is getting' near two thousand and three hundred euros, near three times as much. I tell you, th'industry is gettin' stagnated; gettin' stagnated, so it is.'

But his father had not finished. 'Another thing too. If the vet finds more TB in the herd, that's it, we're fucked!' He turned and glanced at Rose-Ellen who moved uneasily in her seat.

Danny realised his father was talking sense. His fine black breeding bull and two calves had had to be put down last month as they were TB reactors.

Josie lay down her knitting and got up and stretched herself. His father put his glasses away, got his coat and went out, followed by Mattie.

Danny turned to Rose-Ellen. 'Would ye fancy a trip to Scotland?' Rose-Ellen realised that he had never been abroad; he did not even possess a passport. He had once been to the Isle of Man with Mattie for the sheep trials, but they said it had been a complete fiasco.

'To buy breeding bulls? Ah no, Danny, that wouldn't really be my scene. Forget about that! Why don't we just spend the weekend together, just the two of us; no milking, no tractoring and no Mammy! How about it?' She was anxious to spend time with Danny as even though they would be married soon, she felt recently that they were living parallel lives.

'What had ye in mind?'

'Lots of walks. We'll go for dinner, and just talk as a couple!'

On Saturday Rose-Ellen prepared a picnic and they drove to the sea in Ballymoney in Danny's Volvo. After a brisk swim, Danny chased Rose-Ellen all the way up a sand dune and they both flopped down on to the tartan rug. Rose-Ellen watched the passing clouds. Her mind wandered back to work. She turned to Danny.

'Danny, sometimes I wish I had a job that I could just switch off when I finished in the evening.'

He was busy unscrewing the top of the flask of tea. 'And haven't you a good job as a nurse?'

She could feel the mild irritation welling up inside her. 'I know I'm a nurse, Danny, but I'm not working as a nurse on the wards. I work in clinical research and if something happens, which is the case now, well, it just doesn't go away. The problem lingers.'

But he was not listening to her. He sipped some tea. 'Where are the sandwiches?'

She looked at her watch. 'Ah, it's too early for lunch, Danny, and I didn't bring sandwiches. Wait another hour.'

There was silence between them. He got up and started to draw some shapes in the sand with a stick he had picked up. She noticed how big and strong he was, a fine man in his prime, apart from a slight paunch that was beginning to develop.

'Danny, did you hear what I said about my problems at work? Put away that stick and listen to me, will you please?' she called.

He threw away the stick and came close to her and took her hand in his. 'I love you, Rose. I live for the weekends when you come down from Dublin,' he said, stroking her hair.

She turned to him. 'Ah, I know that, you're one of the best.' He leaned over and kissed her.

'I could make love to you here and now,' he whispered in her ear. He moved closer and lifted up a flaxen lock of hair moving his tongue around her ear and neck.

'Not now, Danny, and certainly not here. We're not sixteen for heaven's sake!' she said, sensing that he was becoming aroused. She could get the faint sweet smell of silage from him. She knew that he was spending each morning in the pit with Conor making silage.

'What! I thought this was some sort of a love weekend ye had planned. I mean, just the two of us.'

Rose-Ellen got up and put on her rubber sandals. 'I'm going for a walk, do you want to come?'

'Ah no, the clouds are passing so I'll soak up the sun for a while,' he said lying back.

Rose-Ellen took off briskly by the seashore, mulling over all the skulduggery that was going on in DCH. She wished she could talk to Danny about how she felt, but while he loved her she felt that he did not really understand her needs or the life that she led. It felt good to walk through the foamy water as it swirled around her ankles sucking in the sand and ground shells as it tugged and swished back to the sea. A seal bobbed its whiskery head up a few hundred yards out, barked and then disappeared, while overhead a flock of plover flew in perfect convoy. After what seemed like ages she made her way back to find Danny fast asleep on the rug, snoring his head off. She gave him a poke with her toe. He woke up suddenly as if he did not really know where he was.

'Jaysus, I was dreamin' about us, Rose. We were on our honeymoon and stayin' in a hotel where everything was made of dark chocolate. But it must have been a nightmare 'cause the chocolate started to melt and I was drownin' in a vat of the damn stuff. It's a good job you woke me.'

Rose-Ellen lay down beside him. 'You've been watching too many of those animated programmes, I suspect,' she said, thinking of the enormous television which dominated the kitchen in the Redmond house.

Looking at her watch, she said, 'What about lunch?'

'Good idea,' he muttered.

She laid out a picnic of smoked salmon, ham, various salads and home-made brown bread. Danny popped open the non-alcoholic white wine and they clinked glasses.

'To us, Rose,' Danny said, pouring the frothy liquid into the tall glasses.

Rose-Ellen took a sip.

'Danny, I'm not happy working in DCH. In fact I'm under terrible pressure with work, and I'm having difficulty with somebody at work.'

She watched him as he gulped the bubbly from the thick glass.

'I thought you were getting on great at your job. Jaysus, this isn't bad for a non-alcoholic drink.'

'Danny, did you hear what I said about my work and the fact that I'm not happy?'

'I heard you but what do you want me to do about it? Sure, we'll be married soon and you won't have to work any more. Can't you get a nice cushy job down here in a nursing home. I hear these jobs are perfect and then if we have kids...'

'Stop it please! I'm talking about the here and now; the fact that my life is hell at the moment in DCH and you, my fiancé, don't seem to be one bit concerned about how I feel.'

'I don't know why work is so important to you. Most women in your position, waitin' to be married, would be busy with makin' preparations. Mammy keeps asking me about the date for the weddin' and I have to keep makin' excuses.'

'I'm sorry, Danny, you're right. I should get my priorities right. But supposing I was worried about something, not necessarily to do with work, would you listen to me? I mean when we are married there will be times when I will need to talk to you about something, or you to me. After all, that's what marriage is all about, sharing the joys and the angst between a couple.'

'Look, let's enjoy the day that's in it and don't be bringin' bad luck with this kind of talk, Rose-Ellen. Sure, we'll cross these bridges when we come to them. I know I'm not as grand or as sophisticated as some of the men you've met, Rose-Ellen, but I'll be as good to you as any man and I promise I'll always be there for you. I know you work very hard at your job and you take great pride in what you do. Sure, I never stop pinchin' myself thinkin' that you're going to be my wife. I sometimes think that I'm the luckiest man alive.'

Rose-Ellen looked over in his direction. 'Come here, Danny, and give me a hug. Oh, Danny, Danny. You're so uncomplicated, like your cows and the animals and you've a good heart and you're the best.'

He came over and kissed her and she lay in his arms while the gentle breeze rustled the long grass around them.

Towards four pm just before gathering up everything, Rose-Ellen stared out to sea and the same old feeling of despondency hit her. She wondered what her life would be like once married, and she became a trifle uneasy.

Chapter 22

It was Friday in mid-June and the beginning of what promised to be a scorching weekend. Rose-Ellen met Pierre coming along the corridor flanked by a group of eager, serious-looking junior doctors. They were heading into the large auditorium where a breakfast conference was to take place, at which Pierre was giving a lecture. He appeared to be in animated conversation with one of them.

Catching Rose-Ellen's eye, he called out to her. 'See you after the conference,' and turned the corner with his white-coated entourage. Then she remembered that a lady from the Cytu AB trial had been waiting in the research department since seven-thirty.

'Good God!' she muttered to herself and fled down the corridor recalling that the patient was fasting. The *petite* lady had developed ovarian cancer at the tender age of thirty-eight. Her prognosis was poor and the cancer had spread considerably throughout her body.

Having already been briefed on the trial and having signed the consent form some days ago at the clinic with Pierre, the lady sat in the day room looking out of the window at some birds pecking on the ground near the bushes. She was nervously fiddling with a row of pearls around her neck. She turned and smiled at Rose-Ellen who came in to the room. Rose-Ellen appreciated that the road ahead would be a difficult one for this patient.

'Good morning. I'm Rose-Ellen Power, the research nurse and I'll go over everything with you about the study. How are you feeling?'

But the lady had a distracted air about her as if she wanted to remove herself from the immediate anxiety of what was about to unfold.

'I love looking at the birds,' she said. 'They're always the same; never get down like us humans.'

'Now, about today. I'll just go over everything again with you and make sure that you know exactly what's happening,' Rose-Ellen said.

But the patient folded her hands on her lap. 'There's no need, love. Doctor O'Hegarty explained everything to me at the clinic. He's a true gentleman. Nothing could have been too much trouble for him. Now, I don't know much about these things, except to say that I don't feel well,' she said, opening the clasp of her handbag to get a tissue inside.

'Are you quite sure that there's nothing you want to know before I do the usual procedures?'

'Oh no, the dear doctor explained everything to me so clearly and…' she clutched Rose-Ellen's sleeve, and whispered, 'I'll do whatever has to be done. I've resigned myself to my fate, said all my prayers and made my peace with God. *Que sera sera*, as the song says!'

'I understand,' Rose-Ellen assured her. As Rose-Ellen took her bloods she thought of the sadness of this case. This lady, with the figure of a girl, had worked as a cook in a large boarding school from the age of sixteen and had devoted all of her working life to the children, but now to be diagnosed with cancer seemed unfair and unjust.

Rose-Ellen took a sample of blood for analysis, performed an ECG and arranged an X-ray. After the lady left, Rose-Ellen went upstairs to the oncology ward to check on some patients. The day case patients sat receiving their chemotherapy regimen; many of them bore the shaven heads and had that gaunt, frightened look resembling prisoners of war.

She could hear the familiar sharp, hoarse voice of Gertie halfway up the corridor. Gertie was a lady in her late fifties from the inner city who was in hospital with suspected bowel cancer. Tough and feisty, she was having a run-in with a big lump of a woman pulling the tea trolley. Gertie shouted after her, 'Come 'ere, you. Are you bleedin' deaf? I want fuckin' soup, not fuckin' tea!'

The tea lady turned and stared at the diminutive figure standing in the doorway of the ward, clad in a bright pink dressing gown, with a mound of rollers perched under a white hair net.

'You're on a liquid-only diet, and that means tea or coffee, no soup,' the tea lady said with great authority, pulling the tea trolley after her.

Gertie spied Rose-Ellen coming up the corridor. 'Here, Rosie, tell dis bleedin' harpy that Dr O'Hegarty said I could have a bit o' soup for me lunch. Go on tell her, 'cause she won't effin' believe me!'

Rose-Ellen looked through Gertie's medical chart to see what she had been ordered.

'Gertie can have some soup and I'll change the diet label on her bed to semi-solids. She's just come off her IVs, so she can have soup, rice or jelly and ice cream,' Rose-Ellen said, returning to the tea lady while smiling at Gertie.

'I'll bring the soup over to you when I'm finished with the teas,' the tea lady said harshly to Gertie, giving Rose-Ellen a look that would have blasted granite.

At lunchtime, Rose-Ellen stuck her head into Pierre's office. She noticed his shirt was splattered with blood and guessed that he had probably just come from the ICU. He was busy writing up some notes and did not bother looking up. Screwing up a piece of paper he had just torn into a tight ball, he threw it into the waste-paper basket. He then put down his pen, let out a long sigh and looked intently at her. She could feel the tense atmosphere. Rose-Ellen had never witnessed him so downcast. He got up and put away the patient's chart and she noticed how pale and drawn he appeared.

'The trial's a mess, Rose-Ellen, a bloody mess. At least McAdam's gone for good from this place. He'll now have to answer to the Fitness to Practice Council here.' He banged the filing cabinet shut. 'There were just too many unanswered questions.'

She sat down.

'I feel exhausted even thinking about it.'

Pierre looked at her gravely. 'Give the audit report top priority. Any problems you have, you are to contact me or Dr Doolan.'

'That is a lot. I really don't know that I'll be able to give it my full attention with all of the other work I have to do around here.'

'Please. This is too important.'

She said nothing, but realised that the audit report had priority in her work schedule.

She left for lunch and met her friend Siobhan. 'It's the talk of the place,' Siobhan said. 'Pierre getting McAdam sacked from his post. Is it true?' She was curious to find out more.

Rose-Ellen knew that she would have to be very circumspect about what she said. 'Yes, it's true, and I can't really talk about it, Siobhan. A lot of things have happened recently.'

'You can say that again! I know Shay has his faults, but some patients really trusted him, particularly the old ones. Wouldn't have anyone else, so you never know, do you?' Siobhan said, cutting her ham roll into three pieces methodically, her small hazel eyes peering at Rose-Ellen over her glasses.

Rose-Ellen envied Siobhan, so confident with her own certainties, working up there in endoscopy, each day the same as the next.

'I suppose he had a glib way of putting patients at ease, as long as they didn't know too much about their situation,' Rose-Ellen said.

That afternoon, Rose-Ellen and Pierre worked together in silence in each of their offices until there was a knock on the door. Rose-Ellen opened it and Moira stood there. She was beaming with excitement and radiated a carefree abandon.

'Hello. I hope that I'm not disturbing you,' Moira said gleefully.

Rose-Ellen welcomed her. 'Oh, no, not at all, come on in.' Moira breezed in past Rose-Ellen making her way into Pierre's office.

'Hello, darling,' she said, gushingly as she gave Pierre a kiss on the cheek. He got up and closed the door of his office. Rose-Ellen could hear them chatting and laughing. Soon they got up to leave.

On the way out, Pierre placed a firm hand on Rose-Ellen's shoulder. 'Have a good weekend, Rose-Ellen,' he said, and left.

Rose-Ellen made herself another cup of coffee, sat down and started to finish some paperwork before heading off for the weekend. If she were to drive to Wexford now she would only hit the traffic heading south to Brittas. At five o'clock she heard footsteps and wondered who could be around the office in the hospital at this hour as most of the staff had left.

The door of the office opened and closed. Before her stood Shay McAdam. He had a malevolent expression on his small, vulpine face accompanied by a rictus of a grin.

'I didn't expect to see you here now,' she said nervously.

'Well, now that I'm here, you can listen to what I have to say. Thanks to you, recruitment to the Cytu AB trial has been stopped. O'Hegarty has suspended me from my job and all my research work has gone wallop, and the site will be audited by the bloody FDA. These are big guns. Have you any idea what you've done, you stupid bitch?'

Rose-Ellen froze in her chair as he moved nearer and stood over her in a threatening fashion. Rage seemed to seep through those razor eyes. She realised that there was nobody in this part of the building at this time on a weekend, and mustered up her reserves of courage. She realised she should not betray her fears.

'Me? What have I done? I've done nothing! How dare you barge in here to my office and speak to me like that!' she said.

'How dare you snoop into my office and discuss me with anybody you like without my permission. And by the way, I've reported you to management in the hospital so don't try and pin this whole sorry mess on me alone. After all, you were trial co-ordinator. And another thing, it was you, you little ferret who snooped around my office and got into my computer, went through my private correspondence and then went off blabbering around the place about me.'

She felt her blood run cold. 'I did no such thing. The internal audit picked up what you had been up to. Not me! You're just paranoiac now that you've been dismissed.'

McAdam moved over and slid himself onto her desk leaning his ugly face down again to eyeball her in a threatening manner. She could see every vein of his mottled skin, the pale, cold eyes and tiny white flecks in his irises and wide pupils, almost black, like a cat, still and focussed, ready to pounce on unsuspecting prey.

'This won't end here, believe you me. You see, my solicitor is on to this and you will end up in court trying to defend yourself against a top barrister,' he hissed.

She bristled with indignation at his proximity but tried to remain composed. Above all she could not afford to let her guard down. He was breathing near her and her heart began to pound. He moved his face even closer, almost touching hers, his pointed chin emphasising his ugly, vulpine features.

She fiddled with some papers on her desk. 'You forget it's not me who's suspected of tampering with the data.'

His thin, bloodless lips managed a leer, only adding to the repugnance she felt towards him. Flashing a mocking smile, he put his hands through his gelled hair.

'Tampering with the data? Who knows what you enter into the computer?' He had relaxed slightly from his original position of preying cat.

She leaned back in the chair. 'That's ridiculous and you know it. All my work is monitored by the company who check what I enter into the computer against the patient notes. But nobody can ever check if the original medical notes are correct or not. You could be making it all up as you go along, which is what I and others suspect, particularly for those patients with the small folders who have no hospital number. Do you know what I think?'

He looked at her and laughed. 'Who cares what you think. You see, you're not that important, even though you think you are!'

But she continued. 'I think that quite a few of those patients don't exist at all; they were made up by you to swell the numbers of patients enrolled at this site. And it was probably your own blood you spun down and sent off for those patients you fabricated.'

He pounded the desk with his clenched fist. 'Watch your tongue, you slanderous bitch.'

She stood up and folded her arms.

He slid off the table and stood there glaring at her; his soulless, limpid eyes skewered her and his sinister smile made Rose-Ellen apprehensive. She hoped he did not sense her nervousness. She had never liked him, and at this moment detested him completely.

He continued to stand there, his legs parted slightly and his hands on his hips. She looked down at his shoes. Recalling this episode later she wondered why she did this; perhaps it was to avoid his gaze. She noticed that they were cheap, scuffed and dirty. She always knew he was a phony.

He pointed a finger at her. 'As for what you call thievery, I had permission to help myself to those funds.'

'What about the drugs you collected from the pharmacy with your own prescriptions? Or those drugs which never made it to the pharmacy but were shipped off to unsuspecting women all over the world – poor desperate women with little hope. Where are these drugs? Did you sell them? Maybe on the black market? There are lots of unanswered questions.'

'I'll be answerable to the powers that be, but not to a bloody nobody like you. Don't you ever, ever interfere with me or what I do, because if you do, I'll kill you! Do you hear?'

He was shouting now, his voice having reached a new pitch of ire.

She needed to remain calm and in control.

'What difference does it make now? You're history.'

As he made for the door, he called back to her, 'Acting like a detective isn't looked on very kindly in a place like this…Think about it.'

'Nor is fraud!' she retorted quickly.

Rose-Ellen maintained a patient and watchful *sangfroid* as he made his way out of the office. She was trembling with fear as she helped herself to some water from the small fridge close by. She swallowed a few gulps and took a long, deep breath, waiting a while until her composure returned before getting ready to leave. She had not realised that Shay McAdam harboured so much resentment.

Calmly, she put on her jacket and locked up. She was barely able to concentrate. Her driving bordered on the hazardous; one irate man gave her the 'v' sign and cursed her as he vroomed into the fast lane. Her hands trembled on the steering wheel.

Driving to 'The Potter's Wheel', a pub off Baggot Street, she parked her car badly on the side of the road, went inside without putting any money in the metre and ordered a family-sized gin and tonic at the bar.

The place was full of *bonhomie* as people looked forward to a lazy, warm June weekend. Some were sitting outside under parasols, others were content to remain inside away from the sun's glare and the heat. Groups of office girls with their bright colourful shopping bags sat around together laughing and giggling.

The gin gave her some composure while reflecting on her life, her job and wondering where she was heading. She had given the job in DCH her all and where had it got her? Nowhere! It would be better to pack in her lot and look for a more secure career. A career where she would not have to take the flack for another's incompetence and dishonesty, where she would not feel threatened and abused, but mostly where her work would be valued.

She thought of Pierre and wondered what he was doing. She felt that working with him was one of the positive aspects about her job in DCH. He had taught her so much about clinical research but more importantly she had learnt about the things in life which matter: honour, integrity and dedication. She felt deeply for him, that was sure, and at times she could think of nothing else only him. His very presence seemed to dominate her thoughts be it in his role as doctor or else mucking about uncoiling ropes on a boat, or just sitting with her in the office when they both silently worked together. She wondered if he thought of her at all when they were not at work and supposed not, but then she reflected on those intimate moments shared and felt that he must feel something for her, and her heart gladdened.

She then decided to call Danny. 'Hi, love,' she said. She could hear cows bellowing in the background.

'Hi, Rose, how are things?'

'I'm not happy about what's happening at DCH. I can't sleep and the least thing makes me jump. There's a lot going on, Danny and it just seems to be all getting on top of me.'

'Well come down here, love, and I'll cheer you up.'

He lived in his own safe, secure world of farming at home as regular and comforting as the seasons.

'No, Danny, I've arranged a pile of things here for the weekend. How are the plans for the house coming along?'

'I'm advisin' the builders on the foundations. It won't cost much because the land is mine.' As well as having the large farm, the Redmonds also owned much land over by Monamolin, and so Danny and his siblings were each given large parcels of land when they had reached twenty-one. Danny had decided to design the house according to the local council plans, dispensing with the services of an architect, something which had infuriated Rose-Ellen.

'We'll have it north-facing so that ye can have a south-facing garden at the back. That'll get the sun all day for your plants, and whatever ye want to grow,' Danny chuckled.

She sighed as she took another sip of her gin.

'You seem to have thought of everything, but I don't like those council plans. I'd like to hire an architect so that we can design our own house. Those types of houses are a blight on the countryside, and once built there's nothing you can do with them. We'll just end up extending and trying to make something of it, and all the time it will be just what it is, a small dull plain house.'

'No, I'm havin' none of that! It's too costly hirin' an architect.'

'OK, I'll pay the architect then.'

'Haven't you enough to be payin' for with the weddin'?'

'Ah no, Dad's paying for that,' she said matter-of-factly.

'You just want to be different. That's all. Jaysus, when I think of what I could buy with the fees you're goin' to splash out on an architect; a new trailer for the tractor that could fit up to thirty bales of hay, an extension to the pen for the ewes or that fabulous five-star Charolais bull that had caught my eye over in Ennistymon a few months ago.'

She could barely hear him with the noise in the pub. 'I won't live in any old bungalow like thousands of others dotted around the countryside; ordinary mean little houses. I just wouldn't be happy in it, that's all. Can't you see that?' she shouted at him. People looked in her direction.

Irritated with him now, she roared, 'And what's more, you can get somebody else to live in your little *bothan*!'

'OK, I get the picture, but you can pay the feckin' architect,' cause I won't. That's for sure.'

'Fine, I'll pay him,' she said stubbornly.

'Look, Danny, I have to go. I'll see you next week,' and she snapped her phone shut. She now felt more distressed than ever. She was sure that her state of angst was compounded by Danny's complete indifference and disregard for her feelings. If she could not turn to him, her fiancé, in her deepest, darkest hour, then it was time to reappraise their relationship. As she gathered her bags her heart was heavy, and she dried a pearl-like tear that had formed.

Chapter 23

Pierre came in early on the following Monday. Rose-Ellen knew that he would need to go to the wards to check on any patients admitted over the weekend. He seemed cool and detached towards her. She felt that their professional relationship had become somewhat fraught over these past few weeks and she presumed that this was the reason for his frostiness. After she had made coffee and sorted out a few outstanding issues from the previous week, she decided to broach the subject of her encounter with Shay McAdam.

'Pierre, can we talk? I need to speak to you about something.'

He sat down and for once did not open any of the charts in front of him. He folded his arms and stared at the wall in front of him. His reaction was one of cold, stiff politeness. 'Of course, but if you could be brief as I have a lot to attend to this morning.'

She drew a deep breath.

'When I was here alone last Friday Shay McAdam came in and threatened me. He became quite abusive.'

He looked down at the bundle of unopened charts on his desk. 'What was he doing here? He has no business being in this hospital while he is suspended from his job. His threats are not to be taken lightly,' he said. His expression softened. 'Always keep a pager or mobile with you and I'll alert security. That sort of behaviour is unacceptable in any civilised society.'

However, Rose-Ellen had not finished.

'He seemed to resent me reporting him, but I was only doing what I felt to be right. I'm sorry that it had to come to this.'

She stopped as she knew that this was not quite true, and Pierre would probably sense it too.

But Pierre seemed anxious as he turned to face her. 'How are you getting on with the audit findings?'

'Nearly finished. Most of the issues have been resolved.'

'That's good. Because it is important that all issues will have been addressed before the international audit or indeed if the FDA decides to audit this site.'

He hesitated and then continued. 'Oh, and about the research funds. I've transferred some money from the general research fund into the Cytu AB account, so you should have plenty to cover patient travel expenses. I've given the bank strict instructions that no more money from the research account is to be withdrawn without my being informed, other than by you for patient expenses. In the longer term, once we've assured IQI Pharma Corp that we've addressed all concerns and issues, and they are happy with our progress, then we can proceed with recruitment. With McAdam gone things should now progress smoothly.'

Rose-Ellen nodded and returned to her desk. She noted the amount of post awaiting her attention. At least the temporary suspension to recruitment of any patients to the study would allow her to catch up on things. Pierre came over and sat on her desk.

'Another thing. Helen has done a bit of detective work and has discovered that there were patients who had all been dreamt up by McAdam to increase the numbers in the trial. This so-called GP surgery was a complete figment of his imagination. This is extremely serious. It's fraud in its purest form. The company, the authorities and of course the hospital management have been informed.'

She looked up from the pile of unopened letters on her desk.

'How did she find that out, I mean about the GP surgery? I can't believe he'd do this. God, I have had to pinch myself lately to make sure I'm not imagining all of it,' she said tiredly.

'Apparently there is no GP surgery that would have referred these patients. Helen did some good detective work on her own and of course it helps that her brother is a GP in west Dublin. There were just too many inconsistencies. Dr Doolan and I will oversee those ongoing patients in the trial. He has been thoroughly briefed on the patients in the Cytu AB trial and this is where you come in; to be alert to any protocol violations. But get the audit report out of the way first.'

'Well, at least recruitment has been suspended, so I can concentrate on the ongoing trial work.'

'Precisely. Dr Doolan and the company must be kept up-to-date at all times about trial matters.'

Pierre continued, 'Basically, what I'm saying, Rose-Ellen, is that I'm putting you in charge when I'm away.'

'Away?' she asked.

'Yes. Do you remember the Circle of Ireland race? I'll be gone for a week towards the end of June.'

When she heard that Pierre was giving her full control over the management of the trial she felt a great swell of pride. 'You need have no worries when you're away. I'll address all audit findings with Dr Doolan.' At last she could show him her worth; how she could be entrusted to run things on her own.

He looked at his watch.

'Now I really must head on up to the wards.'

Despite all that he had to contend with, Pierre had resolved the issues created by McAdam, and she was grateful to him that he had shown her the respect that was her due. Now she could concentrate on the important tasks at hand.

Chapter 24

'Oh, Mam. Danny is being very awkward about the plans for the house and he seems to deliberately find fault with all my suggestions. He has the entire Redmond family behind him and I feel I can't win no matter how hard I try, and God knows I do. We quarrel over the least little thing, and sometimes I wonder if married life would be one long episode of giving up my independence, but then I suppose most couples have these pre-wedding tiffs.'

Kitty Power listened to her daughter's concerns as they sat in Rose-Ellen's bedroom at home.

'I don't know what it is, but the relationship is not going well, Mam. It's not as if I'd be marrying him, I'd be marrying a lifestyle. And there's his family. He's tied to them – mother, father and all those brothers and that suspicious sister. We just don't seem to agree on anything any more. Sometimes I feel as if I don't really know him at all. You could say I only know him superficially, but the more I see of him and his ways the harder it is. I wouldn't have a hope.'

Her mother came over and held her. 'There, there, my pet. You don't have to do anything you don't want to, and I'm behind you all the way.'

Rose-Ellen continued, 'I also like living in Dublin.' She saw a slightly hurt look come into her mother's expression.

'Ah, Mam. I didn't mean it like that. I love coming down to see yourself and Dad, but to live here in Wexford all the time, well, I'd miss Dublin. Maybe I'm just becoming a bit more independent, like living on my own, preferring my own company and doing my own thing. When I go to the Redmonds I feel like I'm somebody else; like wearing some kind of a mask. I'd have to survive down here by becoming like them.'

As her mother stroked her soft curls and kissed her forehead

Rose-Ellen felt the tears welling up in her eyes.

'There, there, Rose-Ellen, dear. Don't worry, pet. If you don't want to go through with it, then don't. Only you know best. You know, if you do go through with the wedding, it will be very hard to get out of it. It's never easy to divorce and marriage is a legally binding contract. It involves families, property and rights, and it's not all about love you know. Oh, I hate to sound unromantic, but when reality kicks in it can kill all thoughts of love.'

Rose-Ellen let her thoughts flow freely. After all, if she could not say these things to her mother, who could she say them to?

'I'm not sure that marrying Danny is the right move for me. You see I don't want to rush into anything. At least we haven't set a date for the wedding.'

Her mother held her daughter's beautiful face in her hands and looking into her eyes said, 'You don't have to do anything you don't want to do, and if you really want me to be honest I wouldn't mind one bit if you called the whole thing off. There, now I've said it!'

Rose-Ellen looked at her mother.

'You don't really like the Redmonds, do you?'

'Well, put it this way, they wouldn't be my cup of tea, and with your looks and brains, darling, you could do a lot better than that big coarse fellow, Danny Redmond. Ah, don't get me wrong, he's a fine fellow in some ways, but he's not for you. I didn't like to say it. Well, I thought you were mad about him and your father was delighted with the engagement, but then men are different. They don't see things the way we do.'

She watched her mother sitting on her bed looking out at the garden with that wistful look she knew so well.

'Your father would be seeing the Powers and the Redmonds related as a result of this union; two old Wexford families, and that would be it.'

Rose-Ellen reflected for a while on what her mother was saying. Kitty turned and looked at her daughter.

'You know, another thing is that I wasn't at all happy about him building a house on their land. It's just a bit too close. Much better to keep the in-laws at a respectable distance.'

'Mam, I'd no idea that you felt that way about Danny. You see, I've had doubts for a few months now. I don't know what exactly, just little things, and they keep cropping up all the time, eating away at the romance.'

Rose-Ellen got up from the chair and looked at herself in the mirror and then at her mother. She had a determined look about her. 'No, that's it, my mind's made up. I'm going to call the whole thing off. There's no point, and the longer it goes on the more I'm convinced it would be a mistake. It's only fair to tell Danny now and not lead him on.'

Her mother's eyes seemed to follow Rose-Ellen as she moved distractedly round the room. 'Look, darling, you must do what's best, but don't rush into anything you might regret either. Have a think about it, but remember, nobody can lead your life for you and, after the big wedding and all the fuss, it's you and him together. There will be nobody to help you, and then when children arrive, well, that's it.'

There was a moment's silence.

'It's the woman who takes all the responsibility there; minding them, teaching them what's important in life, manners and how to behave, because I can tell you, they won't learn much from the Redmonds about the finer things in life.'

She felt a shiver as she tried to envisage the uphill struggle she would have teaching their children about such things. Trying to imagine what life would have in store for her in several years' time. Being beholden to Mrs. Redmond and that entire family convinced Rose-Ellen more than ever that she simply could not go through with the wedding.

'I'm going over to the Redmonds to tell him.' Then she had a slight faintness of heart.

'Or maybe I'll write to him.'

Rose-Ellen remained on the bed while her mother got up and started to tidy things around the room. She folded one of Rose-Ellen's cardigans to put it away and turned and faced her daughter.

'No, don't write. It's better to have the courage and tell him honestly to his face. Many things are better not written down. Look, love, don't be too hard on him. It's not his fault. It's just his way. Say it gently. There's no point in causing offence. Don't forget, we have to live down here with them.'

Rose-Ellen realised that she would need to tread carefully. After all, the Redmond and Power families had known each other for generations.

'Trust me, Mam, I won't,' Rose-Ellen said, and with that she started to get her things ready for her return to Dublin. As she packed she tried to think of what to say and imagined Josie, Redmond and all of them surrounding her and protecting one of their own. The thought of breaking the news to Danny terrified her. The beautiful engagement ring perched on her finger was sparkling in the evening sun and, overcome with sadness, she cried into her pillow. Her mother quietly left the room and came back with a small glass of hot whiskey and honey.

'There, there, love, drink this little hot whiskey. It will give you strength and courage. It's not an easy thing to break off an engagement, that's for sure, so be brave. You'll be fine. After all, Rose-Ellen, it's not to be.'

Rose-Ellen sipped the honey-flavoured whiskey and felt better after it. It seemed to give her some inner strength. She got dressed and cleaned her tired face.

Her mother gave her a hug before she got into the car. 'Thanks, Mam, for all your advice. You're right. I know deep down that what I'm doing is the best for both of us.'

'Well, if you don't feel one hundred per cent sure then it's best not to go through with something that you might regret later on. At least you're following your head as well as your heart. Be brave, love. You're a smart girl; you'll be fine. Don't worry, it'll all work out for the best.'

Rose-Ellen put the car into gear and headed towards the Redmond farm. As she drove, she tried to think of what to say, the right words, words which would cause least offence, but the nearer she came to the farm, the more her resolve failed her. She veered off the slip road and turned the car and headed back up on the N11 to Dublin.

Once back up in Dublin concentration eluded her. She felt rudderless, unsure of her relationship with Danny and emotionally drained after all that had happened.

On Thursday evening Danny phoned her. He seemed unusually confident. 'Hello, love, how's it goin'? Will ye be down soon?'

She seemed to be caught off guard by his call. 'Why, Danny, is something up? I was only down last weekend.'

'Well, I'd like you to meet me new girlfriend, Barbara-Ellen.'

Rose-Ellen removed her earring and replaced the phone to her ear. 'Who's Barbara-Ellen?'

'Ah, she's the grandest little greyhound I bought! She'll be great when she gets going. I'm thinking of going into dogs, ye know, runnin' them, coursin' maybe. And didn't I call her after ye?' he said with a chuckle.

That was enough for Rose-Ellen. Any misgivings she had harboured about Danny up till now were finally confirmed at the mention of Barbara-Ellen. She would not marry anyone who would indulge and breed greyhounds for the cruel sport of tearing apart innocent hares for people's relish and to make money. She remembered her uncle and his smelly greyhounds – exercising them every morning, the muzzle barely concealing their viciousness – and how it used to send shivers down her very being. She recalled the constant whiff of urine from these dogs as they sat in the family estate car snarling through the grill, their eyes trained to chase and follow the darting, weaving, frightened hare, nostrils flared for the whiff of blood.

'I'll be down next weekend, Danny.'

'Ah, that's great, Rose-Ellen. Ye'll love her. She's an absolute pet. Well, goodbye, love, see ye at the weekend.' Rose-Ellen hung up. There was no going back now. As far as she was concerned the die was cast and Barbara-Ellen was the catalyst.

On the following Friday she finished early and set off for the Redmond farm over by the Blackstairs. Her arrival was timed to coincide with milking. At least this way she did not have to go to the house and suffer the wrath of the Redmond clan.

She drove over the cattle grid and into the muddy yard. Danny was standing by the gate watching her, stick in hand. Swinging her small Peugeot 204 to face the gate, then turning off the engine, she watched as the cows strolled in a line into the milking parlour. They each knew their way and ambled slowly along with bulging udders and bony hips swinging in an elegant fashion. They would clamber up on to the milking platform with their gentle, shifting hooves making minimal sound. Soon he would attach the clusters of cups to the cows' teats and they would stand placidly as the white milk flowed into the tank, their soft breathing barely audible against the whoosh of the milking machine. She had seen it so often before. She watched as the last of the cows made their way inside.

Danny had a surprised look on his face as clearly he was not expecting her. Sensing that something was amiss he came over to where she had parked and stood fixing his eyes on her. She got out.

'I didn't expect to see ye here at this hour. Ye must have left work early!'

'Danny, we need to talk,' she said, getting out of the car. Rose-Ellen did not know whether to continue or not and for a brief second panicked. Her nervousness was palpable and her voice started to quiver. He seemed to pick up on her unease. She needed to be brave and get it over with. His expression was one of confusion and concern.

'I don't know how to say this, but I'll be as kind as I can. The fact is that I want to break off our engagement.'

Slowly his expression changed to anger.

'What! Aren't we engaged? Haven't I been buildin' a house for us these past few months? Jesus Christ, what more can I do?'

'I know that, Danny, and that is why I need to come clean with this now before you make any more preparations for our marriage. Look, it's how I feel, not what we have. I can't go through with it. Can't you see we're totally different people? Maybe we got on when we were younger, when we were in school and played together all those years ago, but I've changed. Can't you see that we've grown apart?'

He seemed utterly dazed. There was a look of complete bewilderment on his face. His pale blue eyes narrowed in fury and indignation.

'Changed? Ye can say that again! You're not the girl I knew, that's for sure! Ah, Dublin's ruined you, the good life and high flyin'. I can see that.'

There was no point in talking to him. He was sour and hurt now. She looked down at the ring and tried to get it off her finger, but it refused to move. Despite twisting and turning it the marquise stone remained defiantly stuck providing the final ironic twist. Maybe it was the heat of the summer's eve and her finger had swollen. Her eyes avoided his stare.

'I want to return the ring.'

'I don't want the bloody ring. I just want us to be together.' He was edging towards her. 'Ah please, Rose-Ellen. Look, maybe I know I'm a country fellah, but you'll have a good life with me, and you'll want for nothing, that's for sure.'

She briefly thought of the life they might have together, but maybe having all the material things and comforts in life were not enough. She looked at him standing in front of her and realised that if she married him she would be trapped for the rest of her life down here – with him, his cows and the farm, their life dictated by the relentless rolling seasons and the demands of dairying.

Finally the ring came off her swollen finger. She looked at it for the last time as it twinkled in her palm.

'No, Danny. I'm sorry to end things like this, but I feel it's better to be honest with you now, rather than later. Yes, I have changed. Whether it's for the better, I don't know. I'm sure that you'll meet somebody else and be very happy. You'll be a good husband and father, but we've grown apart, and people do change in life. I don't want to go into something that I would regret. It wouldn't be fair to you.'

He took the ring without even looking at it as if she had handed him a pebble from the beach. He seemed genuinely hurt. She could hear the bawling of the cows inside waiting patiently to be hooked up to the milking machines.

'Mammy and Daddy will be very disappointed. What am I goin' to say to them? You've brought shame to this family with your behaviour. We were good and kind to you.'

His voice was near breaking. Rose-Ellen had to look away. She wanted to get away, anywhere, she did not care, just to get out. Danny went on, 'Why…why Daddy even gave us some land to build a house on. Jesus, ye bloody women. There's no pleasin' ye!' With that he walked away resignedly, head bowed, into the milking parlour to his patient cows.

Rose-Ellen felt a tinge of shame as the Redmonds were indeed a good family – the salt of the earth – who had been kind to her and treating her like one of the family. But that was not enough to get married to him. Rose-Ellen had taken the decent and honourable path by returning the ring and being honest with him before any wedding plans were finalised. He would meet somebody else and now Rose-Ellen felt some sense of relief as she turned and got back into the car and drove bumpily out over the grid and onto the road back home.

Chapter 25

The next Sunday, the last one in June, Rose-Ellen, accompanied by Siobhan set off to Wicklow for the start of the Circle of Ireland race in which Pierre was competing. They positioned themselves up on the headland and watched the spectacular scene through binoculars away from the crowds.

'What was the name of Pierre's boat?' Siobhan asked peering through the binoculars.

'Blue Orca. A fifty-foot Cookson, I think it was.'

'Oh, I think I can see it. I can just about make it out.'

When all final checks were done, the colourful flotilla of boats assembled near the starting line at Wicklow harbour. Hundreds of spectators lined the quay and cliffs overhead to watch the wondrous spectacle. Flags flew and horns sounded, and the harbour master and President of Sail Ireland gave speeches over a tannoy. Seagulls squawked across the roaring crowds on this great and momentous day. The coastguards, Sailing Club, Civil Defence and Royal National Lifeboat Ireland crew were on hand if any difficulties arose.

Exactly ten minutes before noon, the ten minute starting gun boomed. This meant that all spectator boats had to get out of the pathway of the great balloon-like boats as they assembled for the race behind the imaginary line. Then the final gun went off and the almost hemispherical, balloon-like spinnakers lifted the yachts lightly off the water as they thrust forward on their great voyage.

Rose-Ellen grabbed the binoculars from Siobhan. 'Here give us a look.' She could see Blue Orca, a tall elegant boat first off the line with its massive billowing blue and white sails, and she thought of Pierre.

Overhead she could hear the drone of a 1966 Piper plane and stared spellbound by the aerobatic manoeuvrings of a Tandem two-seater plane.

Up and up soared the silver plane into the dark grey clouds letting off jets of smoke periodically, which, according to the voice on the tannoy, was made by the periodic ejections of tractor diesel released by the retired Harrier jump jet pilot in the cockpit. As the boats sailed past the harbour at Wicklow on to their gruelling Circle of Ireland round trip, Rose-Ellen blew a kiss from the headland.

'Goodbye, Pierre and good luck!' and waved with the rest of the crowd at the fleeting flotilla.

Chapter 26

'I feel as though in some ways the damn thing, beautiful as it was, had entrapped me,' Rose-Ellen confided to Olivia on the phone when she had returned to Dublin on Sunday night. But she felt strange arriving into work on Monday morning without her beautiful ring. Once proudly displayed on her fourth finger, she now did not seem to miss it that much.

The phone rang in her office at nine-thirty am sharp. She picked it up. 'Rose-Ellen Power. May I help you?'

'Good morning, Ms Power. Ms Horne's secretary here. The Director of Nursing would like to see you at ten am in her office.'

Rose-Ellen knocked on the door and the prim, pert secretary opened it. Rose-Ellen noticed her deferential air, and presumed that servility and secrecy had become second nature to her from working with Ms Horne.

'Ms Horne will see you now,' the secretary whispered in barely audible tones.

The Director of Nursing sat back in her chair and scrutinised Rose-Ellen carefully.

'How is everything in the research department?'

'Fine thank you, considering everything.'

'I won't waste time as to why I asked you here, Nurse Power. Dr Shay McAdam has made a complaint. He said that you got into his computer by using his password and read his own private diary, and from those actions made fraudulent accusations against him.'

'Got into his computer? I don't know what you're talking about! I never went near his computer. That's ridiculous! I have no idea what his password is. That is highly confidential. Dr McAdam has been suspended because of quite serious irregularities regarding the Cytu AB trial, in other words, fraud,' Rose-Ellen replied.

The older woman glanced at Rose-Ellen over her thin fine glasses. 'I hardly think, Nurse Power, that it's up to you to question another's integrity, certainly not a doctor's, and not one as hard-working and as diligent as Dr McAdam. You know he was held in very high esteem here both by the medical and nursing profession and patients alike until his suspension. Words like "fraud" are very strong, and unless you have sound proof of this you should hold your judgement. Do I make myself clear?'

'Ask Dr Doolan, the CEO and Dr O'Hegarty. They'll all back me up on what I am saying. And another thing, I was threatened by Dr McAdam one Friday evening here before going home,' she said.

The Director of Nursing leaned forward on her desk, straightened the corners of the bundle of papers and looked intently at Rose-Ellen. 'You will not be the arbiter of what has taken place; that will be left for higher authorities. I am only concerned with the fact that you, Rose-Ellen Power, have not only accused someone of fraud, but you also got into their computer unknown to them, and then you denigrated the good name of a very hard-working professional. Dr McAdam said that you had made very serious accusations about his alleged professional misconduct to members in this institution and to those outside.'

Rose-Ellen then remembered the audit and what must have come out in the report. She took a deep breath to camouflage her nervousness.

'If you're talking about the element of professional misconduct, well, during the audit I alerted the auditor as to the irregularities regarding how the trial was conducted. If Dr McAdam chose to believe this to be an accusation of his professional conduct then I think that you need to speak with the auditor.'

She knew by Ms Horne's expression that the woman had no intention of taking matters further and least of all with an external auditor.

'I feel under the circumstances that it were better if you were to move to a ward away from trials and audits. This is an extremely serious matter. The geriatric ward is always short-staffed, so you can start duty there next week,' Ms Horne said triumphantly.

Rose-Ellen felt numbed. She had not spent the past few years in the difficult and demanding world of clinical research to end up on a geriatric ward looking after elderly patients. She thought of the hours spent checking the data for the Cytu AB trial and how in her search she had uncovered the lax and sloppy work of another. And where had her probity got her? It had cost her her job, integrity and good name. She could see that all her work to date at DCH could be lost because of this woman's unyielding and uncompromising behaviour.

'If Dr McAdam has been suspended from his position as Registrar in the hospital that has nothing to do with me.' She could only presume that Ms Horne was opportunistically availing herself of the situation to have her finally removed from her research role.

'I am moving you from your position because you cannot be trusted with computers, nor can you be trusted to hold your counsel, blabbering to outsiders about those who work in the hospital, and interfering in another's affairs. I understand that you consistently undermined Dr McAdam and were constantly correcting him about his work.'

'I did not discuss anything about Dr McAdam with anybody outside. I said what I had to say to the auditor, that is all. I found Dr McAdam to be lax in his clinical research work and as study co-ordinator it was my duty to point out certain irregularities to him when necessary.' Rose-Ellen looked down at her hands folded on her lap. She sighed as she thought how little this woman understood the intricacies of clinical research. 'And what about all the patients for the trial whose visits have been scheduled while Dr O'Hegarty is away? Who is going to look after them? And besides, I am not employed by the hospital. My salary is paid from the research funds so you have no say in what job I shall perform here.'

Ms Horne concluded, 'I have nothing further to say on this matter. You may clear out your things and leave your office this morning and start in the geriatric ward. It is not up to you to question the motives or *modus operandi* of another. You need not try to be some kind of a whistle-blower. The hospital management will ensure that people like you, who make accusations on very flimsy evidence, are dealt with in the appropriate manner. An agency nurse or one of the relief nurses can do your clinical trial work. After all, there is nothing too involved as far as I can see other than taking vital signs, meeting the patients and giving them their study medications.'

Such cold comfort indeed being moved to the geriatric ward. Her high moral rectitude had meant nothing in the whole scheme of things; on the contrary, it had jeopardised her future. Surviving was about being politically correct, saying and doing what was popular, even if one did not believe it, and keeping one's head below the parapet. But still, Rose-Ellen could not be silenced.

'Please let me explain. There was fraud uncovered and I was concerned for the overall welfare of patients. Why was Dr McAdam suspended? It was because Dr O'Hegarty believed that he was not conducting the trial according to Good Clinical Practice'.

'That's enough!'

As Rose-Ellen stood up to leave, she said, 'And I won't be taking up this position on the geriatric ward. I'm not interested in looking after old people. As I said, I'm not employed by the hospital, and besides, Dr O'Hegarty will decide what happens to me. So we should wait until he returns.'

Ms Horne was taken aback at Rose-Ellen's refusal to take the alternative position offered to her. 'Dr O'Hegarty is not here and so I shall deal with matters. You will be temporarily suspended from your research position until such time as Dr O'Hegarty returns,' Ms Horne said, leaning forward on her desk.

Rose-Ellen felt that Ms Horne was relishing her position of authority. She looked at the clock on the wall and then turned back to the Director of Nursing.

'I have no intention of taking a position unsuited to my specific qualifications and training. I'm sure that Dr Doolan will agree with me. After all, he's in charge now while Dr O'Hegarty is away.'

'I don't wish to involve Dr Doolan. You will not resume your research duties until Dr O'Hegarty's return. Then a decision can be made as to what will become of you.' Her ample bosom heaved with indignation.

'Dr Doolan knows all about Dr McAdam's conduct. Dr O'Hegarty briefed him thoroughly on the goings-on. I'd rather leave this place than work where I'd have to be beholden to you and your deputies. I've worked too long now in an independent capacity in research roles to accept this kind of stop-gap job, so I'm giving in my notice.'

'You will leave today if that's what you want. I'll get the accountant to settle up your final salary and prepare the paperwork. That is all.'

She realised that there was no point in arguing with someone whose ulterior motive was to have her moved. Rose-Ellen was let out by the secretary who barely acknowledged her and she returned to her office. As she tidied up and made some last minute calls her heart was heavy. She looked round at all the files, a testament to the hard work she had put in, the hours toiled, the endless and painstaking notes and rigorous attention to detail, now to be handed over casually to a nurse from the wards with little or no experience of the management of clinical trials.

Rose-Ellen phoned Siobhan in the endoscopy department. 'Siobhan, can you meet me for coffee in about ten minutes? I need to speak to you urgently.'

'Give me twenty minutes. I have a few scopes to clean after today's list. I'll see you at a little after eleven.

They met in the small coffee room on the ground floor. 'Your ring, what's happened?' Siobhan gasped looking at Rose-Ellen's left hand.

'Oh, Siobhan, where do I start? I've broken off my engagement with Danny, and I've left my job. Madame Horne wanted to move me to the geriatric ward where I suspect she can keep her beady eyes on me.'

Siobhan put the frothy coffee to her lips, barely touched it and set the cup down gently in front of her. 'Steady on there. You're not making sense. What happened for God's sake?'

'That scoundrel McAdam has reported me. But Horne never liked me; she's always been so cold and unforgiving towards me and this is her golden opportunity to finally get rid of me.'

Siobhan was shocked. 'Jesus, this is mega! Geriatric ward! How insulting! Where is Pierre in all of this? After all, you were only doing what you thought was best, and besides, if all that underhand stuff was let go undetected, wouldn't you all be in a right stew?'

Rose-Ellen stirred her cappuccino distractedly and scooped the foam into her mouth. 'Sometimes by doing what's best you pay the price.'

'What about the union? You could always go to them. I don't think you can be suspended like that; you have grounds for appeal. It just doesn't seem right to me. After all, you've done nothing wrong that would warrant a suspension. A suspension usually means that you've either done something you shouldn't have, or not done something you should.'

'I haven't paid my membership for a few years and I'm not employed by the hospital. I mean, my salary is paid for by the research funds. So I haven't a leg to stand on.'

'All the more reason why that old bitch can't just temporarily suspend you.'

'I think she can until Pierre comes back.'

'That's ridiculous. I never heard such crap in my whole life; you're nothing but a scapegoat.'

Rose-Ellen knew that Siobhan was probably right. Until Pierre returned, her options were few.

'Oh, I wish Pierre were here, but he's away sailing round Ireland at the moment. He'll be away for the next week.'

'Typical, bloody typical! Away sailing, and all this going on! I think it very unfair that you have to take the brunt of this with your own job. But do you know what? He'll be OK. Guys like him always are.'

'And to make matters worse, he's not contactable. Dr Doolan is looking after everything while he's gone. I thought of going to him and discussing my position, but what's the point? I know he wouldn't do anything and I couldn't bear to involve him in things of this nature. He'd only make it worse.'

Siobhan rolled her eyes at the mention of Dr Doolan's name. 'That's just great, bloody great. Pierre drops you into it and heads off on some stupid yacht race! I wouldn't care if the fellow is churning in the Atlantic at this stage. I'd contact him.'

'I can't, he's out of reach. He's not responding to any calls and besides, I don't think that they can take calls out at sea in that kind of race.'

'Let him take the flack for this when he comes back. I wouldn't get involved, but it seems such a terrible shame about the suspension. When is he back?'

'I don't know exactly. It depends on this damn race and when it finishes.' Rose-Ellen felt that everything was caving in around her. Siobhan was right. Men like Pierre, whilst academics, were ultimately career builders.

'But tell me what happened between yourself and Danny? Oh, Rose-Ellen, I'm so, so sorry.'

Rose-Ellen fiddled distractedly with her paper napkin. 'I don't know. It was becoming more and more difficult every time we met. We disagreed on everything; we just seemed to have grown apart. I suppose I never really knew him, but since we got engaged I was becoming more involved with his life and I realised that we had very little in common. You know, small things, they all add up. I just know that deep down I wouldn't be happy with him.' Rose-Ellen smoothed out the napkin. 'Then there was his family. He's so tied to them. We'd be building a house on his land, close to the family, and I would have no peace between his mother and father and the brothers, not to mention that bitch of a sister.'

Siobhan put out her hand and placed it on Rose-Ellen's. 'I'm so sorry about this, and when it rains it pours. But you know, it's not the end of the world. You'll get another job. Listen, think of your strong points. You're attractive with a good personality, and it won't be long until you meet someone else, I'm sure of it. And besides, if your heart isn't in it then it's best you don't go through with it.'

Rose-Ellen started to cry. 'Thanks, Siobhan, it's great to talk to someone. I was beginning to wonder was it me? Was I jinxed? First the broken engagement and now being suspended from my job!'

'Nah, it's not you. It's just that you're more honest than a lot of women in your situation, and the other is just bad timing coming so soon after you've broken off the engagement. But you'll get over that, I know you will. You'll bounce back. After all, you're still young. And look on the bright side, isn't it best you realise now that you didn't really love him or want to go through with it in the first place, rather than finding this out a few years down the road with a couple of children in tow?'

Rose-Ellen dried her eyes with the napkin. 'You're right.'

Siobhan looked at her mobile to see if she had any messages and then put it away. 'Listen, when Pierre's back you'll be re-instated. I wouldn't worry about it too much. And besides, you're well qualified. If all fails you'll get something. Can't you do a bit of agency nursing to tide you over?' She drained her coffee cup before Rose-Ellen had time to answer. 'Now I really have to go. I'll keep my ears to the ground about another position; anything that comes up. You know what the endoscopy unit is like, it's a hive of gossip, nothing escapes me up there, so if I hear of any positions going I'll let you know!'

'Thanks, Siobhan. I can't go home because my parents will suspect something.'

Siobhan stood up, threw her cardigan casually over her shoulders and reached for her bag. 'But you might get your job back. Things will be different when Pierre comes back from holidays surely?'

'To be perfectly honest, I don't think that I would return here to work in any capacity after what's happened. It would be too difficult. Ah, it's not just old Horne, although she would continue to make my life miserable and she'll be Director of Nursing for the next twenty years. It's the whole McAdam thing as well. The job has turned sour for me now. Even when Pierre comes back I'm not sure I'd want it. McAdam could be re-instated; you never know, doctors are in short supply and he's very popular so it would appear.'

'I'm sure it won't be easy for that bastard to get his job back again. Those days are gone!' Siobhan said assertively.

'At the end of the day IQI Pharma Corp needs the patients to prove the worth of Cytu AB, and a replacement for me will be found quickly so they get their numbers in. I'm dispensable in the greater scheme of things,' Rose-Ellen said resignedly.

'You shouldn't be so hard on yourself.'

But as she got up to leave too, Rose-Ellen wondered if the trial would continue at all after everything which had gone on. 'No, I might as well cut my losses and leave this place'.

'Ah, Rose-Ellen, forget about them all. None of them did anything for you. You're on your own now and don't look back.'

'That's for sure!'

'Listen, I know things have been awful for you, what with everything coming together. I think that you should go home, lie low and tell your parents the truth. They'll understand.'

'No, maybe Mam will. At least she did about the engagement, but my Dad will only just be getting over the break up with Danny. If he hears now that I've been suspended from my job and the circumstances it'd ruin him, that's for sure.'

Siobhan checked the time. 'I have to go. I'll keep an eye out for anything, but in the meantime have a good think. It's been a terrible shock to your system. I'll give you a buzz soon, but look, love, take it easy, have a rest and clear your head.'

Siobhan left to return to her world of scopes and probes in the endoscopy unit. Rose-Ellen needed some time to take stock of all that had taken place. Right now her thoughts were furiously hurtling through her mind and she was not thinking logically. She had given no thought to the repercussions of what she had done. Now it was all beginning to come home to her. At this precise moment she wanted to get away from DCH and all that it represented – disappointment, dishonour and discontent.

Chapter 27

Watching a dog chase a line of seagulls out as far as the eye could see reminded Rose-Ellen of sketching. She drove south in the direction of Dalkey with her paints and there positioned herself in a quiet part of the beach so that she could slop around with watercolours before committing any image to canvas. The weather was mild with a sprinkling of clouds. There were the usual veterans of all year round bathing, children screaming when they had unearthed some poor unfortunate crustacean from its home in the rocks and a loose dog madly chasing squawking gulls who were impervious to its wretched barking, their sole immediate focus on the relentless quest for food.

Trying to concentrate on a scene was difficult as her mind failed to connect with the surroundings. She thought of all that had happened in that small office, how she had come to enjoy working with Pierre and how everything had turned so nasty culminating in her departure. She marvelled at how her world had been crammed into this tiny intimate area and reflected back on the days spent there; some difficult and unpredictable, but many peaceful and satisfying. Now such times were only bittersweet memories. She resumed her painting, but the perspective was either wrong, or colours were too stark and bright for an Irish watery sun, or she was just not concentrating on the task at hand. How could she function when her life had suddenly taken a road to nowhere? Remembering happier times only distracted her; a time gone by when her uncluttered mind could produce beautiful scenes from nature – a ladybird climbing up a stalk, clumps of bright pink dahlias in her mother's garden, roses drenched with dew or an oak standing strong with its grand yet simple majesty.

In the middle of the week Rose-Ellen decided to go home to discuss the situation with her mother, but wondered what to say about losing her job. Perhaps some vague notion of how the research funds had dried up at DCH would explain all, but her mother would probably not believe her, because Rose-Ellen had often talked about how Pierre was attracting more and more research proposals globally. It was better to come clean with the truth – her mother had a knack of prising the truth out of people. Hopefully her father could be kept in the dark until she had a permanent job. To him one job in a hospital was the same as another, and as long as she was gainfully employed in a respectable position he did not really give it too much thought.

Putting her key into the home front door, Rose-Ellen was filled with trepidation. She stood in the hall and took off her coat as the cool glittering voice of a soprano on the radio filled the air. The smell of freshly baked bread drifted from the kitchen beckoning Rose-Ellen there.

Kitty called out, 'Is that you, Maurice?' and Rose-Ellen tiptoed into the kitchen. Kitty was surprised and yet delighted to see Rose-Ellen, who put her arms around her mother and kissed her.

'What brings you down here to see us now, pet?' Kitty asked, looking at Rose-Ellen with that suspicious look she used when she had doubts. 'I'll just put the finishing touches to this cake and then put on the kettle, and then we can have a chat,' Kitty said busily.

Rose-Ellen noticed all the paraphernalia needed for decorating a cake; piping bag, colourings, bags of icing sugar, lemons and an assortment of tubes and nozzles. Her mother was putting the final touches to a cake decorated for a couple's thirtieth wedding anniversary. As the water was boiling she observed the diligence with which her mother worked placing the piped violets, forget-me-nots, rosebuds and lilies of the valley onto the frosting on the cake. Dipping a soft toothbrush in powdered carmine, Kitty drew her finger across the bristles so that the powder flew on to the roses, creating a deeper shade of red. Then she perfectly piped in scroll lettering the words 'Happy 30th Anniversary' in pale pink, and afterwards outlined them with a deeper shade of pink, finally placing a golden bow delicately around the finished work of art.

'Mam, that cake is too good to eat. If I bought it I'd put it in a glass case and look at it forever,' she said, and came over to admire it.

Her mother smiled at her. 'Darling, I've been icing and decorating cakes for years. I love it and there's nothing like a fresh home-made cake lovingly baked. Those bought cakes are all powder, chemicals and dried eggs. It's not the same as the real thing. Now once I get this into its box we can have a nice cup of tea together and you can tell me all the news.'

Once the cake had been wrapped and boxed, they sat over their cups of tea at the kitchen table.

'Oh, how do I begin, Mam? I've lost my job. It's a long story really, but to cut it short they wanted to move me to a geriatric ward because of the various goings-on in the research department, and I refused.'

Kitty looked at her daughter suspiciously. 'What goings-on!'

Rose-Ellen helped herself to a cherry bun from the plate. 'There was a recent audit and things came to light. I was very upfront about one of the doctors there and I told the truth about things he was doing. I can't really go into it, and of course at the end of the day, when you're seen to be rocking the boat, well, the management in the hospital don't like that and that's why I was moved.'

Her mother was shocked. 'It doesn't seem right that your honesty was rewarded like that, but that's the way these days. Sometimes you're better off to say nothing and keep your head down. But we're not like that.' Kitty put her hand out and squeezed Rose-Ellen's. 'And we thought you were getting on so well there. Look, you have your health and something else will turn up, it always does, and that nice doctor will give you a good reference and you can move on. At times we have to compromise in life, and make the best of the situation, and remember nothing is forever in this life.'

Rose-Ellen wondered how Pierre would react when he heard what had happened. Would he have let her go so easily? He would of course give her a reference, but what would she do in the meantime? She did not want to alarm her mother either.

'Oh, Mam. I'll get something, but that could take time and I hate drawing the dole.'

'Don't you worry about money, and you'll have as much food as you want to take back with you, so come down here every weekend and we can see you through the week. I won't have any of my own going without, that's for sure,' Kitty said supportively.

What would she do without her mother? Rose-Ellen thought. There was no one like her.

She passed the weekend as if in a daze, and her mother made no demands on her. She avoided her father's gaze and pretended to him that she was here because she had a few days off. On Monday afternoon Kitty filled Rose-Ellen's car boot with the provisions from Power's Emporium.

She reflected on the impasse she had reached in her life and tried to think of what she would do now. However, now that she had lost everything and was only just managing to hold on to her self-respect while drawing the dole, the thought of setting up a business in France became more and more probable, while finding a research position receded.

Rose-Ellen sat back with a cup of tea in her flat and opened the evening paper. The leading article on the front page read, '*Yachtsman Doc fights for life following shooting*'.

Turning up the light she continued to read:

Dr Pierre O'Hegarty has been shot on the boat Blue Orca. *He was airlifted to the Wexford General Hospital where he is said to be critical. He remains unconscious. Dr O'Hegarty had come second in the prestigious Circle of Ireland yacht race, and was found drifting out to sea when help arrived.*

Unable to take in all that she had just read, Rose-Ellen got up and wandered through the flat checking on her plants and flicking between channels to take her mind off what had happened to Pierre. Wondering how she would ever get through the night she tried to remain busy, but the hours dragged on and concentration eluded her.

That afternoon Rose-Ellen drove over to the hospital. Pierre was in the intensive care unit. Making her way up the corridor, she noticed a young Garda on duty outside the unit and approached him and asked if she could visit Pierre briefly. He looked suspiciously at her.

'I'm a nurse and I used to work with Dr O'Hegarty,' she assured him.

He looked at her woodenly. 'I'm sorry but we have strict instructions that nobody is to go in to see Dr O'Hegarty except immediate family, given the circumstances,' he said authoritatively.

'Would it be possible for me to speak to one of the nurses in ICU?'

'I don't see anything wrong with that,' he muttered, and went over and knocked on the door. A nurse came out holding a tray with some cotton wool balls and bandages. She seemed slightly flustered. He whispered something to her, and she then looked over at Rose-Ellen. The nurse went back into the ICU and closed the door. The Garda turned to Rose-Ellen. 'The nurse is going to her break in a while and will talk to you then.'

So Rose-Ellen waited outside until the nurse re-emerged. She came over to Rose-Ellen, ignoring the Garda.

'I'm going for a cup of coffee if you'd like to come with me.' They walked down to the coffee room saying little on the way. Then the nurse turned to Rose-Ellen. 'Oh, by the way, I'm Patsy.'

'Hello, Patsy, I'm Rose-Ellen Power. I'm sorry to come here like this, but I live out by Loughbow and have recently worked with Dr O'Hegarty, so naturally I was shocked when I read the papers.'

They sat down in a quiet corner of the hospital restaurant. Patsy put down her cup.

'It's been hectic all morning. We've had press, Gardaí and detectives.'

'I can imagine. How is Dr O'Hegarty?'

'He's very weak but he's heavily sedated. The consultant doesn't know how he made it. There is talk of sending him up to Dublin because post-op he still has internal bleeding from his liver.' Rose-Ellen was disturbed at the news, but at least Pierre was alive.

'Patsy, I'm very grateful to you for this information, especially when I just called on the off chance of finding out about him. The Gardaí won't let me near him; they say only immediate family, but I'm just wondering if I could visit. I'll only be a minute, if that would be possible?'

Patsy checked the time on her fob watch. 'I and another staff nurse are on this evening, so there shouldn't be any problem. But please, just for a few minutes, OK?'

'Of course. I'm not sure if he has any relatives here.'

'Yes, here and France. Oh, and a sister in England.'

'Thanks, Patsy, I can't tell you how much I appreciate this. I'll call back at six-thirty this evening.'

Patsy finished her cup of coffee. 'When you call just knock on the door and I'll let you in. I'd better get back. See you later.'

As Rose-Ellen returned to the ICU at six-thirty pm, she noticed a man standing outside talking on his mobile. He looked at Rose-Ellen as she knocked on the door which was opened by Patsy, who let her in.

Rose-Ellen tiptoed over to the cubicle beside the window where Pierre lay, and approached his bed gingerly, drawing up a chair alongside him and sitting down. Everything was hushed and still in the unit. The nurses moved like shadows in the sterile, clinical world among those frail, ill and vulnerable patients, utterly dependent on their care.

'At least he's breathing,' she consoled herself. *Alive and breathing*; these words full of explosive power and meaning took on a greater poignancy as she stared at him lying on the bed. She noticed his pallor and the skin on his face seemed to have shrunk. Droplets of sweat gathered on his forehead. His shallow breathing was barely audible. She watched him for a while and wondered if he would pass peacefully from this life, slipping quietly into the anonymity of eternity, to become the sweetened distillate of the man she had come to admire. Pierre looked frail, imperfect, yet utterly real, lying in that white starched hospital bed, a fan whirring gently nearby to keep him cool. Rose-Ellen thought how easily life could be snuffed out. She could hear the hiss of the morphine pump and wondered if he were in pain or even if he were conscious or not. She could not bear the prospect of him dying; it just all seemed so shocking and unfair. There were too many dependent on him. The clock over the bed seemed to stand still, as if time were on hold. Feeling restless, she got up and touched Pierre's pale, limp hand gently.

'Is everything OK?' a voice cried. It was Patsy at the open door. Rose-Ellen had to get away before her tears betrayed her feelings.

'Yes, yes, fine. I'm just going,' and with that she picked up her bag and left the ICU. As she left, the man outside snapped his mobile shut and put it in his pocket. He approached her.

'Hello, I'm Detective Finn O'Donnell. I understand that you're a friend of Dr O'Hegarty. As I'm investigating the case, I need to talk to as many friends and acquaintances of the doctor as possible.'

She nodded.

'Your name?'

'Rose-Ellen Power.'

She noticed he looked at her intently.

'Do you have a minute now where we could talk?'

'Sure. I'm just going down to my car,' she said, taking out her car keys from her bag.

'Fine, I'll follow you,' he said, as he motioned her forward.

O'Donnell was friendly in a professional way. They went as far as her car in the hospital car park.

'Now start at the beginning and tell me how you know Dr O'Hegarty, and anything else that might be relevant to the shooting.'

Taking a deep breath, she pushed her hair back off her face.

'Dr O'Hegarty and I worked together in the clinical research department in DCH. We worked with another doctor there, Dr Shay McAdam, who had been suspended from his job recently.'

'Why so?' O'Donnell asked taking notes.

'Oh fraud, doctoring the data.'

'Did Dr O'Hegarty have anything to do with this person's suspension?'

'Yes, he did.'

'I see, so this person could be a suspect then.'

'I suppose so. Look, I'm afraid that I have to go.'

'Thank you. I'd like to call you over the next few days to ask you more about your working relationship with the doctor and this fellow McAdam. We intend to interview everybody who has had any dealings with Dr O'Hegarty, either professionally or socially or to do with the yacht race. We have to cover every angle.'

'I understand. If I can be of any help, I'd be happy to oblige,' she said, providing him with her mobile phone number.

'In the meantime, if you come up with anything new, or if you can throw any light on what has happened, give me a call,' he said.

He handed her his card. She put the card in her bag, thanked him and said that she would be in touch.

But two days later he called her.

Chapter 28

O'Donnell and Rose-Ellen met at a Garda station in central Dublin. 'Glad you could make it. Now, for the record, I'm not into formalities, so if it's OK with you, I'm Finn.'

'Hi, Finn,' she replied, as he motioned her to sit down.

A young Garda brought him in a cup of tea. She declined any refreshments. O'Donnell took off his jacket and sat opposite her. Finn O'Donnell was a man in his thirties, medium height and build. He could be described as attractive rather than handsome. His hair was a salt and pepper colour and his green eyes had an alertness that one associates with those of sharp intelligence and a curious mind.

'So, how are things with you?'

'Look, this may have no bearing on the shooting, but I need to tell you this. Oh, I'm still so frightened and nervous when I think about it.'

'Why so?'

'Well, basically, I was intimidated by Dr McAdam, the one who had been suspended.'

'Why did he intimidate you?'

'He felt that I was the one who had spilled the beans on his activities in the research department, and that I had contributed to his suspension, but I was only doing my job. I don't understand it. Even in a shop the other day, I felt the little creep was following me, as if he were still stalking me.'

As she spoke about all that had happened in DCH, O'Donnell said little, his focussed eyes never straying from her, noting down the odd comment here and there. She stopped, sensing that she had rambled on. He put down his pen and looked at her.

'It's common enough to feel like that after some traumatic event. The thing can take hold of you, as if you're re-living the whole experience in your mind all the time. It's quite plausible that this McAdam individual may have had something to do with Dr O'Hegarty's attempted murder.'

'There was some tension in the department, and it is pretty serious for a doctor to be suspended from his professional duties. It could be years before he practices medicine again.'

He sat back in the chair and closed the file in which he had made notes. 'I'll speak to this McAdam individual and caution him about his intimidation. But attempted fraud is potentially very serious and his temporary suspension could be considered a motive.'

'I feel very upset about what happened, and my leaving my job; it's as if there's a shadow hanging over me professionally.'

'But why did you leave your research job? I don't quite understand!' he said, frowning a little.

'There were difficulties within the department and Dr McAdam was, how shall I put it, a bit lax and more, while I was trying to do things according to the book. You have to be careful in the world of clinical research; there is no room for error. I really can't say too much at this stage, if you know what I mean.'

'I can imagine that it is a highly regulated industry. And you were the fall guy. Not that uncommon.'

'You could put it like that.'

'But you got on OK with Dr O'Hegarty, or did you?'

She was surprised at this remark. 'Of course, why wouldn't I? We worked closely together on the same projects.'

'I'm just covering every angle. Anybody who worked with him could be considered a suspect until we eliminate them.' She reached down to get her bag as she did not want to stay a minute longer with this detective and his suspicious mind. O'Donnell looked at his watch.

'Where did the time go? Let's break off now. I'm sure you want to get away on this lovely weekend.'

Rose-Ellen smiled at him. She was relieved that the interview was over. 'At least I'll have missed the main N11 traffic,' she said.

He got up and put on his jacket. 'Thanks very much for this information, Rose-Ellen. Every little thing helps. You can get in touch with me directly on my mobile or through any Garda station. They'll just ring through to me. As you know, it's sometimes the tiniest detail or observation that can swing a case.' He put out his hand. 'Well, have a nice weekend and we'll be in touch.' They walked out together and over to her car. She climbed in. He leaned in through the open window and smiled at her. 'Don't worry about anything. If you do, just give me a ring. OK, I'll be in touch. Safe driving,' he said, as he tapped the side of the car. Then he was gone.

Rose-Ellen turned the engine and watched him as he crossed the street and disappeared in the relentless stream of cars whose anxious occupants wanted to leave the city for the weekend.

Chapter 29

Rose-Ellen watched Pierre sleeping peacefully in a private cubicle, his tired face and shallow breathing a testament to the brutal treatment he had endured. She felt a rush of emotion for him as he lay there so helplessly. She wanted to reach out and touch his feeble hand – marble-white, on the bedcover. It was purple in spots where they had tried to take bloods. She touched the tip of his fingers. They felt cold to touch. She tightened her grip and a faint smile came across his face.

She got up from the hard chair, leaned over and whispered in his ear. 'Hi, Pierre. It's me, Rose-Ellen. Can you hear me?' and he nodded slightly. 'Oh, Pierre, I can't believe this happened to you! Who on earth could have done this?' she murmured, her voice tapering down to a barely audible whisper. She sat beside the bed on the hard hospital chair and looked at him lying there and thought of how fleeting a life is, and how it can be snuffed out in a brief second. Rose-Ellen realised now that they would probably never work together again. They were both at cross-currents in their lives and she was suddenly overcome with a great sense of loss. She got up and moved over to the window, watching the visitors heading across the car park to the main door of the hospital. She realised that it was time to move on; move away from the disillusionment of the present.

'Rose-Ellen.'

She moved over to his bedside. 'Yes, Pierre, what is it?'

'Can I have a sip of water please?' he said faintly.

'Of course,' she said, pouring him some fresh iced water from the jug at his bedside. After a few sips he lay back on the mound of pillows.

'I never thought I'd wake up again.'

'What happened?'

'It's all a haze, but I can still hear the shots,' he said tiredly.

'Oh my God! I can't believe that anyone would do this to you. But why?'

'Why indeed? I wonder! Who knows why I was targeted, but I'm lucky to be alive.'

'That's terrible.'

Just then there was a knock on the door. Rose-Ellen went out, opened it slightly and there stood Finn O'Donnell.

'Hello, Rose-Ellen.'

'Oh, hello.' She was surprised to see him.

'I wonder if I could come in to have a word with Dr. O'Hegarty, if he's up to talking.'

She turned and looked over at Pierre in the bed, and then opened the door more fully before Finn walked in. He pulled up a chair alongside the bed. Rose-Ellen stood by the window.

'Hello, Dr. O'Hegarty, I'm Finn O'Donnell, the detective on the case and I would like to ask a few questions, if you are up to speaking.'

Pierre sat up despite his weakness. 'I'll tell you what I can.'

'I want to know exactly what happened. In other words, if you can start at the beginning and tell me what took place. Take your time, just tell me what you are able to, as I appreciate that it is still early days since the shooting.'

'It was the day after the Circle of Ireland race. I was checking the instrumentation on the boat, when I felt it sway. I sensed that something was up and went to investigate. I looked up the stairs and got a boot in the chest.' He hesitated as if trying to recall. 'There was a tussle between myself and the intruder as I tried to grab the gun from him. It was then that I was shot.' He took a long breath, lying back on the mounds of pillows as he looked up at the ceiling. 'I tried to get up but I was bleeding profusely from my stomach; I couldn't stop it. I started to take off my shirt, but he came at me again, laughing as he pumped another bullet into my leg. Then I lost consciousness and dropped to the floor, and the gunman fled. I'm haunted by what took place in the small, confined cabin of the boat. Flashbacks of those fleeting seconds come and go all the time: the cracking thump of the gun, the hard cabin floor, the copper smell of my blood as it drenched my shirt.'

Rose-Ellen came away from the window to his bedside and gripped his hand as he continued. 'His ice-blue eyes fixed and focussed with gun poised. I see him all the time in my dreams; it's as if he haunts my every waking hour. I can't escape these flashbacks,' he said, looking out the window. 'But life must go on,' he said, turning to Rose-Ellen.

'Take your time, you're doing great,' O'Donnell said reassuringly.

'I knew that if I didn't call for help I would have bled to death, so I remembered the VHF on channel sixteen and managed to call giving my position. It was a matter of time as I could hear the swish of the water, and knew that the boat was drifting, and then I must have passed out.' Pierre took a sip of water. 'The surgeon said that if the bullet had been another centimetre towards the centre of my liver it would have hit a major blood vessel, and I would probably have bled to death.' Rose-Ellen drew a quick intake of breath as she thought of the tenuous balance between life and death.

'Can you describe the man?' O'Donnell asked.

'Mean looking, black brown greasy hair, about five eleven.'

'Anything else; distinctive features?'

Pierre thought for a while. 'A gap in his front teeth.'

'Anything else?' O'Donnell asked, taking notes.

'Oh yes, a silver earring in one of his ears. I think it was his left ear, yes left one.'

Rose-Ellen observed O'Donnell as he took notes. She noticed the awkward way he held the pen in his left hand. She turned her head when he looked up and smiled at her occasionally. After a while, she got her jacket and bag.

'I think that I'll go now, Pierre. You must be tired,' she whispered.

O'Donnell stood up. 'Thank you very much for your help, doctor. If you can think of anything else, please get in touch with me,' he said, reaching into the breast pocket of his jacket and leaving his card on the table at Pierre's bedside. 'Thanks again, you'll need your rest.'

Rose-Ellen came over to Pierre. 'I'll call again, Pierre. Let me know if you need anything.'

He reached out and took her hand in his. 'Thank you, Rose-Ellen.'

As she made her way out, O'Donnell followed. 'Would you like to go for a drink?' he said, as they walked down the long corridor. She thought him a bit forward asking her for a drink when he was investigating the case, but life was too short for procrastination, and besides, nothing seemed to be going according to plan in her life at the moment so she might as well go and have a drink with this total stranger.

Chapter 30

'Maybe now that Danny's gone, I'm just getting interested in other men,' Rose-Ellen mumbled.

Her mother fixed her with a firm look. 'Well you can put that Danny fellow out of your mind, darling, because it didn't take him long to find someone else.'

'What do you mean?'

'Isn't he going out with a bookie's assistant in that betting shop that's opened up on the main street? A young slip of a thing, cute one too; the sort that would be eyeing up acres of land before she even contemplated romance. You're well out of it; let him off with himself.'

Carrying the crystal vase of sweetly scented roses into the drawing room Kitty turned and said, 'You deserve better than the likes of Danny Redmond.'

Rose-Ellen sat down in front of the television. Restless and confused, she could not believe that Danny had found somebody else so soon. It only seemed like yesterday that he had stood outside the milking parlour pleading with her not to break off their engagement.

She watched the evening shadows draw patterns on the lawn outside *Uisce Gaire*. She loved this time of day, when each large tree stood erect and tall over its elongated shadow in the fading, slanted light. Six blackbirds hopped around the lawn, cocked their heads and listened for worms among the shifting shadows, then moved off as if propelled by some automated mechanism; stopping and listening again. The blackbirds were joined by a thrush, all happily listening, moving and pulling worms and insects from the earth.

Danny had got himself another woman, she had finished with clinical research in Ireland and Pierre had nearly died. She wondered what lay ahead for all of them and realised that so much can be changed in life by whim and circumstance. Having dreamt of running her own business, she felt that now was the time at this unforeseen juncture in life to realise her wish. But buying a business premises would be too difficult in Ireland at the moment, and besides, she wanted to get away from this country where all her dreams and hopes had crumbled to dust. She was at cross-currents in her life, rudderless and confused. She had often toyed with the idea of running her own business. Perhaps it was in the blood, and she had always wanted to give living in France a go, a dream she harboured, since she had spent three months in Paris as an *au pair* girl after doing her Leaving Certificate. However, she would need funds. She had some savings from her time in America and she still had not touched any of the inheritance from a grand-uncle who had left her some money, and her Aunt Peggy's shares might come in useful.

Chapter 31

Pierre had requested few visitors while in hospital, only close friends and his sister, but his small private room was adorned with prayers for the sick, get well cards and letters, some of which remained unopened.

'Rose-Ellen, you've been so good to me coming here. I don't deserve it. It's has made such a difference. I'm sorry about…' he said one day to Rose-Ellen who sat at his bedside.

'Please, Pierre, it's OK.'

'It feels so unreal, even now.' He wriggled in the bed and managed to sit up. At least he was down now from his IV therapy. 'That's better. I can't tell you how much your visits mean to me.'

'When I think of all you've been through,' she said, reaching over and giving him a kiss.

As she withdrew, he pulled her to him. 'Thank you so much for all the visits, Rose-Ellen. I lie here and wait for you in the evenings. But enough of me! Tell me about yourself.'

She held his hand. 'Well, as you may know, I have left DCH. Things just got completely untenable for me and now I am doing nothing with myself. Well, I am making plans for another stage in my life.'

'I am sorry that matters did not work out for you. If I had been there, things might have been so different. If I had more energy now… He stopped and reflected a little. 'But now the dice has rolled to you and you must seize this opportunity to do something worthwhile with yourself. Oh, don't get me wrong, the work in DCH was fine, but you deserve better. So what had you in mind?'

'I have always had a yen to start up my own business. I suppose it's in the family, and now at this juncture I see that the opportunity has come my way.'

'Sounds wise.'

'It would be something in the food line, starting a deli or coffee shop, but not here, no way, not in Ireland. I was thinking more of France.'

He whistled. 'Wow! Going to France and starting a business. I wouldn't discourage you. I have seen how efficient you were at work and if this efficiency could be brought to a business, you would do very well. You know, Rose-Ellen, your professional life is over, here in Dublin, so I would say go for it while you are still young.'

A lump started to form in her throat as she listened to him. She realised that they would never work together again and this would be goodbye; they would each plough their own furrow in life and that made her sad. 'Why do we always dread change, even though it is for the best,' she said, barely concealing her disappointment.

'The last thing you want to do is to lie on your deathbed and say, 'Why didn't I do this, or that? No procrastinations now; that time is gone! Seize this window and go for it. And please don't worry about me, I'll be fine. My Aunt Grace is here and my Uncle Geoffrey in France has been terrific.' Then there was silence as Rose-Ellen reflected on the future. After a while, Pierre whispered, 'Now I am must rest, but I hope that you will heed me. Please!'

'Yes, Pierre, you are right.' She put on her jacket and kissed him on the forehead and let herself out of the room.

As she drove home she tried to evaluate her feelings for Pierre; his many attributes and skills and wished that their lives were not going separate ways. She had come to rely on him in so many little subtle ways; his knowledge, careful judgement, counsel and most of all his integrity.

Chapter 32

The next time Finn O'Donnell contacted Rose-Ellen, she was at home in *Uisce Gaire*. 'I'll meet you in Wexford,' he said. 'It'll only take me a little over an hour.'

'That's too far. We can compromise. Let me see, what about Greystones?' she suggested.

'You know, it's years since I was there. OK, could we say tomorrow afternoon? I'm tied up all morning,' he said.

The old *La Touche Hotel* was gone, Rose-Ellen thought. 'Let's meet at the coffee shop over by the bridge, close to the church, at say three o'clock.'

'Grand! Looking forward to it.'

She wore a new pair of jeans and a fuchsia pink blouse with a three-quarter length casual burgnundy coloured jacket. As a final touch, she tossed her head so that her hair tumbled down around her shoulders. She then drove up to the pretty village of Greystones.

It was a Saturday afternoon in mid-August when Greystones was thronged with people out for the day on the DART from Dublin. Young backpackers chatted in groups on the main street, elderly couples walked hand in hand window shopping and a group of tourists who had taken the train as far as the last stop to visit this pleasant seaside village. Finn was sitting outside the coffee shop smoking a cigarette. She noticed that he had discarded the tired, ill-fitting tweed jacket; instead, he was now sporting a smart navy blazer, crisp white shirt, lemon tie and casual dark green cords, and he looked well.

He smiled as he got up to greet her. 'Great to see you, Rose-Ellen.'

'Hello, Finn, I hope you weren't waiting too long.' Sitting down, she placed her bag on the back of the chair and looked around at all the cars parked alongside the road. 'Greystones has got very busy. I suppose it's all the buildings that have sprung up here these past few years. I'd prefer it as it was before. Now it's just too busy; it's almost impossible to get parking anywhere.'

'And you have to pay. It's the same everywhere. Oh sorry, I forgot. Do you mind if I smoke?' he asked.

'I hate it, but it won't make any difference. You'll smoke them anyway.'

'It's a bad habit. Some day I'll give them up. Well, let's see, what would you like to do? It's a lovely day. Would you fancy a walk on the beach?' He leaned back and pulled out a red and white pack of cigarettes from his pocket. Flicking the bottom, a cigarette jumped through the air and he caught it in his lips. He leaned back studying her.

Rose-Ellen could just about make out the glittering blue sea with a few cotton wisps of clouds overhead. 'Why not?'

Lighting his cigarette from behind a cupped hand, he snapped the blue lighter shut. 'So that's settled then. A long walk it is.' He inhaled a lungful of smoke.

After their coffee, they walked along by the sea passing the huge grey boulders and massive concrete blocks awaiting the building of the new marina. As they strolled Finn talked to her of his childhood. 'My mother used to bring myself and my brother Liam to Bray for the odd treat when we were children. We didn't have much growing up, but Bray was paradise to us inner city kids; dodgems, sea, candy floss and ice creams!' He seemed quite animated while reminiscing. She noticed how he could name the birds wheeling and circling the rocks in repetitive, patterned flights and marvelled at his enthusiasm for life and how he took delight in the smallest of gestures. He took up a stone and did what most men do – skimmed it along the surface and succeeded in making it hop six or seven times. They went up through the narrow path, higher and higher into the fields along by the coast. Bray Head was visible in the distance beckoning to them.

Finn removed his tie and blazer and slung the latter over his shoulder. Rose-Ellen noticed his great stride when walking and how his hair shone in the sunlight. She could barely keep up with him as they manoeuvred the stony and rough terrain of the cliff walk. The soft breezes ruffled her hair, and she felt the sudden freedom and abandon of youth. For a brief moment she thought of her childhood; racing through the waves being chased and splashed by her father and felt a certain contented nostalgia.

'It's great when there's a bit of heat in the air,' she said, looking around. He held her hand as she climbed the stile and she felt a shiver of delight at his touch.

'Mind the step on the other side.'

'So you lived in Killiney?' she said.

'That's right. My brother and I bought a semi-detached house in a quiet *cul-de-sac* in Killiney in the late nineties when such good solid houses were still within the purchasing power of the ordinary PAYE worker's salary. It was fine for a few years, but when my brother got married I was left with the mortgage. But, I wasn't there that often, and to be perfectly honest I had no peace because of noisy teenagers, their drums and bass guitars.'

'So you settled for the anonymity of the city where nobody knew your name, let alone your profession,' Rose-Ellen said, as she tripped along the field beside him.

'That's it. My mother wondered why I was still unmarried by the time I was thirty.'

'So?' Rose-Ellen asked.

'I simply never met the right girl because of the constraints of the job. But I…Ah, it doesn't matter,' he seemed to hesitate and then stopped. Rose-Ellen blushed and moved along ahead of him. Finn continued to hold her hand as they made their way along the cliffs. Rose-Ellen delighted in the whole experience of being so high up over the sea, and yet felt a strange sense of trepidation due to the nearness of the cliff edge. She felt a sense of belonging, closeness to another, as they walked. Neither felt the urge to say anything.

They did not seem to notice how far they had walked until she could see the guillemots and cormorants dive from the large jagged cliffs hanging over the sea. Looking back, the speck of Greystones harbour shimmered in the sunshine, its cranes and boulders dwarfed in the distance, surrounded by the glittering pale turquoise sea. She realised that they had walked almost to Bray.

The Dublin to Greystones train passed by, and like a child Rose-Ellen looked up and waved at the passengers, but they were only fleeting shadows as it sped by. 'We're nearly in Bray. Look, see down there, the town.'

'God, you're right! I had no idea we'd gone so far, and isn't it a lovely day for it too?'

They made their way down the cliffs. She was glad that she had brought her flat shoes and so was able to negotiate the steep decline to Bray, its splendid Victorian pier beckoning to them. They stopped inside one of the tiny *cafés* on the seafront for tea and scones a little after five o'clock. Four tables were squashed inside the neat and sparse cafe.

'It's a change from some of the more sedate old hotels on the seafront where you've to wait a while for lukewarm tea and a plate of limp sandwiches,' Rose-Ellen said, smoothing back her hair.

'God, that sort of walking would keep you fit,' he said.

'It's nice here, and the place all to ourselves too. The Bray walk is so popular in summer. I'm famished,' she said, looking over the laminated menu. They ordered tea and scones. A pot of tea, and freshly baked scones with cream, home-made strawberry jam and butter soon arrived. Finn scooped some cream on to the scone and then placed a large dollop of strawberry jam on top of that before putting it into his mouth. He quickly removed any traces of cream from his lips with his napkin.

'That tasted good. I was starving,' he said.

Rose-Ellen thought of her own present predicament. She had recently started to give serious consideration to going to France and starting a business. 'I've a plan a foot for myself,' she said, pouring herself more tea from the round, blue teapot.

'Tell me more.'

'Well, I am thinking of going to France and starting up a business, maybe a coffee shop or deli. I have to do something with my life. I can't be hanging around her for ever, that's for sure.'

'I suppose you have to follow your dreams when you are young. The force is full of types who clock up the years working away for the pension, can't bloody wait to get out, as if they were wishing their lives away. Then some of them are only retired a year, and they drop dead. It's ridiculous to live one's life waiting for a pension.' He then went silent as if her plans had a somewhat negative effect on him.

After tea they joined the other strollers along the pier. Finn held her hand and chatted about anything and everything. Down near the dodgems he bought two large cone ice creams, and they walked back to the railway station, clutching the swirling creamy cones and holding hands to take the train back to Greystones.

Chapter 33

'With your experience you should be able to get yourself something that's more permanent and interesting. It's not as if you're a plain, dull girl, but you're not getting any younger and you need some stability in your life if you want to settle down and maybe get married. Or if you don't want to get married what about a little business, something in the food line, after all, people always need to eat. You've a good head and you're a resourceful girl. Think about it!' Kitty Power said, as she sat with her daughter in the dining room at *Uisce Gaire*.

'Mam, I have been thinking about a business, I have told nobody about it, but I've made out a business plan and am going to discuss it with a marketing and business manager.'

'Oh! Tell me more!'

'Well, it wouldn't be here, it would be in France. Something like a deli or coffee shop.'

'Well, aren't you the dark horse! I think that is not a bad idea at all. You need to get a direction in your life, otherwise you're just going to drift and that would be fatal. Now listen to me, pet. I have some money put by, ah, nothing much, something for my old age, but well, what good is money if it is not used, and so I would like to give you this money.'

Rose-Ellen sat down and stared at her mother. 'No, Mam, I couldn't take that money, that is yours.'

'It is no good to me. I'm giving it to you because it would make me the happiest mother alive if you would start up your own business, and in such a lovely country as France. Oh, I have such fabulous memories of our honeymoon there. The enormous fields of rich scented lavender and gorgeous sunflowers; only images one can dream of.' Her mother had an impish grin. 'Now don't start me on the cheese and the French bread. Oh, it was magic, sheer magic.' Rose-Ellen had never heard her mother speak with such animation before.

Imagining O'Hegarty lying helplessly in a hospital bed fighting for his life, with the long tedious road to recovery ahead of him, gave McAdam a certain vicarious pleasure. There were many things Shay McAdam resented about Pierre, but being suspended by him had fuelled a deep desire for revenge. He took a long drag of his cigarette and stared at the ceiling. After a while he sat up and eyed the half-drunk bottle of whiskey on the table. His thoughts turned to that fool with his 'fuck you' expression and dull cold eyes, his face simmering with rancour. The man was cunning and with no scruples, without the brains or nerve to withstand pressure. McAdam wondered if such a pathetic individual could be trusted. McAdam wanted to give O'Hegarty a hiding, but two bullets was overdoing things. And now he came out in a cold sweat at the prospect of O'Hegarty dying. The Gardai would leave no stone unturned to solve such a heinous crime: the killing of an eminent oncologist gunned down so mercilessly. What if that idiot came back looking for more money, blackmailing him? He poured himself a whiskey and pondered on the future.

Detective Finn O'Donnell sat in his bachelor flat overlooking the docks in Dublin. He sipped his Bushmills, with one cube of ice, and watched the lights twinkling in the bay. Savouring his drink, he marvelled at all the changes that had taken place in the city. He remembered the dreary old derelict docks with rows of drably painted giant containers awaiting shipment, sad dirty yards where unwanted mean pink weeds pushed their way through slats in walls speared with pointed glass, where anxious dockers lined up for work, and where the disenchanted took the cattle boats in droves to England. The old Guinness barges, or the greasy, rusty trawlers languishing in the port were mere memories now.

But the dynamism was palpable everywhere these days with huge cranes poised against the sky, geometric gleaming glass buildings, sturdy steel and stone structures whose reflections shimmered in the evening light, more redolent of New York or Hong Kong.

The Liffey lights were starting to glow as the evening traffic moved slowly, lumbering itself out of the city like a giant silver serpent. He was cooking dinner for Rose-Ellen in his apartment. As he let her in, she could smell the familiar aromas of mediterranean food suffusing the air, to the strains of Mozart's Horn Concerto. In Rose-Ellen's eyes it was a typical bachelor pad: minimalist, sparse, storing only that which was necessary for the present, where everything was arranged and ordered. The view over the Liffey was wonderful. A handsome man in uniform smiled benignly from a photograph on the mantelpiece. He bore a remarkable resemblance to Finn.

'Who is this?' she asked, taking it up and examining it more closely.

'My father. My mother had a hard time keeping him away from the women. He was a holy terror when it came to the fair sex,' he said, with bracing candour as he stirred a pot with a large wooden spoon.

With a wistful smile, she turned to him. 'I'm not surprised; he's very handsome. Well, don't they say that women love men in uniform?'

'That's true, although I don't think the old Garda uniform ever did much for me.'

Rose-Ellen smiled again and looked away. She noticed how the books were arranged in alphabetical order in the small bookcase by the wall. She realised that she was hungry.

'Mmm,' she said. 'It smells delicious.'

'Won't be a minute,' he said, tasting the sauce.

'Can I make myself useful? Here, let me carry some things in for you.'

He presented her with a small tray on which the cutlery, glasses and napkins were placed. 'Thanks, I'd just started to lay the table.'

The table was near the window overlooking the river. She saw the sails of small boats flapping in the wind on the Liffey, and could hear the faint tinkling sounds of the halyards against the masts. It was almost dusk and everything moved with its own rhythm in the glow of evening.

He opened the wine. 'Dinner will be ready in a few minutes.' Rose-Ellen turned away from the window and he motioned for her to sit at the table. 'Please, please sit here.' He had cooked Italian beef stew and baked potatoes served with a green salad. Rose-Ellen thought it was delicious and took her time, savouring each morsel. When they had cleared up Finn brought over the coffee.

'We'll sit over here,' he said, directing her to the pale yellow sofa. He sat alongside her and proceeded to pour the coffees.

She thought about his job. 'So what sort of crime are you tackling these days?'

'Oh everything from VAT fraud to counterfeit.'

'Counterfeit?'

He opened a packet of cigarettes. 'Yes. See these cigarettes? Well, I've no guarantee that they're not counterfeit; did you know that one in four packets of fags in this country is counterfeit?'

'Are you serious? Why do you smoke them then? If the real ones are bad for you, God knows what's in the counterfeit ones!' she exclaimed.

'Precisely. I wish I could give them up. I've tried everything: patches, will-power, yoga, acupuncture, but nothing works,' he nodded and laughed ruefully.

'Ah, you're an addictive type and that's all there is to it. Speaking about crime, have you had any leads on McAdam?'

'We've built up a profile on him. Likes to gamble at cards, big time, I mean internationally. I was in a poker club last week. An undercover job on some racketeering and he was there.'

Her blood went cold but still she could not resist drawing Finn out. 'Tell me more.'

'What do you want to know?'

'Maybe about the gambling, or what kind of a joint a creep like him would frequent.'

'If you don't mind I won't mention the name of the place. But he's a typical poker junkie, sits and waits for his next move, like a stalking cat. Then when the moment is right he strikes and makes a good kill at the pot.' Finn put down his coffee cup.

'He's calculating. He'd approach poker in a mathematical way,' she said, recalling McAdam's penchant for statistical analysis of clinical research results.

'They say that's the only way to win. All this talk about watching your opponent's expression across the table is a load of bull; that's what you see in films, but not in real life,' It's all very calculated,' he said.

She looked past Finn through the window. The view was really breathtaking from where she was sitting. She looked around at the neatness in Finn's apartment and wondered about his family. 'What about your mother?' she asked tentatively.

He took a drag of his cigarette. 'She passed away a few years ago.'
'Oh, I'm sorry. And your Dad?' she asked.
'He died a long time ago. I never really knew him. He left my mother for another woman.'

She detected a slight tinge of regret in his voice.

'That's the way it is in life. You can't choose your parents,' he said.

As he poured himself more coffee, his eyes wandered down to her legs as she crossed them, where a slit in her dark navy dress revealed a long slender calf.

She was anxious to change the subject. 'My mother thinks that I'm drifting. I've decided to fulfil my life's ambition, start up a business, but not here.'

He took a deep breath.

'Jaysus, Rose-Ellen, I don't know. Where will all this capriciousness lead you? First of all you leave your research job, now you want to head off on some hair-brained scheme – to France if I recall. What about money?'

'For God's sake, don't you start!'

He leaned back on the sofa and looked up at the ceiling. 'I mean, you're not going to swan around backpacking for a few months. This is serious stuff, Rose-Ellen.' He leaned back and looked up at the ceiling.

'Ah, *La Belle France*. Oh, how I love that country, everything about it. I'd love to have a go at living there; see how it'd work out.'

He turned and looked intently at her. 'You know, Rose-Ellen, so many people spend their lives in the relentless drudgery of a mere existence, and they're full of regrets in the end, and it doesn't have to be like that. I've become a lot more reflective lately. I suppose I'm just getting on in life, but of course, with time, one's priorities change.'

'How's your French?' she asked.

'Not bad, could be better, but improving I hope!' he replied.

She had a gleam in her eye and with abandoned gaiety added, 'Maybe I could open that deli I've always dreamed about.'

'I presume you've thought all this out and that it is not some instant reaction to you losing your job,' Finn said.

'Follow our dreams, not leave things until we're too old and set in our ways,' Rose-Ellen said firmly.

He moved closer to her on the sofa, and placed his arm around the back of it.

'Well, maybe we could go to France and do something together. How about it?'

She smiled at him and wondered what he meant. 'It's only a thought, a dream,' she said, resting her head on his shoulder.

'You're a restless soul, Rose-Ellen.' And as he held her close she moved her lips up to his and they kissed, softly and sweetly, and then lay in each other's arms watching the dancing reflections in the shimmering light of the Liffey.

A few days later Finn called unexpectedly to Rose-Ellen's flat in Sandymount. She answered the door in her dressing gown, while holding a bowl of cereal.

'Get dressed, I'll wait outside,' he ordered.

Quickly throwing something on, she wondered what he had in mind as she banged the front door after her. She slid in beside him in the front seat of his old Audi. He was sitting in the car with his shades on listening to some violin music on Lyric FM. 'Oh, that Brahms violin concerto just sends me to a different stratosphere,' he said. 'The power and sheer musicality of the piece; it's bloody great.' He looked at her and gave her a radiant smile.

'We're going for a little drive, my pet!'

She sat back in the seat. 'Did you have anywhere in mind?'

'Not really, I just feel like taking you for a spin.'

So they drove along the coast. They stopped at a small coffee house in Dun Laoghaire. As usual they had to sit outside as Finn wanted to smoke.

'Well, any news?' he asked as he struck a match.

Stirring the coffee slowly she looked at him. 'Yes, I'm going to France on a ship as part of a crew.'

Rose-Ellen had answered an advertisement for an assistant crew member on a sturdy cruiser, a forty-two foot Beneteau, sailing to France, *An Faoilean Ban*, owned by guy who ran a successful offshore sailing company. They planned to sail down from the south-east of Ireland, through the Channel, past the west coast of France and finally arrive at the port of La Rochelle at the end of September.

Taking a long drag of his cigarette Finn half-closed his eyes, and leaned back a little, as if not believing what he had just heard. He looked up at the awning and whistled. Then he looked at her. 'You can't be serious.'

'I am, and what's more...'

'Are you crazy or something? Do you know what you're doing? Rose-Ellen, this is wild talk. You're leaving your parents like this. I'm, well, gutted.'

'But what's so strange about this idea? It's only for a few weeks, and if it doesn't work out in France, well, I'll just come home. Look, Finn, I'm sorry, but I'm very unsettled at the moment. I haven't worked in a while now and I need to move on. I've become disillusioned with the whole hospital scene in this country; it has all gone sour and I am at a juncture in my life, and then breaking off my engagement with Danny. Can't you see I need to move on and it would be better for me if I found new pastures and leave this whole damn sorry mess? This is the time in my life when the window of opportunity beckons and I need to take it, *carpe diem* and all that. I'm fond of you Finn, but I need to do this. I mean, find myself, do something worthwhile with my life before it's too goddamn late.'

'I see. Well, have it your own way. You obviously didn't even consider me in your wild schemes.'

She looked at him and realised that he was hurt now. 'What do you mean?'

'You know damn well what I mean. You surely don't think that I've been arranging to have coffees with you or to keep you updated on the dear doctor's shooting!'

'As I said, it'll only be for a few weeks, unless I decide to stay there.'

He looked at her with a crestfallen expression. 'I'm sorry, Rose-Ellen, you're right to do what you want. I would just be...it's OK.' She could see he was visibly upset and moved her hand across the table and touched his. He lifted her hand and placed it to his lips.

Finn dropped her home as usual that night. In the car, before getting out, she watched the minutes on the dashboard clock tick away, and felt compelled to say something. 'Look, Finn, I'm sorry if I didn't consult you about my plans for France, but well, I didn't think you'd really mind. I thought you'd be happy for me that's all.'

Putting his arm around her, he whispered, 'It's OK, love. You do whatever you want. It's your life.'

'Yes it is', she said rather wistfully.

'Do you have any more information about Pierre's shooting?' she asked.

He was looking straight ahead. 'The guy who shot Pierre was found dead in the park the other day. Killed with an overdose through the neck.'

'Overdose of what?' God, how bizarre!' she murmured.

'We'll see what the post mortem throws up.' But he said no more. He turned off the radio and looked at her. 'Rose-Ellen, think seriously about going to France. You know, I'd be devastated if you were to go.'

There were things she would have liked to have told him; how she felt about him and had come to rely on his trust and genuine care for her. He had come into her life by serendipity through a horrible shooting of a great and wonderful man, and she did feel for him. 'Oh, Finn, you've been so good to me these past few months. In fact I don't know what I would have done without you being constantly there for me, giving me encouragement, and there's a little bit of you I've kept in my heart. But there's so much happening in my life at the moment. I feel I'm living some kind of a crazy souped-up dream. I mean, I feel a kind of a lightness as if I don't want to stay here any more, but my emotional life is still here in Ireland, and I just need to get away and follow wherever it is that my head is leading me. It's so hard to explain, but I know that it's the right thing to do and yet, at the same time, it's breaking me inside. There are times when I feel so down and afraid of the future, fearful that my dreams might just crumble and die, and I'll just have to start all over again.'

'That's life when you're young and you're gambling with your future, but if you don't do it now it will gnaw at you for the rest of your days.'

'I can honestly say that you've been just fantastic to me this past while. I'd never have managed without you. But you must understand my needs as well. I am only just over my engagement with Danny, and I have to come to terms with that. Then there is Pierre and the shooting and me losing my job. Jesus Christ, how much more can I take on?'

Finn reached over and smoothed a lock of hair from her face. They kissed in the car in the murky light and then she put her fingers to his lips. His arms went around her slim waist again. 'Oh, Rose, you drive me mad. Your voice and your smile. I was fine trundling along with my job and my few pints at the weekend until I met you, the beauty with the beguiling smile.' Then he raised his hands to hold her face.

'Finn…I…'

'Shh, baby, Rose-Ellen. Some day I will take you, take you in my arms, and love you and cherish you when the time is right, so let's not spoil things tonight. You know my mother instilled into me that the best things in life were always worth waiting for. So I'll wait for you, Rose-Ellen, no matter what it takes.'

He left her at the front door of her flat. As she watched him go her heart was light, and she was happier than she had been in a long time. She gazed at the rug by the fireside and noticed all its strange images: exotic birds, luxuriant leaves, swirling acanthus plants, fantastic designs and faces all fused together. Trying to decipher the various shapes in this sea of coral, pale blue and cream, she reflected on her own life, one interwoven with spells of happiness and angst, disappointment and unexpected delights. She realised that she was at cross-currents in her life and that the time had come to leave Ireland and to forge a life of her own elsewhere, one where she could make her own decisions independently without being beholden to anybody.

Chapter 34

'Oh, she's a beauty,' Rose-Ellen whispered to herself as she clambered aboard *An Faoilean Ban,* feeling her way around the deck.

'Welcome aboard, Rose-Ellen. Jerry O'Neill, your skipper for the trip,' he said, holding out a strong hand to Rose-Ellen. She was here to take a short tour of the boat with the others who would sail to France.

'Hi, Jerry. Wow! It's a fine boat, and everything seems so neat and tidy,' Rose-Ellen said putting, down her rucksack and looking around the deck.

'Ah, we sailors have to think minimalist.' She noticed the double polished stainless steel sink microwave and oven. Further inside were the bunks. She was curious to find out what was kept on board and opened up drawers and pulled out hatches. Each space was jam-packed with storm outfits and other nautical gear.

On the wall she read out loud the list of essentials they would need on board : 'Blankets, rugs, rainwear, dried foods, tea, coffee, clothes, socks, sunglasses. The list seems endless.'

'You can't afford to run out of anything way out in the ocean so we have to keep lists of all we need. I only hope that the weather stays calm for the journey down, but it's been mild enough so far,' Jerry reassured her.

'So, two days to go and prepare everything,' she said.

'Precisely,' he said.

On the last Saturday of September, a small crowd of well-wishers assembled in Dun Laoghaire to bid the sailors goodbye before the trip to France. Finn was there and when he met Kitty and Maurice the introduction only seemed to add to their confusion as to why Rose-Ellen was leaving Ireland.

'He's a lovely solid man. You're mad to be leaving him, that's all I can say,' Kitty said, looking out to the horizon and barely holding back her tears.

Maurice clasped his daughter to his chest. 'Best of luck, my angel. Keep safe, and stay in touch. I'm always here, and you only have to say the word and I'll come if you need me.' He released her and for a brief interval scrutinised her. 'Darling, you know we all love you very much and are going to miss you.'

'Thanks, Dad. I'll be fine, don't you worry.' Rose-Ellen said, trying to put on a brave front.

Finn tried to be as calm and practical as usual, but Rose-Ellen could sense the emotion in his voice as he wrapped his arms around her. 'I'll miss you, love, but it won't be long. I'll take some leave and come out and see you.'

'That would be great, Finn. Promise now?'

'I promise. You know that I'd do anything for you, Rose-Ellen.'

Despite all the self-delusion that Rose-Ellen was independent and brave, when it came to the crunch, she had become dependent on Finn's company, his reliability and good humour. They had become very close these past few weeks as Finn introduced her to his world of opera, film and the French language. She had started to become dependent on their regular walks and chats and she found him stimulating and amusing in so many ways.

'Goodbye, Finn, and take care. And as soon as we land in France, I'll be in touch,' and she blew him a kiss.

As they drifted out farther beyond the harbour, Rose-Ellen could barely see the small figure of Kitty waving from the quay, and her eyes started to glisten over with emotion. She was full of sadness and had mixed emotions at departing. She was leaving behind all her memories; those of Finn, Kitty and her Dad and the last memory she had of Pierre sitting up in bed still in plaster, taking her hand in his and telling her to go and follow her dreams, and she was doing just that. But on the other hand, she was venturing down new untrodden paths and this gave her buoyancy that helped keep her spirits up.

She had to learn quickly about life on board. Jerry knew that a storm was forecast and was making the usual preparations. For the first few days, with a good calm sea and fine weather, Rose-Ellen took to her galley duties enthusiastically. The other two on board, a man and woman, were well acquainted with this geographical area, and as they passed Land's End one of them pointed out some landmarks to her. The sea around Cornwall and its various landmarks were like set pieces from a fairytale to him as the guy pointed out stone formations emerging from a sea bed that had stood the test of time.

'See here, this rock, the one sticking up? That's the *Armed Knight* and that one over there is the *Irish Lady*.' Rose-Ellen could see the jutting shape out yonder, the white marbled sea churning around, heaving up on its sides and withdrawing as it swirled around it. 'You can just imagine her reaching out and desperately hoping that she would be rescued, and nobody able to get near her because of the ferocity of the waves. So she eventually perished and they say that every so often her voice calls from the depths,' he said dispassionately. Rose-Ellen moved away as witnessing the ominous rock, black and perilous, its white spume lashing and receding against its striated surface, she felt a strange sense of doom.

As they left the jade-green waters of the English Channel, the seas around the French coast turned a deep Prussian blue where the different currents met and created a frenzy of furious seas.

On the third day, disaster struck.

'It's here, the dreaded storm,' Jerry shouted.

'Christ, that's all we need!' somebody shouted, folding up some sail.

'Right, better be prepared and take down the main sail,' Jerry shouted, looking out at the horizon. 'Cause it'll be too damn difficult when the wind changes.' They looked at him and wondered what the immediate future held for them. Rose-Ellen surveyed the sky and the broody sea, which had taken on a sinister blue-black hue. Then she felt the hard thud of a wave hit the hull. The tow was strong with four-metre high waves hissing and spitting behind the stern. The surging tide started to heave, creating a great swell in the ocean, and at one stage the boat seemed to move sideways like a car skidding on ice.

'Oh my God!' she said, blessing herself quickly while thinking of her mother at home, and wondered what she was doing on board with these men whom she barely knew; complete strangers.

Jerry took the wheel and Rose-Ellen helped pull the ropes, tightening up the sails into the wind and all this time the boat was buffeted by colossal waves, some towering ten feet in height. When the boat sank deep down into the trough of a massive wave Rose-Ellen saw herself drowning, but then Jerry righted and steered it up again into an oncoming crest. It was a terrifying experience, rising to dizzying heights and then falling again.

She staggered round the deck, anxious to be of help whenever needed, only to be slapped unmercifully from behind by a huge wave that hit her like the crack of a whip. She lost her bearings trying to hold on to the guard rails and slid across the saturated deck nearly hurling herself overboard. Fortunately Jerry managed to catch her jacket in time.

'Got ye, that was a close shave. Are you OK?' he asked sympathetically.

'Yes, yes, I'll be fine,' she said, feeling rather dazed.

Afterwards, when it was calm and the storm had abated, Rose-Ellen lay down in her bunk and thought about her move to France. She had enough money saved and had some on deposit still from her aunts and uncles which was not spent. Then there was the cheque from Kitty. She knew it would be difficult at first in France, a country she remembered now from her teenage years, a time idealised. She had been foundering on the cusp of a rudderless, carefree life when all her friends were setting goals and targets and getting on with their lives. God knows she had given DCH the very last fibre of her being, and where had it got her? Only down a *cul-de-sac* like a cornered, frightened animal. Every ounce of energy had been expended on a job for the corporate sector who in the end did not care a blind whit what became of her. But she must not dwell on the negative aspects of the past year, but rather preserve her energy now for more important and greater things in her life – setting up her own business in France and starting afresh. She had to focus on the present and not reflect back on the past with its ghosts, shadows and soured dreams.

Chapter 35

After two weeks at sea, the *An Faoilean Ban* cruised into La Rochelle. Jerry and the crew continued sailing down to the Med, but Rose-Ellen remained in La Rochelle. She booked into a small hotel, *La Coquille*, to regain her strength and composure, freshen up and decide on the future.

Over the next week she strolled through the small narrow streets of La Rochelle pondering on her recent trip. She had her business plan with her having studied it thoroughly, and agonised over all possible scenarios regarding setting up a business. She used to go to the same coffee shop each day, not far from the hotel, and sit and watch people pass by. She felt at home here, and realised more than ever that it was in this region in France that she wanted to fulfil her ambitions and set up a small business.

Finn phoned her one night on her mobile. 'Well, how are you? Did the sail go OK?'

'Oh fine, Finn. I'm so excited to be here and have been doing a lot of thinking and planning my business. This place is perfect; near the sea, nice climate with an interesting mix of culture and business. So, if you wanted to come out, maybe we could look at a few properties together. My French is shite, so you could help out in the area.'

'You sound so cheery and confident, and that's good. Well, let me see. I could manage a few weeks leave. I'm due some time off and things are quiet here for a change.'

'It'd be great if you could come out, Finn.'

'Listen, pet, leave it with me. Isn't there an airport in La Rochelle?'

'Yeah. There's also one in Bordeaux or you could go to Paris and get a train down.'

'I miss you, Rose.'

'I'll say goodbye, Finn, and keep in contact,' she said, and hung up.

Her conversation with Finn, that link with Ireland, made her feel nostalgic and sad.

Without any friends in France, Rose-Ellen felt alone. Having only mediocre school French added further to her isolation. After she put the phone down a wave of sadness hit her, and she was overcome with emotion and burst into tears. She thought of Pierre and wondered how he was coping with his injuries.

Within two weeks, Finn had joined her in La Rochelle. Having only been communicating in bad French for the past few weeks, Rose-Ellen's eyes sparkled with enthusiasm as she told Finn her plans. They were sitting in the foyer of *La Coquille* drinking coffee. 'Well, it's like this. I thought of opening a kind of Irish deli here in La Rochelle. It'd be different and this place is always busy with trade and people sailing by and…'

'What did you have in mind?' he said, adding two lumps of cubed sugar to his coffee.

'I have some money saved and I could buy a reasonable premises here and do it up. I mean, I could get a bank loan here in France, and I'm not bad with my hands.'

He sat back and took a deep breath and looked at her. 'Rose-Ellen, my pet, have you thought in depth about this? I mean, this would be a huge undertaking. Listen, buying a premises alone would be a huge commitment, never mind setting up a business as well.' He looked at her sternly as he continued. 'Don't get carried away with France and all the lovely things you see here. Dear God! You've only just arrived. This would be serious hard work and running a small business anywhere is not for the faint-hearted, never mind in another country whose language is not your mother tongue.'

'Finn, please don't bring your negativity from Ireland with you. I'm hell-bent on making a go of things here and I don't want you, or anybody else for that matter, messing things up with their cautious advice. All my life I've had to listen to "don't do this, don't do that, be careful of those", and frankly, I'm sick of it!'

'Quite the determined little madam, aren't you now! Or maybe I just never really knew what mettle you were made of! Point taken, Rose-Ellen. I'll shut up as there's no point in arguing with one so adamant!' He put out his hand and touched hers. 'Love, I'm sorry. I don't want to be such a damp squib, but you'd need to do your research carefully. You hear some difficult and sad outcomes of the best laid plans of people trying to set up a business abroad.'

'Oh, I know what you're getting at and maybe I'm just being naïve; impressed by the French way of life, the atmosphere, that indefinable *je ne sais quoi*. But so what! If I don't do it now, I never will. There's no such time as the right time.'

'Whatever you decide to do, I'll help you as best I can. I know that you have some experience in this area and buying a business premises in Ireland would be nigh impossible at the moment'.

'Hear, hear' she said, touching her coffee cup with his.

'They say that the best way to find out anything in France is in the local hostelry. Anybody in a pub or a café will put us in touch with the right people; apparently that's how business is done here.'

She smiled at him. 'Well, aren't you full of great ideas!' she ventured.

'It's amazing what you pick up as a detective, and haven't I a couple of friends in the Gardai who bought places here? Mind you, it wasn't exactly a bed of roses. It's not that straightforward.' She licked her spoon and smiled naughtily. 'You little devil,' he said, reaching over to kiss her.

'Can you stay for a few weeks? We could look at places together!' she said, stirring her coffee again.

'I have no plans, love, except to be with you. We'll play it by ear. I've an open ticket.'

An open ticket? She wondered how long he intended to stay. 'Living here would be about enjoying the good things that life offers: peace, harmony, a more sedate way of life,' he said, stretching himself on the chair.

'I'm glad you've come over; it's much better to have a second opinion. I think La Rochelle is very expensive and there'd be too much competition. I've hired a car and drove around for a few days and came across a lovely village about half an hour from here. It's just perfect, on a river, and well, I just fell in love with it.'

'OK, let's see it then.'

They drove south along the coast and then farther inland for a while, until they came across a charming village, tucked away, nestling among the soft green fields on the banks of the Charente River. Rose-Ellen veered into the car park under the sycamore trees. They strolled along and sat at an outdoor *café* near the park. It was a typical French *café*; a few chairs and tables arranged sporadically on the street outside, each with check tablecloth and condiments. It seemed dark inside with a large awning overlooking the entrance with the word *Brasserie*. Rose-Ellen could hear the muffled sounds of chat inside and the sound of cutlery on plates. Finn looked around and then produced a large map of France from his coat pocket. 'Isn't this a lovely village, so typically French! Just right, not too far from La Rochelle or the sea,' he said, casting his eyes around the square.

'Finn, they're all lovely villages to us, who come from ones at home only as old as the turn of the century, but I particularly liked this one,' she said.

'Look, here it is on the map, not too far from anywhere. Perfect for business,' he said, pointing to its position in the Poitou Charente region of the map which he had spread out in the car. They then went to the nearest estate agent and looked at some houses for sale in the window. Finn examined each sign carefully. 'You'd be paying at least ten per cent commission to these fellahs and same again to the *notaire*, so you need to allow for this. Leave this to me now.' She nodded in agreement.

They strolled along the scurrying streets and just seemed to drift into a local restaurant in the middle of the town. There were some people dining, and several men were standing at the bar with short liqueurs. One large man was cutting a roll of white goats' cheese with a knife and scooping it into his mouth. The weather was still warm, a bit breezy, and so they decided to have lunch inside. Afterwards Finn went up to the counter to pay, and before long he was engaged in conversation with some of the men there, including the barman, all of whom were only too willing to impart any information they had. They were pointing him in the same direction: down straight and turn left and then right. Rose-Ellen could not quite make out what was being discussed and she was curious to find out.

Finn returned to her table. 'Well, I've got the name of the *notaire*.'

She smiled at him. 'We'll go to his office and make an appointment.' He gathered up the map and the car keys from the table.

The *notaire*, Monsieur Leveque, had his office on the edge of the town. They did not have an appointment so the lady at reception asked if they could come back after four o'clock and she would try and arrange for them to meet the *notaire*.

At four o'clock promptly they arrived at the *notaire's* office and were soon called in to meet Monsieur Leveque. He was a quietly spoken, middle-aged man with the formality and politeness of French people. He greeted them gestured them to sit down.

Rose-Ellen spoke. 'Do you speak English?'

'Yes, but slowly. Now how can I help you?' Monsieur Leveque asked.

'Eh, I'm thinking of starting a small business, something like a deli with a coffee shop and would like to view some suitable properties, preferably old ones in the village, but which don't need too much work on them and within budget of course.'

'How much did you want to spend?' he asked, looking at her and then turning to Finn.

'My limit is one hundred and twenty thousand euros, 'Rose-Ellen said.

'Over the next few days, I can take you to view some properties in the afternoon. I am not available in the mornings.'

For the next few days, they accompanied Monsieur Leveque around the village viewing properties but none were suitable. Finally, they were down to the last house on their list, and Rose-Ellen had become dejected with all of the properties seen so far. 'It used to be an *épicerie* on a corner off the main street in the village and the owner has retired from his business, but he and his wife continue to live in the house where they have raised their family. It looks a bit tired and weary, probably needing some work. But I think you should see it,' Monsieur Leveque said enthusiastically.

'I suppose it'll be more of the same: old electrical wires dangling from open holes in ceilings, dark, dreary, pokey little rooms, with rickety stairs and no central heating,' Rose-Ellen whispered to Finn, as she settled into the back of Monsieur Leveque's estate car.

'Now, don't jump to conclusions. Sure, you've seen nothing so far!' Finn said, taking her hand in his. They drove a short distance and came to the premises. As she got out Rose-Ellen thought the place had character, with a vivid red creeper hugging the stone wall outside, rose trees abounding to the front, although their summer blooms had by now faded, and bunches of still healthy looking lavender plants with their seed like heads swayed against the front of the house. The house stood on a corner at the end of a side road off the main street in the village. A smaller street, a *ruelle*, meandered down from the back of the house to the river. There was a massive oak standing majestically on the street at the back of the house, its stately branches covering part of the roof of the premises.

'Oh, Finn, isn't the garden lovely! It'll be a riot of colour in summer,' Rose-Ellen piped up.

But he was more cautious. 'Steady on there now, love. We'll need to see the inside of the premises firstly.'

Monsieur Leveque knocked on the door of the house and an elderly man emerged wearing an open-necked shirt and a wine-coloured cardigan. He was Monsieur Vincent, the owner. With his shock of grey hair, brown eyes, sallow complexion and soft expression, he appeared to be the archetypical rural Frenchman.

'Ah, *bonjour*,' the man said, putting out his hand to greet Monsieur Leveque who did likewise, and made the formal introductions. Monsieur Vincent greeted them warmly and led them inside. Madame Vincent was a *petite* lady wearing a grey pinafore tied in the middle.

They then toured the house at Monsieur Vincent's invitation. Finn went around tapping walls and looking out for any signs of dry rot or dampness. It was more spacious and less dark than the previous properties they had viewed.

Mounting the stairs, Finn whispered to her, 'Very sound, with loads of potential!' From the upstairs they looked outside on the garden which was dotted with a line of tall stately poplar trees. A large weeping willow stood proudly near a murky pond with tall reeds where some brown ducks swam. To the rear stood various outhouses which probably at one time housed pigs and poultry.

Monsieur Leveque caught up with them. 'And now we shall take a tour of the garden. Please, after you,' he said, motioning them to go outside.

They passed a small wooden hut. 'That reminds me of a *Hansel and Gretel* house,' Rose-Ellen whispered to Finn.

'And there's a bread oven for your gingerbread men,' Finn joked pointing to an in-built furnace in the side of the hut. Monsieur and Madame Vincent proudly showed their vine trees and small orchard. A pair of rabbits munched in their hutches and beautiful plump black and white hens scratched whatever it is that hens find so attractive on the ground. A disused dovecote stood proudly at the end of the garden.

Over the fence to the rear, Rose-Ellen noticed the grandest manor house imaginable with a hexagonal tower that reminded her of a fairytale.

It was cream-coloured with a dark grey perfectly constructed roof and pale green shutters. 'Wow, what a house!' she gasped. Its colourful garden lent it an enchanted look. Nothing had been left to nature's hand.

Finn whispered to Rose-Ellen by one of the poplar trees, 'Well. What do you think? Would you be interested?'

'It's hard to say at this stage. It's certainly the best of any we've seen so far,' she said.

After some time, Madame Vincent arrived with a tray of glasses and a bottle of the local liquor, *Pineau des Charentes*. Monsieur Leveque helped *Madame* serve the drinks and then sat down. 'They tell me that they are selling with certain reluctance but neither of them is getting any younger and *Madame* in particular is very restricted due to her arthritis. Their children want them to go into a *Maison de Retraite*,' Monsieur Leveque said. *Madame* spoke in French to Monsieur Leveque and he translated to Rose-Ellen and Finn. '*Madame* said that they are proud of all that they have built up over the years and are sad to be selling. It will be like leaving part of their lives behind, their memories to be entrusted to another, so they hope that you will appreciate their home if you do buy it.'

Having quaffed his liqueur, *Monsieur* cleared his throat. 'And now we come to the delicate subject of the price. *Madame* and *Monsieur* are asking for one hundred and forty thousand euros.'

'That is far too much; way out of my price range,' Rose-Ellen blurted out, shaking her head slightly to register her misgivings with Finn and he in turn had words with Monsieur Leveque. Whilst this would not be considered much for a house in Ireland, in France it would be a sizeable sum. Finn quickly scribbled one hundred thousand euros on a piece of paper and pushed it over to Rose-Ellen. She agreed that this could be their first offer and said, 'We would like to put in an offer of one hundred thousand euros.'

There was silence and then the Vincents started to argue. *Monsieur* threw his hands in the air and said in French, '*Mais non!* We couldn't settle for this. It's too little. When I think of the work...' But his wife quickly put her hand on his.

'*Cheri*, we don't have to sell for this price. It's fine. We'll wait.' Drinks were replenished and the atmosphere became lighter and more conducive to *negocier*.'

Monsieur Leveque talked to Rose-Ellen and Finn and agreed another amount. 'They have said that their final sum is one hundred and ten thousand euros,' Monsieur Leveque said.

'Ah, *mais non*,' the little man said, laying down his glass firmly on the table. '*Oh la, la,* we'll be here for a long time,' Monsieur Vincent said firmly.

Then Rose-Ellen spoke. 'Look, I really do like this house, and so my very last offer is one hundred and fifteen thousand euros. No more!'

'Too much, way too much,' Finn said.

'I'm buying and that is what I'm prepared to pay,' she said to him curtly.

'OK, it's your choice,' and he remained silent.

So this final sum of one hundred and fifteen thousand euros was mutually agreed.

Although the house needed some work, structurally it was a sound building, in a good location, on a quiet corner off the main street of the village which was not far from the sea and La Rochelle. Also, it came with plenty of land to the rear for growing vegetables and keeping some chickens. 'It's a good solid buy. You can't go wrong from any perspective,' Finn said buoyantly having polished off his third liquor. Rose-Ellen tried to figure out how much she would have to scramble together for the deposit.

'Finn, what have I done? I'm going to have to charm some bank manager here for a loan.'

'Ah, no bother to you!'

They said goodbye to the elderly couple and left in Monsieur Leveque's car and resumed the paperwork at his office. Monsieur Leveque described the purchase as a *Coup de Coeur*, one from the heart. Rose-Ellen and Monsieur Vincent signed a *compromis de vente*, which was the initial agreement between both parties. 'You have a week during which you can change your mind,' Monsieur Leveque said, handing her the forms to be signed.

They said goodbye to Monsieur Leveque outside his office. Rose-Ellen was as happy as a kid goat as she skipped down the road. Finn caught up with her. 'Can you imagine at last owning my own place!' She linked her arm with his and swung her bag over her shoulder. 'I can't believe it. Oh my God, what have I done!' She stopped and stared at him in disbelief. Taking her by the shoulders, he took in her anxious look.

'It's a good investment and, as my mother always said, one can't go wrong with bricks and mortar'.

'It's not your money.'

'True, but it's a good buy, though. Jesus, those liqueurs were very strong especially so early during the day. I feel like going to bed.'

'No wonder you're so happy. God above, this isn't like going a bit crazy on your credit card. It's a major investment.' She lapsed into silence, preoccupied with her latest venture.

Rose-Ellen phoned her parents that night and told them what she had done. 'I hope you're doing the right thing. You have a week to think it over and if you have any qualms at all, pull out of it,' her mother said cautiously. But her father's reaction was different.

'I think it's a wonderful idea, pet, and I'll help you with whatever you want. Sure it's a big undertaking, but don't you know about the grocery trade, and haven't you worked in this place for years? And of course, it's in the blood!' he shouted triumphantly emphasising the last word.

'You know, Finn, as the days go by, I'm kind of getting used to the idea of owning my own little spot in France, and it's not a bad feeling either,' Rose-Ellen said, as they walked by the house and on down to the river in the village. The deposit was finally made up from various saving funds she had set aside, and the sale was set in motion. 'So what will we call the house? After all, a good name is vital to a business.'

Finn smiled at her. 'What about calling it after yourself?'

'What do you mean?'

'Well, it's yours now. I mean, *Chez Rose-Ellen.*'

She thought about it a while. 'Too cumbersome. I like *Ellen*, though.'

Finn's face lightened up. 'That's it, *Chez-Ellen!* I like it, oh, I like it,' and with that he lifted her up in the air and twirled her around.

'Finn, it's perfect!'

'That wasn't too difficult now, was it?' Finn said, with a glint in his eye.

Chapter 36

A week after the *compromis de vente* was signed, they were walking down the main street in the village when Rose-Ellen turned to Finn, 'Did you notice the house next door called *Avalene?* The garden is so romantic. I wonder who lives in it!'

'A rare beauty indeed, and with its own chapel. Now that's posh! Well, one sure thing is that you won't suffer from bad neighbours.'

'As soon as I spied it, it struck me as being something special, different, and yet…' she stopped.

'Go on…'

'Something timeless, I suppose. Glimpses of a lost or imagined past.'

He lit a cigarette. 'Ephemeral I would say. It's a lovely building and so very French,' he said, catching her hand as they crossed the road.

Soon it was time for Finn to return home. 'Oh, Finn, I'll miss you very much when you go. It's been lonely here for the past few weeks with nobody to talk to, but sure I expected that. It's not just that, I mean…' She trailed off and looked at him.

'What do you mean? Are you having any regrets?' he asked in a somewhat bewildered way.

'No, no regrets. It's just that there was so much going on at home when I left. It's only since coming here, that I started to think back on everything – me leaving my job, Pierre's shooting and breaking off with Danny. It's just been an awful lot to cope with and now I have to think of trying to survive here.'

'True. A lot happened together for you. It all just seemed to stack up at the same time. 'Now, it's best to be active and busy at times like this otherwise you'll just get morose and close in on yourself. I'll be back. I might even give in my notice when I return home.'

'Now don't do anything hasty. Remember, you've a good pensionable job.'

'True, true, but couldn't I come out here for a year and give it a try? What have I to lose?' he asked.

She looked at him wistfully and wondered about the future.

Chapter 37

Siobhan arrived shortly after Finn went home. 'God, you're a dark horse, Rose-Ellen. All the time you were in DCH your little brain was scheming up this great venture. I think the place is fabulous! You've a great solid premises here. Must be near three hundred years old I reckon; the walls are as thick as a dungeon.'

'I've been reliably told that it'll be warm in winter and cool in summer,' Rose-Ellen said, as they sat out in the garden and sipping from *coupes de champagne* in the clear crisp October evening. 'I'll have to go to the Chamber of Commerce and sort out my tax. I bet you didn't know that there is a social worker in every district in France to help people set up their own business,' Rose-Ellen said.

'Well, isn't that just great. It takes the French!' Siobhan sighed. She watched as Rose-Ellen moved her pencil round the drawings she had made of the premises with dizzying speed, measuring and calculating while utterly absorbed in the design of her dream. 'You love this whole adventure, Rose-Ellen. So tell me, what possessed you to do it? I mean explain to me the transition from the good or maybe not so good job in DCH and starting a coffee shop cum deli in a country you hardly know and where you can't speak the language. Knowing the French, you won't get far here without the language.'

'I had mulled over the idea of starting my own business for a long time. It was always a seed in my mind, and then when everything just seemed to collapse around me – Danny, the job and then Pierre – I decided to go for it.'

'I think you're one in a million to do this. I always knew you had it in you, but it takes a lot of courage to do what you did, and I hope it will work out for you. In fact, I know it will because, well, you're just special and it's a gut feeling I have.'

Rose-Ellen reached out her hand and touched Siobhan's. 'Thanks, Siobhan for the encouragement, and I really appreciate you coming out here, taking your precious time off. It's good to have friends around in situations like this, starting afresh in a new country. I was so lonely when I came out at the beginning, but Finn came out and that helped a lot.'

'Finn sounds nice,' Siobhan said, squinting up at the passing clouds.

'I had started to think of Pierre. I can't seem to get him out of my system. I just hope he recovers fully. It was a brutal thing to have happened to him. I still wonder who on earth would have done such a terrible thing to a man who has given so much of himself to people.'

'The whole shooting business is the talk of the place at home. Nobody can make any sense of it all. Pierre, of all people! If it had been a gangland shooting nobody would have batted an eyelid.'

Rose-Ellen started to cry. 'Oh, Siobhan, I get so upset when I think of him lying in that hospital bed with nobody there to comfort him. He has so few relatives.'

She dried her eyes.

'Sorry Siobhan. Anyway, tell me about yourself. How are things with you?'

'Me! If I didn't come out here I'd only be going off with "you know who" and playing boring rounds of golf and sampling expensive wines, and listening to him moaning about his kids and how demanding they are,' Siobhan said matter-of-factly.

'So give him up then!' Rose-Ellen said, refilling the flutes with champagne.

'That's just it, I can't. We've kind of got used to each other. But it's a funny thing, when I see what you've done here, how you've taken the plunge to change your life completely, I might just give him the heave-ho.'

Rose-Ellen looked sceptically at Siobhan and wondered.

Kitty and the family were preparing to come over. 'Now, darling, we've arranged for Uncle Michael to take care of the emporium, while myself, Olivia and Brendan travel to France for the opening,' Kitty said, during one of her many phone calls to her daughter.

'Mam, that's great. But I haven't opened my business yet. It's early days. I'm only being handed the keys. Monsieur and Madame Vincent will bring all of their children with them; as part of the next generation by law they have to sign over their interest in the family home and there'll be quite a few locals as well; the *notaire* and the mayor, so it should be an interesting day,' Rose-Ellen said.

'Still, it's an important day for you, my pet.'

Finn used up all his annual leave and overtime to pop over to France for the final handover of the premises to Rose-Ellen. He phoned her the night before his departure.

'So, we're celebrating the handover, is that right?'

'Yes, that is correct. Signing and taking the keys in France is a big event here. It's no big deal at home, but here in France it is, so that is why I want it to be a memorable day. After all, it's the first house I've ever owned, and the end of an era for the Vincents. Also I suppose I want to say thank you to Monsieur Leveque and the mayor for all they've done; everybody's been fantastic.'

'It sounds great. I hope it stays fine.'

'So far so good; touch wood,' she said.

Kitty travelled over with Olivia and Brendan by car from Rosslare to Cherbourg, and was very excited. Brendan gave Rose-Ellen a big hug when they arrived. 'I've brought over all your orders: Irish flour, mince pies, Christmas cakes, jams and chutneys, maple cure rashers, sausages and puddings. The car and its boot are stacked with stuff. I could feel the car's suspension take a nose dive at one stage.'

'Brendan, you're fantastic! Here, let's unload it. I'll get a few of the men to help us,' Rose-Ellen said, calling over Finn and her father.

On a fine crisp day in late October, the various interested parties signed the formal paperwork and the Rose-Ellen hosted a small drinks party followed by a lunch in a local restaurant, *Le Grand Chêne*. As Rose-Ellen wandered around among the guests, Kitty grabbed her arm.

'Oh, darling, I've drunk too much champagne and the bubbly has simply gone to my poor head.'

'Mam, I think you should maybe lie down.'

'Not at all,' Kitty protested. In poor French interlaced with English, Kitty was discussing with Monsieur Leveque a holiday she had taken in France many years ago. He was too polite not to afford her his full attention. 'Oh, the markets,' she said. 'I couldn't take myself away from the cheese stall. Where was it again? Somewhere in the south…oh I can't remember!' Cocking her head at Maurice, she called out, 'Maurice, where was the market in France where we came across that divine cheese?' But Maurice was too engrossed in demonstrating the various methods for dry-curing ham to Monsieur Vincent. Turning back to resume talking with Monsieur Leveque, Kitty was in full flight. 'Anyway, it was a type of creamy goats' cheese in different shapes; oh I loved the heart-shaped creamy one! And you know I've never been able to get my hands on it again; delicious, simply delicious, the texture,' she said, bunching her fingers together and placing them to her lips, supposing this was the extravagant way people described things on the continent. She started to giggle as the waiter replenished her *coupe de champagne*. Kitty Power had not felt so giddy since her wedding day. 'Oh, I'm really not used to drinking so much during the day, but well, it's not every day that one's daughter is handed the keys of a fine premises in France.'

Rose-Ellen moved off and chatted away to some of the younger Vincents while Finn got into heated discussions in French with the secretary from the mayor's office about the political situation in France and the forthcoming local elections. Olivia and Brendan went over to Kitty who at this stage had been deserted by the *notaire* who made his exit discreetly and politely.

After the celebrations, Rose-Ellen, Brendan and Finn went for a walk through the town. The weather was surprisingly mild for October. Rose-Ellen strolled between the two men. 'I think I'll be happy here. There's something about this village, old-fashioned in a charming way, where the people are keen to preserve traditions and practices handed down for generations, and avoid the temptations of becoming a large industrial town.'

'It's a lovely village with the blend of modern houses and the old medieval buildings. I like the different styles and colours,' Brendan said, noticing the white houses with their pink roofs and green shutters.

'Well, that all ended very well and without any problems. Thank God! I was scared that the surveyor would find fault with the building it being so old, or that there might be some legal problems,' Rose-Ellen said.

'And what now? When do you officially open for business?' Brendan asked.

'That will take some time. First there'll be the renovating and modernising. The answer is, I don't really know. I'll have to get a professional to help me with my tax and get sorted out with my health and pension and all the other bureaucratic bits and pieces.' She looked wistfully at him and then away. Her small nest egg would probably be swallowed up to plough back into the business. 'But surviving in the meantime and getting through the winter will be a priority,' she said feebly.

They resumed walking out by the river, all the while Rose-Ellen rambling on with her lists for this and that, her plans both immediate and for the future. 'I'll be here for another fortnight, so anything that you need doing let me know. I'm good with my hands, can fix anything, and as you know my French ain't half bad,' Finn said, placing his arm around her shoulder.

Brendan hoisted himself on to the wall overlooking the river on the edge of the town and said reassuringly, 'You'll be fine, Rose-Ellen, there is no competition here. You're not far from La Rochelle, and if you hang in and work hard you'll succeed. I know for certain you will. Sure, it's in the blood!'

She reached over and touched his arm. 'Thanks, Brendan for bringing over all the stuff. It was a great help.'

Rose-Ellen had bought some kitchenware and linen from the local *brocante*, junkshop, and the Vincents had left some of the less sentimental furniture behind, so at least the house was habitable at the time of takeover. Late that night, when all had quietened down, Rose-Ellen and Finn made their way to the premises. 'It seems so different to when we first viewed it. Somehow it looks bare without the familiar dresser and little mementos on the wall,' Finn said.

'Some of the rooms upstairs have not been occupied for a long time and are a bit musty. Still, it's mine and that's the most important thing,' she said, grabbing Finn and waltzing around the living room with him.

He looked around the place and let out a long whistle. 'You are now the proud owner of a piece of France, and fair play to you, girl', he said, clasping her to him with a big bear-like hug. They walked through the various rooms in a state of numbed silence. Rose-Ellen looked up at the large ceiling with its strong wooden beams and buttresses, brown with age and smoke, and swags of cobwebs here and there. In the corner she noticed the remains of a pine marten's nest, long abandoned.

She then turned and looked at him. 'I can't believe that this is mine, all mine, Finn!' He gently pulled her to him and gave her a kiss. Spying a small white envelope peeping out from under a bottle of champagne on the table, she slid from Finn's arms and opened it. A small pale lavender card read:

Bienvenu! Nous espérons que vous serez très heureuse ici

It was from the Vincents. A tear came to her eye as she placed it on the mantelpiece. There was food in the fridge and a dim fire was still burning in the grate. 'Tonight's for celebration, so leave all cares and worries until tomorrow,' Finn said, opening the champagne. They found two mugs in one of the many boxes Rose-Ellen had brought with her. 'Here's to you, Rose-Ellen,' he said, tapping his mug against hers. She took a sip, but felt cold. Finn noticed that she was shivering slightly and started to poke the fire. 'Now that fire's pretty miserable, where are the logs kept?' Rose-Ellen remembered that the stacks of wood were in the outhouse. Placing her mug on the mantelpiece, she located the torch.

'I know where the wood is kept. Follow me,' and they ventured out together in the dark, cold air. Rose-Ellen led Finn to the woodpile in a small hut by the dovecote. Finn brought in several logs and got the fire going again in the enormous grate in no time with some rolled up newspapers to start it. After a little nurturing, and with the draft provided by the glass cover, the fire blazed hot again.

Reclining in the large armchair, sipping his champagne, Finn removed his shoes. 'Here's to you, my sweet. I wish you the very best, Rose-Ellen, 'cause you deserve it.'

He reached over and took her hand and kissed it. They watched as the flames danced in the large grate. 'It's funny the things you remember when you have a drink of two,' she said, warming her feet at the fire.

'Or a bottle or two,' he said, stretching himself out.

They both stared at the great blazing fire behind the glass door until Rose-Ellen broke the silence. 'Do you remember that fellow who was killed in the park, the one who tried to kill Pierre?'

'Indeed I do. Why do you ask now?' Finn said, sitting up.

'Well, did they ever find out who did it?'

'Not yet, but we're working on it. The lads in the force have a few leads.'

'It gives me the creeps even thinking about it. Sometimes my imagination can go wild, and I think the strangest things, trying to piece bits together about the plot to understand what may have happened.'

'Well don't, my sweet, this is time for you to be thinking about your glorious new house,' he said, looking up at the dark brown wooden beams and polishing off the remainder of his champagne.

Chapter 38

Rose-Ellen struggled as she tried to settle into a new country and become integrated into French village life. Finn took a long weekend away from work to spend some time with her and presented her with a stone plaque engraved with the words:

With the kiss of a sun for pardon, and the song of a bird for mirth, you are nearer to God's heart in a garden than anywhere else on earth…

Rose-Ellen was charmed with his gift.

'Finn, thank you so much. It'll look lovely in the garden, but how on earth did you manage to carry such a heavy piece over with you?'

'I wouldn't compromise on weight for you, Ms Power. I saw it in a garden centre and liked it and thought that it would be a nice feature in your garden,' he said, stealing a kiss from her. They walked around the garden and then she spied a spot peeping out from under a clump of greenery on an embankment.

'Look! Here! When the violets come out in the springtime it'll look perfect,' Rose-Ellen said, lifting some of the withered strands. Finn placed the plaque firmly on the ground, securing it well with a firm boot. Rose-Ellen bent down and read the lines again. 'There, that's the right place for it. It seems as if it's been there for years. It'll remind me of you.' He looked at the plaque and then at Rose-Ellen as she walked along the garden path, humming to herself with head held high.

'A reminder, a memory, is that all I'll ever be to you?' he called, slowly following her up the garden. She stopped by the large bay leaf tree, pulled a leaf off, broke it in two and smelled it.

'Finn, I get so down, you wouldn't believe it. You see, in order for me to understand the French and their way of life, I'm just going to have to learn the language, and that's all there is to it. That won't be mastered in a few months. In fact it'll probably take me years.'

'Give yourself time. You've only just arrived for God's sake!'

'It's always the little things that affect me. Sometimes when I'm struggling with the correct French word, say for example in a shop, the salesgirls impale me with the usual '*Quoi?*', then roll their eyes up in desperation and continue chatting without so much as looking in my direction. It can be so disheartening.' She started to cry.

He came over and put his arms around her and ran his fingers through her soft hair. 'I've missed you these past few weeks, everything about you, your smile, your voice even your perfume, just little things.'

He bent down and kissed her and she took his hand. 'Thanks, Finn. It just feels so lonely here with nobody to talk to for days on end.'

'That's the way when you move away from home, from the safe and known.'

'Finn, how are things at home?' Any news?'

'News? Let's see, *beaucoup de* news. Do you remember I told you about a body found in the park some time ago. Well, it was that of the man who shot Pierre. It was a cold-blooded murder. I'd say almost clinical.'

'What!'

'He was killed with an overdose of insulin.'

'Insulin? Why insulin? Somebody who clearly knew what they were doing, and with some knowledge of medicine.'

'Indeed. Injected through the jugular.'

'Are you thinking what I'm thinking? McAdam could have done it; he'd know exactly where to find a vein in the neck and he would have access to insulin. I'd say it was a slow painful death, he wouldn't have died that easily.'

'Probably not, it was a few days before they found him. McAdam has jumped ship, he's in the south of France, last seen gambling high stakes with the Russian mafia.'

'Jesus, the unfairness of life! And Pierre, how is he?'

'As far as I know he is recovering well over in England. I think he's staying with his sister, but it'll take him a while to recover from his injuries.

He was lucky that he didn't bleed to death; they say it was a close shave. He'll need a lot of physio to his leg. I gather he still walks with a slight limp. He told me he'll go back to the hospital to work probably with reduced hours.'

At the mention of Pierre's name she became distracted and strolled off back down to the house. What was it about him that set her heart into a quick pace. She knew that she could not entertain these thoughts any more of Pierre as their paths were now on divergent courses. Even though he was now only a memory, it was one that was embedded in her psyche and would be for a long time to come.

Her commercial licence came through and she had registered with the RSI, *Regime Sociales Independents*, to help with setting up a small business. Soon the builder would hopefully start with the renovations. In her quest for work Rose-Ellen contacted all the business people in the village who might require an English speaker. The local estate agent just happened to be looking for somebody to take prospective buyers, mainly English, to view houses in the locale. It was proving difficult to find any French people who would be willing to work at the weekends or who had sufficiently good English.

'Don't be doing anything on the internet. You need to engage with the locals even if your French is not good. Look, darling, people are the same the world over, and what they want to see is a face and hear a voice, not some faceless person writing sweet nothings on a computer', her father said to her one day, during their twice weekly calls. She knew that he was right as usual.

The local primary school, *Maternelle Primaire*, needed somebody to help out and supervise the children after school for a few afternoons a week. Rose-Ellen talked to Madame Claudette Launay, the *directrice* there, and despite Rose-Ellen's paltry French she was successful, but this paid poorly. However, she felt it was a start. Then, making her way to the local *Maison de Retraite*, the retirement home in the village, she produced her nursing certificates and managed to secure work for two nights a week there.

'At least I'm getting an income, but even more importantly, I'm more confident speaking the language and I'm becoming known here. Gaining the trust of the locals is absolutely essential if I'm to succeed in business,' she said to Finn on the phone one night.

'Good, as I said it'll take time and patience.'

'Oh, and I'm taking French classes two nights a week.'

'Dead right, it's the only way to improve. Take the classes, there's no short cut that's for sure, otherwise you're only practicing your mistakes,' he said.

Rose-Ellen stayed in France over Christmas, and the few days coming up to Christmas time were busier than ever. She had not a minute between taking prospective house buyers around for the local estate agent, supervising the local children after school and the long hours of night duty in the retirement home. There were festivals in the local village, choirs in the great church in the town, walks and visiting peoples' homes.

Christmas Day was quiet and Rose-Ellen went for a walk with some of the locals in the afternoon. A few days after Christmas Monsieur le Maire, the mayor, and his wife led a small party through the fields and across the river. Rose-Ellen could hear the crack of guns in the distance over by a large forest against the background of barking frenzied dogs and then the triumphant sound of a horn probably heralding some poor beast's fate.

The mayor turned to her. 'They have sighted a stag, it won't be long now, and they will bring it through the village to show it to everybody. They like to do this, it is traditional here.'

'Oh, I see,' Rose-Ellen said, looking into the distance.

The quiet days following New Year gave her time to reflect on her decision to come to France as she spent time making and bottling jams from the preserved fruits donated kindly to her by the Vincents. January was freezing and Rose-Ellen had difficulty trying to keep warm as the temperature plummeted to minus zero.

February arrived and the bitter cold continued, but at least it was the beginning of spring. Rose-Ellen knew that she would need to buy a car if she were serious about setting up her own business. She still had some money in Ireland on deposit and arranged a transfer of funds to her bank account in France. She was walking back home one evening when she spied a violet *Deux Chevaux* Citroen car parked badly on the side of the road. But her attention was drawn to the sticker at the back: 'Well behaved women don't make history'. She scribbled down the contact number and that night phoned the owner. 'Hello, I am enquiring about the violet car for sale,' she said, in her best French possible.

'Oh yes, I detect you're not French from the accent,' came the retort in a clipped English accent.

'That's correct. Are you the owner?' Rose-Ellen said.

'I am. When did you want a spin in it?'

'Right away, if that's possible,' Rose-Ellen said

'My, my, you are anxious to get wheels. Where are you? I'll come down tomorrow in the morning and we can go for a drive.'

'How much are you looking for it? And what's its mileage?' Rose-Ellen was anxious not to waste time on an old banger.

'Look, it's like this, I'm heading back to England. I've just broken up with my French boyfriend and I want to get the hell out of here as fast as my legs can carry me. So it's a good little car, won't let you down and it has only had one owner before me, and I've treated my car like a baby, so let's say seven hundred and fifty euros.'

Rose-Ellen gasped at the price. 'But at that price it must be falling apart.' She started to think of the bangers at home that would cost a lot more.

'Look, it's yours, darling, take it or leave it. I want to sell now. I'm not hanging around here. Where are you?'

So the next morning Rose-Ellen and the English lady vroomed through the narrow streets of La Rochelle and Rose-Ellen loved the car from the first time she slid in to the driver's set. They exchanged bank details and within two days the sale was complete.

'Hello, Mam, it's good to hear you.' Rose-Ellen looked forward to hearing her mother's soothing voice, during their twice weekly calls.

'Love, I miss you so much and especially now with the beginning of spring. Ah, it just isn't the same without you, my pet,' Kitty said.

'Guess what!'

'Tell me dote.'

'I've bought an old *Deux Chevaux* Citroen, lavender and cream, from an English lady who was returning to the UK after years in France.

'You'll need a car, good idea,' Kitty said.

'I'm going to call the car, Violetta.'

'I can just see you, pet driving around in Violetta. You'll be known as the girl in the lavender car. Let me know if you need anything, anything at all, and I'll send it over.'

'No, Mam, I'm fine now. It's just a matter of cutting back and managing the bills.'

'We're both so proud of you, darling,' Kitty said.

Rose-Ellen could sense that her mother was choking back the tears at the other end of the phone.

Chapter 39

Spring arrived with a lingering frost. Rose-Ellen began to despair that she would ever see builders on her premises. She spent the interim period carrying out small tasks in the house such as painting, sanding down the wooden beams and buying furniture. The four bedrooms upstairs were reasonably spacious. Two of the rooms were *en-suite* which she had painted pale lavender during the long cold evenings of winter. She bought two four-poster beds made of walnut and hung some pretty pictures on the walls. Scattered around the rooms was furniture of different styles and periods that she had purchased in the local *brocantes* and *vide greniers.* A medium-sized bathroom was at the end of the corridor and a large turquoise clawfoot bathtub reigned majestically in the centre. Rose-Ellen had it found at the *déchetterie*, the local dump, and it gave the room a touch of luxury and a hint of decadence. Having learnt the art of trading and bargaining, Rose-Ellen was able to buy fine old pieces of furniture for very little. In her spare time during the bitter winter evenings, she cross-stitched cushion covers and bed linen creating her own unique designs.

Proving to be popular in the village, it was suggested that she join a choir. But still her poor French was preventing her from having any kind of reasonable conversation with the locals. One evening she was invited to a party by a member of the choir and the conductor approached her. '*Le beau pays d'Irlande*, ah, *vraiement un pays romantique*!' She opened her mouth and suddenly stopped. Oh, why didn't the words come to her in French?

'*Oui, un pays, tres beau,*' she hesitated and then remembered. Then she thought of the reasons why French people usually came to Ireland. 'Fishing, it is very good for fishing.' Soon she was in animated conversation with him, and one or two others joined them. She told them there were many things she loved about her new way of life in France. She longed to hear the sound of the beautiful white owl at night as it emerged from its nest in the great chimney pot of the beautiful house next to hers. He would circle the sky with his magnificent wingspan and white breast and call to his mate from the high trees in her garden. She had not heard the sound of an owl in Ireland for years and it reminded her of how the French managed to conserve the land and its wildlife.

They listened to her and Monsieur Arnaud, the conductor, said soothingly. 'I must congratulate you on your French. It is not bad, not bad at all. I cannot tell you how important it is to *"faire l'effort"*, here in France. That is why so many people who speak English find it difficult to get along with us French people, and why they do not like us or trust us. It is because we feel that they do not bother with our beautiful language and culture.' She nodded and became heartened by his kind words.

Finally, planning permission was granted for the renovations to *Chez-Ellen*, with some slight provisos, and the builders started renovations on the premises. Finn was true to his word and phoned her every week. She became accustomed to his phone calls and if he delayed or missed one, she became despondent

'So how are the improvements going?' he asked eagerly one evening after her choir practice.

'The builders removed some of the interior walls to create space inside, while managing to keep the old French wooden beams, which I've treated with preservative.'

'You're not one to waste any time, that's for sure,' he chuckled at the other end.

'You know, Finn, I have never seen so much plasterboard, rolls of insulation and gigantic bags of powdered concrete, which the builders have unloaded.' She thought of the new French doors that they had put in on the ground floor, letting in much needed light.

'It's lovely and airy now, lots of light. But the builders are very temperamental,'

'Why so?'

'They arrived one day in a van with all their tools and equipment, but then left to buy supplies and did not return because it had started to rain – a downpour which lasted two days, but they work well when it's fine.'

'Ah, well sure that's the main thing, getting the work done. Sounds as if you're managing them well, despite your French.'

Then she thought of the cloud of dust lingering in the air like an unwelcome guest, settling everywhere and creating a film of fine grey powder. 'I can't wait to see the front of the premises transformed from four poky dark rooms into two large, bright and airy spaces for the restaurant and the deli. The endless drone and whine of the drill sometimes drives me mad. I've to go round sometimes with ear muffs. The builders must think I'm a right bossy bitch.'

'Why so?'

'Ah, I don't know, I follow them everywhere. You have to, to make sure that they are doing things your way and not theirs!'

With time, she came to appreciate that the front of the premises belied the amount of space within and to the rear, and it was here that the produce would be sold and the food served. A room at the side was converted into one large room with a small adjoining kitchenette for her own private use. The kitchenette, where she would spend most of her free time, would have to be comfortable, inspirational and timeless. The original pale sickly orange colour on the walls had to go and in its stead she decided on a yellow gingham-effect giving the tiny room a bright sunny feel. This was a difficult undertaking involving paint rollers, a craft knife, plumb-line and spirit rule. It took Rose-Ellen almost two weeks of painstaking concentration and accuracy, but finally, when she marked the horizontal lines in pencil and painted them yellow, the effect was magical.

She wished to have as natural a look as possible to the main premises so she used wood and stone with different textures such as fibre matting and pattern weaves. Cream and white and soft greys gave the place a natural light, tranquil and airy feel. There was also sufficient space to accommodate five tables each seating four people, plus three tables outside in the summertime. Wanting the place where customers dined to have a country-style feel to it, and having borrowed a sewing machine from Madame Vincent, she set about making frilled seat covers in cream and coffee-coloured fabric, creating a pretty and homely feel to the place. When completed the floor was pale ochre brickwork, and the walls rendered, revealing the facing of the original stonework. The shutters, window ledges and borders, as well as the large pole in the centre, were painted a soft green; *Provence verte*. The warm blends of colour, stoneware and wood created the effect of a charming old manor house. The back of the premises would be used for storage.

Delphine Vincent was married to one of the Vincent sons and was proving to be a good friend to Rose-Ellen, introducing her people in the village and helping her with translations as Rose-Ellen tried to understand the often circuitous route of French bureaucracy. After what seemed an enormous amount of paperwork and French bureaucracy, permission was granted for the sale of food and a licence for a small restaurant. One day in March, *Chez-Ellen* was finally completed and opened for business. Olivia and Brendan had come over the week before with more supplies. 'You know, Rose-Ellen, I could easily go into the haulage business. Olivia loves the ferry and you'd want to see the wine we bring back. We're like a floating off-licence,' Brendan said, sitting down to a cup of tea after they had arrived and unloaded the car with all of the produce brought over.

'It's such good wine compared to the rubbish at home,' Rose-Ellen said, as she placed a lime-candied mini rose on a lemon cake and set it on a cake stand. Rose-Ellen had stayed up practically the whole night before the opening frantically baking cup-cakes. The opening was scheduled to take place at four pm. Finn came over the night before the opening. She had invited all of the local people for a glass of wine and finger food to help her celebrate her first venture. As she put the final touches to the spread of mouthwatering savouries and sweets, she looked around at the immaculate coffee shop and felt so proud. Finn arranged delicate china teacups in mathematical rows and gleaming glasses waited to be filled with bubbly.

'Finn, I think you worked in catering in another life,' Rose-Ellen said, kissing him lightly on the cheek.

He looked at her as he neatly arranged wisps of cress around a plate of dainty salad sandwiches. 'Ah, well, if you do something, you might as well do it well.'

Monsieur Leveque dropped in, as well as members of the Vincent family. Rose-Ellen's beautifully wrapped boxes of home-made cup-cakes sold out within minutes, as well as the large quarters of Kitty Power's famous fruit cake. The selection of Irish foods brought over by Brendan and Olivia the week before, included dry cured Irish ham, smoked salmon, shortbread biscuits and a variety of teas which proved to be very popular. Also on sale were Rose-Ellen's jams and chutneys made with the last fruits of the garden which the Vincents had collected and preserved.

Rose-Ellen was whirring around with plates of home-made brown bread when Madame Leveque stopped her. *'C'est delicieux,'* pointing to the salmon.

Rose-Ellen gleamed. *'Saumon Irlandais,'* she called excitedly, and quickly moved on.

Olivia was pouring tea from a large pot trying not to spill it on to the delicate china saucers, while at the same time endeavouring to balance plates of home-made shortbread. Brendan came to her rescue. 'And I thought the French were coffee drinkers,' he said, gently taking the almost empty pot from her hand.

'Thanks, love, I need a re-fill quickly.'

While Olivia followed her beloved Brendan, who retreated into the kitchen, Rose-Ellen caught her by the sleeve. 'Can you hand round some of these salmon sandwiches? I need to replenish the white wine. Where's Finn?'

'He's around somewhere. I saw him a while back heading off somewhere with several bottles of champagne.'

Rose-Ellen found Finn in animated conversation with the Vincents. They were roaring laughing at whatever he was saying. 'Finn, a minute please,' Rose-Ellen said.

He turned and noticed her anxious expression. 'Oh *un moment,*' he said, to the by now surprised Vincents, as he put down his glass of bubbly. 'Is everything all right, love?'

'No it isn't! We need more of everything and I was wondering if you could go and make up more sandwiches. They are going down very well,' she said crisply.

'No problem, just relax,' he said, excusing himself and retreated into the kitchen to make up some mixed sandwiches. The evening went well as people chatted and laughed and drank champagne and tea.

When the last guest left, Rose-Ellen sat down and poured herself a glass of champagne. Finn was busy polishing glasses. 'Finn, you've been fantastic helping out today, thank you so much.'

'Well, you never know. If you do well and make a go of it, and things are looking good, I might just pack in the detective business.' He watched her as she took a sip of the iced champagne. Her feet were tired from walking around with plates and pots of tea. 'I would give up everything to be here. Can't you see, Rose-Ellen, how much I want to share my life with you here?' He stopped polishing and scrutinised her. 'I don't know; my heart isn't in the force any more. I've been passed over a few times for promotion.' Rose-Ellen was not surprised at this. Finn had a very sharp mind with a quick intelligence and worked diligently, but he was not cunning. 'I speak my mind, and I think that's why the top brass feel it best to leave me where I am. I'm good at my job, and they need people like me on the ground.'

'Finn, I hope that you wouldn't dream of throwing in a good permanent job to come out here on this wild venture of mine!'

He looked at her in earnest. 'I'm deadly serious. I'd still get a bit of a pension, not as much as full service, but goddamn it, life is for living not for hanging around for a bloody pension that I might be too old or infirm to enjoy. After all, none of us know how long we're going to live, that's for sure.'

'Are you being truthful with me, Finn?' she asked.

'Would I lie to you? And besides, I miss you at home. I'll be crossing off the days in the calendar until the next time I'm coming over.' He held up the wine glass and turned to her. 'In fact, Rose-Ellen, I've never been more serious in my life. I like it here from what I've seen so far, and like you I love the finer things in life which France has to offer. I think that the French have the right blend, not too commercial, time for themselves, things like that.'

She got up beginning to feel a trifle uneasy with the way the conversation was developing. Rose-Ellen liked Finn, but she did not want to give him any false hopes by inviting him over here indefinitely, as this gesture would imply a more permanent and serious side to their relationship. She became unnerved when he spoke like this.

'Finn, it's like this. I love it when you're here and it's great having you about, but it's, well, moving over here is a different matter altogether. I'm just not ready for any kind of emotional commitment at present until I get the business up and running.'

He watched her as she moved around the place with her glass of champagne in her hand. 'Well I might as well be honest with you, Rose-Ellen. I'm not hanging around for ever until you get your business sorted out or until you have fulfilled whatever dreams you have inside that head of yours. I mean it and that's that,' he said, replenishing his glass with more champagne.

Chapter 40

'So how's the *restaurateur*? Isn't that what you'd call yourself now, or maybe *restaurateuse*?' Finn asked her during one of their phone calls.

'Oh fine. You know, Finn. A woman without a man, like me, seen brandishing an electrical drill, hammer, pliers or other such instrument, with a bunch of nails in my mouth humming to myself is something that the traditional male French mind finds hard to fathom. Here in France, men do these things!' she said proudly.

'Well, necessity is the mother of invention and there is no reason why you couldn't do them, and save yourself a fortune. You're dead right!'

'I'm getting ready now to open the restaurant, but there's so much to do, you wouldn't believe the amount of preparation that's required. I've also got more ducks and chickens and some bantams.'

'You'll have your hands full, that's all I can say. You'll love the chickens, my mother kept them, and there's nothing like a freshly laid egg.'

'And two goats; both females.'

'You're stark raving mad, getting bloody goats, 'cause you'll have nothing left in your garden.'

'They say they're very easy to keep and not hard on the grass. I'm taking lessons on milking them, and I think I've finally got the hang of it. They're hilarious. I've called them Niamh and Edwina.'

'Oh, I hope they're well fenced in because goats are master escapers.'

'Don't worry, I've a state of the arts enclosure made by one of the builders and they can't get out. They seem pretty content there in each other's company.' She also had a cat, Padraigin, a little red fluffy waif of a kitten she had found running frantically through the heavy traffic in La Rochelle one Saturday afternoon.

Preparing the menus was something Rose-Ellen enjoyed. Delphine came upon her one day surrounded by sheets of paper, crayons in various colours, felt pens and geometric instruments.

'*Mon Dieu* what's this?' Delphine was intrigued.

'I hate those typed up menus, the same boring ones week in, week out on laminated paper. No, I want creativity and ingenuity so I'm doing up my own menus.' Rose-Ellen said, vigorously cutting some shapes from a lime-green paper card. Delphine sat down at the table and watched Rose-Ellen cut, write out and underline each menu with attractive little images of the food on pink and green paper. Picking up a menu, which showed a courgette pie and a green salad holding hands lovingly, a strawberry ice dancing with a glazed peach, and a jester rolling *Tartes Tatin*, Delphine exclaimed, '*Cherie,* this is a work of art!'

Rose-Ellen was proud of her artistic flair and was determined to put it to good use. 'You'd want to see the childrens' menus,' she laughed handing her a sample. Delphine stared in amazement at the image of a clown juggling tiny sausages with chips, a seal balancing a hamburger on his nose and a ballet dancer holding a dazzling wand springing out of a huge ice cream float slathered in chocolate and strawberries. 'You'll have none left; they'll all just come here to make off with your menus.'

'Maybe so, but at least I'll get them into the restaurant. I have to use my artistic talents somehow. Oh, before I forget, I was wondering if you could help me with designing the boxes for my cakes.'

Delphine expressed surprise. 'Buns, boxes, tell me more!'

'Well, I want to design a box for my cup-cakes and I was thinking of the colours green and pink, maybe with a golden border and some pink flowers. What do you think?'

'It seems a lot of trouble for a few little cakes, is it not?'

'Maybe so, but I believe that it's the little things that count, particularly here in France.'

'OK. What do you want me to do?'

'Right. First thing we need to do is to see where we can source the boxes. Look, this is the drawing. Then we need to bring them to a packaging place or whatever.' Rose-Ellen flicked through her various designs and found one for the boxes.

Delphine scrutinised the designs. 'They're lovely, Rose-Ellen. You know how we French love everything packaged prettily.'

'Yes the *emballage* is so important here in France!' Rose-Ellen said.

'I wonder where you could get them made up,' Delphine said. Then she thought and after a few moments exclaimed, 'Ah, I know.'

'Where?' Rose-Ellen asked while scrutinising her colour chart.

'There's a small packaging factory outside of La Rochelle. My sister used to work there for the summer when she was in university, and they'll make up anything for you and they're not expensive. I'll find out from her and get back to you.'

'Would you? That'd be great, Delphine.'

Every morning Rose-Ellen rose at five o'clock to bake scones and breads and display them in the shop by eight-thirty, when *Chez-Ellen* opened. A few days later, Rose-Ellen was negotiating with Monsieur Gremont over the price of green beans. Rose-Ellen bought her vegetables and fruits from the Gremont's farm. Monsieur Gremont was related by marriage to Monsieur Leveque, whose sister was married to Monsieur Gremont's brother. They were interrupted by a large heavyset man.

'*Bonjour, Monsieur, voici le jambon.*'

'*Ah, bonjour, merci Monsieur, une seconde s'il vous plait.*'

Rose-Ellen studied the stranger beside her. She noticed the lettering on his van which read: '*Charcuterie de la Ferme Dempsey*'.

'Dempsey. That's an Irish name,' she murmured.

He put out his hand. 'Ollie Dempsey, pleased to meet you.'

'Rose-Ellen Power, from Loughbow in Wexford.'

'Be God, it's a small world. So what takes you here to this neck o' the woods?'

'I'm trying to set up a small restaurant/café and I might be in luck as I'm wondering where to source my bacon.'

His pale blue eyes lit up with the prospect of another customer. 'Look no further, I'll supply whatever ye like. We have the best organic pig farm around. We're based near Rochefort. Myself and the wife, Charlotte, process all our own meats and produce *terrines, pâtés* and *charcuterie*.'

'That's fantastic. I'll give you my card and maybe we can talk', she said, reaching into the bottom of her bag and handing him a card.

'It's nice to hear an Irish accent around here. They're not that plentiful, mind you!' He pointed to the van. 'Ye have my number on the van.'

'That's great. I'll be in touch,' she said, as they shook hands.

Although she would not be accountable fiscally until the following year, Rose-Ellen was acutely aware of how important it was to keep the books in order for the taxman and to keep up her monthly mortgage repayments to the bank. Frugality would be essential if she were to survive, retaining enough each month to plough back into the business. Ollie and Charlotte Dempsey were proving to be a great help with their contacts and local knowledge.

It was May, that time of year when the tourists came. Rose-Ellen would need some help in the shop. One day she spied a scrawny youth in jeans, his long black hair tumbling down his neck as he pressed his face against the window. She ignored him but a few days later he returned, and her curiosity got the better of her. She went outside.

'Hello, can I help you?' His face seemed familiar and she wondered where she had seen him before. He seemed embarrassed.

'*Pardon, Madame,*' he stammered.

'Come inside and have a coffee, I think you could do with one.'

He introduced himself as Jean-François Launay, the youngest son of the principal in the *Maternelle Primaire,* Claudette Launay, where Rose-Ellen had helped out some afternoons every week when she arrived at the village initially. Rose-Ellen invited him to take a chair and poured him a coffee.

'So tell me, what do you do?' Rose-Ellen inquired sitting opposite him.

Stirring the coffee with his teaspoon, he looked around the place and leaned back on the chair. 'I'm not doing anything since I left school, but I'm good at cooking and I thought maybe you could do with some help.'

'And how could you help me?'

'It is a busy place and you need somebody here every day, and I live locally.'

Rose-Ellen realised that what he said was true. He was the son of a well-respected member of the village and seemed a nice, well-mannered boy.

She closely observed him. 'OK, I'll take you for a trial month and see how you get on. I do need somebody during the busy hours, from eleven to four. You'll have to hide the long hair I'm afraid; not allowed with food. OK? How does that sound?'

His face beamed and she thought he had the sweetest smile she had seen in a while.

The shop closed on Sunday and Monday, like so many small French businesses. Jean-François started his month of duty on the following Tuesday. He had a pleasant demeanour and was polite and courteous, but like many teenagers he was inclined to be slow and forgetful. On the third day, she found him chatting to two young girls while the vegetable soup boiled over, congealing to solid lumps that would have to be scrubbed off the hob. On another occasion he talked at length on his mobile when there was a queue of anxious customers waiting to be served. She took him aside.

'Jean-Francois, you will have to concentrate on what you are doing. Now, I am laying down a few rules and one of them is this,' she said, waving his turquoise mobile in front of his eyes, 'No mobile on duty. Got it?'

He nodded and put the offending article away in his pocket.

Chapter 41

Rose-Ellen became acquainted with her neighbour, Madame Madeleine de Saint Amour, who lived in the stately elegant house, *Avalene,* to the rear of *Chez-Ellen. Madame,* its sole occupant, usually parked her car on the narrow road leading down to the river and slipped through the side gate and into the back of the house.

Madame 'Tondeuse', lawnmower, Rose-Ellen preferred to call her. The reason being that – at the princely age of eighty-two, when the grass was a decent ten centimetres in height – Madame de Saint Amour, with beautifully coiffed hair and drop earrings, a string of pearls elegantly set on perfectly matching cashmere jumper and cardigan, would mount her large ride-on mower and manoeuvre it delicately between her stately rose trees whose majestic, yet fragile heads of oyster, magenta, crimson and apricot, vied for the ever changing sun's rays. There was not a hair out of place on *Madame*'s aristocratic head. Recently widowed, her late husband had been involved with the design of the remarkable fast trains, TGVs. Devastated by his death and having no children, *Madame* was thus reliant on some distant relatives for help, but they were usually too busy with their own lives. Inevitably, Rose-Ellen lent a helping hand in whatever way she could.

Avalene was magnificent. A classical building with terraced gardens and a pond, pretty box hedges arranged like a maze in the front, surrounded by elegant plants of the old French variety that had withstood the vicissitudes of time and weather. To Rose-Ellen it represented all that was peaceful and charming in an otherwise stressful world. To the side stood a tall tower, complementing the elegance of the rest of the building. Most of *Avalene* had survived the French revolution and two world wars, but it was now a little tired despite its grandeur.

Sturdy wrought iron gates, centuries old, which had once welcomed all to this French retreat, now remained locked. Sometimes as Rose-Ellen stood in front of *Avalene* it was like gazing at another time; a different world. Massive flowers and colourful shrubs danced in the soft breezes from large urns which had withstood aeons of weathering.

But there was restlessness about *Madame*. She recalled how one Sunday afternoon in October last year, *Madame* had called on Rose-Ellen to introduce herself and to welcome her to the village. The following week when Rose-Ellen was busily prising open walnuts with a nutcracker, which had just fallen from the enormous walnut tree at the back of *Chez-Ellen*, *Madame* called again.

'Rose-Ellen, my dear, I was wondering if you could please help me today. You see, I would like to move the large painting which is over the *cheminée* out to the hall. It is getting smoke from the fire and it would be better in the hall. If I move things around it will make the room livelier.'

'Of course I'll help, *Madame*,' Rose-Ellen said, putting down her nutcracker in the basket and following *Madame* into *Avalene*. There they wandered through the house glittering with antique chandeliers, vintage cut-glass and the finest old French silver. They moved the painting, and then the sofa, and finally the small *bibliothèque*. Once *Madame* started changing pieces around, she was relentless in her quest for order and symmetry.

Rose-Ellen glanced around the room, beautifully arranged in rich red and gold with cushions which would almost whisper and invite you to sit on them, and rich brocade curtains sweeping to perfection covering the large ormolu windows.

'*Parfait*, and now we shall have an *apéro*,' *Madame* said, opening her finest champagne to help celebrate the movement of *les meubles*. Rose-Ellen's entreaties to reserve the champagne for family occasions fell on deaf ears. 'You are *ma famille*, Rose-Ellen. I want to share my finest champagne and wines with you, my dearest. Come, let us drink and we can chat.' Uncorking the champagne, *Madame* filled Rose-Ellen's glass and they sat down on the comfortable cream *chaise longue*.

Rose-Ellen felt that *Madame* had not had it easy with her neighbours across the river who would not permit her to park her small car at the back of *Avalene*. They claimed the river-way as theirs having deliberately fenced it off to avoid the day trippers who made regular forays down to the embankment at the back of the houses. *Madame* spoke to Rose-Ellen about them as she imbibed the cool champagne. 'I have asked them so many times to remove their *Droit de Passage,* right of way, so that I can park my car at the back of the house. For twenty years they have refused and I am forced to park on the road at the side of the house. But *malheureusement* I am no longer young, so I find the walk to the back of the house very difficult, especially with my arthritis,' she said, rubbing her right hip.

Rose-Ellen recalled how Delphine said that it was nothing but a grudge towards *Madame*. '*Madame's* grandfather had at one time been the local mayor and he owned many of the houses in the town in the 1900s, running several large businesses, including the only hotel for miles around, so they are resentful.'

Madame spoke excellent English so communication between her and Rose-Ellen posed no problems. After a while and noticing the empty bottle, *Madame* brought out another one. Rose-Ellen recalled being barely able to stagger back to *Chez-Ellen* after the drink-laden afternoon.

Madame struggled valiantly on her own. On a Monday afternoon at the end of May, when Rose-Ellen was preparing to wade through mountains of paperwork, a knock came to the door. It was *Madame*. 'Rose-Ellen, I have just opened my special walnut *eau de vie* and wondered if you would like to help me sample it,' she said, with a twinkle in her eye.

'Why that would be lovely. I can't think of anything nicer! Give me a half an hour and I shall be with you,' Rose-Ellen said, realising that she would probably be there for quite a time.

Soon Rose-Ellen joined her and they clinked their tiny liqueur glasses as they sat on the large sofa. Rose-Ellen noticed a pile of books on the table. 'My dear, I am a true Gaullist. Nobody wants to listen to an old woman any more; they are not interested round here. Oh, there is something I must show you. I have this marvellous book by Madame de Gaulle, written about the life of your wonderful Monsieur Daniel O'Connell, *un vrai* republican, a man whom I greatly admire. What is it they called him? The...'

'The Liberator!' Rose-Ellen exclaimed, remembering her Uncle Arthur who often mentioned the great man.

'Yes, of course, that's it,' *Madame* said, getting up and leaving the room briefly to return with a small stepladder. She positioned the ladder next to the vast shelves of books which lined one of the walls in the room. She climbed the ladder and reached for a beautifully bound book, clutching it protectively to her bosom. Steadying herself as she descended, she handed the heavy leather-bound copy to Rose-Ellen who leafed through its old pages; browned in spots with age.

'I can only imagine the admiration that Madame de Gaulle must have felt for Daniel O'Connell due to the care and attention lavished on each page and the wonderful illustrations.'

Coming over and sitting beside Rose-Ellen, *Madame* poured herself more of the rich velvety liqueur. She had a photographic album on her lap. 'In the forties I spent my honeymoon in Ireland. It was a poor country, I remember, but we had a wonderful time; so little money, but such high hopes and of course we were very much in love.' A tear came to her eye and she reached out and touched Rose-Ellen. As she did, some hand-written cards fell from the album on to the carpet and, bending down, she picked them up. They were individual menu cards, executed in exquisite handwriting, each with an image of an elegant lady in Edwardian attire, or a magnificent house and garden. 'Oh, I wondered where they were – my mother's dinner party menus,' *Madame* exclaimed excitedly.

Rose-Ellen reached out and took one. It had an eight course menu on a small white card with a drawing of a lady in a turquoise dress and grey fur, wearing a large pink hat with a black bow. It was dated February, 1913. 'Did your grandmother write out each of these invitations? How many people were at the dinner party?' Rose-Ellen asked, studying the card.

'Yes, she did. My dear, these were the days when it was difficult to have things printed and she painstakingly drew the images and hand-wrote each menu. It took her hours and sometimes there were ten to twelve people at these dinner parties. Oh, these were different times! But then the war came and there were no more parties,' she said, quickly gathering up the cards and putting them away in a drawer with the album.

Rose-Ellen then remembered all the paperwork and the myriads of things awaiting her: letters to write, suppliers to be paid, fees for water, waste and other amenities. Replacing her empty glass on the table, she got up to leave. 'Thank you, *Madame* for a wonderful afternoon, but I really must go., I didn't realise it was so late,' she said, barely able to stand up after the strong concoction of drinks.

'Oh, I adored having you. It is so lonely here on my own and I love to have somebody to talk to,' *Madame* said, clasping Rose-Ellen to her bosom.

As Rose-Ellen waved goodbye at the forlorn and lonely figure of the old lady in her doorway, she thought of the wonderful parties and times which *Madame*'s family must have hosted many years ago in *Avalene*. As she made her way out she wondered if she would ever be able to own something as timeless and beautiful as this magnificent house, right next door to her.

Chapter 42

Finn decided to take some unpaid leave to spend time with Rose-Ellen. He had saved enough money to take this break. If Rose-Ellen did not change her mind about their relationship, he would travel around Europe. He had seen too many friends die without enjoying any of their well-earned pensions. Finn had missed Rose-Ellen all this time and his telephone bills were mounting because she still had not managed to have a phone installed; instead he was having to ring her on her French mobile. Still he loved her with all his heart and it seemed a small price to pay to hear his beloved's voice.

'There's nothing I like more than being with you, my girl with the mesmerising eyes, you know that,' he told her one night during one of their phone calls. 'It gets harder being a detective the older you get, and criminals are becoming more violent now; much more vicious. It's appalling.'

'Finn, it'd be good to see you again.'

'Listen, Rose-Ellen. You know it doesn't have to be like this. If you'd only let me stay and help you.'

'Look, Finn, don't be expecting too much from me at the moment. I've a lot on my plate trying to get this place up and running. You've got to understand that it's all absorbing.'

'It doesn't have to be though, if you'd let me stay here all the time with you.' A few days after his arrival, Finn got stuck into the various chores from the long list Rose-Ellen had prepared. If he was not touching up the paintwork he was helping Jean-Francois, who needed a lot of encouragement and guidance, or he was giving advice to Chantal, the young girl who was employed to clean the tables, take the orders and stack the huge dishwasher.

'You've a great way with young people, Finn, but I suppose that's probably from having to deal with all types and ages in the Gardai,' Rose-Ellen said to him over dinner one night.

'Ah, I'm a sensitive old eejit,' he said, taking her hand and putting it up to his face. 'I'd love to know what is going on in that pretty head of yours, Rose-Ellen. I'm wondering if you care about me at all, and if you do when are you going to be serious about us?'

'Oh, Finn, I'm sorry if I appear to be preoccupied, but there is just so much to do all the time, things to think of, lists to make up, I...'

He put his finger to her lips. 'Stop, will you! Making excuses, that's all they are! You spend more time with those bloody animals than you do with me. You can still save something of yourself for me, and the business will always be here. Now, why don't we give it a try, I mean, you and me, and if you get sick of me, or meet a suave Frenchman, well, there's always the detective business for me,' he said, somewhat cautiously.

She laughed, 'Meet a suave Frenchman! Not likely here, unless I fall for some of the local men – the plumber with his horrible French accent who fancies himself in his tight jeans. Or the swaggering electrician with the gammy eye with his coarse wife and half a dozen children. Or the sleepy-eyed brother of Jean-Francois, who, if given any encouragement, would hop into bed with me,' she said, getting up and removing the plates.

'God above, Rose-Ellen, you can be a hard-hearted bitch at times, but maybe that's why I like you.' Finn got up and kissed her seeking her neck under a stray lock of hair, but she gently moved away. He caught her as she put the plates in the sink, 'Don't always be moving away just when I'm getting romantic,' he said, holding her tenderly and kissing her on the lips.

He held her tightly and felt her relaxing as he caressed her. 'Take it easy, love, it's OK.' He kissed her again on the lips and neck letting his tongue travel down her soft clear skin. He could feel her respond to his touch and he continued to kiss her gently.

She was giggling now. 'Finn, you're driving me wild, mad, crazy,' and put her arms around him and they continued to smooch in each other's arms while the stewed apple turned brown on the stove.

As well as scones Rose-Ellen baked lemon and coconut macaroons, fruit cake and vanilla fingers, and her lavender honey ice cream made from real lavender flowers was proving to be very popular with children. But hungry tourists and customers would look for something more substantial than tea and coffee and a dessert. Delphine had an idea.

'What about Charlotte Dempsey, Ollie's wife. She is a wonderful cook,' she said, one day to Rose-Ellen while buying some preserves.

'Great idea, I'll ask Ollie,' Rose-Ellen said,

So Charlotte Dempsey was commissioned to provide *'les plats'* for the midday meal. Each morning, Ollie arrived in his van with light and airy quiches, onion and mushroom tartlets, delicious chicken stew in white wine and cream, as well as Charlotte's two favourites: guinea fowl in red wine sauce and pork *cassoulet*. These were on the daily menu, or for take-away portions.

Rose-Ellen's own *pâté* made with chestnut, blue cheese and chives in a colourful ceramic bowl was a favourite and firm seller. She called it, '*La Spécialité de Chez- Ellen*'.

Chez-Ellen was going from strength to strength and proving to be very popular in the village and around. But the preparation and cooking of food and all that running a business entailed was taking its toll on Rose-Ellen.

Chapter 43

Finn thought that Rose-Ellen was working too hard because she seemed always to be harassed and strained. Money was a constant issue; financial matters and the taxman loomed ominously in the background. Small businesses had to pay enormous amounts of tax in France; often sums that did not reflect actual profit. Then there were the goats.

'I'll take a gun to that Niamh one day,' Finn had said to Rose-Ellen, after chasing the goat through the village after she had escaped from the enclosure. Niamh had munched her way through a plateful of macaroons left out in the store room, and then made off with a bag of walnuts in her mouth. Sometimes Rose-Ellen was so preoccupied with the business that she did not seem to be listening to Finn. At other times she could be downright irascible and bad-tempered towards him. But he had to be patient; after all, she had invested time and money in the business and the first few years would be crucial to its success. One evening, he had carefully prepared a meal with a bottle of excellent wine, but Rose-Ellen just ate the food staring straight ahead and soon afterwards retired to bed. Another time, he took her in his arms, caressed and stroked her hair, but when he tried to kiss her she glanced downwards with the same distant expression that had become so familiar.

'Rose, would you not take things a bit easy?' he'd said to her. He had taken to calling her Rose.

'Finn, you know I hate being called Rose. It reminds me of the Redmonds. Now please, Rose-Ellen from now on.'

'OK, Rose-Ellen. As I was saying, it would have taken somebody years to have done what you've done!'

'I know, but I want to get the place up and running and then maybe I can take things easy. I know this dream I have to start my own business in

France is taking up all my energy, but it won't be forever.'

'What about a little dog? Sometimes animals can have a calming way with people. You could take it for a walk, get you away from this place,' Finn said.

'I have Padraigin and she's enough, and cats are easy. Besides, dogs have to be taken for walks. Anyway, animals are a bind. At least a child of three can open a packet of cereal!' She sighed, making out her weekly order for Ollie Dempsey.

'Still, a little dog would be lovely around the place,' Finn said.

She looked up at him. 'I'm sorry, Finn, you must think me a heartless bitch and maybe I am. I would love to give a little dog from a rescue centre a home, but it wouldn't be fair, not now. Maybe later, I agree. When we're…I mean, when I am more established. And besides, from a health regulation viewpoint, that mightn't be a good idea.'

He hoped that things would improve with time, but still he had no regrets about taking his entire holidays for this year to spend with her. Other times there was the old Rose-Ellen with the mesmerising eyes with whom he had fallen in love in Dublin, especially when she was away from the business, walking across the fields with him or sitting by the fire, enjoying a glass of wine after a long day, or reading a book under the weeping willow in the garden at the back, free from worry and the immediate cares of the business.

On the twenty ninth of each month, the biggest fair in France was held outside the small village, Les Herolles in La Vienne. Les Herolles was about two hours from Chez-Ellen. Rose-Ellen wanted to find out about French country produce, so she and Finn set off early in the morning. By the time they were up and organised most of the French farmers had already arrived in their trucks and trailers and had their pens prepared. The place was heaving and cars were parked in fields for miles around. The trading had begun at seven am and everything was in full swing. There was a huge open courtyard with cattle, sheep, donkeys, goats and fowl. Rose-Ellen had never seen anything like it before. The French farmers chatted amongst themselves whilst partaking of the local liquor. Others sat on the railings guarding the pens, their sticks slack, engaged in the whole trading business. Brown, black, and grey donkeys stood subdued, motionless, their heads bowed, impervious to the odd pat on the head whilst the goats 'baad' nervously. A large nanny snapped at her little kid each time it moved away from her. The frightened sheep, with perfectly shorn wiry coats, bleated in large pens, their rapid breathing indicating their fear and discomfort.

A beautiful blonde Aquitaine bull, golden wheat colour, seemed to be the centre of attention as he stood majestically in his pen, his enormous neck and large head distinguishing him from the graceful cows. He had four red and gold rosettes pinned to his harness which were a testament to his marvellous pedigree. Rose-Ellen wondered how his stocky, sturdy legs supported his mighty weight, his shiny, snow-white fetlocks and hooves buffed to perfection, a testament to the care and attention his proud owner lavished on him.

The place was a riot of colour and sounds as the slow, well-practiced art of trading was carried out against a background of bellowing and bleating in the hot noonday sun.

Rose-Ellen moved about the place with Finn. There were stalls selling every delicacy; all kinds of sausage, cured hams, truffle oil, rose jam, chestnut beer, artisans' cheese, jars of stag *terrine*, various blends of *pâtés*, *confit* of duck, and huge rounds of country crusty breads. She turned to Finn who was looking at the hunting knives. 'Dad would love to be here. He often decried the fact that many of the old artisans' ways were dying out in Ireland.'

'I'm afraid that the EU has put an end to a lot of the small local enterprises which is a real shame,' he said, holding up a knife with a large sickle-like blade.

There were beautiful white cocks and hens strutting imperiously around in pens, their heads held high with bright red gleaming coxcombs. They were not like the enormous black turkeys next door, their wattles quivering as they cackled loudly, turkey-style.

Rose-Ellen moved on. People shoved plates of food under her nose to sample, big brown and white mottled and curved sausages the size of drain pipes, pudding, goats' cheese or wild boar *saucisson*. Men with corpulent bellies cheerily tucked into plates of frogs' legs fried in butter and garlic, scooping up the cream sauce with hunks of bread; others were savouring plates of *boeuf flambé*, washed down with dark red wine, and groups were standing at various stalls and counters sipping small glasses of *crème de menthe*; others partook of Armagnac to celebrate the day's transactions.

They sat in the blazing sun and had a pizza and beer. Rose-Ellen laid two big bags of purchases on the ground, while Finn gently placed two standard yellow roses carefully beside his chair and away from passing crowds. 'Now if we lived here, pet, we could go to these fairs around the country and sample French rural life at its best.'

Rose-Ellen wondered why Finn talked about them settling down together when he worked in Ireland with a good permanent responsible job, but still it was heartening to know that he loved her and would do anything for her. 'Isn't it a riot of colour and sounds, Finn? I'm so glad we came; nothing sanitised about this lot!'

'*Au naturel,* that's the French,' he said, finishing off his coffee.

One evening, they went out for a meal in the local hotel. They both had the beef wellington and two bottles of wine. Staggering out of the place, Rose-Ellen was barely able to walk, tottering on her high heels and singing loudly in the street. Finn held her by the waist guiding her over the cobbled streets. 'Careful now.'

Arriving home, he put on some Irish music and opened a ten-year-old bottle of whiskey. Rose-Ellen attempted a few jigs and then flopped down on the sofa. Then getting a new lease of life she jumped back up and danced around the place, swinging to the song *I Will Survive* while holding a large tumbler of whiskey. Finn kept replenishing her glass. Rose-Ellen was really letting go; her hilarity was infectious and irrepressible. Leaving the empty bottles and tired remains of a wonderful evening they mounted the stairs to Rose-Ellen's bedroom, the lavender room.

Finn could not contain himself any longer. He had waited long enough for Rose-Ellen and now was his chance. He sidled over to her on the bed where she lay and stroked her hair.

'I'm mad about you, Rose-Ellen, do you know that?'

She was barely listening. 'I'm so, so tired,' she yawned and turned over to go to sleep.

But he was not going to be dismissed so easily. 'Listen, Rose, I'm sick of being told you're too tired…another time…you're too busy. For feck's sake, what am I supposed to do? I'm a man for Christ's sake, with a man's desires and passions.'

But she was out cold.

'It's always the same old story, too tired, too this and too that,' he sighed.

The next morning was a busy Saturday morning, when the housewives came by for their usual purchase of her fresh scones and shopped for the weekend, but the shutters to *Chez-Ellen* were firmly down.

Madame Blanchard was a neat little lady who had run the *patisserie* for many years and had only half-heartedly welcomed Rose-Ellen to the village. She took great pride in her array of colourful and elaborate tea cakes all neatly arranged under the glass counters: cherry and apricot tartlets, light and airy *millefeuille* pastries, *paris brest* and the rich *choux* pastries with their comical appeal: either *'Les Religieuses'*, – éclairs in the shape of a nun's habit, in coffee and chocolate with a swirl of whipped cream on top, or *'Divorcées'*, – éclairs, half coffee, half chocolate, divided by a cream strip, and stacks of baguettes and country breads, all made by an artisan's hand.

Finn and Rose-Ellen both slept in. Monsieur Chabot's cock crowed and crowed but Rose-Ellen still did not wake so deep was her sleep. Finally, a little after ten o'clock, she emerged from her deep, hung-over sleep. Finn was stretched out on Rose-Ellen's bed snoring beside her. Her head ached and her mouth was parched. For a brief second she could not recall where she was and looked around the room, barely able to focus. 'What time is it?' she said, peering at the clock. 'Oh Jesus!' she shouted and jumped out of the bed making her way to the bathroom. Her head was throbbing.

She went downstairs and made a cup of tea and brought one up to Finn who had woken by now and was sitting up on the bed smoking a cigarette. People were talking outside. She sat down beside him in her dressing gown, her hair tumbling down over her face as she sipped the warm tea. 'I just don't have the energy to get up day after day and do this.' She yawned. 'It's a killer.'

Finn put down his cigarette and pulled her towards him. 'Darling, that's what business is all about, hard work and commitment. Look, it was a one-off last night. I suppose it was my fault starting on the ten-year-old whiskey after two bottles of wine.'

She looked at him through her fallen tresses. 'What? Finn! Whiskey after all that wine! No wonder I feel rotten.'

'So what? It was one of these spontaneous things. I'm just looking at you and wondering if you realise how truly lovely you look, even if you feel rotten. Rose-Ellen you have the translucence of the naturally beautiful.'

'Come off it, Finn. I'm trying to build up a business and if they find that I'm unreliable, well, they'll just go over to *Madame Flimsy Culottes* across the way,' she said, looking out of the window at the *patisserie* where a small queue of eager customers were forming outside *Madame*'s shop. She could see the housewives now making their way over to the pretty *patisserie,* muttering to themselves, when they found *Chez-Ellen* had not yet opened.

'Do you know why Delphine christened the prim Madame Blanchard *Madame Flimsy Culottes*?' Rose-Ellen said, as she brushed her hair.

'No, why so?' he asked.

'Well, one day as she was passing by the *patisserie*, the door to the back of the shop was open and she had noticed *Madame*'s washing line in the back garden. Pegged from the line in perfect symmetrical formation was the neatest row of beautifully designed French style panties: skimpy, ultra-feminine in soft pastel colours, with lace, bows and spangles. Delphine roared with laughter as she felt it was probably her way to instil some passion into her marriage with that dull, predictable husband of hers, a little bald-headed man whose daily commute to La Rochelle on the same train, in the same carriage, is about as exciting as watching a slug devouring a lettuce leaf.'

'I find her OK, mind you,' he said, taking a pull of his cigarette.

'Darling you're a man! She's polite and crisp to me. I know all about shopkeepers and how they are privy to all sorts of gossip. Behind the dark *façade* of her lace-bound windows, I'd say *Madame* keeps a note of everything that goes on in this small French village, even if she appears as stiff and starchy as her *meringues*. Will you put out that cigarette for feck's sake, Finn? It's making me sick.'

'Ah, you're just jealous. Come away from that window and lie down here beside me,' he said.

But Rose-Ellen continued with the gossip. 'It's rumoured in the village that *Madame Flimsy Culottes* entertains a certain gentleman during those hours in the afternoon when *La Patisserie* closes and before her husband returns from his government job in La Rochelle. While the pots are simmering for the evening meal she indulges in a little frivolity on the side with *Monsieur le Coiffeur.*'

'You mean the guy who owns the only half decent hairdressing salon in the town, and who is free to indulge as he pleases?' Finn asked.

'Precisely!' *Monsieur le Coiffeur* had been married one time, but was now free to engage in a bit of titillation without any real commitment. According to Delphine he would leave his soaps and all his paraphernalia and set forth to the *patisserie* for an afternoon of unbridled bliss and thrills with Madame Blanchard. Rose-Ellen came and sat down on the bed beside Finn. 'They say he has snipped and spruced his way in to *Madame's* life and on to her couch, nipping across to her in the quiet of the late afternoon. Their affair has continued for years and people from the village seem to turn a blind eye,' she whispered.

'My God, have you women nothing better to do only gossip? It's probably all very harmless!'

'I'm sure there are rumours and some have had their suspicions, perhaps even *Madame's* boring husband, but homes aren't being wrecked, children are not being displaced and *Madame Flimsy Culottes* is receiving unbridled pleasure from the attention of *Monsieur le Coiffeur*,' she laughed out loud.

'Sounds very French indeed,' Finn remarked.

She turned to look at him, her eyes wide with excitement. 'Delphine said that *Madame* confided to somebody in the village that *Monsieur le Coiffeur* brought her to delicious heights of passion down at the back of the *patisserie*. Can you just imagine the goings-on of the pair of them?'

'Stop it, Rose-Ellen, enough said. I don't want to hear another word out of you. I'd better watch what I say to that Delphine one, and her salacious gossip. You have a business to run here so you should be more circumspect.'

She went back over to the window. 'Oh, what did I tell you? *Madame Flimsy Culottes* is benefiting from our hangover. Look at that queue! I know what I'd like to do.'

'Pray tell me!' Finn said, putting his hands up to his temples.

'Oh nothing, it doesn't matter.'

Finn sprang up out of the bed and looked onto the street below. 'You're a blow-in, pet, and also you're not French and there's no arguing with that. You'll never be totally accepted and you have to understand that; it's important from a business point of view that you cultivate her.'

'She is only too happy to make a sale and as long as I'm buying from her and not taking her loyal customers she continues to smile her saccharine smile. So what if I'm not French; am I not learning the language? It just takes time.' She remained at the window looking at the snake-like queue outside the *patisserie* across the road. 'Can you just imagine her now, peering across the road through the slits in her blinds, as the disappointed women firmly clutching their baskets and intent on the morning shopping leave *Chez-Ellen,* and cross the road to her shop, muttering words of disgruntlement.'

'Surely you can't blame them, for God's sake, if you're going to take the odd lie-in. After all, buying bread in France is part of an age-old ritual,' Finn said, yawning.

Rose-Ellen put her hair up with a clip she had been fiddling with. 'She doesn't like me and that's that, but you know people change and besides it's in her interest to like me,' she said, glaring at him.

'Suit yourself, I'm just letting you know,' he shrugged.

'Well don't, if you're not going to be positive,' she snapped at him.

'Anytime we need extra bread for the *café* or cakes, I'll nip politely over to her and buy whatever is needed from *La Patisserie*, as I have done in the past and after a conversation of pleasantries and the odd flattering compliment, to which *Madame Flimsy Culottes* is not averse, I'll just make my way back. It pays to be polite in this small place, Ms Power!' He looked at her and his expression softened. 'Sometimes it's not a bad thing to just let go, and by God, Rose-Ellen, you were some sight last night, prancing around scantily dressed, and in your spangled shoes, singing away.' He had a devilish look on his face as if he knew more than he pretended.

'Ah, stop it, Finn. I don't want to hear about last night, I'm mortified! Now I had better go downstairs and open up this shop before Jean-François arrives.'

Just then they could hear banging outside in the garden. 'What's that?' Finn asked.

'It's only the goats. They want to be fed. I'd better get up.'

Finn wiped his eyes and shook his head. 'That's better, gets the blood vessels going. No, Rose, stay in bed awhile. You're tired.' He put his hand through her hair and pulled her gently on to the bed beside him. He bent down and kissed her gently on the lips. They kissed and he could sense Rose-Ellen letting go and responding to his touch. Finn flickered his tongue over her ear lobes and down her neck. 'Rose-Ellen, you drive me crazy, you know that.' Then they heard a knock at the door. 'Who is it?' shouted Finn. It was Jean-Francois.

'Just coming,' Finn shouted back, getting up off the bed and straightening his hair before going to open the door. Rose-Ellen vaguely heard something about deliveries and laid her head on the pillow and drifted off to sleep.

Some days later Rose-Ellen was explaining the *a la carte* menu to a Spanish couple in *Chez-Ellen*. It was just after two pm and Jean-Francois was cleaning and tidying up after people had had the set lunch and went about their business. Rose-Ellen looked up and saw Madame Blanchard standing at the doorway with a stony face that would have stopped a herd of thundering bison heading over the plains. She excused herself to the Spanish couple and marched over to *Madame*.

'*Bonjour Madame,* may I help you?'

'*Bonjour Madame,*' Madame Blanchard said frostily and asked if *Monsieur* were here.

'He's around, but is there anything I can help you with?' Rose-Ellen asked politely.

'Why must your customers, particularly at lunch time, park their big cars and jeeps on the footpath in front of my *patisserie*? It is very difficult for elderly clients or young mothers with buggies to get into my shop.' Rose-Ellen was just about to open her mouth and protest but Madame Blanchard continued. 'And another thing, the music at lunchtime here is very loud, too loud; people are complaining about it. You must understand *Madame* that this is a quiet village and we are not used to this kind of lifestyle.'

Rose-Ellen thought of Jean-Francois and his penchant for loud music at lunchtime. She had tried talking to him about it but to no avail. She could hear Finn whistling in the background. 'Finn, have you a minute?'

'Coming,' he called back.

When Finn came in to the restaurant, *Madame's* face lit up and gone was the angst ridden expression she had adopted for Rose-Ellen. She smiled as sweetly to him as if she were cooing over a basketful of kittens.

Rose-Ellen turned to Finn and said in English. 'Can you talk to her about jeeps on kerbs and loud music please or whatever else she can think of, while I see to our customers,' and turned on her heels and returned to the Spanish couple. After a while *Madame* left and Finn came over to where Rose-Ellen was furiously whipping up some cream for a strawberry roulade. 'Well, I hope you sorted that one out. She rubs me up the wrong way. I simply can't abide her and her syrupy smile.'

'I told her I would have a word with Monsieur Beaudry about the cars parked on the footpath outside of her shop; maybe put up a sign such as *For Patisserie Customers only*, and I'll get on to Jean-Francois about that heavy rock music he's so fond of. Christ, it's like a bloody disco here sometimes in the middle of the day!' He held her by the shoulders and looked at her. 'Love, I know you don't like her, but damn it, you have to live alongside her and it's important that we are at least seen to be doing something about her damned kerb or whatever else she wants. There's no point in making enemies and I think you could be more polite to her,' he said.

'We have no control over who parks their cars where and how! And how does she know where these people go after they've parked their cars? I suppose she's watching them with her binoculars to make sure that they end up at *Chez-Ellen* so that she has more ammunition to hurl at me.'

Finn looked at her, shook his head and walked away.

Chapter 44

In July, Rose-Ellen and Finn took out *La Sirene,* The Mermaid, a sailing boat belonging to Monsieur Launay, Jean-François' father, around the harbour in La Rochelle. Although not a seasoned sailor, Finn used to sail over and back to Howth with a Garda colleague, so he had enough experience to sail off the coast of La Rochelle, but Rose-Ellen was ever mindful of Pierre's warning words to her of the perils of the ocean:

'You must respect the sea, because it respects no one, least of all the inexperienced; it exacts its merciless toll'.

They made their way to the harbour in La Rochelle. *La Sirene* swung in to its mooring in the harbour. She climbed on board from the rib and laid down her paints and canvas. It was a twenty-two footer, compact but sturdy enough to withstand the unpredictable winds around La Rochelle. Putting on her life jacket, she tied herself to the lazy jack. Finn put up the sails and undid the rope warp from the mooring. Releasing the tie-ups on the boat he hooked up the jib sail first, hoisting it by the halyard, and then securing it by tying a stop knot. She then fed through the main sail. Having the main sail secured, Finn then winched it so that it reached the top of the mast. Tugging on the halyards with all his might, he secured the ropes to the cleats on the side deck. *La Sirene* was cast off and they sailed out beyond the harbour of La Rochelle heading the boat nicely off into the wind until they reached the wide open sea.

Such peaceful solitary times were like jewels, without anybody trespassing on Rose-Ellen's thoughts. Lately the bank, customers, the endless banter, requiring her to be all things to all people, the relentless struggle to keep standards high and of course the animals were beginning to take their toll and she cherished these solitary idle moments. She had so much to do and preferred to work well into the night and get through her various tasks so that she could relish those heady sunshine days such as today.

It was a day full of hope and the sun broke the blue water with a million speckled sapphires and diamonds, sparkling and dancing as *La Sirene* sailed leisurely along the tranquil sea. The wind was light so they dropped anchor when a perfect view of the port came into focus. She commenced painting on canvas. The serenity of the surroundings helped her concentrate on the outline.

Finn was busy acquainting himself with all the equipment on board. 'I hope that wind doesn't change that much, as I'd say it could be tricky here if anything happened.' As the day wore on it became colder as the wind altered, and the once calm tide turned whipping up a squall. Deciding to motor back, Finn moved to the stern to start the engine. It puttered a few times and then faded, dead.

He then unscrewed the cap of the petrol tank and looked inside. He checked the level of petrol by peering deep inside the outboard engine. It was empty. 'Oh, for fuck's sake!' he muttered and sank back on his heels.

'What's wrong, Finn?'

'No petrol.'

She cursed Jean-François' father. 'Monsieur Launay told me it was all ready for sailing. He had not refilled the tank.'

'And we had not bothered to check how much was there before setting sail,' Finn said, looking out at the horizon. A chill wind sprang up as the sun began its descent. The once-friendly whispering waves now became white-tipped, menacing little urchins, dancing in a frenzied fashion. But the sails kept flapping in the furious wind and Finn could just about manage to steer the boat. She took out her mobile and rang Jean-François but there was no reply. The boat swayed as the wind rose, and Rose-Ellen almost fell over. She knew that she must try to remain calm. As the wind whipped up, Finn reached over and pulled up the anchor and tried to manoeuvre the boat back towards the shore which was slowly disappearing before their eyes due to the north-easterly direction of the winds. *La Sirene* seemed to have a will of its own.

Beginning to be fearful, Rose-Ellen hunted around for any supplies that might help. There was no emergency flare, nor was there any radio, and she remembered that this was odd that there was no radio on the boat.

She took out her phone and dialled Jean-François' number again. Still no reply. Jean-François, the callow youth, unused to responsibility, who at times drove her mad with his dreaminess in the shop, was turning into their only hope.

The once calm surface gave way to a more sinister rolling sea and ominous clouds cast a dark shadow. The water took on a deeper and dangerous hue. *La Sirene* dipped into a deeper trough furrowed by the relentless waves that lashed against it. She looked around frantically to see if she could at least call to somebody, but there was not another boat in sight. Their only companions were the squawking gulls and gannets overhead intent on diving spear-like into the perilous sea. At one stage, she imagined herself slipping beneath the waves and disappearing without trace.

The waves danced around them, performing their merry dance of doom. Rose-Ellen lay crouching in her wet, salt-laden clothes, her mind began to play tricks. Images danced before her tired eyes and sounds emerged out of nowhere, but all was eerily quiet but for the restless sigh of the sea and the whispering of the waves. 'Now listen, pet, we must think clearly and not panic,' Finn said, holding her by the shoulders. 'We'll get out of this, but please stay calm. We need to lower the main sail, so I'm going to reef it down, at least then it will stop us falling over.'

The jib was a furling jib on a swivel rolling up on itself. Finn attempted to furl it to a smaller size by pulling on the furling drum at the bottom of the jib on deck on the bow. That seemed to steady the boat. Rose-Ellen steered the boat in a straight line to a dot in the harbour that she could barely see, but remained fixed and focussed all the time as Finn battled with the sails. She kept silently mumbling prayers over and over again that they would get home safely.

All this time the north-easterly wind tried to push the boat further from the port but Finn steadied it. She could not help but admire his strength and steady hand and calmness in the face of adversity.

With the waning light, a ghostly calm descended with only the perfidious sea and its sly curling waves for company, they eventually made it back to the harbour at La Rochelle. When they steered the boat to its moorings, she stood up and hugged Finn. 'Oh, Finn, thank God we made it. I began to imagine all kinds of scenarios. I remember Pierre once telling me that the seas around La Rochelle…' but she trailed off as she could see the hurt in Finn's eyes at the mention of Pierre. After all, Pierre was not there now. It had only been her and Finn, and Finn had got them out of a very tricky situation.

'There were some fierce cross-currents out there, at one stage, I thought we were taking in water, but then it seemed to calm down I dunno, could be just luck the way the wind changed.' He tried to remain upbeat, but Rose-Ellen suspected that like her he had got a terrible fright.

August arrived and business was brisk at *Chez-Ellen*. Rose-Ellen decided to take up painting again having started classes in the village with a retired artist. Some of her scenes of the lovely old tower in La Rochelle were on sale in *Chez-Ellen*; they had been greatly admired and two had already sold.

Tourists dropped by as well as sailing folk, passing business people and the locals. There were the summertime bikers with their shaven heads and tattoos, or people from the local campsites invariably looking for chips and deep-fried food. Menus had to be translated into English and Madame Launay, who had reasonably good English, was given this task and had provided Rose-Ellen with a translation of all the French dishes. Rose-Ellen quickly had the English menus made up. Finn reviewed the menu one day before handing it out to a couple of bikers.

'What the hell is burnt cream?' he asked, turning to Rose-Ellen who was busy cutting sandwiches.

'Finn, language please! Burnt cream? I have no idea; here show me,' she said, swiping the menu from him.

'There, see,' he said, pointing to the offending name.

'God, I don't believe this. That should be *crème brulée*, not burnt cream. What sort of an eejit is she! Everybody knows what *crème brulée* is; there was no need for any translation.'

'You should have checked the translations before having had the menus printed up in English. I'll go over it tonight and see if there are any other strange lexical conundrums! It's a wonder she didn't translate *pommes frites* as fried apples instead of French fries.'

'Stop it, Finn! I've enough on my mind as it is.'

'Darling, you need to live more in the present, in the here and now, and savour the moment. You're too bogged down with bloody lists for this and that. Just enjoy.'

'And how is the business going to manage if I don't pay attention to all the details?'

'Trust me, it will! Darling, nobody is indispensable in this life,' he said, pulling her close to him and trying to steal a kiss, but she just continued to peruse the menu card.

Chapter 45

It was the middle of August and Finn and Rose-Ellen were working together in the afternoon; their routine had become so established that they had fallen into an easy working momentum. Rose-Ellen dealt with the coffees and Finn took the orders. Rose-Ellen was so immersed in the noise and steam of the coffee machine that she was working on auto-pilot. But suddenly she felt the atmosphere change as three tall men entered the cafe and she felt herself wake up to the world around her.

The trio took the last remaining table by the window and chatted amongst themselves whilst they perused the menu. Having served the espresso coffees to the other customers, she approached their table. Pierre looked up from the menu card. To her he had aged a little and had lost weight giving him a lean, athletic look. Gone was the healthy glow from the outdoors, and his curly brown hair was now quite shorn enhancing his fine profile. When he saw her coming towards their table he leaned back in his chair, clearly astonished.

'Rose-Ellen, this is a surprise!'

A tremor ran through her as she looked down and smiled at him. 'Hello, Pierre. It's been a long time. How are you?' He stood up and kissed her on both cheeks, and when he moved she noticed that he had a slight limp.

'Oh, I'm fine now, thanks, getting better every day. So, can I presume from the name *Chez-Ellen* that this is yours?' he said, looking around.

'Yes. I've been here now quite a while.'

'What a stroke of luck meeting you here,' he said.

'These are two friends of mine, Nicholas and Pascale. We're heading down to Cognac, but realised we were running low on fuel so came off the main Angouleme road.'

They both nodded and smiled at her. She had hundreds of questions to ask him, but Finn was now looking in their direction and sidled over to the table as Pierre sat down.

She noticed that Pierre's expression changed when he spied Finn out of the corner of his eye. He glanced down at the menu and without looking at her said, 'I'm sure I've seen that chap somewhere before.'

She could sense Finn's ebullient mood nearby. 'Well, if it isn't Dr O'Hegarty! And how are you? I don't suppose you remember me, or do you?'

Then Pierre's face lit up in recognition. 'Of course, Detective O'Donnell. And what on earth are you doing here?' Pierre looked from Finn to Rose-Ellen with a puzzled expression. Rose-Ellen wondered what he was thinking. Why could Finn not have kept away, hidden himself in the background, she wondered.

She sensed that Pierre was probably slightly embarrassed at the unexpectedness of the events. Turning to include Finn, Rose-Ellen said a trifle apologetically, 'Finn is here for a few months helping out.'

Pierre looked away from Finn and perused the menu again. 'Good for you. Well, let me see what we'll have. Pretty impressive menu if I may say so. What's the soup?'

'Tis gorgeous!' Finn exclaimed, excitedly.

She sensed a *froideur* and threw Finn a thunderous look, because she wondered what Pierre would have thought of her entertaining a detective on his case. She was embarrassed now at Finn's presence and could not help disguise her embarrassment. Pierre seemed more interested in the menu and Rose-Ellen suspected it was because of Finn's presence. He looked up from the menu card and smiled at her; that smile she had become familiar with over time.

'I'll try some of the fish pie and a green salad,' Pierre said, closing the menu card.

Rose-Ellen noted this down and then took the orders from the others. She gathered up the menu cards and went back to prepare the food. She thought of all the times she had sat at Pierre's bedside waiting for him to emerge from a coma, and now it was as if she had meant little to him; treating her just like another nurse doing her duty. All this time he had occupied her thoughts and now she wondered if it had all been in vain.

Finn joined her in the back room where they prepared the food. 'Christ, I bet you didn't expect him turning up like that out of the blue,' he said.

'No, and I wonder what he thinks of our little arrangement,' she snapped icily. She wanted Pierre to herself at this time and Finn now seemed to be an interloper. He said nothing.

During the coffees when most of the diners had left and things had quietened down, Rose-Ellen had a chance to sit down with Pierre. 'So, Pierre how have you been? You look well despite everything that happened. God, when I think of everything…I', she then stopped.

'It's good to see you again, Rose-Ellen, and it's great what you're doing. In a way I envy you. I mean, doing your own thing, probably realising a dream. As for me, every day is a bonus; I'll just need to be patient.' He was stirring his coffee. He looked at her and then at her hand. Rose-Ellen blushed and she thought of Danny and that day outside the milking parlour when she had handed him back the ring.

Catching Pierre's eye she said, 'I've broken off my engagement with Danny.'

'Yes, I noticed you were no longer wearing that stunning ring.'

After some small talk, Pierre and his friends left. Pierre drove hard out towards the motorway to Cognac. Rose-Ellen cleaned up and tidied the place before closing up. Finn had taken himself off for a long walk. When the restaurant was closed up for the evening, she sat down with a glass of wine and contemplated everything which had happened. Paidraigin came and rubbed up against her. She bent down and stroked the cat's slightly humped back.

'Oh, Paidraigin, you have no worries; just to fill your little belly all the time.' She felt the same old feeling that she felt before – knots in her stomach whenever she was with him. She thought back on their time together in DCH; little snapshots of him came to her mind: sitting with a patient and listening carefully to their woes, re-inflating a collapsed lung with his slightly long hair curling down over his face or his patience teaching junior doctors and medical students. 'Oh God, it's ridiculous, how I feel, like a sixteen-year-old,' she said out loudly, but the only one who could hear her was the purring cat.

Chapter 46

Rose-Ellen had a distracted air about her and seemed unable to concentrate on immediate matters. She was confused. For her to love Finn, she had to respect and admire him in some way, some would say almost revere him, and while she looked up to Finn and had depended on him in so many ways, and one day could have fallen in love with him, she felt that had all changed now since Pierre had come back into her life again, albeit fleetingly.

Finn had been her confidant and companion when things did not go according to plan, and now he was leaving her. Within a week his bags were packed. Rose-Ellen came over to him. 'I'm sorry about this, Finn, I really am. I suppose I've come to rely on you so much these past few months, but I feel it's only fair to be honest about my feelings. I hope that we can still be friends.'

He was writing his name on his luggage tag and looked at her. His tired red eyes revealed how he was finally reconciled to the end of their friendship, and his voice quavered when he spoke. 'Rose-Ellen, you seem so desirable to me at this moment, but now I feel that you're the woman I'll never have. Friends? That's all we'll ever be! I hate leaving you, Rose-Ellen. I feel in some ways as if I belong here, but I now realise that I don't and that's the hardest bit. Things change. I saw it the day he walked in here. But can I say one thing? For whatever it's worth I'll be there for you, because I love you and I always will, no matter what.'

'I'm very touched by your honesty and forthrightness, Finn.' She put her arms around his neck and whispered, 'You deserve somebody truly special. You've been such a friend to me these past few months. I don't know what I'd have done without you.' Her eyes started to glisten and he picked up on her emotional state and drew her to him when she started to cry. Her head lay against his chest and he stroked her long wavy hair.

'It's OK, love, you know you can say anything to me, anything at all.'

'It's good to be held, Finn, and I'm trying to appreciate this moment for all its worth.'

'Stop it will you, you're just making my leaving so much more difficult,' he said, nearly choking back the tears.

They drove to the airport in silence, each aware that they might never see the other again. Rose-Ellen turned into the airport and said, 'Maybe we could…' but then stopped as she looked for a car space.

'Look, I don't have to go. I can stay, maybe you need more time,' he said, pressing down the button to open the window.

'Please, Finn, don't make it any harder. I need space and time and I just can't deal with my feelings at the moment. OK?' She looked in the mirror. He said nothing. She was aware of the tension in the car, that feeling which arose when two people have said everything and it was preferable to say nothing; both aware that anything uttered might ruin the last precious moments of a friendship about to end. He got out but she remained in the car. 'I know I should go with you, Finn, but if you don't mind I won't. I would just find it too hard.'

He leaned into the window and said, 'I understand, pet, don't upset yourself.'

She started to cry. 'Oh, Finn, this is awful, terrible, what am I doing?'

'Look…'

'No, I must go. I'm sorry, Finn, please try to understand. Let me go, you'd be better off without me. This is so damn hard.' She started to bang on the steering wheel as she screamed, 'I'm in bits, bits, bits!'

'Rose-Ellen, please, love.'

She reached up and pulled him down and kissed him. 'Goodbye, Finn, and take care.'

He tried to hold on to her, but she put the car into gear. 'Safe home,' she called and sped off.

On the way home, she could hardly drive as the tears almost occluded her visibility. She found a parking space on the side of the road and drove in and cried her heart out, big, large, loud sobs. She sat in the car park wondering about her life and where it was going as the light faded. She wondered if her romantic life was jinxed and why she could not meet somebody to have a loving, lasting relationship.

'Poor Finn, he was such a good man and I just let him go like that. My God, what have I done?' She then got out her phone and sent him a text.

'*Sorry Finn! I hope some day you can forgive me. Love RE*'. A terrible wave of grief seemed to descend on her as she put the car into gear and sped off out on the highway to more immediate cares.

Chapter 47

In some respects, Rose-Ellen missed Finn's quiet, easy ways and laid-back charm, but she desperately needed to get more help now that Finn, her guiding light and helpmate, had gone. Rose-Ellen gave Chantal more responsibilities while employing Monsieur Beaudry's niece, Nadine, to do a lot of the menial jobs, such as emptying the dishwasher and cleaning the kitchen. All of the French ladies wondered what had become of *'le bel Irlandais sympathique'*. They could not understand how Rose-Ellen could have let Finn drift out of her life.

But it was Delphine who did not spare any ire in telling Rose-Ellen how she felt about her callous treatment towards Finn, but Rose-Ellen just ignored her friend's admonishments. This was something she would have to come to terms with herself. She felt guilty about having invited Finn to stay in the first place, especially when he made enormous sacrifices and contributed to the business. Rose-Ellen sat almost crying as she thought of how good and constant Finn had been in her life, and wondered how she could so heartlessly have let him go. She wondered if she were becoming cold and brutal in the cut-throat world of business. She realised that she bore the ultimate responsibility about what had happened to Finn and his departure from her life.

The seasons came and went and Rose-Ellen continued the daily grind of running *Chez-Ellen*. Finn had been gone almost a year now and she had to struggle on her own, cooking at all hours, running the place, managing Chantal, Nadine and Jean-Francois, doing the stocktaking and being kind and charming at all times to customers. Despite everything that had happened, she missed Finn, his kindness and concern for her and his loving ways.

There were some things Rose-Ellen missed about Ireland – Haydn's fish and chips in Loughbow, the smell of wild clover, the flighty turbulence of the Slaney River, the ever changing charcoal-grey skies, but mostly she missed her mother.

In late autumn she decided to close up *Chez-Ellen* as much of the main tourist trade had eased off by then. Farming Paidraigin out to Delphine and instructing Jean-François on his various chores, Rose-Ellen packed her bags and returned home. She reflected on how Madame Blanchard would relish her departure for a few weeks, but Rose-Ellen was tired and exhausted from the business, and realised in her heart that if she did not go home to Ireland to recharge her batteries and see her family, she would just wilt in France. It was a chance she had to take. It was the first time since her arrival in France nearly two years ago that she was returning home to Ireland, and she was naturally very excited.

Little had changed at home except that Danny had got married and the pair were living in the bungalow that he and Rose-Ellen had originally designed. She saw them one day in a supermarket pushing a large trolley piled high with stuff, but Danny did not see her or, if he did, he chose to avoid her. Rose-Ellen suspected the latter. She stood in the queue with her small basket and pondered on their relationship. Poor Danny with his cows and his family had never encouraged her to dream and to use her imagination. Women need to be seduced and excited intellectually as well as sexually, and Danny had never really ignited any of these desires or feelings within her. She did not care now. It did not really matter anymore as she somehow removed herself emotionally from the past and all that Danny Redmond had represented.

'My God, child, I worry about you. You're fading away, it must be the French food that has you this thin!' Kitty said to her one evening. But Rose-Ellen knew that as well as the French portions it was also the frenetic life she had become accustomed to; endlessly worrying about the business, keeping the taxman happy and above all trying to be on top of matters. So many small businesses around her were crumbling as the French government mercilessly took huge levies from them.

Olivia and Brendan were going to the regatta in Wexford at the weekend, and it would soon be the end of the sailing season. 'Rose-Ellen, you need a break and you need to stop worrying about the business in France. It'll survive,' Olivia said to her sister one evening as Rose-Ellen combed her long hair in the mirror in Olivia's bedroom.

Rose-Ellen put her arm around her sister. 'I know you're right. I promise while I'm here that I'll try to forget about it.'

'Why don't we take a picnic and we can watch the regatta from the headland this afternoon? I'd love if you could come with us. Brendan has to be there. I think he's involved in giving out some of the prizes later on in the day, and there's some kind of a do afterwards in the sailing club. It'll be great fun. Well?' Rose-Ellen looked at her sister, who did not seem to have a trouble in the world, helping their Dad in the emporium, and leading a carefree unfettered life while betrothed to Brendan. She had the best of all possible worlds. Engaged to a wonderful man, but being as free as a bird in the meantime.

'Of course I'll come,' Rose-Ellen enthused.

It was a glorious day and people everywhere appeared happy and relaxed. Rose-Ellen noticed how much more the Irish seemed to enjoy themselves compared with the French where life in rural France was comparatively lacklustre and dull, and where people remained sober and calm for all occasions, their *hauteur* seeming to be more important than the *joie de vivre*. There was eating, drinking and dancing everywhere in Wexford. At one stage, after they had finished their picnic, as Rose-Ellen was walking down the main street linking Olivia, a young man nonchalantly strolled up and took her gently by the hand and they waltzed together in the middle of the street. She then caught up with Olivia. 'Oh, I just love the spontaneity, the familiarity and the almost wild abandon of Irish life, and realise that this was something I have missed in formal France where one casually defies the rules of courtesy at one's peril.'

'I suppose that's what makes this country so unique,' Olivia said, hopping down from the pavement to make way for a young girl with twin buggies.

'Do you know that although I am now well known in the village in France, the locals still refer to me as *Mademoiselle*,' Rose-Ellen said, as they both queued for cone ices in Downe's ice cream parlour.

That evening there were to be celebrations in the club house for the regatta. Rose-Ellen dithered as to whether she should go or just let Olivia and Brendan go off on their own.

'I'm not taking no for an answer – you're coming with us and that's it,' Olivia said. Rose-Ellen opened up her wardrobe and wondered what to wear as most of her clothes were in France. Everybody would probably be dressed casually if smartly for the club house, so she chose a pair of white trousers and a forget-me-not blue silk top. 'You look stunning, sis,' Olivia said, putting her arms around her sister.

Rose-Ellen sat in the back of the car while Brendan drove them to the clubhouse. They fought their way through the crowd, many of whom had that soaked look as if they had been drinking since mid-afternoon. She chatted to a few people whom she knew and then Olivia and Brendan disappeared to talk to some friends, and Rose-Ellen found herself on her own. Carrying her glass of white wine, she wandered over to the club house's large bay window. Looking out on to the seafront, she thought of France and experienced a pang of loneliness as she no longer felt part of the Wexford scene, having become accustomed to the tranquil life in France. Rose-Ellen turned around and looked back at the bar and spied a group of men laughing at the counter. The tall one was explaining something with a beer mat to the others. The barmen were pulling pints and putting ice into tall glasses. She could not believe it, although of course it was quite probable that he would attend a boat regatta. After their meeting in France she thought that he might not have too much to say to her. She made her way up to the bar.

'Hello, Pierre,' she whispered nervously behind him.

'Oh, hello, Rose-Ellen, this is a surprise. I didn't expect to see you here,' he seemed a little perplexed as he turned around to face her.

'Me neither,' she said, trying to keep the colour from her face. After a while, she wondered if she should move away as he preferred to discuss sailing matters with his friends. But in the end she decided to stay. She did not really know what to say to Pierre after all this time and in this rather public place. He seemed polite but distant.

'Let's go sit by the window,' he suggested. She heard his voice again and remembered its warmth.

'Good idea,' she said.

He looked better than when she had met him in France over a year ago; tanned and having put on some weight which suited him. They made their way through the crowd over by the window. He sat astride a low stool and pulled one up for her. 'So, how are things? It was so good to see you last year and to find you running your own business. How is your business doing? You must have closed up shop for a brief period like most of the savvy French. The French are not slaves to work and commerce like we've become.'

'True, but it is never easy running your own,' she admitted. She wondered what he was thinking after their brief encounter in *Chez-Ellen*. His expression softened and he smiled at her.

'You're very brave taking on the complications of the French bureaucratic system. I always knew you had a lot of go in you. So it was OK to come over here and leave it for a while, or is your friend looking after it?'

She brushed her long hair back from her face and took a drink, replacing the glass gently on the coaster. 'My friend has gone back to Ireland. He'd only taken a few weeks off work to help me, and he's gone back to his job. It was always my venture and mine alone. You seemed anxious to get out of the place with your friends as if you were in a hurry.'

'Well what did you expect me to do, for heaven's sake? There I was having lunch with my friends in your restaurant, and I see a detective who was investigating the shooting, and he was giving me a funny look, so can you blame me for wanting to get out of the place quickly? And he may be involved with you, I don't know. Is he?'

'It doesn't matter, Pierre.'

He said nothing but took a swig of his drink. Rose-Ellen felt uneasy and was wondering if she should leave. He took up a coaster and tapped it on the table. 'I've been doing a lot of thinking lately. I suppose having had a lot of time in hospital makes one reflect on one's life, what's important and what isn't. I had been meaning to apologise for everything that happened, you losing your job, and the awful Cytu AB trial business, but I couldn't contact you and then when I met you in France...' Rose-Ellen still had some tiny grains of bitterness buried deep in her heart about her departure from DCH, particularly in relation to Shay McAdam. She was full of contradictions, and had learnt that most people's lives were laced with complexities and ambiguities. She too could understand Pierre's frailties and now his remorse. 'Look, please believe me when I say this, but I regret very much your suspension and then McAdam's involvement with the

IQI Pharma Corp and the management at DCH. I learnt about what had happened when I returned to the hospital. It was a dreadful business.'

She wondered how he invariably managed to infuse a certain delicacy into something he desperately wanted to say, adding to its poignancy. Somehow the admission of guilt and his apology had become all the more powerful and sincere. She wanted to give him a big hug and tell him that everything was all right. No matter what had happened at DCH, she would always feel something for him. She took a long drink from the cool glass of wine.

'You know, Pierre, it's all water under the bridge, and does it matter? Life is strange. If I hadn't been let go, I'd still be in DCH, struggling for deadlines and satisfying auditors. Instead I'm working for myself, doing something I enjoy, being in control of my own destiny, so I can't complain.' He said nothing but listened. Rose-Ellen continued, 'I was very upset when I left DCH initially, more at the way I had been treated than anything else. It took a long time to get over it, but I've moved on.'

He placed a hand firmly on hers. She felt her whole body tingle with the warmth of his strong hand on hers. 'It's a pity that things didn't work out, though. Oh, I had great plans for the research department in DCH, but life never turns out as we hope.'

'What do you mean?'

'When something like this hits you in life,' he said, 'a bolt out of the blue, you get a sense of priorities. I suppose my own brush with mortality brought home to me what matters, and it was touch and go for a long time as to whether I would make it. When I returned to DCH, my heart wasn't in it anymore. The accountants became more involved in running the department, and so I quit.'

She looked at him and thought of the man she had known and worked with. He who had the drive and energy to take untrodden paths that no one else would venture down; to pioneer tricky, challenging trials, some with potential risks for the patients. Without researchers like him, whose courage, originality and forward thinking was crucial, medical research would remain forever stagnant.

'I can't believe that you're saying this to me,' she said.

'I also learnt that the person who tried to kill me had been paid by Shay McAdam and his cronies.'

A cold shiver ran through her at the mention of this name. Even his uttering it made her tremble slightly as she thought of McAdam's vulpine face when he threatened her that day in the office. She replaced her glass on the coaster with such force that the drink slopped a little on the table. Pierre continued, 'McAdam was siphoning huge sums from the research account and that's why he was enrolling patients so vigorously. Trial drugs had gone missing too and they would have fetched a high price on the black market. I should have seen it coming. He even had the hospital accountant fooled and was able to forge his signature for the release of funds from the research account. He was developing a taste for extravagance, luxury and all the things he had probably been denied in his youth. The elixir of power and its trappings.' Rose-Ellen listened closely to Pierre's every word. 'You never got the opportunity to defend yourself and I take full blame. He made sure to have you side-lined, but he had more pleasurable things in line for me. And I'm sure that when things died down in DCH he imagined himself stepping into my shoes, when old Doolan had retired.'

'I can't believe McAdam would have paid to have you shot. My God, it's unbelievable!' she almost screamed.

'Unreal! You wouldn't believe it if you read about it! If I had died, he would have been charged with being an accomplice to murder, and would possibly have faced life behind bars. Men like McAdam are smart, but thankfully not that smart.' She could see that Pierre was affected by recalling these sordid events. 'Your pal O'Donnell and his colleagues were instrumental in tracing his link to my attempted murder,' he said.

'I believe it was McAdam who carried out the Phoenix Park murder last year by means of a shot of insulin in the jugular,' she said.

'Murder, conspiracy to murder, attempted murder or whatever. They're all there, and McAdam is in the thick of it! He won't practice medicine ever again if he's caught! But the boys are on to him. I understand that your pal, O'Donnell, has been instrumental in tracking him down,' Pierre said, stretching his long limbs.

She recalled Finn talking about McAdam gambling in the south of France. Rose-Ellen listened with meticulous attention and cupped her face in her hands, full of disbelief at what Pierre had just revealed to her. 'I can't believe this. It's shocking,' she said, pushing her hair out of her face.

He looked at her fair hair falling down round her innocent surprised face. 'Can I say that…' and he stopped. Rose-Ellen blushed and lifted her glass to her lips. 'It's a funny thing, I never ever expected him to turn out like that. While I never liked the chap, I was astounded at what he'd done. And to think that patients were under his care,' he continued.

'You would wonder why somebody like that ever chose to become a doctor in the first place.'

'Who knows why indeed! It's very perplexing. Once the detectives had worked on the case thoroughly he was found to be an accomplice in my murder and the actual Phoenix Park murderer. Well, it was only a matter of time.'

Rose-Ellen leaned forward. 'So who was this man who actually shot you and who was murdered by McAdam?'

Pierre took a long gulp of beer and placed the glass firmly down on the table in front of him. 'Apparently he owed money to McAdam, a bet that he couldn't pay. So McAdam asked this chap to "teach me a lesson", you know, rough me up a little. Despite having been pumped with two bullets, I remember the fellow quite clearly. He was not unknown to the Gardai; a petty thief, a minor criminal. The wretch paid with his life for his debts. I suspect McAdam was afraid that he'd talk or maybe blackmail him as is often the case, and of course to inject someone with a fatal dose of insulin would require some knowledge.'

'Clearly some medical knowledge,' she said, moving her bag to make way for somebody passing by with an armful of drinks.

'Precisely. But it would be a slow agonising death. I gather the man was not found for a couple of days and without medical intervention, his fate was sealed. McAdam knew exactly what he was doing when he injected the fatal dose.'

'But maybe he hadn't meant to kill him,' she said.

'I shall not defend the indefensible,' he retorted.

Rose-Ellen regretted her remark.

'So how was the link established between McAdam and your shooting? How did they find out McAdam was behind the whole thing?'

He smiled at her. 'I must say you look lovelier and younger than ever.' She blushed.

Pierre stopped momentarily as if remembering something. He sounded bold almost as if he were trying to be brave, yet she detected a slight tinge of regret in the pause which followed. 'He was careless, though, and was probably not a trained hitman. His DNA was found on the boat and the bullets matched his gun, a Beretta, when he was identified. Also he stupidly made calls to McAdam on his mobile immediately after the shooting, and these calls were easily traceable. I'll never forget the man's blue eyes, as hard and cold as the Arctic sky in sunlight.'

'Wouldn't you think he would have deleted the calls?'

'Even if he had, that didn't mean that the calls weren't hidden on the chip somewhere and besides, the Gardai have the authority to ask the phone company for records,' Pierre said.

Rose-Ellen could not take in everything Pierre was unravelling before her eyes. 'My God, who would have thought it? I didn't like McAdam, but I had no idea he was that type.'

Pierre looked over her head and into the crowd. 'It was well known that McAdam was an ace poker player. The world of poker can be easily infiltrated by the undercover intelligence section of the Gardai. So McAdam was a marked man, and a suspect from early on in the investigations, and would have been under heavy surveillance by the Special Branch.'

'God this is unbelievable!' Rose-Ellen sighed, as she recalled Finn's involvement in the case and suspected that he would have marked out McAdam as a suspect when she had initially told him of her mistrust of him.

'Like all these types, their past stalks them for the rest of their lives; they never manage to shake off the shackles of their former existence,' Pierre said.

'Still, I can't understand how McAdam thought he would get away with everything. I mean, just sail into your post with you out of the way. Surely he would have reckoned he would be a suspect after you had suspended him.'

Pierre looked at her kindly. 'Rose-Ellen, you have to understand that men like him feel they're invincible and that's their undoing in the end.'

'So once the detectives were on to McAdam, it was curtains for him. Is that right?'

'Pretty much so. He was uncovered and his world collapsed overnight. Oh yes, it was quite a sensation!'

She wondered why Finn never spoke of this to her, and then she remembered the long calls on his mobile sometimes well into the night, but he was always very guarded, at least towards her. She supposed that he was too emotionally involved with her to have informed her of anything to do with Pierre. She felt a pang of remorse when she remembered Finn now, and how Delphine's bitter words about her treatment of him had affected her. She realised that she had treated Finn harshly and had misjudged him in so many ways; how deeply he felt for her and how he had worked tirelessly to bring McAdam to justice. She was ashamed of her behaviour, and in particular at her callous disregard for one who had shown such loyalty and genuine concern for her welfare and that of Pierre. She could not resist the urge to move her hand across the table and touch Pierre's. He seemed endeared by this gesture. 'So what are you doing now?'

'I'm acting as a locum clinical lecturer in the Eastern Infirmary, and once I'm fully recovered…well, who knows what the future will have in store. I'm glad to be back at work, and I like this hospital; it has none of the baggage of DCH.' He moved back on the stool, stretching his long limbs. His face seemed slightly contorted with pain.

'I'll do something else long term. I'm working on a few plans.'

'It was terrible, the shooting. It must have affected you in lots of ways,' she said.

'You bet!'

But she knew that he was unlikely to dwell on the past and smiled her sweetest smile.

'I'm so glad things are getting better for you, but it was a difficult time. I mean, at the beginning, as a patient in the hospital.'

In time she would ask him more about his health, but for the moment she would let things settle. She noticed how he had changed – the stern focussed gaze was gone. Perhaps he had learnt to let go and not to challenge fate. And yet there was something inscrutable in his expression, an uncertainty at times.

It was his turn to lean forward now. 'So, enough about DCH. Tell me, what possessed you to do it. Was it on a whim? Or had you always had it in mind to run your own business? And why France? I'm intrigued!'

So she told him about how she had left the sailing crew and the difficulties of buying and setting up a business in France and the pitfalls encountered in the process. 'I still struggle with the language. Every day

I think it's getting worse and then I'm told that my French has come on enormously. It's been tough, very tough, but I'm glad I did it, although at times I missed home so much. I just wanted to run away from it all. I mean the responsibility, but it's not like a job, it's twenty four seven.'

He seemed genuinely interested, listening eagerly. She painted life in a small, rural town in France, describing the various characters. 'Mam thought that she was back in the fifties in Ireland with the women still wearing pinnies, feeling and smelling peaches and nectarines to make sure that they are just perfect'.

'Oh, I can imagine life down there in rural France. A bit like being transported back in time. Will you have another drink?'

She looked at her almost empty glass. 'Why not?'

She watched him as he strolled up to the bar. Pierre seemed to know everybody, and it took nearly twenty minutes for him to return such was the eagerness with which people greeted him. 'Sorry about that! My boat came first yesterday so I have to go and be presented with the cup shortly, but we still have time.'

The place became more animated and Rose-Ellen had to raise her voice to be heard. After a while, Pierre looked at his watch. 'Do you remember me talking about my Uncle Geoffrey? Well, he's not great at the moment, and I promised him that I would go out to France, maybe do some locum work and help him with the business. He's getting on and needs somebody around until he decides what to do with it. I'll tell you more later, but I must go now.' Then he stood and kissed her on the cheek before walking briskly away.

Later, after the presentation, Rose-Ellen met up with him again and introduced him to Brendan and Olivia, and they chatted until it was time for them to leave. As he was putting on his jacket, he said, 'When are you going back to France?'

'I'm here until the end of the month.'

'Would you like to go sailing with me sometime before you go, just like old times?'

'That would be lovely. I'll be at home or helping Dad in the shop and even if I'm not there, leave a message.'

He gave her another peck on the cheek and then sped down the steps.

The days passed and in no time Rose-Ellen would have to return to France. Disappointingly she had heard nothing from Pierre. 'He's not for you, my pet, a man like him; just not your type,' Kitty said dismissively.

Two days before she was due to leave for France, the phone rang. It was Pierre. 'Rose-Ellen, I'm so sorry. I meant to call you, but I got completely tied up with work, preparing research presentations, correcting papers and the finals. It's been hectic, but I hadn't forgotten that you were leaving at the end of the month, so how about dinner tomorrow night?' She had so many things to do on the night before she was to leave for France, but as she was unsure when they would meet again, she agreed.

'I'd love to, Pierre,' she replied.

So it was arranged that they would have dinner in a restaurant overlooking the pier in Wexford.

'What am I going to wear? I've packed everything for returning tomorrow. What about my simple black dress and a white scarf?' Rose-Ellen said to Kitty.

'No, not suitable attire for the evening. Too stark and severe, something more casual would be preferable.'

'No, that's it. I don't have time to go through my wardrobe.' Rose-Ellen had packed most of her clothes and she could still manage to fit into this black dress.

That night Pierre dropped by to collect her in an old Audi that had seen better days. Her mother watched from the window as the car swung into the driveway. 'Well, he might be into boats, but he's not in to cars, that's for sure.'

Rose-Ellen turned to her mother and said firmly, 'Mam, please.'

Her mother smiled and went to open the door. 'Good evening. You must be Dr O'Hegarty. Please come in, you are most welcome. I'm Kitty, Rose-Ellen's mother.'

Pierre greeted her warmly with a shake of his hand. '*Enchanté, Madame,*' he said, bowing slightly.

'Oh, I love a man with exquisite manners,' Kitty smiled. 'Rose-Ellen, Pierre is here to see you,' she said.

Kitty led him into the dining room and Rose-Ellen came from the bathroom where she had been combing her hair. Pierre smiled as he saw her and came over and greeted her with a kiss on the cheek. He wore a beige wool jacket with an open-necked shirt and light brown trousers. After some polite chatting with Kitty they left for the restaurant.

His car was untidy, a nautical smell pervaded the inside, and it had bits of rope and oilskins in the back. But she did not mind in the least and was just glad that he had contacted her again. He chatted on about various things, how his life was so busy and then he turned to look at her. 'How do you feel about returning to France after your long break?'

'Partly dreading it because I know that there will be so much to do, but I'm looking forward to it as well. It'll be good to get back,' she said, looking over at him and smiling.

They arrived at the restaurant on the quays. Rose-Ellen had known of its existence, but had never been there before. The cheerful waiter led them to a discreet table for two in the corner with a reserved sign. Pierre pulled back her chair and she sat down. The waiter handed them two large menus. Pierre perused the wine list and then the waiter arrived to take their orders.

Rose-Ellen relaxed after a glass of wine. Pierre laid his glass on the table and leaned back on the chair. 'I'm glad that I caught you before you returned to France.'

'But you know where my business is in France,' she said. She had stopped eating now, and laid her knife and fork on the plate.

'Rose-Ellen, I wanted to thank you for visiting me all those times when I was sick in hospital. I wasn't fully aware of who came in and out, but I do know that you were there a lot of the time, as was Moira. My sister Catherine and my Uncle Geoffrey told me which reminds me to give you back your stole, which you left one night.'

She put down her knife and fork at the mention of Moira. 'How is Moira?'

He twirled his wine glass. 'Oh, Moira. Well, dear Moira had to decide between me and those wretched horses of hers. I'm afraid the horses came first. She's a fine girl, really, but we just drifted further and further apart. Once she went over to the UK she became totally bound up in the whole competitive thing.'

'Oh, I'm sorry,' she said lamely.

'She's very happy over there, believe me. Suits her really.'

Rose-Ellen wanted to change the subject. 'Will you stay as a lecturer or have you other plans?'

'No, the lecturing is only for a while. As I said, I'll be going to France for some months shortly to help my uncle. He lives in the south of Brittany and is getting on. He wants to retire and get into something else, something a little less stressful. So I promised him that I would go over there for a few months and help out in the wintertime to close up the business. So perhaps when I'm in Brittany I'll drop down and pay *Chez-Ellen* a visit.'

'Well, you'd be most welcome,' she said, dabbing her lips.

'I'm setting up a medical consultancy. You know, if people want papers reviewed, corrected or edited, or writing up papers, either in French or English. The joys of the web, one can work *n'importe où*.'

Thank God, she thought to herself. She had at least managed to converse and understand everyday French and did not balk at Pierre's use of occasional French expressions. But it was cold comfort to her that her French was still in dire need of improvement. 'It would be very nice if you could visit me in France. It can get very lonely sometimes without anybody to speak English to, though my French is coming on slowly. I still find it hard, but I'm glad that I've taken the plunge to do what I want.'

'So is it easier now living in France?'

'Indeed it is.'

'Is it where you want to live or just to be based for the time being? I mean starting up a business there would imply some type of permanency,' he said.

'Home will always be Ireland, it's where I grew up and where my parents live, but France is now where I want to live and I suppose it's another type of home, but real home is here in Ireland. And what about you?' she asked cautiously.

'My home,' he smiled, 'that is a good question. I've never really had a home as such like you; perhaps that's why I love the sea so much. Now, before I forget let's exchange mobile numbers.'

She reached down and got her handbag from under the table. 'Quite. If you don't give me your mobile number now, I'll forget about it!' she said. 'My memory's gone to the dogs lately. I suppose having to remember everything.'

'Comes with running your own business, I suppose,' he said.

They entered each other's phone numbers in to their mobiles, and the pleasant evening passed too quickly for Rose-Ellen, and soon it was time to leave. Pierre remained silent in the car as he drove her home.

When they arrived at *Uisce Gaire* all was in darkness, and only a dim street light guided her way to the front door. She searched for the front door keys and as usual they were buried at the bottom of her handbag. Oh, why did they always disappear just when she needed them, she wondered. She rummaged and fumbled and ended up taking most of the contents out of her bag, placing them on the wall until she found them. All this time, Pierre stood and watched the performance and smiled. Shoving everything back into the bag she turned to him and said, 'I'm always the same with keys. I'll have to get a whistle or light for them. Pierre, thank you again for the lovely evening. I really enjoyed it and I'm glad that we were able to meet again.'

'So am I, and it was my pleasure. It's the least I could do for visiting me all those times in hospital…' And then he stopped.

She looked at him wistfully now, and wondered if he had only taken her out for dinner out of gratitude for her having visited him in hospital. She felt hurt. He seemed a bit embarrassed. 'Of course I wanted to invite you out tonight, Rose-Ellen; that wasn't the only reason,' he added. Her expression softened. 'Anyway, it's late,' and he drew close to her. She could see his expression and outline under the street light. He was smiling now. 'Come here and let me kiss you goodnight,' he said. He put his arms around her waist and kissed her. She responded by putting her arms on his shoulders. She could have kissed him for ever there and then, just the two of them, so delicious was that fleeting moment in the dark as he held her in his arms. 'I'll see you in France,' he said. 'I know where you are, and don't worry. I'll be in touch.' Then he strode towards his car and before getting in, turned and waved to her.

Rose-Ellen mounted the stairs that night still savouring the kiss with Pierre. It was all that she had thought it would be. She was deliriously happy with the evening. The thought made her tremble with excitement.

Chapter 48

Rose-Ellen had returned to bedlam at *Chez-Ellen*. Mounds of bills awaited her from builders, suppliers, telephone and electricity companies, invoices for this and reminders for that, but most worryingly, there was a letter from the bank to say that she had defaulted on her mortgage payment for last month, the month of August. After pouring herself a glass of champagne, she strolled out into the garden and wondered how she was going to pay these outstanding bills.

Jean-François had been assigned to look after the ducks and chickens when she was away and he had at least cut the grass, but the place had an untidy and neglected air about it. Faithful clumps of lavender were growing everywhere, their long spears of two-toned deep mauve flowers swaying as brown and white butterflies flitted and danced in the long sheaves, like coins falling in slow motion.

She checked on the goats and found that they had vanished. She could see where one of them, probably Niamh, had made her way out under the wire fence which was only a gap of several inches. Edwina must have jumped the enclosure that Finn had built. She wondered where they could have gone. Grabbing her car keys she hoped that as both were female and thoroughly spoiled they would not have gone far. She drove round and round out to the countryside calling them by their names, but to no avail. She was worried as Monsieur Gremont had warned her about the many plants that are poisonous for goats. Then just as she had given up all hope while returning *via* another route, she spied the pair of them, on the side of the road reaching up as far as they could stretch over a ditch, feasting on brambles and some wild gorse.

'Niamh, Edwina!' she roared out the window, but they turned away and resumed munching. She then got out of the car with the rope and called soothingly at them, waving the bag in which she kept their treats. They were just about to continue munching when she rattled the goody bag. Niamh looked at her and then glanced at the bag and, within nanoseconds, they both scampered down the ditch nuzzling up and nibbling at her hand while trying to grab the bag. 'Oh, my little darlings, what if anything had happened to you!' she said, rubbing them furiously. As they were happily nibbling on the treats she tied the rope to their collars and led them to the trailer and then shoved them in, but in doing so noticed how long and mangy their coats had become and how they both desperately needed to be milked.

When they returned, Rose-Ellen put the pair back in their enclosure and got almost three and a half litres of milk from each. She suspected that Jean-Francois still could not milk them despite all the lessons she had given him. With their udders empty and their bellies full, the two goats skipped and danced as if delighted at the resumption of the routine life that they had been denied for the past month. Rose-Ellen did a temporary job on the fencing. She realised that she would have to trim their hooves which were becoming curly.

Relishing the cool champagne and listening to the quiet whisperings of the last of the season's wildlife and insects, Rose-Ellen contemplated the future. It would be so tempting to walk away and close the door behind her, but sooner or later the unpaid bills and other demands would haunt her.

That afternoon Delphine called around with Paidraigin in her cat box. 'How are you, *ma cherie*?' Delphine said, hugging her friend with the customary French greeting.

'Oh, my time at home was wonderful, Delphine, just wonderful, but so, so short!'

'Well you have a certain, I'm not sure what it is, let's say a certain look that seems to indicate that something romantic happened when you were in Ireland. *N'est ce pas?*'

'Well, yes. I met Pierre and we went out one night, and guess what?'

'Tell me and don't tell me!'

'He's coming to France to work for his uncle!' Rose-Ellen clapped her hands and laughed as her face lit up with glee, but Delphine sat there implacably and said nothing.

'Pierre's Uncle Geoffrey asked Pierre if he would come and live with him in Nantes for a few months to help out with his business, and Pierre agreed. His uncle is old and becoming frail, and life on the sea, whilst once exciting, is now becoming difficult. Pierre will carry on his medical consultancy from France at the same time.'

'That is very convenient for you, *n'est pas?*' Delphine watched Paidraigin who had wandered off. 'I think she is more interested in the smells in the garden than in you, her mistress,' Delphine said coolly.

The next few weeks were hectic as Rose-Ellen tried to make up for the time away. She became quite despondent; anxiety about the taxman, bills to be paid, trying to catch up on tasks unfinished all weighed heavily on her mind, and at times she wondered if her hard work had all been in vain. The bank manager was less than supportive as she tried to explain the difficulties she encountered running the business, but he just removed his glasses and said laconically to her, 'Starting a business here in France is not easy, and you must realise that if you default any more on your monthly payments we will have to involve a third party, and this is not a very pleasant experience for anybody as they will want to see all of your payments, expenses etc.' She was terrified that all her hard work would founder in a short while if she did not take stock.

'I'm sorry, I did go away to Ireland for a month, but I had not been home for nearly two years and my parents are not getting any younger. I will ensure that there are sufficient funds for payments each month. I'm sorry that this has happened.'

But he looked at her sceptically and said, 'This is a warning to you not to default. You could lose everything. Perhaps you do not realise that it is extremely serious in France to be overdrawn in your bank account. We do not tolerate any kind of defaulting of this nature; it is simply not in our culture.'

Her frustrated desires caused her to snap and appear short-tempered to those around her. While Jean-François was gentle and polite, he was young, immature and self-absorbed, only undertaking what he had to do. 'Sometimes I wonder if you understand me at all or else you just care to ignore me, Jean-Francois. I wonder which it is, or is it a bit of both?'

There were times when Rose-Ellen craved for the simple joy of peace and quiet as she sat in the garden and listened to the gentle hum of the evenings while rubbing Edwina's head on her lap. She loved the rustle of the shimmering leaves of the poplars, or the gentle plop of the plums as they fell to the ground. The day-to-day cut and thrust of surviving in business made her truly relish these moments of silence alone in her garden. She watched the little squirrel with his white tuxedo scampering around the garden picking up those uneaten fruits, quickly soaring up a tree at the least movement.

Rose-Ellen contracted a severe chest infection within a few weeks of returning home. She suspected she might have got something on the plane or her immune system was compromised with the stress of running her business on her own. She was on a second course of antibiotics, but her chest rattled and she nearly choked each time she coughed. Kitty Power came over to be with her daughter, but insisted on travelling alone.

Once in France, Kitty rolled up her sleeves and tidied, cleaned, scrubbed and dusted the place, preparing hot drinks and light meals, changing the sheets every day and sweeping out and airing, *Chez-Ellen*, so that it was spic and span. 'I don't want you getting any infections, any MRSA or whatever they call it,' Kitty said.

'Mam, you only get that in hospital,' Rose-Ellen said, flicking through some magazines Kitty had brought over with her.

'Still, there's no point in taking any chances,' Kitty said, punching a huge square-shaped pillow and sending up a cloud of fluttering feathers.

'You won't be able to keep this up, and I'll just get used to it.'

Kitty looked at her sternly. 'You're doing too much as it is. You need to rest, even at your age,' Kitty said, firmly pointing a long orange and brown feather duster at her daughter.

Jean-François, who was running *Chez-Ellen* with the help of Charlotte Dempsey during Rose-Ellen's recovery, tried to keep out of Kitty's way. Charlotte Dempsey baked breads and cakes for *Chez-Ellen* as well as her own *'plats du jour'* and Ollie kept up the stock. Chantal ran the restaurant and Kitty lent a hand anywhere she was needed. Ollie Dempsey agreed to look after Niamh and Edwina as they had escaped again and had wandered into Madame Blanchard's *patisserie* and the mayor had been called.

Six weeks after her ordeal, Pierre phoned to say that he would drop by and arrived in the evening from work. Rose-Ellen was up in bed touching up her make-up. Pierre arrived up the stairs and kissed her as soon as he came into the room.

'Hello, *cherie*, how are you?'

'Well, I'm much better thank you, Pierre, and I'm being utterly spoiled here,' she said, glancing over at Kitty who was smoothing the bedclothes. 'Sit here and we can chat,' she said, patting the bedclothes beside her.

'The tea's all ready downstairs. I'll go and fetch it and then head off for a walk. I won't be long, love, but I'm sure you both have a lot to catch up on,' Kitty said, and then went downstairs.

'Thanks, Mam,' Rose-Ellen called after her.

Rose-Ellen reached out and took Pierre's hands in hers. 'It's so good to see you again, Pierre.'

'You've been unlucky, Rose-Ellen with that nasty chest infection. I can still hear it.'

'I've been quite worried about the business, so have been neglecting myself.'

'Stress! That dreadful common denominator of all our woes. You must look after yourself; there is so much depending on you,' he said, as he sat down on the bed.

Kitty came back into the room at that moment and laid the tray with the tea and china service on a small table near the bed. 'Well, I'll let you two catch up with the news and the gossip,' Kitty said.

Pierre gave Rose-Ellen an amused smile and thanked Kitty. He then poured the tea and handed a cup to Rose-Ellen. They both burst out laughing. 'Your mother is…em, how shall I say? An amusing character,' he said.

'Oh, you wouldn't believe how she is relishing her new role of nurse to me. She's like a spinning top; up and down the stairs, dusting, polishing, sweeping. I think she loves the idea of being here with me in France, and getting away from Dad and the deli. She's become an authority on all brands of detergents and cleansing liquids here, threw out all the ones I had, and now the place is smelling like a public lavatory with all the bleach she's lashing on everything.'

He smiled at her. 'How are you feeling despite everything?'

'Well, I got some dose of it. I've never felt so low and the antibiotics drain one.'

'Yes, I'm afraid that's to be expected.'

'But I'm on the mend. Think positively, that's my motto.'

She looked at him over the rim of the china tea cup. 'How are things working out for you? You must be busy with your uncle's new venture.'

'Indeed. But you know, I actually like this type of work. I didn't think I would, and of course he needs all the help he can get.' He looked out of the window. 'My poor uncle. I wish that he would retire and take it easy. He's seventy-eight, for goodness' sake.' He turned to her and smiled. 'But you know the French, they think that they can live forever. He has great plans for setting up a school for mariners and this is where I could help, but at least the boat-building business has now finally gone down to Monaco.'

'That's great. I know it had been a worry for you. I mean, trying to sell it.'

'Precisely. And getting the right price, too. After all, the business was like his child and he hated letting it go, but time marches on and he simply doesn't have the energy or drive any more for running a business.'

'Don't I know!' she said, laying her cup on her bedside table. 'And you? Are you getting any work with the medical consultancy?'

His expression softened. 'Yes, it's not bad. I'm also getting quite a bit of consultancy work in French. I'm also doing some locum work in hospitals in Nantes and La Rochelle. Oncologists are in big demand.'

'That's terrific!'

He came over and sat on the bed. 'Look, Rose-Ellen, I want to tell you something and that is, well, how shall I put it?' He took her hand in his. She watched him as he stroked her hand. 'I want to be near you so that we can spend more time with each other, and so I have decided to base myself permanently in La Rochelle.'

Rose-Ellen leaned over and gave Pierre a hug. 'Oh, Pierre, that would be wonderful if we could be together.'

'It's a big country France and I want to be near you. It would make me very happy,' he said, lifting her moist hand to his lips. 'It would make sense and I realised how much you meant to me when you visited me in hospital, and then when we met in Wexford I started to think about what was important in life. Oh, darling, I hope that you don't mind me being candid and telling you how I feel,' he said.

'Oh, Pierre, I'm just so happy that we'll be near each other and that you feel that same way as I do,' she said shyly, reaching out and clasping him to her. They talked for a few hours about all that had happened until such time as Rose-Ellen began to experience a wave of tiredness that seemed to envelop her.

'Pierre, I'm sorry, would you mind if I had a little snooze? I seem to tire easily since my illness. I feel quite exhausted,' she said, lying back on the pillow.

'It'll take a while for you to get back your old energy. Try and get as much rest as you can in the next few weeks. Your system has been through quite an ordeal, so patience, *ma cherie*.' He gave her a kiss, got up and returned the cups to the tray. 'I'll call soon again.' He knotted his scarf. 'I'm with a friend of mine, Pascale, and will head on up towards Nantes in the morning.'

'I understand, it's a fair way to go.'

'Goodnight, and I'll see you soon,' he said, as he blew her a kiss in the doorway.

Later that evening Kitty sat with Rose-Ellen. 'I must say Pierre is a fine gentleman if ever there was one, and so handsome. I never realised he was so tall. God almighty, his legs seem never-ending.'

'Yes, he's a handsome one,' Rose-Ellen said.

'Now, to other matters. I'll have to go home soon. Ah, you know your father can't cope without me and I think you're over the worst. Just one piece of advice, darling. Look after yourself and be good to Pierre, because I think he's very fond of you, and indeed I know a lovelorn soul when I see one. Believe you me!'

'What do you mean Mam?'

'Oh, I think you know damn well what I mean. I don't have to spell it out.'

Over the next few months, Pierre moved down to La Rochelle where he based himself managing to get a temporary research position in one of the large hospitals there. Having slowly regained her strength, Rose-Ellen resumed work again at the same fretful speed.

They sat one evening in *Chez-Ellen*, Pierre in the armchair and Rose-

Ellen resting on the rug at his feet, looking out at the back garden. Pierre stroked her hair. 'You know,' she said, 'I never visualised us here together in France like this. I remember that awful time in DCH when you would hardly look at me over the whole Shay business.' She turned to face him. 'Does that surprise you?'

He moved forward and drew her to him. 'Yes, it was a dreadful time and one best forgotten. I was a different person then. I could only see what I wanted to see, and that was that the department was crumbling. Dr Doolan was hardly able to cope and smack in the middle of it all stood a very unreliable and selfish person.' He put his arms on her shoulders and she leaned back and looked up into his eyes. They had that sad look that she had occasionally noticed. 'I didn't appreciate all that you were doing at the time, and then there was Moira with all of her demands,' he said wearily. She manoeuvred herself up and sat on his knees. He kissed her on the forehead and then on the lips. She could feel his mouth on hers, eager and longing. He brushed her hair back and spoke soothingly to her. 'Rose-Ellen, I can't tell you the number of times I lay awake and thought of what you'd gone through, and I blame myself completely for it.'

'Don't, Pierre, it doesn't matter anymore. What is done is done and now we are here. That's all that counts,' she said, snuggling up against him. Now they would have no secrets.

'You know what I love about you, Pierre, is that you're not judgemental. Then there's all the unpredictability of my life, breaking it off with Danny and then Finn, You must think me a heartless bitch at times, but you're… well, how shall I put it? You're too much of a gentleman to keep reminding me of my failings I suppose.'

'Well, you broke off your engagement to Danny and so that is past, but what about O'Donnell?' he asked.

Rose-Ellen thought of Finn and how she had just brushed him out of her life when Pierre dropped by into the café. 'Oh, Pierre, I feel terrible about Finn, he was so good to me and helpful. I still can't believe that I just casually invited him out here and yes, I'll be honest, we were involved, but then when you came by that afternoon with your friends, I started to feel differently towards him. I can't really explain.'

He looked at her. 'I don't understand, *cherie*.'

'Pierre, when you were ill in hospital I came to visit you many times. Sometimes you were aware of me being there, other times not, but over the weeks, my feelings for you changed, maybe your vulnerability, who knows, but I knew that something deep and profound was happening to me regarding my feelings for you.'

'And your feelings for O'Donnell now?'

'Of course I can't just forget Finn. You can't just airbrush somebody out of your life like that. I am not that clinical and cold!'

'I wonder if you know what you want, Rose-Ellen, maybe grasping at something elusive.'

'You see, I don't know how to say this but I suppose I have grown to love you a little more each day. When we were in DCH our relationship was different, professional, but over the last few months I have seen another side to you, a vulnerable side too, and I realise that I have very deep feelings for you. Now I've said it!'

He drew her to him. 'I thank you for your honesty, my love. You know the first time you came for the interview at DCH, your beauty, carriage and liveliness attracted me, but we were working together in the straight-laced atmosphere of a hospital and I had to behave in a certain way. I couldn't let my feelings run away with me. But one day we were out on the boat together and I nearly let my emotions fly away with me, but I remembered that you had a boyfriend. You must have picked up on my responses. Do you remember that day?'

'And then there was Moira,' she said.

'True, but Moira is very different to you. She is hard and tough, needing to be so focussed on that Olympic Gold for eventing. One has to be almost ruthless and that is a side to her that I was seeing more and more of as time went by. You know, I started comparing her to you consciously, and then I dismissed this idea of comparison as I realised it was hopeless. You were engaged to Danny and then we lost contact. When I met you in the restaurant that day, and you were with O'Donnell, that was the end as far as I was concerned, until of course we bumped into each other in Wexford.'

'And things could have been so, so different,' she murmured.

'Ah, such is life.'

Rose-Ellen was thrilled that Pierre had come to stay in La Rochelle and their love was taking on a new dimension. She loved having him close to her knowing that each time he left it would only be a short time when they would see each other again. No matter how weighed down she became with the business, she could rely on Pierre's love for her.

Although Pierre was based in La Rochelle he spent most of his free time either sailing off the coast or with Rose-Ellen and her menagerie in that charming French village. She suspected that it was the first time in many years that Pierre had felt some kind of homeliness with her in *Chez-Ellen* despite its mad and frenetic pace with the business and the animals. They explored the surrounds on bikes and occasionally she went sailing with him, but mostly they were content to sit at the fire and relish each other's company. He also taught her to love the French language. '*Cherie*, you must enjoy speaking this beautiful language. If you do, it will come to you, don't resist it.'

She looked at him and wondered if he knew the constant struggle she was having with masculine and feminine nouns, tenses and the subjunctive. 'Oh, Pierre, you make it sound so easy, but I find it endlessly difficult. Just when I think I've mastered it, I turn on the radio and feel as if I'm listening to double Dutch,' she sighed with dismay.

'It will come slowly and gradually, but,' he held her close and looked at her, 'you must be patient. Excellence only comes with time, application, dedication and a huge amount of patience.' And patience was something she was learning all about in France.

Rose-Ellen had always prided herself on being a *connoisseur* of the finer things in life. However, it was from Pierre that she learnt to truly appreciate the pleasures of wine: when to drink it and with what, good and lesser vintages, storing it, but most important of all, its taste. He introduced her to the world of wines from *Tuscany* and *Alsace*, as well as the *vin jeune* of the *Franche Compte* and the delicious and refreshing wines of the *Savoie*. One day after sampling an array of wines which Pierre had produced from Uncle Geoffrey's cellar, Rose-Ellen was feeling somewhat maudlin.

'I've learnt so much from you, Pierre, darling Pierre. Oh, I'm sorry. I've probably drunk too much, but I had to tell you how much I love you and appreciate everything I've learnt from you since the first time I met you in DCH. Now I've said it,' and with that she collapsed on the sofa.

'*Cherie*, don't apologise, it is nothing and if I can help in any way, I'm always happy to do so, and then again it gives me so much pleasure to look at you when you are happy, to see your eyes sparkle with a certain radiance. So regret nothing, *cherie*,' he said, sitting down beside her and taking her in his arms.

Chapter 49

One night warm night at the end of November, Rose-Ellen invited Pierre to dinner. She spent hours preparing a delicious meal, ensuring everything was perfect: candles, her finest lace tablecloth and napkins, a warm fire, and a fine selection of the best wines. Pierre arrived shortly after eight with a beautiful bunch of her favourite white roses, sprinkled with gardenia and some greenery.

'I simply love fresh flowers! Thank you so much, Pierre, you're very thoughtful,' she said, as she took them from him.

'The pleasure is all mine, *cherie*,' he said, giving her a big hug. He looked around the place. 'I love this room, Rose-Ellen! And each time I come, you have done a little more with it,' he said.

She watched him as he stood beside the beautiful pink and cream *Sèvres* china coffee set on the dresser, admiring the paintings of elegant ladies with their parasols, coiffed heads under elaborate hats and flouncy dresses billowing on a beach. His eye took in the graceful organdie cream and gold curtains which hung elegantly in folds from the high wooden beam, and the lovely old pink and lime floral chintz settee. But most of all he admired her own paintings. 'I love this one in particular,' he said out loud.

'Which one?' Rose-Ellen said, mixing *Dijon* mustard and a little white wine for the sauce.

'The rich red cherries sitting in the blue bowl beside a block of real butter.'

'That's one of my favourites and it was done here in France when the cherry tree was bursting with rich ripe fruit. I just plonked a bunch of cherries into the first bowl I saw and then I thought that the rich red, pale blue and yellow were a lovely combination.'

He noticed the others: the weeping willows leaning into the Charente River as it meandered through lush green parklands with pretty houses set back off its embankments, or the placid herd of peaceful cream-coloured cows in a meadow under a large oak tree.

Dinner consisted of oysters in champagne, followed by guinea fowl with grape and thyme, perfectly matured local cheeses and carefully chosen wines to match each course. Everything went perfectly well until the coffee was poured. Rose-Ellen had relaxed for the first time in many months but had drunk too much. She brought her coffee over to the fire and laid the cup gently on the saucer and said, 'Pierre, I never really told you how angry I felt about the whole business at DCH. I suppose I was afraid of dragging up the past again. I didn't want to upset you, when all the time I was the one who had been hurt.' She looked at him and her voice had a strange, deep timbre. 'Do you know how that affected me? Have you any idea? I felt like the scapegoat.' She abstractedly got up and rearranged some of the flowers in the large crystal vase, then took her wine glass from the mantelpiece.

Pierre stretched out his legs while looking into the fire which had now lost its blaze. 'Rose-Ellen, looking back, I know that I should have been more vigilant about what was going on in the department. But I trusted McAdam, as, by the way, did many others in the hospital. He had us all fooled.' She could sense that he felt slightly unnerved as she stood in front of him. 'But you know, hindsight is a wonderful thing, and as you said yourself you've made a complete turnaround of your life for the better. Now, please, *cherie*, don't dwell on the past, you've got to move on,' he said, looking at her. He reached out his hand to hold hers, but she ignored this gesture.

'Life for the better, complete turnaround? Oh yes, things look lovely and rosy to you and to everyone else from the outside here in this place, but believe you me it's been an enormous struggle and mighty difficult sometimes. I could be facing bankruptcy,' she said, her voice almost cracking with emotion. He eased himself up from the chair by the fire.

'Darling, don't cry. I hate to see you upset like this, he said, trying to reassure her. 'I remember those unpaid bills some time ago, Rose-Ellen. It's not like business in Ireland. It's as if they don't want you to succeed here in France. I don't understand it. My Uncle Geoffrey had an endless struggle trying to set up his business. He was always borrowing from my father. I remember it so well.

'I've seen my French family members go under here for not paying their bills. You'll lose everything in the end if you're not careful. It's time to stop the sweet talk and face up to reality. I want to help you, if you'll allow me. Look, I'll even put up the money for you and we can come to some arrangement,' he said, looking deep into her eyes.

But she was furious now. How dare he decide that she was incapable of running her own affairs and needed to be bailed out! She picked up her wine glass and took a large gulp. 'For Christ sake, don't you start! You're as bad as the rest of them with their bloody bills and *factures* for everything here. I'm bloody well sick of it! I'm paying those effing bills bit by bit, but then there's always something else to pay. It's never-ending!'

'Please, Rose-Ellen, listen to me, for God's sake. Don't let pride take over and dictate things. I only want to help, you know that. I hate to see you upsetting yourself needlessly. Yes, needlessly, because it doesn't have to be like this. Listen to me, will you, please!'

She looked away from him and into the fire. She was very sensitive when it came to *Chez-Ellen*, after all, it was hers and hers alone, not his or her father's, and nobody would tell her how to run things, and she certainly did not need anybody's charity, even if the intentions were well meant.

'I wouldn't say these things if I didn't care about you and wanted to help. Please believe me,' Pierre said, trying to offer some reassurance.

She looked at him coldly. After all, it was really none of his concern. 'I know what you're thinking,' she said. 'That I can't manage my own affairs. Isn't that it? Well, it's not like that. I want to do something worthy with my life. I don't want to be continuously beholden to others, or to some kind of authority all of my life. God knows I had enough of that in nursing, and, well after DCH, you should understand my feelings more than anybody else.' Tossing her head she said, 'And another thing, where were you when I had to take the flack for that bastard McAdam? Off sailing around in a bloody yacht race!'

She had landed a blow. Her anger about her spell in DCH had been simmering all this time and had now come to the surface. She was at breaking point and the tone of her voice reflected her anger. All the resentment and regret she had harboured since her departure from DCH was now emerging like some wretched boil in need of lancing.

'I'm sorry if I've offended you. No hurt was intended. I was merely trying to help.'

Pierre reached for his jacket and made for the door, but before leaving he turned and looked at her. 'I was hoping for some change of heart, a spark of clemency perhaps. Oh, darling, please don't spoil the night. Look, what's done is done and I'm trying every day to make it all up to you and help. Please, can't you see,' he said, returning and placing his coat on the back of the chair, 'I'd do anything to erase the past.'

But all this time she remained implacably staring into the fire, an almost empty wine glass in her hand. 'You're just like the rest of them, fending for yourself. All the work I put in to that job, doing my best for the patients and the auditors. And all for what? For bloody nothing!' she said, staring at the flames. She was fuming with anger.

Pierre looked at the floor, downcast. 'Rose-Ellen, I understand that you're angry, and rightly so. I'm sorry – I did leave a lot to you and if I could have that time back again I'd make it up to you a hundredfold. I'm going, but please know that I've had many regrets since the shooting, regrets about you, and the job, what could have been. Oh, I could go on.' He stopped and then opened the door and let himself out.

When he had gone she watched him through the window as he got into his car and sped out of the village. She returned to her seat and polished off the remainder of the bottle of wine. Furious with everything, her life and now the business, she screamed in exasperation and threw the glass against the mantelpiece. It splintered into tiny pieces, the fragments of crystal a reminder of the night's blighted end. Having exposed her vulnerability and a nastier side, Rose-Ellen hoped that she would not live to regret her bad behaviour. She looked into the dying fire and all she could see was the mendacious smile of McAdam among the ashes, and she froze. She mounted the stairs to a cold bed to find Paidraigin waiting for her, tidily curled up in a neat little ball, enthralled by the luxury to which she had become accustomed and oblivious to the awful troubles of her owner.

Rose-Ellen woke the next day with a heavy heart, and the bittersweet tang of self-pity enveloped her. She felt wretched both from what she had said but also from having drunk too much. She took two painkillers which only shifted the pain from the front of her head to the rear, but at least gave the illusion of having worked. In daylight, and able to focus more clearly, she realised that last night's behaviour would only alienate those nearest to her. Stubbornness and arrogance were her Achilles heel and her father had warned her that they would be her downfall. *Chez-Ellen* was dominating her thoughts and very being, and she wondered if it had made her as tough and unyielding as steel, unwilling to listen to others or to relinquish her new grasp on power.

Her self-disgust gnawed away at her all day and the next, and she could not concentrate. Although she sought to justify her outburst with Pierre, in fact, there had been no reason for her bad behaviour. Rose-Ellen was ashamed of her selfishness. Had not Pierre suffered far more from McAdam than she ever would? He had nearly died. She doubted if he would ever forgive such pettiness, and why should he be bothered with her anymore?

Alone in France, struggling to make ends meet and having nobody with whom she could really communicate had made her independent and isolated. She confided in Delphine who listened carefully and then spoke solemnly to her. '*Cherie*, if you are interested in having a relationship with Pierre, you must learn to be more considerate. After all he has been through perhaps you could show a little more sensitivity. It was a pity that you had taken so much wine. A little wine is good, but too much…we get…how do you say? Sentimental and aggressive.'

Despite certain reservations and misgivings she had had about what had happened at DCH, Rose-Ellen still harboured deep feelings for Pierre. Now she had ruined it all in one night because of an overindulgence in drink and self-pity. Because of her unwillingness to compromise, to take advice when it had been given so generously, Pierre was gone. It appalled her how she had thrown back his offer of help almost begrudgingly. She realised that she ought to have been more sensitive to everything that he had been through: the nightmare scenario of having been shot and almost killed by some crazed madman, the lingering injuries and the psychological trauma of such an experience. She supposed that she would never see Pierre again. The trust and friendship built up between them would be lost, and harder to regain. Their past together would only be a memory now.

While Rose-Ellen liked the idea of owning her own business, she was slowly coming to terms with the toll that such an enterprise took. It would have been so much easier in an ordinary job, working for another, to up and leave and go to La Rochelle and make herself available to Pierre. But she simply could not walk away from her responsibilities. Contemplating everything she had done in her time in France, if she did not take stock, it would all simply vanish. Reflecting on the hours spent creating the business, all the little touches which she had added to the place, the devotion to her customers, all meant little to her now. Her fragile relationship with Pierre was ruined – shattered – in a moment of madness. She would write to Pierre, but would he reply?

Getting through the rest of the week and the following one was unbearable, but when she had regained sufficient composure she decided to send him a letter. After several attempts at writing, she tore up the pages.

But he never did contact her again and the days rolled by into weeks. Unable to sleep, Rose-Ellen rose in the middle of the night and paced the floor of the bedroom, mulling over what had happened, re-living the events of the last dreadful encounter with him, finally dragging herself back to bed to cry hopelessly into her pillow.

One day in December, realising that Pierre was probably gone forever, but determined to make one last chance at contact, Rose-Ellen picked up pen and paper and started to write. She thought of losing him and what it would mean. Being apart from him filled her with dread. She tried to push through the dark shadows that lurked deep within her, so that she could put her thoughts down on paper, but it was not easy.

Dear Pierre,

I am sorry about my outburst to you after our dinner together. I realise that I acted hastily and appreciate that you were only trying to assist someone who is too stubborn and proud to accept help when it comes her way. I am under a lot of strain at present, but there was no excuse for my bad behaviour. You are right, I must try and put the past behind me and move on.
I hope that we can meet again.

Rose-Ellen

Folding the page neatly in half, she gently put it inside the envelope and kissed the flap as she pressed it, recalling their sweet moments together. She went down to the post office to post the letter.

He would receive her letter; how he would respond was anybody's guess. She had to wait now; he was hurt and it would be a long time before he would consider contacting her, if ever. Rose-Ellen knew that in order to understand Pierre, his reserve, his independence and his *hauteur*, she would have to change towards him and make a place for him within her own heart. If she really loved him, his uniqueness would need to be respected.

In hindsight, she realised that Pierre was wise and correct in his thinking. After all, he had lived here in France for a large part of his life, and was half-French. He knew and understood the French way of life as she never would. In trying to set up her business in France, she was losing sight of the enduring things in life: friendship, trust, loyalty and love.

Chapter 50

A week later, Rose-Ellen returned from several gruelling hours of ordering stock and settling her finances with Ollie and Charlotte Dempsey. She was tired and lately felt depressed. She saw that her message light was flashing on the phone. She pressed the play button to hear the recorded message.

'Hello, Rose-Ellen, Brendan here. I'm afraid that I've some bad news. Kitty's been taken ill. To cut a long story short, she's in hospital in Wexford in the ICU. You should come home as soon as you can. Don't worry about getting home to Wexford. We'll collect you from Dublin airport. I don't like relaying bad news, but try and get on the next flight if you can'.

She flopped limply on the sofa; numb. It did not sound good judging from the portentous tone of the message. She tried to call her father but there was no reply at *Uisce Gaire* or in the emporium. Olivia's mobile rang out as well. Finally she called Brendan back.

'Ah, thank God you've called. I was getting worried,' he said.

'What happened? How's Mam?' Rose-Ellen's voice was nearly breaking with emotion. She could sense Brendan taking a deep breath.

'I don't want to alarm you, but you need to come home right away. Apparently your mother got a pain in her chest the other day out in the garden, a sort of tightness. Olivia called the doctor immediately. Kitty's had a heart attack.'

Rose-Ellen froze when she heard the words 'heart attack'. She tried to let the dreadful news sink in. She had known that her mother's two brothers had both died in their fifties from heart-related causes. Then she recalled her Dad's words, 'The Whelan men have strong bodies but weak hearts'.

As Ollie drove her to the airport, Rose-Ellen could barely hold back the tears. All she wanted to do was to see her mother. 'Oh, Ollie, I can't believe what's happened. Mam was never sick a day in her life.'

Ollie kept his eye on the road to the airport. 'I'm sorry for your trouble, Rose-Ellen, really I am. I'm not good at this sort of talk, Charlotte is better. I'm sorry she couldn't be here with you. But they can do a lot for heart attacks now; it's not the end of the road by any means. I remember my own father had a heart attack and lived for fifteen years after it.'

But Rose-Ellen was not listening to him. She dried her eyes with a piece of tissue paper, wet and in shreds from crying and looked out the window, her mind miles away.

Brendan and Olivia met her at Dublin airport and they drove straight to the hospital. Hardly anybody spoke on the way down. Rose-Ellen looked at Olivia whose young, soft eyes looked tired and red from crying and sleepless nights. Kitty was in a private cubicle in the coronary care unit in the local hospital. Rose-Ellen sat at her bedside and clutched her mother's cold hand. She sensed that Kitty was aware of her presence as every now and then she could feel her soft voice trying to talk to her under the oxygen mask. Rose-Ellen asked the consultant after rounds the next day as to her mother's prognosis, but he was not hopeful.

'Your mother's had a major heart attack I'm afraid. If she survives this, her quality of life will be poor.' Then he looked at Rose-Ellen sternly, the way doctors do when imparting grave news, and said, 'I think you should be prepared for the worst.'

Rose-Ellen stayed with Kitty for two days, barely leaving the small cramped cubicle with its various machines. Maurice wandered in and out, mumbling to himself. He had not shaved for a few days and stubble was bristling on his still fine skin. His thick grey hair was uncombed and his jumper had fresh stains on the front. He seemed to be in a world of his own and sometimes Rose-Ellen felt he did not really understand the gravity of the situation. But she could only think of her mother. Olivia seemed to be permanently in a trance and jumped with fright every time a nurse came into the cubicle. One afternoon, Olivia sat on one side of the bed clutching Kitty's hand. Rose-Ellen sat on the other side.

'Oh, Mam, please, please don't die. I'd be devastated if anything happened to you. What would we do?' Olivia said, turning her tearful eyes to Rose-Ellen, who mechanically flicked through a glossy magazine as she tried to take her mind briefly away from the immediate drama.

Rose-Ellen woke with a start in the early hours of the morning of the third day when her mother gripped her hand tightly. Kitty thrust aside her oxygen mask and seemed to rally.

'Mam, are you OK?' Kitty sat up in bed, gasping for air. Her colour was a pale ashen grey. 'Nurse!' Rose-Ellen shouted. The nurse left her desk and rushed to Rose-Ellen. 'Get a doctor, I think my mother's going,' Rose-Ellen said frantically to the frightened young nurse.

Rose-Ellen held Kitty and cried. 'Oh, Mam, please don't go, hang on in there. Someone will be here in a minute. Please, please, Mam don't go, not yet.'

Within several minutes two doctors arrived to find Rose-Ellen holding her mother and weeping inconsolably.

'It's too late, too late. She's gone!'

She would always remember sitting with Olivia and her Dad in the day room in the hospital after Kitty had died. A nurse had brought in tea and biscuits. 'I can't believe I'll never see her again; out in the garden or baking. It's so unreal,' Olivia said, crying, her head on Rose-Ellen's lap. Rose-Ellen felt as if her life was temporarily on hold. She wished that she had seen Kitty alert and like her old self before she had died. After a while she got up and walked to the window and looked out.

'Yes, that's the worst part,' she said. 'Knowing I'll never see her again.'

Maurice sat there numbed by the whole traumatic almost dreamlike episode, popping the digestive biscuits mechanically into his mouth and taking great gulps of milky tea.

All around the house lay reminders of Kitty's untimely demise: the unfinished cakes and half-knit pullovers awaiting completion by the master's hand. A final testament to how active their mother had been until her final hour.

One day, a few weeks after, Rose-Ellen placed a loving arm around Olivia.

'I can't believe Mam's gone. It doesn't seem real!' But Olivia was in a world of her own, dealing with the fact that her only sister was now permanently in France and her dear mother would never smile at her again.

'Rose-Ellen, why did she have to go so soon? She was fit and fine and never complained. She was only sixty-three for heaven's sake.'

Rose-Ellen mulled over her mother's sudden death. 'Olivia, I'm so sorry that she won't be here for your wedding. She would have loved it. She was so looking forward to the big day. I know she never complained, but on the odd occasion I noticed she used to drink milk at night for her indigestion, and now I wonder if it was indigestion. Maybe it was her heart and she wouldn't let on.'

Olivia looked at her sister, her face full of the confused strain she was feeling at the moment. 'You mean Mam was in some kind of denial about her heart condition?'

'I honestly don't know. She would have known about the family history. I mean, her brothers. Why had she not confided in us? Did she even know? Did she have any symptoms? I don't suppose there's much point in asking Dad.' Going over all these possible scenarios nearly drove Rose-Ellen mad.

Olivia drew her cardigan around her shoulders. 'Ah, that would be no good; he's not with it half the time since Mam died. Sometimes I think he doesn't even know what day of the week it is anymore.' Their father was in a permanent daze, having taken to the whiskey bottle. They wondered if Kitty's death had sunk in with him as sometimes he absent-mindedly addressed Rose-Ellen as 'Kitty'.

Just before Rose-Ellen was due to return to France, the news reported a severe storm lashing across France and northern Europe from the south-west with winds gusting at over one hundred kilometres per hour. The weather played on her mind as she tried to sort out Kitty's belongings and wondered about *Chez-Ellen*, and then there was Maurice to think of too. Rose-Ellen noticed quite deterioration in her father's condition since Kitty's demise, but at least Olivia and their Uncle Michael would run the emporium for the time being.

After three weeks in Loughbow, Rose-Ellen returned to France. Ollie collected her at the airport in La Rochelle and was unusually reticent, but Rose-Ellen suspected his reserve had to do with respect for her grief. She tried not to think of her mother, focussing her eyes on the photograph of Ollie's two smiling little girls holding their baby brother on the dashboard of the car, as well as a statue of Saint Christopher and various football emblems.

'They're lovely children Ollie,' she said casually, trying to sound a bit normal.

'Ah, they're lovely now. I wish they'd stay this age for ever, but kids grow up and change like us all. Ah, but I'm mad about them.'

Upon arrival at *Chez-Ellen* she sensed something was wrong. She looked at Ollie who stared straight ahead. Without another word she got out of the car and went around to the side of the house and let out a gasp. What greeted her would remain imprinted on her memory for a long time to come. A huge branch from the massive oak tree had fallen directly on to the side of *Chez-Ellen*. Its wood was rotten inside.

'Oh my God!' she exclaimed. Ollie came over and put his arm around her shoulder.

'We didn't want to alarm you because we knew you were grievin' for your mother, but there was a terrible wind here a while back and it did mighty damage to many houses right through this part of France. I'm so sorry. It's awful bad luck.'

'I didn't think...' And she stopped and burst out crying.

Ollie peered in at the garden and then turned to her. 'Christ, this is terrible, Rose-Ellen, and so soon after your family's grief. God knows, it's the last thing you needed right now. Myself and a few of the lads from the village managed to pull out your car, but to be perfectly honest, I think it's banjaxed.'

Full of trepidation Rose-Ellen opened the door of *Chez-Ellen*, and while most of the front of the premises was untouched, the massive branch from the great oak had fallen on the garden to the rear. Some of the windows and shutters were broken and smashed. The great hulk had flattened anything that came in its path; its gnarled and knotted branches spread out, claw-like, poking through the shattered windows of *Chez-Ellen*. She sat down and looked around at the state of the place. Rose-Ellen wanted to run away, or return to *Uisce Gaire*, despite the air of sadness that had hung around the home she had just left.

'The mayor is gettin' on to it as soon as possible, but there were a lot o' buildings in the village that were hammered. Charlotte has the chickens and I've been looking after the two goats and Jean-Francois' Mam took the rabbits. Me and a few of the fellahs from the village will cut up the tree and hopefully your insurance company will pay for any damage.'

She glanced at him wistfully. 'I wonder about that. It was an act of God. But thanks, Ollie, for removing the car. You've been great.'

That night she stayed with Ollie and Charlotte and the next day, Ollie and Monsieur Launay and a few of the other men from the village came with their chainsaws and removed the massive oak, presenting her with a haul of immense logs. But even after a few days there was still no sign of any builders. As there were many premises and homes damaged in the storm all builders were in demand. Finally after a week and much cajoling and pleading, two apprentice builders arrived and began to repair the parts of the roof which were damaged by the wind. Many of the tiles had blown off with the force of the wind and her satellite dish had been completely ripped from the side wall. The builders worked well and replaced the broken windows and wall, so at least Rose-Ellen felt safe at night. The great oak which had stood majestically for centuries by the side of the road had two huge chunks ripped from its side. It now looked forlorn having lost its lovely rounded shape. It would be some weeks before the wall would be repaired by the local authorities, but in the meantime she needed a car.

Some in the village were not so lucky. Monsieur Cabot's roof was completely gutted, and Delphine's cousin's house was flattened to the ground with the force of the wind. Madame Blanchard's chestnut tree's great branches had fallen on her pretty garden crushing her glasshouse, and destroying many of her prize cuttings and plants.

Violetta, Rose-Ellen's faithful old Citroen, was beyond repair so pleading with her local bank manager, she arranged a loan and bought a hardy second-hand Peugeot 205 from the local garage. For the next few weeks Rose-Ellen could barely cope. Jean-Francois and Charlotte had been marvellous in keeping the business going while she was away. The young man had got up at the crack of dawn each morning to bake Rose-Ellen's much loved scones and muffins, and Charlotte continued with the *plats du jour,* while Chantal was becoming more and more efficient around the place. She had taken to bossing Jean-Francois much to the dreamy youth's dismay. Delphine did all of the stocktaking and ordering and became the manager and general factotum around the place. Siobhan, her best and oldest friend came out to be with her and helped Rose-Ellen to try and get her life back together again.

'Oh, Siobhan, I am devastated at Mam's death. The one thing that had kept me going here all through those dark bleak months, when I knew nobody, had been the regular phone calls from her. It was she who had encouraged and listened to me from the outset. I now realise that I'll never hear my mother's consoling voice again and that breaks my heart.'

Siobhan came over and took Rose-Ellen to her and caressed and rocked her like a baby. 'Shh there. It's hard I know, and time will not heal, but it will make it more bearable, so be patient with yourself too, Rose-Ellen. You're inclined to drive yourself all the time and sometimes it is good to just let others do the worrying too.'

'You're right, I should learn to let go, but then when I do there is something else pulling at my energy.'

'So learn to switch off. The people who live the longest in this world are those who just switch off. Sure, when you're gone, that's it. Somebody else will just take over.'

To add to her anxiety the insurance company would not pay for any of the damage as the winds had exceeded a hundred kilometres an hour. This added to Rose-Ellen's anxiety as she was heavily in debt for the business and owed money to several lending institutions.

People in the village were very supportive and understanding, but during the lonely dark hours of night Rose-Ellen cried herself to sleep. She sought to take her mind off her mother's death, but concentration eluded her as despair and regret dominated her every hour. She missed Kitty terribly and nothing could compensate her for the awful chasm this loss had left in her life.

Chapter 51

It was early January and Rose-Ellen realised that she had to try and concentrate for all her worth on *Chez-Ellen* despite the overwhelming grief which seemed to engulf her. There were times when she was tempted to throw it all in and run home to Ireland, but to what? Kitty was gone. Then there were the premises itself, always in need of repair and updating, and she wondered if there would ever be an end to the constant maintenance required. The moss on the roof would have to be treated, the gutters and drainpipes cleared, and there was water trapped under the new floorboards upstairs from a leak caused by a faulty tap during the frosty spell. It was like walking on a sponge. She could not even think of the rising damp in the 'cave' – downstairs. She was in dire straits financially, the devastation caused by the storm having taken its toll. She talked to Delphine one day of the depression she felt at times because of all that had happened to her. They were sitting out at the back of *Chez-Ellen* after a particularly busy day.

'I can't describe how I feel most days. I mean, my mood, everything is just a sort of grey and more grey. I go round each day doing my work but sometimes I feel as if I'm sleepwalking. I can't seem to get worked up about anything anymore; just despair. The fact is that I feel empty inside. I feel so empty now that my mother is gone, and I did not really talk to her before she died. That's so hard.'

Delphine got up and came over and placed her arms around Rose-Ellen. 'Oh, *cherie*, you have been through so much recently. First of all Pierre and then your dear mother dying and you didn't really get any time to grieve. You ought to have closed up this place for a few months and stayed at home, but I know, you, like the rest of us have bills to pay and it isn't easy. I can't offer you any solution except to say that as your friend, you can talk to me whenever you like, day or night. I hate to see you like this. You who are always so full of joy, and what is the word, full of *"le craic"*!'

Since Kitty's death there were few things that seemed to buoy her up. She closed her eyes to try and remember her mother; images of Kitty walking the beach or knitting by the fire; images so homely and natural. She had thrown herself into the business, anxious to take her mind off her own immediate sorrow, but the great chasm of grief seemed to hit her after a while and she wondered if she would ever be able to get on with life again. At night she talked to Kitty in her dreams and hoped that her mother heard her in her deep, dark, fretful hours.

Chapter 52

Winter passed and it was a constant struggle as Rose-Ellen worked relentlessly to keep *Chez-Ellen* afloat. By late spring she was at last making ends meet. She had turned the business around and was now managing to pay all the bills on time. One hectic morning in April, Rose-Ellen went to the *Trésorerie Publique* as she needed to discuss something with Monsieur Beaudry there. The villagers normally paid their bills at the *Trésorerie Publique,* the local civil service office. Monsieur Beaudry was a typical French civil servant whose appreciation of the letter of the law was renowned. He was in his late fifties, tall and pale, with sharp features, aesthetic and scholarly, with tiny spectacles perched on his long nose giving him a stern expression. He was a stickler for grammar and fastidious when it came to almost everything pertaining to the French language. Rose-Ellen was anxious not to delay, but he insisted on discussing the subtleties of French syntax with her, until finally at eleven- thirty am she looked at her watch.

'*Mon Dieu, Monsieur,* I must fly, as customers will be arriving shortly for their lunch,' and she grabbed up all her paperwork and fled out the door, leaving Monsieur Beaudry to his pluperfect subjunctives and other syntactical delights of the French language.

Rose-Ellen returned from the *Tresorerie,* plonked her shopping on the table and put away the paid bills. Jean-Francois was whistling in the kitchen preparing the *menu du jour* and Chantal was busy laying out the tables.

'Jean-Francois, were there any messages for me while I was out at the *Tresorerie?*'

'No, *Madame,*' he answered languidly.

'The customers will be arriving shortly for their lunch, so you need to start heating Charlotte's *plats*. That pork casserole needs to be well cooked by twelve-fifteen, so pop it in to the oven now please,' she said, rolling up her sleeves and donning her customary pink and yellow apron.

After some time as Jean-Francois was pouring some *vinaigrette* dressing over little bowls of green salad he turned to her and said casually, 'Oh, I forgot, a *Monsieur* called today. He said he would call again.'

'*Monsieur* who?' Rose-Ellen asked, pulling out her selection of copper pans from the cupboards.

'His name was Pierre.'

'What did he look like as there are several Pierres around here. I mean, did he give a surname?' Rose-Ellen felt continually exasperated with Jean-Francois' vague and casual manner with regard to things which did not directly affect him.

'He did, but I cannot remember, but he was very tall, he had a coffee and then read the paper for a bit and got up and said he would call you.'

'Damn, damn, damn that bloody Beaudry and his pointless grammar. Of all the mornings to be stuck with him! Thanks, Jean-Francois,' she said, putting the copper pan on the gas and heating up the cream of mushroom soup. Her one chance to renew her friendship with Pierre had been ruined by a pedantic civil servant.

A week later Rose-Ellen was in the middle of making a liqueur with brandy from her peregrine peaches, her hands sticky from the beautiful soft yellow fruits, when the phone rang. She fumbled with the phone, but it went to voicemail. She quickly washed her hands and phoned back the number which had come up.

'*Allo, oui?*'

'Hello, I'm returning your call.'

She took a deep breath and felt her body tense. She could not mistake that silky voice.

'It's been a while,' he said, 'so I wanted to call you.'

She felt herself brimming with joy that he had called and could barely concentrate. Nevertheless she kept her guard up. 'Did you get my letter?' There was a brief silence at the other end. 'You never replied to it,' she said.

'Maybe we could meet,' he said eventually.

'Maybe,' she said.

'What about next Monday,' he ventured.

'How about one-thirty on Sunday?'

'That would be fine. I'll look forward to it.'

'Great, see you then.'

'I'll call for you and we'll take it from there. Maybe go for a sail.'

'OK sounds good.'

The prospect of meeting him again after all this time filled her with trepidation…and yet she was also exhilarated.

When Sunday arrived, Rose-Ellen felt nervous although curious and a little excited too. The clock struck one-thirty but by two there was still no sign of Pierre. She wondered what had happened because he was rarely late. She looked out of the window and paced back and forth the front room until finally he turned the corner a little after two-fifteen. She opened the door and there he stood, dressed in sailing gear.

'Hello, Rose-Ellen, sorry I'm late, things always seem to crop up at the last minute when you want to get away.'

'Hello, Pierre,' she said shyly.

He moved towards her and she noticed how healthy he looked.

'It's good to see you again. I'm glad we agreed to meet,' he said. He stood there unsure of what to do.

'I won't be a sec. I'll just get my things and we can be off.' She could barely concentrate on what he was saying as she was so excited at seeing him again after all this time.

The weather was mixed as they set off. On the drive to La Rochelle he seemed initially reticent towards her, but Rose-Ellen acted as if little had changed between them. Somehow, their breakup seemed to have less significance in the light of her mother's death. Nothing could ever be as bad as the last few months had been.

Rose-Ellen had not returned to La Rochelle since the day with Finn on *La Sirene*, but it was heartening to see the small square inlet dominated by the round towers again. In some ways she had missed the city's vibrancy, the rash of masts pointing upwardly on white fibreglass lined, with almost mathematical precision. Everywhere the Sunday throng was evident; people strolled or sat leisurely in the afternoon sun, with the fresh tang of seafood lingering in the air. Seafront restaurants were full as slim waiters dressed in black with crisp white aprons hurried like bees between packed tables armed with plates or busily taking orders.

Getting into the boat brought back memories of their first sailing trip together in Ireland off Lambay which she had pushed down deep into her subconscious. The sails flapped in the soft breeze and Rose-Ellen could hear the soothing lap of the water against the sides of the boat. Watching Pierre preoccupied with the sailing gear on the thirty-foot boat, she supposed that like her, he felt a little awkward. But she sensed that she had to trust her own instincts even though she had a great urge to hug him and tell him of her remorse. She would wait until the moment was right.

Out beyond the harbour, Rose-Ellen leaned over the side of the boat and let her fingers touch and drift through the sea water that was sparkling with dappled sunshine. She could feel the sea's cold tingle as the water flowed through her splayed hands carrying its surging swell of fathomless secrets and mysteries beneath. As she spread her fingers and lifted them out of the sea, watching the water drops fall, inky black humps dipping and surfacing came into view.

'Oh, my God, how fantastic! Look at them! What are they?'

Pierre was letting out the main sail when he saw the beautiful, graceful backs moving in unison. 'Dolphins. They'll be curious to see what we're up to. They'll only stay with us for a while, and then they'll get bored and move on.' The boat caught up with the dolphins and kept pace with them, a school of about forty, moving in parallel through the dark water. It was an amazing sight. The dolphins upped and splashed, snorting, clicking and blowing. A calf glided gracefully next to its mother, weaving, dashing under her and emerging again to touch her.

Rose-Ellen observed their playfulness in amazement. 'Look, Pierre, see over there, you'd think they were dancing and jiving with our boat.'

'We're probably pushing all of the plankton forward with our bow waves,' Pierre said, smiling, and reached down to touch a large dolphin that had come within a few feet of the boat. Then he glanced at Rose-Ellen. It seemed to her as if these beautiful mammals were portents of some kind. 'I got your letter,' he said. 'And thank you. I was busy, very busy, but I kept thinking about how we had parted and I was sad at what happened.' She moved closer to him. He put his arm around her and said, 'I decided to let things be for a while, because I wasn't sure how you'd react if I got back in touch straight away.'

She looked up at him. 'You don't have to explain. I said too many things that night that I regret now. Look, I'm really sorry for my behaviour. I don't know what got into me.'

He took her in his arms and held her. 'It's OK, I knew you were stressed.' They watched the mammalian shapes as they broke the surface of the sea with their uniform and circular movement. Pierre had a slightly lost and forlorn look; she'd seen that vulnerability before. 'What are you thinking about?' he asked, moving a curl from her face as she looked out on to the horizon.

'A lot has happened to me since we split up and I suppose my life will never be the same again.'

'What do you mean?'

'My mother died since I saw you last and now everything has changed; some things that appeared important before just don't seem so anymore.' She could feel her eyes welling up, but tried to stop the tears because she did not want to cry in front of him. 'Oh, I don't mean you, I'm glad you contacted me.' Her voice was quavering now and the tears started to come quickly. He held her more tightly.

'Darling. I'm so sorry.'

Taking a tissue from her pocket, she blew her nose. 'I have to move on because of the business, but sometimes I miss her so much.'

'If only I'd known. I thought about you after we parted, wondering how you were, and how you were coping, but I wasn't sure about our relationship. I'm so dreadfully sorry about your mother. I know how close you were to her.'

She wiped away her tears with her fingerless gloves. 'I thought that you would never want to see me again. I mean, after what happened.'

His mouth traced her perfectly symmetrical features until his trembling lips found hers. 'Darling, I missed you so much,' he whispered. She felt a surge of emotion, the desire to put her arms around him and whisper to him all the things she had dreamt of in the past few months.

'Pierre, I can't begin to tell you how happy I am that we've made contact again.'

They were oblivious to everything, with only the gentle dolphins and friendly waves to keep them company. Drops of rain splattered and Rose-Ellen pulled the hood of her windcheater up over her head. As the evening drew in, a rainbow appeared in the blue haze and Rose-Ellen delighted in its glorious display. 'Oh look, that's a lucky sign,' she said, and they watched as it faded, both feeling that it was a portent of goodwill. When they docked and moored the boat, they heard a voice call out.

'Pierre, hi! Over here.'

Rose-Ellen glanced over at a group of about six people who had just docked. They were in sailing gear. *'Salut'*, Pierre called back to them and waved. They were soon joined by the group who were friends of Pierre's from Nantes and who were down in La Rochelle sailing for the day. The older man of the group invited Pierre and Rose-Ellen to join them for a drink in a local nearby pub in La Rochelle.

Pierre turned to Rose-Ellen. 'Why not?'

But Rose-Ellen was uncertain and hesitatingly said, 'Oh, I don't know, maybe you should just go on your own.'

'Oh come on, darling, just one, I promise, *c'est tout*.'

The *brasserie* seemed an unprepossessing place from the outside, dull almost, but was lively inside despite its darkness. *Le patron* greeted Pierre like a long-lost son. Pierre introduced Rose-Ellen. 'I would like to introduce you to my friend, Rose-Ellen.'

Le patron stretched out his hand and heartily shook Rose-Ellen's.

'Enchanté, Madame!'

Casting her eye around, she noticed several people drinking in little groups and another lively group at the end of the counter. Soon a large bosomed lady with bright red untidy hair approached them and hugged Pierre. She was the sort of woman whom one associated with running a pub, the watchful eye, pleasant but restrained with customers, her mind always on the business with the same shrewd, shallow, all-seeing expression that misses little. They spoke briefly to them, laughed loudly and then moved off.

'What would you like to drink?' Pierre asked her before going to the bar.

'Just a coffee thanks,' she said, putting her sunglasses away in her bag. They moved down to the other end of the bar where Pierre introduced her to his friends. There were six in total, four men and two women. One of the men kissed Rose-Ellen's hand and smiled, *'La belle irlandaise!'* Rose-Ellen was getting used to such flattery and French charm, and noticed the unfinished bottle of white wine and the remnants of some oysters on a plate on the counter. The women were outdoor types, strong and athletic with pleasant wholesome faces. One of them had a dark complexion and her hair tied back in a ponytail. She raised her glass to Pierre.

'*Salut*, how was your day?'

Pierre clinked her glass. 'Excellent, the dolphins have returned.'

She threw a sideways glance at Rose-Ellen.

'That's a good sign. It means plenty of fish,' she said.

They all laughed and chatted amongst themselves. Rose-Ellen wished that she could understand them as they spoke quickly and in a colloquial style. Getting only the gist of the conversation she felt out of contact, and started to experience that loneliness one feels when one cannot enter into the spirit of things. Pierre wandered over and offered her a stool. She looked at the amber brandy in his glass and then smiled at him in the mirror.

He whispered, 'It's OK, *cherie*, we won't be long. I said I'd have a drink with them.'

The other girl in the group was blonde, tall and confident, with the windswept look of the very healthy. She glanced over at Rose-Ellen but did not smile. Rose-Ellen continued to sip her coffee and wished that she could be on her own with Pierre. Then the man with the almost finished plate of oysters moved around to be next to her. Pierre introduced them.

'Rose-Ellen, may I introduce you to a friend of mine, Marc, who is a surgeon in Nantes and who has collaborated on some research projects with me.' Pierre moved back to the group.

'Pierre tells me that you run your own business here,' Marc said.

She smiled and stirred her coffee. 'Yes, it's called *Chez-Ellen*, a coffee shop and delicatessen.'

'Well either you're disillusioned with your own country or love it here… or perhaps there's another reason…' He was smiling now and looked intently at her, his dark eyes almost penetrating her soul.

She looked back at him. 'Yes, it's been a dream I've harboured for a long time.' She was aware that he was hoping for more information, but she was guarded. He poured the remainder of the wine into his glass.

'You know Pierre, he's a great guy, a little crazy sometimes, but he has a big heart,' he said, pressing his palm to his chest.

'Yes, I think so, too.'

'He likes it here in France, but we don't know if he'll stay. He's restless;

there are times when he wants to be somewhere else.'

Rose-Ellen had an idea what he meant.

'When he's here and happy and doing something he likes, that's wonderful, but after a while he wants to do something else, a new plan, always a plan, a change. Since his accident I think he likes to move. He needs a…what do you call it in English?' He looked at the floor as he searched for the word. 'An anchor, yes that's it. He is like a ship, he needs an anchor.'

At that point she looked in the mirror and noticed Pierre laughing with the blonde girl and a swarthy heavyset man.

Madame la patronne came down the counter to their group, her brandy bottle poised to replenish glasses. She produced a glass for Rose-Ellen, who demurred, but then the lady looked questioningly at her, glass poised and asked with a half smile, '*Et pourquoi pas?*'

Rather than appear ungracious, Rose-Ellen agreed and the woman poured. Marc finished his wine and had some brandy.

'You love him?' he asked. 'I can see it.'

Rose-Ellen smiled timidly.

Marc took her hand in his.

'Please, I know, I sense it in your eyes. Maybe you love him just a little bit, but it will grow.'

She looked at him, his lined tired face from too many cigarettes, wine and too much responsibility. Rose-Ellen was heartened by what Marc said. Marc moved away and Pierre joined her. Soon the little group broke up, each going their separate ways. Pierre and Rose-Ellen headed back to *Chez-Ellen*, and as they approached the turn-off Rose-Ellen turned to him and said, 'Fancy something to eat? I've made something that can be heated up in a few minutes.'

He pulled in and looked at her with a smile. 'Sounds fine to me.'

She opened the door of *Chez-Ellen*. But he reached out and took her in his arms and held her. 'Darling, I'm so glad to be here with you again. You see, I was afraid of losing you.'

Rose-Ellen searched his face and drew her index finger down from his forehead to his chin. He kissed her lightly on the nose. 'Now let's get out of these clothes and into something more comfortable,' Rose-Ellen said, removing her jacket.

Pierre got a fire going in the old grate, as there was a chill in the evening air. Rose-Ellen put on some music and they danced slowly together by the fireside while the food was simmering. She noticed how he moved, his lithe body pressed against hers. She rested her head on his shoulders and moved slowly in time with the music. It was so good to be touched again, to feel and caress him. She thought of the lonely, bitter hours she had spent in the house, the cold evenings stretching slowly into night, awaiting the first bird call, all the time wondering about where she was heading, whether there would be any end to the constant anxiety of keeping everything afloat. Now she had Pierre, at least for this brief interlude.

After dinner, they sat by the fire, chatting and drinking wine. He seemed relaxed and content as he lay back on the old chair. He began to talk of his childhood in France, growing up the son of an Irish diplomat and French mother. 'Oh, the life in Paris was good, we wanted for nothing, but it was cold and lonely. I...' He paused and took a sip of wine. 'I suppose that's why I love the sea so much. The solitude of it away from everything. I became withdrawn after my mother's death. My poor father, busy with government work, had little time for me. That's why I spent so much of my childhood with my mother's brother, Uncle Geoffrey.' Rose-Ellen realised that his world had been one of restrained emotion. He went on, 'Geoffrey was almost like a second father to me, and in some ways I was closer to him growing up than to my own father. Sometimes I feel my father is like a silhouette, a shadow in my dreams and thoughts. And...' He stopped and looked into the fire and then turned to Rose-Ellen. 'I'm sorry, darling, it must be the wine. Please tell me if I'm ranting on. It's insensitive of me talking like this when you've lost your own mother recently.'

'I'd like to know more about your childhood, what it was like growing up in an embassy. I like to hear you to talk. The people around here are great, salt of the earth and all that, but I've been so lonely since Mam's death, just longing for someone to talk to. I mean, someone I can really relate to, who understands me instinctively, without always having to explain what I do and the way I do it.' She laid her head on his shoulder.

'I know,' he said as he stroked her arm. After a while he kissed her again. 'Rose-Ellen, you look beautiful, really beautiful, but then you always did.'

It was becoming warm by the fire and Pierre dimmed the light. Rose-Ellen watched him and stretched out her hand to him. He pulled her up and she undid his shirt. When he was undressed he removed Rose-Ellen's clothes delicately one by one, placing them on a chair, and they lay down by the fire in each other's arms. As Pierre stretched his long, lean limbs out in front of the fire, Rose-Ellen noticed the smoothness of his skin and reaching down, she moved closer and stroked his legs.

She smelled the crackling wood, odours from the burning beech and oak redolent of childhood campfires, and watched the flickering flames. Pierre pulled back her hair and kissed her neck, whispering, 'Darling, let me kiss you.'

She sensed the charged air, the snap of the dry wood as it bristled in the flames and lifted her head, nuzzling into his neck. He closed his eyes for a moment and she moved her hand up and down his right leg. Then she noticed a scar on his thigh. She touched the reddened area. He lay back on his elbows as she looked closely at it. She said, 'It must have been awful. I mean, being shot.'

He said nothing but stared at the flickering flames. She bent down and kissed the scar. It seemed the most normal thing to do. She moved her lips up his leg to his inner thigh. Quivering at her touch, he reached and drew her towards him. Her loose hair fell in folds around her shoulders, and her skin glistened against the fire as he sought her neck and breasts with his mouth.

'Oh, darling, I want you so much,' he said.

He kissed her passionately now, his lips and tongue moving along her shoulders and neck, as far as the point where her breasts met, and ripples of excitement coursed through her very being at his tender touch.

'Let's go to bed,' he whispered. Slowly they stood and made their way up the rickety stairs. Pierre put on the light and the two arm chandelier cast a soft glow around the room. He pulled across the pale organdie curtain, closing off the street lights, and looked around the room, the old walls, with its hardy wooden beams. 'The room is you,' he whispered.

In pockets around the room Rose-Ellen had placed sprigs of rosemary, now dry and crispy. He took up a small rosemary sprig and put it to his nose, taking in its rich mediterranean aroma. 'Rosemary for loyalty. Isn't that what they say?' he said, taking her hand. 'But roses are for beauty, like you, my sweet. You are called after the most beautiful of flowers, tokens of love and sadness, their perfume divine,' he whispered, looking into her eyes.

Pierre guided her gently towards the bed. Pulling back the sheets, she lay down on the four-poster bed, her head resting on the crisp white pillowcase with its border of violets. A feather floated in the air from the pillow and landed on her hair. Pierre removed it and released it into the air where it floated like a snowflake. As she nestled up to him, he brushed the hair from her face and kissed her. She slid her fingers through his hair and kissed him. He moved his hand round her waist and kissed her again – gently at first, then passionately.

'Darling, I have longed for the time when I would take you in my arms and love you completely and unconditionally,' he whispered, as his lips brushed hers. His French accent seemed to her more seductive than ever. 'Oh darling, you are driving me wild,' he murmured, as he expressed his love for her. His lips sought hers and his desire for her was strong. Her heart was pounding. He was stroking her now, caressing and touching her, brushing her gently with his lips and telling her how he had desired her for so long. In the silence of the night he held her close and kissed her tenderly. As they passionately sought each other in the dark, whispering, kissing, touching, she cried out with ecstasy when Pierre made love to her. Rose-Ellen thought that she would never feel as truly happy and fulfilled again. He wanted her more than ever, reaching heights of passion and then drawing back, until finally the great denouement to their lovemaking came to a finale, the intensity of their desires spent after which Pierre held her and cried, 'I can't tell you how I've yearned for this time, my sweet,' he said, as she held him in her arms and soothed him.

He lay back in bed caressing her. 'You know, Rose-Ellen, before the shooting I was always on the go, for ever on the way somewhere else, driven…driven by some strange force.'

'Not living in the moment or smelling the roses on the way,' she said dreamily.

He kissed her lightly. 'Yes, darling, something like that, always wanting to be the first, be the best. But since the shooting I don't look to the future any more, it's elusive.'

Rose-Ellen could feel herself drifting off to sleep while Pierre continued, 'The nights after the shooting were the worst. Every hour that passed made me more fearful. I thought daybreak would never come! The first bird sound brought with it hope. I was melancholy for weeks after the shooting, it seemed to haunt me. But now time is the most important thing, and being alive means more to me than anything else.' He heard Rose-Ellen's breathing beside him and found that she was almost asleep. He drew her closer to him. 'I'll never fear death again. I feel as if I've touched the edge, that precipice between life and death, like looking over a cliff.' But her deep breathing brought him back to the present and he kissed her on the lips. '*Ma belle*, I wonder if you realise how truly beautiful you are. Oh, how I have ached for this moment!' As he lay back and drifted off to sleep, the recent past and its dark shadowy moments became another place.

In the morning Rose-Ellen was woken by the cheap red alarm clock at her bedside. She looked at it, its cheeky little face heralding the day and reminding her of the relentless march of time. She wanted to smash it into pieces and render it silent. She turned in the bed and reached out but noticed that Pierre had gone. He had left a note for her downstairs.

I love you, darling. Pierre.

Throughout the day, Rose-Ellen tingled each time she recalled Pierre's touch. In her mind she was re-living every exquisite moment of their night together. She felt his caresses again and the tender touch of his eager lips on her skin and thought her heart would stop with the desire she felt.

Chapter 53

Because he was able to be flexible with his work, Pierre became a regular visitor to *Chez-Ellen* at the weekends. He and Rose-Ellen sailed around the harbour of La Rochelle or to the surrounding bays and islands whenever Rose-Ellen was able to snatch some time away from the business. Rose-Ellen was in love and because of this nothing seemed insurmountable. Her love sustained her through the hectic hours when she struggled with running *Chez-Ellen* and the French tax system. She looked forward so much to those times with Pierre when she would have him totally to herself. They laughed and loved and were very happy in each other's company.

One day at the end of June, Pierre surprised Rose-Ellen. 'I'd love us to go away together, take a break, so I've booked a romantic weekend away in Saumur. It's such a lovely part of France and there's so much to see.'

But ever the pragmatist, Rose-Ellen had doubts. 'Sounds divine! But who's going to take care of everything here?'

He gently pulled her towards him and said, 'Please trust me.'

'Oh well, I suppose that there's little point in arguing with you when you are like this!'

'Everything is arranged and don't worry, nothing will be left to chance!'

Flamboyant in a panama hat, jeans and cashmere sweater, Pierre drove with carefree abandon along the French roads by the banks of the Loire. He said little on the way, but glanced at Rose-Ellen from time to time. At one stage he took her hand, placed it to his lips and kissed it.

Just as Rose-Ellen was feeling hungry they arrived at Saumur, a stunning city where large white cupolas, splendours from the *ancien regime*, stood out against the skyline, a reminder of times gone by. Pierre was like a man on a secret mission. Even the expression of the *concierge* in the hotel seemed to suggest a conspiracy. That evening they dined in a splendid restaurant on the banks of the river. The menu *gastronomique* was long and extensive, and the number of courses seemed endless. After dessert and before coffee, Pierre reached under the table and took Rose-Ellen's hand, whispering to her, '*Cherie*, tonight is very special.'

'Pierre, what's going on, is there's something that I'm not being told? I feel that there is a tacit display of emotions between yourself and the hotel staff and I am not being let into these little secrets.'

Pierre nodded to the waiter who smiled in acknowledgement and disappeared. The waiter returned with a small plate, which was covered with a linen napkin and a white rose.

'*Pour vous, Madame*,' he said, and ceremoniously laid the covered plate in front of her.

Pierre seemed to lighten up.

Rose-Ellen lifted the napkin and there perched in the middle of the plate rested quite the most beguiling pink jewelled ring she had ever seen. She gasped in shock.

'My God, it's beautiful! Oh, Pierre, this is so wonderful,' she exclaimed and got up and gave him a huge hug. She was ecstatic with joy.

She watched as Pierre tenderly picked up the ring and placed it on her fourth finger. His expression softened and she could feel her heart thumping with joy and the sheer magic of the whole experience. 'Darling this is our engagement ring. It's a topaz stone, most unusual,' he said, taking her hand and kissing it.

'I can't take in what is happening to me. It's so graceful and beautiful. I can't believe that we are engaged. Oh, Pierre, I don't know what to say,' she said, as she stared at the magnificent ring which consisted of dazzling diamonds of soft grey hue set around a deep rose-pink topaz.

'It was my mother's,' he said, 'it's an old rare jewel and has been in the family for generations. Somehow I knew instinctively that the colour and cut would suit you perfectly, my darling.' They touched their golden-rimmed champagne glasses and he toasted their continued love.

'To us, forever.'

'I am thinking about your mother and her ancestors who would have worn this ring, ladies from another era, and I feel truly honoured to be wearing it. I can't take it all in. I am overwhelmed, it's…oh, I don't know,' she said, and started to cry in to her napkin. 'I'm sorry, Pierre, I'm just so overcome and emotional.'

'Apart from this ring being unique, it is very dear to me as it was specially made for my great-grandmother, but darling I want you to wear it always. She would be so proud,' he said, taking her hand and kissing the tips of each finger individually.

Their evening together continued in the pale light of the Loire. That night as they lay in bed, Rose-Ellen listened to his disembodied voice in the dark as he whispered softly to her.

'You know, Rose-Ellen, for many years I had felt adrift in life, never having settled anywhere, either on a boat, an apartment with a view or somebody else's home, and now I crave a place to call my own, a hearth, and somebody to love. I never told you this, but when I was ill after the accident I dreamt about us; you and I being together. It's funny, but the whole time I was in hospital is now just a blur, but that's the one clear memory that I remember very vividly.' He held her close and she could sense his tenderness for her as his hands caressed her body, gently then intimately, and the deep emotional feeling towards him seemed now more important than any physical sensation.

The next day, feeling a little frail from the mixture of drinks, Rose-Ellen barely touched the sumptuous breakfast buffet, except to sip her orange juice and try some of the home-made yoghurt. Pierre had gone jogging. She smiled to herself as she thought of their blissful night together, his tender touch and kisses with his deep passionate desire for her.

Pierre came into the restaurant looking fit and hardy.

'How are you feeling, *cherie?*'

'I'm fine, just overdid it last night. I mean, the drinks,' she added, and he winked at her.

'I thought we might go cycling today, down by the river, and maybe take a picnic.'

She took a small mouthful of the wild berry yoghurt and swallowed it. 'Sounds like a good idea. What time are we meeting your relatives in St. Germain sur Vienne?'

'My cousin Lucille and her husband Didier,' he said, producing a small map of the area provided by the hotel. 'We're here. We'll take the road along the river and at Monsoreau we'll follow the direction for

St. Germain sur Vienne, where they live.'

He took her hand in his and caressed it. 'Oh, I do love you so, my sweet,' and he poured himself a cup of coffee.

'So it'll be a packed day, then,' Rose-Ellen said resignedly.

'Precisely. No alarms to get you out of bed tomorrow and the exercise will do us both good, oh and before I forget, we should try and visit the famous Fontevraud Abbey.'

They set off on their rented bikes at eleven. Pierre looked like a professional cyclist with his bright blue skin-tight suit and sunglasses, while Rose-Ellen wore jeans and a light bomber jacket and tucked her hair under a small sun hat. Pierre secured the small hamper that contained the food to his carrier bag and Rose-Ellen carried the cold drinks in her pannier in front. She was barely able to keep up with him as they whizzed along the banks of the shimmering Loire, leaving the splendid cupola domes of Saumur behind.

At lunchtime they stopped for their picnic, near Montsoreau, selecting a nice quiet embankment upon which to leave the bicycles. There was a single empty picnic table which Rose-Ellen covered with a blue floral tablecloth. She carefully arranged the contents of the picnic basket: a selection of cheeses from the region, a bottle of chilled sparkling water, cold meats and an assortment of salads and a *baguette*.

Rose-Ellen was glad to sit down and enjoy the picnic lunch with a glass of cool spring water as her calf muscles were aching from the cycling. Pierre ravenously attacked a leg of chicken.

'How are you feeling now, everything OK?' he said, clinking her glass.

'Much better, thanks,' she said, although in truth her stomach was still queasy.

'I was reading about the area this morning in the hotel,' he said. 'It's one of the most interesting parts of France where the kings came with the court and went hunting, and did what kings do. Every king each had his own *château* and it must have been marvellous,' he said, wiping his fingers with a paper towel. He stood up and strolled over to the embankment and beckoned to Rose-Ellen. Rubbing a peach on her sleeve she moved over to where he stood, and he took her hand in his. Here and there the river meandered through muddy patches of earth. Fishing boats lay marooned or abandoned and an old fisherman's hut with gnarled ivy growing on one side gave the place a wild and beautiful timelessness. Rose-Ellen leaned her head against his shoulder.

'It's lovely here,' she said. 'It's a wonder more people don't visit the area.'

'Lucille is an authority on the region and we can ask her about it. If we had time this weekend, we could go and see the great castles by the Loire. Another time perhaps.' He reached down and brushed her face lightly with a kiss. 'As we're here we should really try to visit Fontevraud Abbey. We'll head straight for it after lunch, and on our way back visit Lucille and Didier.'

Pierre stole an arm around Rose-Ellen and bent down and kissed her again. All this time the hum of midday traffic jarred the peace and tranquillity of the surrounds, while the smell of hay and peaceful grazing cattle in a field reminded them of the never-ending cyclical nature of life. Pierre held her close as they watched the Loire swirl among the reeds, its great swell tumbling along relentlessly to Saint Nazarre and beyond to the wider Atlantic.

After they had packed up everything, they continued on their journey to the Abbey Fontevraud. After several hours in the abbey climbing old stone stairs, looking up to admire ceilings and carved buttresses, and wandering through the ancient kitchens, medieval halls and garden, Rose-Ellen had regained her strength. 'Isn't it amazing how they lived; they were a hardy lot in those days,' she remarked, smelling a spring of lavender as they strolled arm in arm through the walled garden of the abbey.

'They were indeed a rare breed, Eleanor of Aquitaine and that son of hers, Richard Coeur de Lion, a thug if ever there was one!' Pierre said wryly.

'Couldn't we visit Lucille a little earlier?' she asked, anxious to dispense with the formalities and get back to the hotel for a rest before dinner. Her body was aching from the strenuous activities.

'It's been a tiring day, but my relatives are a rather conservative bunch as are a lot of French people, and certain rules apply, so, darling we must arrive at four. Any other time would be unthinkable. I'd love to see Lucille again and want so much to introduce you to them. I know she'll take to you.'

Towards four o'clock, they made their way to Lucille and Didier's place. They pushed their bikes up a small hill to the house on the edge of the town. Rose-Ellen noticed the sign *'Attention au Chien'* and froze.

'Don't be nervous,' Pierre said. 'It's only old Max and Hugo and they'll recognise me.' As they made their way through the gates, two enormous black dogs came hurtling down the avenue barking furiously and Rose-Ellen remained still. She wanted to turn back as the gates behind them were closing. Pierre stood and greeted the dogs who hurled themselves at him and after sniffing Rose-Ellen, simply ignored her.

Lucille, who was Pierre's late mother's first cousin, greeted Pierre on the doorstep, and then her eyes travelled to Rose-Ellen and she exclaimed, *'Si belle!'* and came and gave Rose-Ellen the customary greeting on both cheeks. She was a woman *d'un certain age* with that fine, slightly olive complexion and delicate features which many French women possess. Her hair was brown and her hazel eyes, although piercing, were kind. Her impeccable suit was a pale grey, and while somewhat worn, bore the trim sophisticated cut of *haute couture*. Her husband Didier, was more portly than she, came to meet them with outstretched arms, giving Pierre a tremendous bear hug, and shook Rose-Ellen's hand, saying *'Enchanté, Mademoiselle.'* They moved inside and then Uncle Geoffrey came out of the kitchen. Pierre rushed to greet him and gave him a hug. Rose-Ellen could see how close they were.

'My dear boy, I bet you didn't expect to see me here, but well, my dear cousin insisted that I come and of course I couldn't resist the opportunity of meeting up with my favourite nephew,' he said, clasping Pierre's hand. Pierre drew him over to Rose-Ellen and Geoffrey bowed and took her hand.

'Bonjour Madame, we met in Ireland under difficult circumstances,' Uncle Geoffrey said, greeting her.

'Delighted to meet you again. Yes, but thankfully everything turned out well,' she said, stealing a glance at Pierre.

They moved into the salon and Rose-Ellen cast her eye around the large room, with its fireplace and period furniture upholstered in a soft pale gold. From time to time she caught Lucille's eye and the latter smiled affectionately. Here and there ornate silver frames displayed family photographs, and one photograph in particular caught her eye, that of two young boys and Rose-Ellen wondered if one of them could be Pierre.

While Lucille went to fetch food from the kitchen, Didier served the drinks. 'Rose-Ellen, what would you like to drink? Some pastis, whiskey or Muscat? What would you prefer?'

Rose-Ellen looked at the array of chilled water and ice cubes, as well as soft drinks. 'I'll just have a sparkling water with ice, please.'

'Certainly,' he said, and proceeded to busy himself with its preparation. Lucille brought in a plate with olives, cubes of cheese, slim slices of dried sausage, some *vol-au-vents*, as well as various dips placing them on the sideboard and handing them around now and then.

Pierre held Rose-Ellen's hand and raised his Kir Royale. 'We have something to tell you all.' Lucille stopped serving and Geoffrey made himself comfortable in the best armchair, while Didier stroked Max. 'I proposed to Rose-Ellen last night in Saumur and we are now officially engaged,' Pierre said, turning to Rose-Ellen and placing a protective arm around her.

'Oh, *mon dieu*, how wonderful, I can't tell you how excited I am about your engagement,' Lucille said, casting her eyes down to the ring on Rose-Ellen's finger and then coming over to hug both of them.

'You know the ring has been in our family for generations. It was Mireille's; she would be very proud.' She smiled benignly at Rose-Ellen and then turned her attention to Pierre. 'Darling Mireille would have been so pleased for you,' and turned away to hide a tear.

'Mireille was my mother,' Pierre whispered to Rose-Ellen.

'Heartiest congratulations, this is indeed wonderful news,' Didier said, raising his glass.

But Geoffrey arose from the deep armchair and came over to Pierre and clasped him. There were tears in his eyes. 'I am totally overwhelmed with the news, wonderful, and she is a beauty too,' he said, winking at Rose-Ellen.

'*Et toi, cheri, qu'est-ce-que tu fais a ce moment?*' Lucille asked Pierre when the congratulations had died down.

'I'm working on a research project as well as doing some locum oncology consultancy in the hospital in La Rochelle. I do some translations and edits in English and French for medical journals and some private consultancy work, and of course I'm helping Uncle Geoffrey setting up his marine school, so I'm kept busy so to speak. Not enough time to spend with my beautiful Rose-Ellen,' he said, curling a tender arm around her waist.

'You lead a hectic life. How is your health now, *cheri* ? Have you fully recovered from those dreadful injuries ?' Lucille asked, reaching out and squeezing his hand gently.

'It seems a long time ago, but of course I still get dreadful flashbacks. Otherwise, I'm almost fully recovered,' Pierre said.

'And they got the person who did this dreadful act, did they not?'

But Pierre did not answer.

Then Didier spoke. 'But why? Why did they do it?'

Pierre looked into his glass and Rose-Ellen reached out and held Pierre's hand. 'Why indeed? I often wonder that myself! The motive seems so utterly ridiculous, it's laughable! Jealousy, insecurity; who knows what motivates people to commit such crimes?'

'Bizarre!' Didier said quietly, making his way over to the drinks cabinet and pointing to the various bottles as he winked at Rose-Ellen. She smiled at him.

'I'll have a pastis this time, please.'

'*Certainement.*'

'I think that the weather is changing. I can feel it in my bones,' Pierre said, as he watched the clouds bundling up on the horizon through the large bay window.

'Ah, you speak like a true mariner,' Uncle Geoffrey said, behind him.

They left a little after six-thirty pm, just when evening was falling. Lucille hugged Pierre and said, 'Darling do please visit us again soon, we always love to see you. Goodbye *cheri*.'

As the evening enveloped them, the temperature dropped and the darkness gathered like a veil around them. Rose-Ellen was tired and her limbs ached as she cycled and she longed for a dip in the wonderful claw-footed bath in their hotel bedroom, but with each minute the weather changed and then a flash of thunder bellowed in the distance. All of a sudden lightening sparkled and crackled in the evening sky, setting it ablaze in the west.

'We'll have to take cover,' Pierre shouted to Rose-Ellen.

But Rose-Ellen was not listening as she was concentrating on the road. Then he swerved off the road down a quiet leafy narrow road and all around them the roll and crack of thunder and lightening resounded and lit up the blood red sky. Pierre stopped up on the embankment. 'We'll take refuge in the troglodyte caves up there; see just up there in the cliffs,' he said, pointing to the hewn out caves which Rose-Ellen could barely make out through the mist and rain. She followed him on the bike until they came to the opening of a cave in the hillside and Pierre pushed his bike in and helped her off hers.

'We'll stay here until the rain passes,' he said, taking off his helmet. Rose-Ellen's teeth were chattering and she was freezing. 'Come here, darling and let me warm you up. You look pale and cold,' he said, taking her in his arms and protecting her from the rain which was bucketing down at this stage. He took off her wet gloves and tried to blow some hot air on her fingers. 'We'll go inside the cave,' he said, drawing her inside. Rose-Ellen rested against the wall of the cave and Pierre put his arms against the wall and shielded her from the sound of the great reverberating thunder overhead. It felt eerie and ghost-like in this long-abandoned hewn out refuge in the cliffs.

'The lightening is about four kilometres away,' Pierre said, wiping the rain from Rose-Ellen's face.

'It feels as if it's overhead,' she said, looking around at the cold stone dome over their heads. She shivered and tried to keep warm. She savoured this sweet moment in his arms as the heavens opened up around them splattering the rain on the overhead rock against the deep thunderous roar in the distance.

'What if we have to spend the night here? But wouldn't it be exciting too, darling?' she said, as she thought of the elemental fury raging around them.

'Rose-Ellen, I couldn't imagine anything more romantic than being here with you just now with the elements. My God, it's wonderful. I feel so alive and in love right now,' he said, drawing her closer to him.

'I was thinking of warm beds and jacuzzis back there on my bike, but this is so much more spontaneous and a little daring too,' she said laughing, and Pierre parted the wet strands of hair from her face and kissed her on the mouth.

When they finally made their way back to the hotel, Rose-Ellen slipped into a hot bubbly bath and thought of the romantic time they had spent in the cave and smiled happily to herself as she bathed in the warm floating silky suds. She looked in her wardrobe for something special to wear and chose a pretty silk lime-green dress with a dropped waist and pearl collar with matching cuffs. Pierre stepped back to admire the dress. 'Now you are *une vraie francaise!*'

'I saw a photo of two young boys aged about ten and a dog in an orchard in Lucille's house, and I wondered if one of them was you,' Rose-Ellen said, as she lifted her soup spoon.

'Yes, probably.'

'It was lovely image of innocence.'

'Ah, yes, me and Antoine, their only son. We're about the same age, and Vanilla the Labrador. I used to stay with them when my parents were away and Antoine and I became very close, almost like brothers, but now he works in Paris as a banker and we don't see that much of each other.'

'I enjoyed meeting Lucille and Didier. They're clearly so very fond of you. And your Uncle Geoffrey; were you surprised to see him there?'

'I did not expect to see him there. I was with him last week and he never pretended that he was visiting his cousins; he likes to surprise! Lucille and Didier insisted that we visit them again and stay the next time. Lucille and my mother were very close, their mothers were sisters, so naturally I spent a lot of time there as a child, but between my hectic schedule lately here in France I have not been to see them for some time now, and so I'm hoping now that we are based here in France that we shall see more of them with time. I'm so glad that you met them too and they liked you, and that's important to me.'

'I can see that. So Uncle Geoffrey was your mother's brother?'

'No, Uncle Geoffrey was my mother's uncle, so he is actually my grand-uncle. He had no children of his own, and so he was very close to me and Catherine.'

Chapter 54

Life took on a very different meaning for Rose-Ellen now that she and Pierre were engaged. Although this was her second engagement it was different in so many ways. She felt very much part of Pierre's world and could not bear to be away from him for any length of time. She never thought that she could become so hopelessly in love with anybody.

On the last Sunday in August, a huge yellow tractor creaked to a grinding halt outside *Chez-Ellen*. Henri, a local farmer, jumped out leaving his little white Jack Russell in the front seat of the tractor. Rose-Ellen was making leek and potato soup which was nearly ready, and when she caught site of Henri she laid another place. Henri would have his lunch with his mother at one o'clock, but Rose-Ellen knew that he would not turn down a bowl of her rich *potage*. The heavy customary knock on the front door signalled Henri's arrival. There he stood on the threshold holding a huge, malevolent mushroom, pale orange with tinges of red. Rose-Ellen stared at this ghastly yet magnificent piece of fungus. He reached out and thrust the dreaded object into her hand as if he were presenting her with a bouquet of flowers, '*Pour toi, cherie.*'

She took the offending piece and laid it on the dresser and thanked him. He then treated her with the customary kiss on both cheeks. It was common knowledge in the village that Henri regularly quaffed his own home brew, *eau de vie*, becoming invariably intoxicated by midday. The strict drink-driving laws that pertained to cars did not apply to tractors in France, so he was free to drive up and down the roads in any state of inebriation he chose without fear of the *gendarmes*.

'*Comment vas tu? Tu es belle, comme toujours,*' Henri said, with a twinkle in his eye.

Henri's flattering words to Rose-Ellen were incessant and unstinting.

He was charming in that old-fashioned Gallic way. She got the impression that there was no love in his life except for his beloved Charolais cows, his Maman and the little Jack Russell. He greeted Pierre with his usual strong handshake. '*Ah bonjour, Monsieur.*'

'*Bonjour*, Henri,' Pierre greeted him warmly.

'Are you going to the *brocante* in the village at the next weekend, where Maman is selling her antique lace? I'll be organising some of the childrens' games,' Henri asked.

'Indeed we shall and I'll have a stall there too,' Rose-Ellen said, ladling out a large bowl of soup for him as he sat down at the table in the kitchen. Rose-Ellen sometimes took a stall at the local fairs and *brocantes* to get rid of stuff she no longer wanted.

As they chatted, Henri slurped down the soup with chunkfuls of home-made bread and then had a coffee. After about half an hour he got up, stretched himself and looked at his watch. 'I need to go to the river and fill up with water for my cows, and then check on the calves. Ah, Rose-Ellen, your soup was delicious as always, a thousand thanks,' he said, placing his red cap on his head. He said goodbye to both and made his way out.

'It's a pity he couldn't meet somebody nice and get a place of his own. I think it would do him good to get away from the mother and to have a family,' Rose-Ellen said, watching him as he mounted his tractor. Briefly she thought of Danny and how his mother idolised him and the other boys in the family.

'He seems pretty content to me. His life could be described as not at all bad; his mother cooks him his meals every day, he is not regulated by timetables, but rather by the roll of the seasons and he is working outdoors in the clear air,' Pierre said, replenishing his cup of coffee.

'But I think that there is a sadness deep down there in him. I mean, why does he drink so much if his life is as ordered and content as that? You know people have mixed feelings about him here in the village. Some think of him as a bit of a clown and prefer to keep him at a distance, but I think he's sweet,' Rose-Ellen said, putting the empty soup bowls into the dishwasher.

'Oh, who really knows what goes on in anybody's life, my dear. We simply don't know,' Pierre said.

'There is a sadness there, but I suppose nobody really knows anybody else. I mean what they are thinking about in the dark, deep hours of night, do they?' she said, filling the kettle and looking out the window and wondering about her own life.

Chapter 55

That winter was particularly cold. Some parts of France recorded temperatures of minus fourteen degrees centigrade. Henri had become depressed with the state of his economic situation and was drinking heavily. They, like the others in the village, watched as he spiralled deeper and deeper down the vortex of ruin and depression. Turning to Pierre, Rose-Ellen said with concern, 'They say in the village that he's finding it harder and harder to feed his cattle. He has become careless and lax. The other day I watched him get down from the tractor and he was practically staggering.'

'He's too young for this level of abuse. He needs help or counselling, or probably just someone to listen to him,' Pierre replied.

'His mother told me one day as she dropped by to buy some scones that she worried so much about him. Ever since his father died there seems to be no consoling him. His *eau de vie* made with their berries and fruits is his only friend. She said that he spends hours making it outside in one of the barns,' Rose-Ellen said.

One bleak cold evening, as the watery sun was setting, Henri failed to return home. The darkness fell and there was no sign of him. Shortly after seven o'clock, Pierre was engrossed in studying a research paper when one of the neighbours, a local farmer, called to the house in a state of anxiety. 'Doctor, come quickly! It's Henri, he's had a terrible accident, terrible!' Pierre followed the neighbour in his car. Rose-Ellen stood in the doorway, the soup ladle still in her hand as she watched Pierre and the neighbour make off down the road. She decided to follow them in her car.

As Pierre followed the farmer up the field, Rose-Ellen went over to a neighbour's house where people had gathered. There she saw that Henri's mother was being consoled by a group of women. She met Madame Leveque.

'Rose-Ellen, the news is not good. Poor Madame, she told us what happened.' She sensed from Madame Leveque's expression that the news was bad. 'Apparently this afternoon Madame was so frightened that something dreadful had happened to her dear boy when he didn't return for lunch. Normally he would have come home to her, rarely missing the large midday meal, but today there had been no sign of him at all. He had told her that he would go to the village to buy some parts for the tractor, and he might not be home for lunch but would see her later on in the afternoon. So in the evening she left all her "marmots", or pots, on slow simmering and put on her boots and went out, turning left past the monastery and on by the fields.' Rose-Ellen made an attempt to interrupt her, but Madame Leveque was intent on regaling precisely what had happened. 'She called him, but only her black hens came, as if expecting some little treat. It was dusk and she knew that she would have to put them to bed. Of course she's not young any more and it would take her longer to do the simplest of tasks,' Madame Leveque said, taking a deep breath. 'She told us that she went in to the first field and headed on further into the inner field. The cows were standing around the tractor and when they saw her, some seemed to move aside. This is the eerie bit. One of the cows moved several paces in the mother's direction, nuzzled up to her and bawled, a cry which gave her a dreadful premonition. She let out a scream as she saw the big tractor rolled over on its side and Henri under it.'

'My God! Is that how she found him?'

'Apparently so.'

It was after nine when Pierre and some of the farmers returned. Rose-Ellen could see the sadness etched on Pierre's face and detected something awful must have happened. 'Poor Henri. I'm afraid he's dead,' Pierre said, taking her in his arms. She felt numbed. It was the same feeling she had when Kitty died.

'Good God, what happened?' she said.

'He had an accident on his tractor. Poor wretch he was already dead when I got to him. He was lying on his side, his knees slightly bent, eyes staring up at the sky. It was as if he had tried to roll out before the great beast fell on top of him, but didn't quite make it. There was nothing I could do, but to pronounce death. I've no doubt it was instant.'

'Oh my God. His poor mother. What will she do now?' Rose-Ellen exclaimed plopping down on the chair.

'Yes, it will be hard on her. He was her only child.'

'Henri didn't deserve to die like this, he had hardly lived. I can't believe that he is gone,' Rose-Ellen said.

'According to the neighbour's wife, his mother stumbled into their house having crossed the fields on her own, shouting and crying with grief. They had never witnessed anything so alarming. Two farmers brought a huge jack and some heavy chains to lift the tractor off him.'

'Jesus, what a terrible way to go,' Rose-Ellen said, and started to cry. Pierre put a comforting arm on her shoulder.

'The spiralling of his drinking and depression cut short his unfulfilled life. Such a waste,' Pierre said, taking a small *aperitif* offered to him by one of the ladies.

The whisperings in the village continued. Things had become too difficult for Henri. In the church people looked grave, but few were grieving. Rose-Ellen watched the men take his coffin to its final resting place from the church. Pockets of melting snow lay lightly on the ground as people came to pay their respects from neighbouring villages. After all, Henri was one of them, a son of the earth. Rose-Ellen felt the tears well up as the clay was heaped over his coffin, while Pierre stole a comforting arm around her.

'I can't believe that I won't ever hear him laugh again in the kitchen or hear the honk of his tractor outside the front door,' Rose-Ellen said. 'Why do things like this happen? And his poor mother, look at her, she has nobody now, she's heartbroken.'

Outside the church, a small crowd gathered around Henri's mother who was weeping inconsolably, drying her eyes with a large handkerchief.

Rose-Ellen and Pierre bumped into Ollie and Charlotte. 'Terrible business altogether. He was the jewel in his mother's life despite his waywardness. Now she'll be burdened with the family farm,' Ollie said, shaking Pierre's hand.

There was a small do in the local *mairie* after the funeral. Rose-Ellen and Pierre were sitting with Monsieur Beaudry and his wife, and Rose-Ellen recalled how kind Henri was.

'He didn't like hunting or any of the things associated with it, and he dreaded the first day of the season because he couldn't bear to hear the guns. He told me that when he was out in the fields in his tractor he would gather up the baby fawns in his arms from the long grass to bring them to their mothers in the woods before cutting the meadow.'

Madame Beaudry patted her eyes. 'Yes, that would be typical of Henri.'

Monsieur Beaudry nodded. 'Before he took to the drink, he was one of the finest *boule* players in the south-west.' There was silence among the small group. Monsieur Beaudry continued with a hint of sadness in his voice, 'His cows come from the some of the finest pedigrees in France, that rare old white Limousin breed. I hope that they get a good buyer, otherwise they'll just end up in the abattoir, their long line gone for ever!'

'He loved those cows, they were like his babies. I remember meeting him one day while out walking and he was swatting the flies away from their eyes,' Rose-Ellen said, recalling too how Henri loved his cows.

'Ridiculous! These animals are bred for the table,' Madame Beaudry said coldly.

'He said that the meat would taste better if the cattle were happy and well cared for and that they would produce the creamiest milk in the county,' Rose-Ellen said smiling.

'It's never a good idea to give farm animals names or humanise them,' Pierre said, putting down his empty glass.

Each wintry day seemed to bring some kind of drama. Once day the phone rang. '*Cherie*, please come. It's urgent,' Rose-Ellen could just about make out her neighbour's Madame de Saint Amour's barely audible voice at the other end.

'Don't move. I'll be right over.' Rose-Ellen said, and asked Jean-Francois to take over while she rushed next door to *Avalene*. She found *Madame* on the floor in the kitchen surrounded by broken plates and glasses. She could hardly speak and seemed to be in great pain and distress. Rose-Ellen sensed that *Madame* may have broken her hip due to the angle of her right leg on the ground and immediately called the ambulance. Rose-Ellen stayed with her until the ambulance came and brought her to the hospital where *Madame* underwent surgery for her broken hip.

A week later, Rose-Ellen visited her in hospital. *Madame* looked regal, beautifully coiffed, her make-up flawlessly applied despite the trauma she had experienced in the past week, but she had an anxious look about her all the same.

'I feel that I can never return to my beloved *Avalene*,' she cried, taking

Rose-Ellen's hand. 'I knew this time would come some day, *cherie*, It has been my home all my life.'

'You've got to get better first, that is the most important thing right now, and I'll keep an eye on the place in the meantime.'

'Thank you so much, you are so, so kind,' she said, reaching out in the bed to hug Rose-Ellen.

'Poor *Madame*, if she could see the place she'd be very upset. Look at it now, a complete wilderness. Do you think she'll ever come back? I mean she's eighty-three, but they live to be over a hundred in France,' Rose-Ellen said to Pierre as she looked out over the hedge to *Avalene*.

Pierre opened up the newspaper and settled himself into an armchair. 'Well it's all changed now that she's broken her hip. Certainly for the time being it would be very unlikely that she'd come back, and besides, it's probably too much for her.'

Rose-Ellen looked him squarely in the eyes. 'Do you think that there's any truth in the rumour that *Avalene* might be up for sale?'

'I wonder what's behind that mischievous smile!' Pierre said.

She went on, 'I really think it's a lovely place. *Chez-Ellen* is grand, but, well, *Avalene* is just different. I wonder if…'

'Rose-Ellen, where is this leading? Are you not happy here?'

'Of course I am, but we could buy *Madame's* house to live in and maybe run it as a small hotel.'

He put down the paper and turned on the television to listen to the French news on television. Undaunted she continued with her grand plans. 'Look love, I don't want to live over a shop for the rest of my life, and we mightn't like the people who move into *Avalene*. I think that we'd regret it if we didn't at least try, I mean put in a bid. I also feel that *Madame* would love it if we bought her place; she'd know it would be well taken care of and she'd give us first refusal.'

'Don't you think you have enough on your plate with *Chez-Ellen?*' he said, flicking between channels.

But she was not listening to him. 'Now at the rate places are selling here, I'd say it'd be snapped up soon by somebody who'd probably only use it as a summer or weekend retreat, and that'd be a shame. It's a lovely house and should be lived in,' she reasoned.

'You seem to have everything worked out in your own mind; always thinking ahead of the next move. I agree that *Madame's* place is absolutely stunning, the grandest house in the village, like the *Hotel de Ville* in any reasonably sized French village.'

Later that evening Rose-Ellen came over and put her arms around Pierre's neck and whispered to him, 'Love, imagine, just imagine, a house with vaulted cellars, marble fireplaces and chandeliers, and the orangery. Do you remember when we were invited to *prendre un verre* with her? Oh my God, and it could be ours...' With her imagination in full flight she moved in front of the armchair where he sat, and knelt on the chequered Irish mohair rug. 'Listen, Pierre, I thought that we could run a little hotel. There isn't a really good one around here at all. I mean there are the usual *chambres d'hôte*, they're ten a penny, and that *auberge* up the road looks tired and dilapidated and I've heard mixed reports about it.'

He looked at her. 'Oh, darling, stop talking like a child of the grand and the opulent. You make me nervous watching those beautiful eyes gleaming with excitement as you imagine herself floating around in such a gilded setting,' Pierre said, folding the newspaper.

'And besides, *Madame* might get better and move back again. She's a tough old bird,' he said.

She looked at him. 'Somehow I think that unlikely.'

She got up and walked over to the window, thoughts swirling in her imagination. She loved Pierre more than anything else and dreamt of their life together, a life filled with beauty and love. She wanted to buy *Avalene* more than anything else and nothing was going to stop her.

Chapter 56

Rose-Ellen and Delphine met for their usual weekly coffee on Monday when *Chez-Ellen* was closed. Delphine smiled as she set down her cup. Rose-Ellen sensed something from her friend's mischievous and perky expression as Delphine glanced over in the direction of *Avalene*. 'I believe Madame de Saint Amour owes money to the bank and the nursing fees are enormous. Of course if I had the money I'd buy *Avalene* myself. It is simply charming. Who knows what will become of it?' Delphine said, shrugging her shoulders.

'Do you think there'd be much interest in it?' Rose-Ellen asked.

'It's hard to tell. It'd be expensive enough but that's nothing compared to what it would cost to keep it going. They say it's in a dreadful state inside!' Delphine said, plopping a sugar lump into her espresso.

'I don't agree. Whilst *Avalene* is old and would require a lot of money to maintain it, it's a sound and solid structure.'

Over the next few weeks, *Avalene* became wild and unkempt. Magpies and crows vied for nesting rights in the tall chestnut trees at the back. Long, straggly stalks and weeds thrived in this oasis of neglect and wilderness, and the permanently bolted gates gave the place an unwelcoming air.

Rose-Ellen continued visiting Madame de Saint Amour who had now been moved to *La Maison de Retraite*. But one evening, she noticed commotion outside *Madame's* room and stopped to ask one of the nurses what had happened. '*Madame* has had a stroke and is to be taken to the hospital. It is serious,' the nurse said.

Madame died two days later.

There were few relatives at the funeral, and not many from the village, certainly nobody from the other side of the river who fought with *Madame* for years over the river rights. *Madame's* two surviving cousins arranged the service. After all the others had left the cemetery, Rose-Ellen stood for a while at the grave. She laid a small bunch of white lilies and roses on the heaped mound of earth. She remembered that *Madame* had always preferred white and never had worn any jewellery around her neck, except for a double row of snow-white pearls, as she considered pearls to be exclusively a woman's jewel.

Chapter 57

Avalene was not put up for sale, but was to be sold discreetly through the *notaire*. As debts had accumulated and bills were mounting, an immediate sale was imminent. It was February and Pierre went to see Monsieur Rousselot, the *notaire* who was handling the sale. Pierre wanted to buy it for Rose-Ellen, but he also wanted to surprise her and not involve her in the purchase and transaction as she had her heart set on it, but he had also come to love it too. Rousselot looked at him sternly when Pierre put in his bid.

Over supper that night Pierre broke the news to Rose-Ellen, 'Tomorrow, we have an appointment with a Monsieur Rousselot.'

About to take a bite of delicately grilled golden sole, she put down her fork and gasped. 'Who's he?' She eyed him closely. 'Pierre, what's this all about?'

He smiled, a smile she knew only too well, filled with expectation.

'I put in a bid for *Avalene* and it was accepted. It reminds me in a strange way of the house I had grown up in Paris. *Cherie*, we shall soon be the proud owners of your dream house. I know that you had always set your heart on it.'

She looked at him her mouth slowly falling open. 'Why didn't you tell me what you were doing?'

'Because I wanted to surprise you,' he said, as he poured her more chilled white wine.

She was dumbstruck. 'There were some other interested parties, but the legal representatives of her estate needed to sell, so I put in a bid. Of course my first offer was rejected, but then we came to a mutual agreement and what's more, for a little extra, the sale includes the contents.'

'Pierre, oh my God! I can't believe this. Can you imagine what it would be like to live in *Avalene*!' She imagined herself looking into the Florentine gilt mirror with its exquisite carving hanging over the sideboard in the hall, or waltzing around on the finely woven gold and pale turquoise Persian carpet, or catching a glimpse at the pale pink chandelier of the finest, old French glass and…She came out of her brief reverie and eyed Pierre. 'How much did you pay for it?'

'Darling, I bought it for you, for us. Now please, let us enjoy the prospect of becoming the *chatelains* of this beautiful piece of history,' he retorted, clinking his glass against hers.

He sat back in the chair and lifted the wine to his lips, his eyes merry with expectation. 'Uncle Geoffrey transferred a lot of the shares in his business to me and I'll sell them. There's little point in holding on to them now. Besides, in case you've forgotten, there's still my apartment in Monkstown. Also I think that running *Chez-Ellen* is too much for you. You need to look after yourself. Some day you can sell it and just concentrate on running *Avalene* as a fine period guest house.'

'Maybe I could franchise out *Chez-Ellen*; get somebody to manage it and we could have some of the profits and still retain ownership of it. I don't think I could ever sell it. I've put too much of myself into it.'

'You should really consider selling *Chez-Ellen*.'

'No, I won't sell *Chez-Ellen* and that's it. Final!'

'But why would you want to run two places, and have you forgotten you will be married to me and we'll have my salary? Also, darling you must not drive yourself too much.'

She sat back in the chair, her eyes twinkling with mischief and excitement. 'Oh, I can't believe that *Avalene* will be ours, Pierre! I'm so excited!'

Chapter 58

Rose-Ellen had great plans to convert it to a fine hotel or luxurious guest house. But major renovations would be required to bring it up to standard. 'I'll have to get another builder, Monsieur Argillon is just too expensive,' Rose-Ellen said one evening poring over sheets of paper from the bank. Monsieur Argillon was the most respected construction builder for miles around.

Pierre came and stood behind her. 'We'll manage. We don't have to do all the renovations at the same time. Let's just do that part of the house which is needed for a certain number of guests. You could just start off with a small number of guests to fill half of *Avalene's* capacity and build it up from there, and of course you will need to employ more people, Rose-Ellen. You can't take on too much, you're doing far too much as it is.' He brushed the back of her neck with his lips and then turned her around and kissed her.

'Oh, Pierre, you have a way of defusing all situations. It comes I suppose with the medical territory,' she said, looking into his eyes.

'Leave it to me, I'll think of something,' she said, folding away her plans and designs.

Rose-Ellen delegated the day-to-day running of *Chez-Ellen* to Jean-François. He had matured over the past year and more so since his engagement to the local primary school teacher. Chantal, who had shown great promise from the beginning, now helped Rose-Ellen at *Avalene* drawing up plans for guest rooms, helping with the decor as well as the finances. Chantal's place at *Chez-Ellen* was replaced by the local butcher's daughter, Elodie, who was interested in food and wanted to make a career in the catering business. Elodie was a big strong girl with plenty of energy and the right attitude and Rose-Ellen felt that she had been so lucky in finding her. So Elodie and Nadine managed *Chez-Ellen* while Rose-Ellen, Jean-Francois and Chantal concentrated on *Avalene*.

The months rolled by and soon summer arrived. Since moving to France, Pierre saw less and less of his sister Catherine who lived in England and who was a successful competitive horsewoman. He was anxious to go and visit her.

'If we go, I'll have to organise this lot first,' Rose-Ellen said firmly, looking from the goats to the hens. They were out in the garden of *Chez-Ellen*, and Pierre had just mentioned a three-day event in which Catherine was competing in Herefordshire.

'Of course, it'll only be for a few days,' he added.

Rose-Ellen appreciated that Pierre had few relatives and was only too happy to accommodate him with regard to meeting up with his only sibling, Catherine. The three-day horse trial was held at the end of May.

At the end of May, they set out for the three-day event in the UK. Rose-Ellen settled herself in the front seat and tried to relax, and not to think of the business back home as they drove from Portsmouth where they had landed by ferry from France, and headed north in the UK.

Pierre reached over and felt Rose-Ellen's arm briefly. 'Darling, I hope that you won't be too bored, but I have promised Catherine for years that I'd attend one of these competitions and I simply haven't had the time before now. She looked after me when I needed to recover from my injuries.'

'Of course, Pierre, I understand. It's a dangerous sport,' she said, watching the line of traffic in front of them and wondered how long it would take them to get there.

'Yes, eventing is one of the most dangerous and unpredictable of all sports, but I'm afraid that I understand little or nothing about the navigational configurations of the equine brain. At least with sailing one was dealing with a vibrant although relatively inanimate medium – the sea – which was not subject to the same fears and whims as a horse. She has few relatives, apart from me, so it's important that I, as her only brother, take an interest in her great passion – horses.'

'I'll just keep in the background for the few days. I've never been to anything like this before apart from the local gymkhanas we'd go to as kids.'

Rose-Ellen wondered how Pierre had met Moira. 'Is that how you met Moira, I mean, through Catherine?'

'Yes, they are still good friends, but I think now that the eventing takes up all of their time. It's very demanding, and of course there's the competitive element.'

After many hours of driving, they eventually arrived at the course. The place was packed with horseboxes. A steward opened the gate for them and once they made themselves known, he handed Pierre a parking ticket for the three days. Pierre then drove across the bumpy field behind all of the horseboxes where the other cars and jeeps were parked and then made their way over to the enclosure. Pierre called his sister on his mobile and after a while Catherine lumbered towards them humping a saddle. She appeared buoyant and confident.

'Hi, Pierre,' she said, dropping the saddle on the ground and rushing to him putting her arms around him.

'Hi, Cath.' He turned to Rose-Ellen. 'I think you've met Rose-Ellen.'

Catherine turned to Rose-Ellen. 'Hello, Rose-Ellen. Yes, we met in the hospital. Congratulations on the engagement.' She came over and clasped Rose-Ellen to her and gave her a kiss. Catherine and Pierre chatted briefly and caught up on the family news.

'I'll get you sorted out with accommodation firstly,' Catherine said.

'So how do you feel about the next three days? I mean, what are your chances?' Pierre said, as they made their way out of the car park.

'The course could be a little tricky for Croga, but then again could be a lot worse with the awful unpredictability of the weather.'

Pierre turned to Rose-Ellen. 'Darling, in case you don't know, Croga is Catherine's wonderful horse, a nine-year old gelding of the famous Trakihner breed, built for Puissance.'

'I'm not sure if this ground will suit him,' Catherine said, poking the ground with her toe. 'It's muddy and sloppy in patches after the recent rainfall around the trial run, and could pull on his tendons.' She turned to face both of them. 'Once I've shown you to your cottage I'll take a tour of the course, and then I'm off to pamper Croga.'

After settling them in the cottage on the grounds where they were staying, Catherine gave Pierre a quick kiss and disappeared carrying a large grooming kit which contained everything she needed to buff and shine her beloved horse: curry combs, sweat scrapers, leather body brushes.

'She's like you in many ways,' Rose-Ellen said to him as she watched Catherine jump into a waiting Land Rover that was being driven by her trainer.

'We've become closer over the years,' Pierre whispered to Rose-Ellen.

They met Catherine early the next day, in the stable, as she was slapping hot towels on the horse's back. Horse smells pervaded the air: leather, saddle soap, wax, hay, fresh dung and horse sweat. Croga's saddle rested on a pole on the wall while the bridle with various curling reins and harness hung beside the saddle. Catherine smiled at Pierre and smoothed out the baking hot, steaming towels.

'Are you OK?' he asked.

'Oh, it's hard work. I still have to plait him, but that won't take long.'

'Is there anything I can do?' Rose-Ellen asked feeling a little redundant being surrounded by such frenetic activity.

Croga started to shake his head and stamp slightly as if somewhat agitated. 'No, no thanks. He's a bit jumpy after the long drive. I think I'll leave the plaiting. I'm just too tired and it's quite tedious.'

Catherine and Croga were the fifth to compete in the dressage section. Pierre and Rose-Ellen had a good seat and watched the start gate nervously. Rose-Ellen thought Croga was a splendid animal, with his long sloping shoulder and good hind qualities. To her he seemed the most perfect of creatures; his beauty, perfection and elegance was a joy to behold.

Pierre waved at his sister, but she was too busy concentrating to return his wave, her nervous smile barely visible through the flimsy net under a tall top hat. She sat poised in a navy riding coat, her snow white stocktie squarely knotted with a gold pin. Her white gloved hands held the reins securely. She pressed her black booted spurs gently into the side of the horse and they got through their paces well and were placed third. Rose-Ellen looked at Pierre and could see how proud he felt of his younger sister. She reached over and touched his hand.

'She looks so beautiful and poised, like a statue.' She thought she saw his eyes glisten.

'For a split second back there, she reminded me so much of our mother,' he said, squeezing her hand.

The next day Pierre and Rose-Ellen strolled around and marvelled at the various dikes and fences that the horses had to negotiate. At one stage, Rose-Ellen texted Jean-Francois to check on the business at home in France, and Pierre came up and put his arm around her. 'Darling you've been so good to come with me, it would have been quite tedious for me, as while I'm very fond of Catherine, I don't share her all absorbing passion for horses. I know it's difficult to take you away from your commitments at home.'

She sent the text and leaned into Pierre. 'Life goes on, Pierre, and it's important for me to be here with you, and besides, I'm quite enjoying the thrill of it all; it's well, different and Catherine's a great girl.'

Catherine on Croga manifested nerves of steel with nearly five hundred kilos of horse flesh to manoeuvre around some difficult obstacles, rotationary fences and sly sneaky stumps of trees. The pair went well and steadily for the first few obstacles. Then, approaching the dreaded ditch and its descent, Croga hesitated somewhat, putting his front two legs forward a tiny bit as if testing the decline. His feet began to slide slightly on the wet surface. It looked for an instant as if he were going to refuse – ears pricked up and slightly back – but his back legs never moved, and Rose-Ellen wondered if Catherine had coaxed him gently with soft words as he slid down beautifully in three short, well-timed strides, straightening himself up at the last. Pierre stood up and watched from a distance with his binoculars and admired the discipline of the duo. Catherine gave Croga enough rein to right himself over the fence at the end of the ditch, and 'bravo', he made it. Pierre shouted 'Well done' and one or two people looked in his direction and smiled. None of the others had managed this one. Jumping well and in good time, they were placed second overall.

Pierre and Rose-Ellen joined Catherine when it was over. Catherine was ecstatic. 'Oh boy, am I glad that's over! I can't believe it went so well. Oh, my darling,' she said, kissing Croga, who shook his head up and down furiously as if in recognition of his achievements.

Pierre put a comforting arm around his sister's shoulder. 'You were great, really great, and it was a difficult course; so many acute angled turns and just plain awkward jumps'.

'I think some of the riders were simply too inexperienced,' she said.

'Or hadn't put in the practice and it showed, so well done,' Pierre murmured.

She was laughing now with Pierre and picking up the reins so that Croga followed, and they all strode off discussing the pitfalls encountered during the round.

The last day was the show jumping and the preferred discipline for both Catherine and Croga. They were eighth out of nineteen entrants. Catherine fiddled with her gloves and adjusted her hat. Number seven was almost finished, having had eight faults. Pierre stood with them. 'I've got to keep calm and be careful. I know he's brave and naturally strong, but anything can go wrong out there,' Catherine said.

He sensed her nervousness. 'All you can do is your best, nothing else. Look, it's not the Olympics. I'm sure everything will be fine.'

As he spoke, the previous rider returned from the ring. Nobody so far had had a clear round and those with the least number of faults would have a jump-off to decide the winner.

'Wish me luck,' she said, and took Croga into the ring. Pierre heard her name and horse being announced over the tannoy.

They started off well. Pierre handed Rose-Ellen the binoculars. Croga was indeed a strong, striding horse, with a good back. He became truly airborne over the jumps, taking them like a stag, a joy to watch while effortlessly negotiating the most difficult ones. He managed the tricky two fence oxer and glided gracefully over the water jump. Perhaps it was the exuberance of the fantastic jump after the water, but his foot nudged one of the copings on the next fence and for a split second it looked as if the tottering object would stay, but then it just fell. Rose-Ellen shouted, 'Oh no, what a shame!' Hushed gasps of disappointment came from the crowd. Still, the two soldiered on and ended their round. They had four faults and were in the lead so far.

When they had finished, Pierre and Rose-Ellen were waiting to meet her. 'Sis, you were marvellous!'

Catherine was breathless from the exertion having negotiated nearly twenty fences, ditches and dikes. Croga was perspiring profusely, with damp pearls of sweat dribbling from his sleek coat and froth foaming from his mouth. Catherine bent down and patted his steaming coat. 'Well done, my beauty!'

Her trainer rushed to greet her. 'Great work, you were fantastic. Let's hope nobody else has a clear round, but it would take an Olympic standard rider to clear that second fence.'

In the final jump-off, the pair had to compete with three others who had four faults from the previous round. Croga jumped well. He had a clear round within the time and won the show jumping. Catherine was absolutely thrilled.

Eventing scores are cumulative, so the pair came second overall in the three days. Catherine was disappointed to have been just shaded by another rider from the North of Ireland on a dappled grey gelding. 'I can't believe that we were within an inch of winning,' she said. 'We were so close, so bloody close! Just a few seconds! It seems so unfair. Oh, it's no good coming second, nobody remembers anybody who comes second. You have to get first, that's what it's all about, winning, bloody winning.'

Pierre reached over and put his arm around her to try to reassure her. 'There'll be other opportunities. Plenty of them, I'm sure of it. Besides you won the show jumping.' But his kind words did little to assuage her misgivings.

'Oh, I know, but it's the cumulative score that's important. Croga's at his prime.'

Rose-Ellen noticed how alike Pierre and his sister were: she was tall and good-looking like him with a fierce competitive streak in her. She had similar mannerisms and had that same focussed gaze. She was glad that she met Pierre's nearest relative and looked forward to having a close relationship with his only sibling in the years to come.

One day in early June, Rose-Ellen said to Pierre, 'Let's throw a party to celebrate our engagement and the purchase of *Avalene*. I'm so excited and these are important milestones, so we must celebrate them.'

He looked at her with some misgivings. 'Darling, don't you have enough on your plate with everything?'

'Not at all, when you run a business, Pierre. You've got to spend and entertain otherwise it'll all go back to the taxman, and better us enjoy it than the French government. So we'll just put all of the catering down against the tax bill, simple really!'

They sent invitations to friends, neighbours, suppliers, family members and Pierre's work colleagues. Olivia and Brendan agreed to come too despite the fact that Olivia was devoting more and more time to running the emporium with their Uncle Michael.

Avalene's garden had a neglected air about it but Ollie Dempsey had trimmed the box hedges and cut and rolled the lawn. On a lovely June summer's day Pierre and Rose-Ellen flung open the large wrought iron gate to the front of *Avalene*, which had been closed for a long time.

As Charlotte and Ollie's maroon van trundled in through the gates Rose-Ellen went out to help, and as she peered inside the van she saw stacks of plates covered in aluminium foil and cellophane paper. Charlotte was organisation personified, but Ollie would not let Rose-Ellen near the food. 'Rose-Ellen, go and pour yourself a glass of wine. We're doing this all the time; leave it to the experts.'

'Oh, God, this is always the worst part, just before the guests arrive,' Rose-Ellen sighed, as she looked yet again at her watch.

Charlotte patted her arm. 'Don't worry, it'll all turn out well.'

Out of nowhere, Paidraigin appeared, jumped up and licked the flesh of the large wild salmon which Charlotte had just deposited on the table. Rose-Ellen let out a scream and whacked her away. 'Cats, you can never trust them, ever!'

Rose-Ellen was dishing out some home-made mayonnaise into little pots and Ollie came over to her. 'I must say, Rose-Ellen, the whole place looks fabulous.'

'And thanks to you the garden is terrific,' she said.

'You've a great spread of food now: wild salmon, chicken *chasseur*, *boeuf flambé*, local cheeses and cakes and *patisseries* to die for. Herself was at the cookin' and bakin' since the crack of dawn.'

'Ah thanks, Ollie. I don't know what I'd have done without you and Charlotte,' Rose-Ellen got up and gave him a big hug. When everything was ready, Rose-Ellen went upstairs and changed into a chic silver grey silk dress with a charcoal-coloured belt.

Guests began to trickle in a little after four o'clock and Pierre greeted them, while Rose-Ellen flew around to see to last minute things. Rose-Ellen could hear her pal Siobhan trying out her French on one of the local *entrepreneurs*. She thought Siobhan looked lovely in an exquisitely cut cornflower-blue dress made of the finest linen.

'I'm so glad everything worked out in the end,' Siobhan said, giving Rose-Ellen a big hug.

'Thanks, Siobhan, you look stunning as usual!'

'This place looks amazing. Fair play to you, girl, you're one in a million,' she said, casting her eye around.

Ollie and Charlotte served the food, and Jean-François was in charge of the drinks, while Pierre helped with the wine. As the place filled, people strolled out amongst the box hedges and garden. Pierre stood on the steps and welcomed everybody. Rose-Ellen watched as he stepped up on to the front. Ollie handed him the roving mike. Rose-Ellen thought he looked splendid in a casual white trousers and pale blue shirt.

'Good afternoon, everybody and you are all very welcome here. Many thanks for coming to help us celebrate the opening of *Avalene* and of course our engagement. I would like to thank all of you who helped Rose-Ellen to settle down here in France to make this wonderful place our new home. I particularly would like to welcome those who came from Ireland. So let's raise a toast to all of you.' To a cacophony of applause and a few whistles, Pierre thanked the musicians, the regular band and the *troubadours* and then made his way over to his relatives Lucille and Didier.

People mingled and chatted until the quiet of the evening, when the furniture was arranged for the dancing on the large *terrasse* in front of the house, and the *troubadours* retired to one of the quieter rooms at the back. People soon drifted on to the tiled *terrasse* to start the night's revelry with a rousing Argentinean tango. Charlotte's brother and his sexy girlfriend, in a red and black polka-dot short frilly dress, delighted the crowd with a spellbinding salsa dance, as they manoeuvred each other effortlessly across the tiles with potent energy, her fish netted limbs wrapping themselves around his slim agile legs. Siobhan shimmied and boogied with the recently divorced Monsieur Argillon, the decorator, who specialised in period houses and who had done the more delicate decorative work to *Avalene*.

Monsieur Beaudry, after several glasses of wine, sidled over to Rose-Ellen. She wondered if he were going to give her a sample of the latest grammar lesson. 'Good evening, *Madame*. It is a wonderful time we are all having and may I commend you on the excellent food and wine, *superbe*!'

'You are most welcome, *Monsieur*.'

He put down his glass. The strains of a slow waltz filled the air. 'I am wondering, *Madame*, if you would do me the honour of dancing with me.'

Although taken aback, Rose-Ellen said, 'I'd be delighted,' and *Monsieur* proved to be a very accomplished dancer. As she glided around on Monsieur Beaudry's arms, she noticed Ollie trying to teach Delphine Irish dancing with little success and Charlotte having a quiet cigarette and drink with Monsieur Launay.

After the festivities were over and the last guest had left, Pierre and Rose-Ellen made their way up to their room. Rose-Ellen stood at the window looking wistfully out on to *Madame's* rose garden at the back, having lovingly been tended for years with its profusion of famous old roses with rich splashes of magenta, crimson, coral pink and primrose yellow.

Turning to Pierre, she said, 'I just get carried away here. Looking out, remembering how things were when I first arrived, and now *Madame* is gone. The roses remind me of how she would gather bunches of them up in her arms and lay a large bouquet in my arms. All the lovely old French roses giving their first bloom in June.'

'I see that you still miss her,' he said, coming and putting his arms around her.

She looked up at him. 'Oh, very much so. I had got to know her very well these past few years and we'd begun to rely on each other in different ways. She was so good, and just made me feel special; it's hard to explain.'

He kissed her gently on the cheek. 'Yes, that is how we often remember those who are gone, how they made us feel, the effect they had on those around.'

'And then I just thought of Mam. How she would have loved this place and would have been in her element here at the party here tonight, talking to everybody and then our engagement, she would be planning all sorts of things…' she then started to cry.

Pierre cradled her in his arms. 'I can sense you feel at home here.'

She rested her head against his chest as he smoothed her hair. 'When I bought *Chez-Ellen* I used to dream of living in *Avalene*, but now it's become more than a dream,' she said, through muffled sobs.

He looked down at the top of her head and then looked out at the beautiful garden as the sun set on it with its riot of colour. They watched the pale pink light fading down around *Avalene*, the subtle eclipse of evening, with the far off sounds of cooing pigeons in the trellised trees, their distinctive call a reminder that evening was folding in.

Chapter 59

Avalene opened as a guesthouse in September. The drab *auberge* in the nearby town referred guests to *Avalene* when it was full. Many people requested dinner and this was proving to be almost a full-time commitment. 'God almighty, if it's like this now, what'll it be like in the summer?' Rose-Ellen said to Chantal, who had just taken a full board booking for three days from a male choir from Austria.

'We'll just have to find another place that we can refer them to,' Chantal said, as she walked across the hall to put the final touches to a bunch of lilies.

'Oh, I hate giving business away, and besides we'd only be referring them to shabby places because there's nothing round here. They would then have to go to La Rochelle. No, I won't have that,' Rose-Ellen said firmly. Chantal looked at her with some concern.

Rose-Ellen was worried about Pierre. She noticed that strange anxious look which had been creeping back to his countenance of late. 'Pierre, I am so happy now, everything's coming along great, but darling I worry about you. Is everything all right, it's just that you're looking anxious lately?'

'Yes, why do you ask?'

'I sometimes sense that you are restless. It's probably just me with my suspicious mind; pay no heed to me,' but still she was worried.

'Darling, living with you is a challenge!' he smiled at her.

'It's just a feeling I have about you, and I hope that I'm proved wrong, that's all.'

But she wondered whether this life was all that he had expected.

One evening the phone rang and Chantal answered it. 'Yes, I'll get *Monsieur* right away, a moment please.' She put down the phone and called Pierre.

Taking the call, Pierre spoke animatedly to the person at the other end, 'That's marvellous! Of course I'll go. I'll make my own arrangements and let you know.'

Rose-Ellen felt a strange kind of unease as she came out to the reception area. 'Who was that?' she asked him.

'The Eastern Infirmary. They want me to go for an interview for a consultant position.'

'I didn't know that you had even applied for a position. Why didn't you tell me?'

'But, darling, I applied for the position months ago and when the interview came up, well, between everything I simply forgot. I'm sorry. I ought to have mentioned it to you. Now they want me to attend the interview.'

'How many candidates will be up for this position?'

'Who knows? A consultant's post will attract many candidates, from UK and Ireland as well as the US and Canada and possibly Australia.'

Moving away from Pierre, Rose-Ellen made her way into the big kitchen. There were tears in her eyes. He followed her. 'I'm sorry, Pierre I can't talk to you now. I must feed the new chickens.'

Carrying a basin of meal she strolled down to the rear of *Avalene* and checked on her new arrivals in the henhouse; her four *Crèvecœur* hens and one cockerel, together with the three Dorking pullets, were scratching away happily. The cockerel was proving to be very difficult and territorial. However, she thought he looked magnificent, his lustrous, iridescent green-black plumage shone in the evening glow and he carried himself with a certain air of authority. But she was distracted now and perfunctorily threw the food in to the henhouse. Letting herself out of the side gate, she crossed over the small road to check on the ducks and rabbits in *Chez-Ellen*. As she approached Edwina, the goat stretched her long neck over the enclosure expecting a pat and some nibbles which Rose-Ellen had in her pocket.

Pierre caught up with her as she was patting the goat. The sky was settling in the evening twilight, changing from aquamarine to lilac and then vermilion. Rubbing Edwina on the nose, Rose-Ellen turned and glanced fleetingly at the sky avoiding Pierre's gaze, murmuring, 'It looks as if it's going to be fine tomorrow. You know what they say, red sky at night is shepherd's delight.' Then, spotting Finn's garden stone, she bent down and smoothed back some of the ivy and weeds that had grown over it, hiding its verse.

As she was busy pulling back the knotted grass, Pierre came and stood over her. 'Rose-Ellen…well…are you not pleased with the news?'

Long wisps covered the stone and she took in its verse and then cast her eye round the place, full of activity, growth and plenty. Her worst fears were realised. Now she realised that their little cosy nest egg that she had worked so hard to build up would probably be no more. She was nearly chocking back the tears. 'I thought you wanted to be away from Ireland and the whole hospital scene there. I mean, after all that happened,' she said.

He crouched down and held her by the shoulders and looked into her eyes. 'But, darling, this is different. This is the Eastern Infirmary and it's the post for consultant oncologist. Don't you see, it's a chance in a lifetime? It's what I've always dreamed of!'

He carried on, as excited as a boy with a new toy, talking about research projects, silver bullet blockbuster drugs…and all the while she said nothing. With a distracted air, she glanced out over at the horizon in the fading light. 'Haven't you a good job here in La Rochelle? And besides, Ireland is all but bankrupt now.'

But she knew that there was no comparison between a permanent consultancy post in the Eastern Infirmary and a contractual clinical research position in oncology in La Rochelle. This was the glittering prize that he had dreamed about.

'Well, you know what that means,' she said, turning to face him.

He was staring at the ground and then he lifted his eyes and glanced around at the well-kept garden so meticulously designed with plants and animals tenderly cared for. 'I do. It will mean the end of all this, this beautiful spot if I'm successful. But I may not be. As I said, there will be quite a few candidates.' He took her by the shoulders and looked into her eyes. 'But, darling, you can have another place in Dublin, a business of your own, or a garden like this. This is not the end; it's only the beginning. We'll work something out. There's always room to compromise.'

Compromise! She could hear Kitty's words again ringing in her ears. Always compromise. Why should she have to compromise! This was her life which had drained every fibre of her being, but which she had felt was worth the effort. But she loved Pierre dearly and would do anything to remain always with him.

She wondered what would become of them and was confused. For the time being it was difficult for her to share his overriding joy. The process was only at the interview stage, but deep in her heart she knew that there would be few candidates who could match his intellect or expertise.

A few days later, Pierre flew to Dublin for the interview. Then over the next few days, there were more interviews by different panels. He phoned her every day and kept her up-to-date with the progress of the interviews. Each hour of the day that he was away she was distracted and jumped every time the phone went. Then on the third night he phoned her with the news, '*Cherie*, I've been offered the post, and while I'll gladly take it, I have to think about us. I know you've put so much of your soul into the business and now *Avalene*, but a whole new life is opening up for us back in Dublin where you'll never need to worry about another invoice again.'

Despite her reservations, she was gracious about his news. 'Oh, Pierre. Congratulations! You deserve it after the last few years.' She meant every word of it.

When they had hung up, she poured herself a glass of wine and sat by the fireside. It was cold outside and watching the flickering flames, her thoughts turned to Pierre and how he had been altered irrevocably by trauma and ill-fate and how her own cosy life had been shaken by circumstance. She knew that if she tried to stop him from taking up this position he would bear a simmering resentment towards her for the rest of his life.

She reflected on all that she had built up here, primarily the business, but also living in the haunting beauty of *Avalene* and in this quaint French village which was very much part of her life now. She felt as if she were at cross-currents in her life; torn between this little jewel in France and her homeland with her beloved. But her love for Pierre was strong and if she let him go she would yearn for him for ever. They would reach some type of compromise. After all she was resourceful and nothing was impossible, so that no resentment or bitterness would exist between them. She phoned Olivia that night.

'Hi Olivia, how are things?'

'Ah, what can I say. I miss Mam terribly, the place is not the same without her. But Brendan has been made school principal and we are planning to get married soon.'

'Oh, that's fantastic news. Sometimes it's so hard here to go on with my life knowing that I'll never hear Mam's voice again.' Rose-Ellen placed the back of her hand to her mouth to stop herself from crying. After a while she asked about their father.

'He's not too bad most of the time, but then sometimes he just relapses and I wonder if he knows that Mam is gone at all.'

Rose-Ellen could sense the angst in her sister's voice. 'I was wondering if I could put something by you. I need your opinion,' she said.

'Fire ahead, I'd be only too happy to help in whatever way I can.'

Rose-Ellen took a deep breath. 'Well, Pierre has been offered a consultant's post in Dublin and you know what that means – it means uprooting ourselves from here and I'm torn between going or staying.'

'Rose-Ellen, since Mam's death, I have put a lot of store on personal happiness and family because at the end of the day, that's all that matters. You don't have a choice! Pierre will be your husband soon and where he goes, you'll have to follow. It's as simple as that. Unless, of course, you're getting cold feet!'

'No, of course I'm not. Well, it's just that I've put so much into this place and to just get up and leave would break my heart,' Rose-Ellen explained.

'Listen, love comes around only once in a lifetime, if even that. You can start a business any time. Now you know what you have to do, and don't start thinking of property and businesses. They'll be around when you die, but relationships are what matter in life.'

Rose-Ellen knew that her sister was right, but she was torn between her love for Pierre and her attachment to this little piece of France. She wanted another opinion so she picked up the phone to speak to her old pal Siobhan.

'How are ye? Great to hear from you! How are things in *la belle* France?' Siobhan was so animated and lively on hearing her friend she sounded as if she were sitting in the next room.

'Things are fine, but well, Pierre has been offered a consultant post in the Eastern Infirmary.'

'That's wonderful news, Rose-Ellen.'

'But it means uprooting ourselves from here in France.'

'So what? It's not the end of the world!'

'I'm not sure if I want to return to Ireland, not now when we've just bought *Avalene*, and well, things are dreadful in Ireland.'

'Well, my attitude is to suit yourself. After all, you've put a lot of hard work into your business and it would really be a shame to just abandon it now that it's getting off the ground. However, a consultant post in Ireland, well, they don't come round that often.'

'Siobhan, it's so hard, so very hard, and this has come at such a bad time. I'll have to do a lot of soul-searching in the next few days. I seem to be at cross-currents in my life when I thought I had settled on a place to live,' Rose-Ellen said.

'Now don't let me influence you. You have to suit yourself, Rose-Ellen, and of course I'd love if you came back, but follow your heart. Do whatever you feel is best deep down; don't be influenced by anybody else.'

Rose-Ellen felt suddenly adrift; unmoored from her surroundings. She could not seem to focus as images of herself as a consultant's wife in Ireland and as a successful hotelier in France drifted in and out of her mind.

She glanced down at her beautiful ring; its rose-pink twinkling against the delicate grey rested neatly on her finger. Casting her eyes around the drawing room, she gazed at the delicate china piece that Pierre had given her; a lady capriciously lounging over a piano as an admirer wooed her with his playing and she became nostalgic. Rose-Ellen sat down and sighed as she thought of how she would have to wrench herself away from such beauty and symmetry.

That evening Rose-Ellen went for a long walk out past the castle on the edge of the town, passing Henri's farm. His precious cattle and their calves would never low again. They were all gone. All was quiet and the place had a deserted air about it. His enormous tractor lay idle, whilst everything seemed rusty and abandoned. Rumour had it in the village that Henri's mother had been so distraught that she had not got round to selling or renting the land yet.

She walked on until she came to the windy part of the road with its serpentine drive leading to a bridge under which the river eddied. A heron perched on a stone, his focussed eye fixed on moving prey, his ungainly grey shape making him almost invisible against the backdrop of great lumbering boulders over the cascading water. Overhead she could hear the whispering call of a bird of prey, a short mewing 'wee-oo' as it glided and flapped gracefully in buoyant flight. She watched as it circled higher and higher cutting quite a dash through the evening sky. It seemed to her a beauty with its white head, chestnut body and forked tail and huge wingspan, and briefly she envied its soaring freedom as it moved out of sight.

In the silence Rose-Ellen tried to think of the future, but it was a silence filled with whispers and evening murmurs as the shadows gathered and dusk enveloped all. Standing on the bridge, and reflecting on the mosaic of life and its trials; how everything was in a state of flux and constantly flowing, nothing ever remaining the same. She thought of how the desire to hold on to things could dominate one's very existence. She realised that she could not continue with this frenetic pace, investing the future with more and more of her energy and spirit, as the present was slowly ebbing away silently and apprehensively, until in time all that she had created would be reduced to the silent world of regrets and heartache.

Whilst it was important to let go, they, like the trail we leave behind, are an intrinsic part of what we are. Her dreams of a life fulfilled in France, where she would never be beholden to anybody, where that barren plain of regret and disappointment would be left behind, would soon be mere embers.

She did not really want to return to Ireland. When her mother was alive that tug towards the homeland was very strong, but now she was uncertain. Her father was old and becoming more forgetful, and Olivia and Brendan were wrapped up in their own busy lives and would soon be married. Then she thought of Pierre and how dull and unfulfilled her life would be without his love.

Something would have to be sacrificed. Like the wild geese as they make their way thousands of miles across vast wastes to feed, or the salmon hurtling themselves upriver against the surging rapids to their spawning grounds, she too would have to make that journey into the unknown to follow her heart's destiny. At cross-currents in her life, Rose-Ellen was filled with a sense of foreboding and uncertainty.

Chapter 60

Pierre was to return to La Rochelle, arriving there at about seven-thirty pm. Rose-Ellen was preparing his favourite dish, *Coquilles Saint-Jacques a la Parisienne* – scallops in white wine. She had laid out the table with care and attention to detail: the finest *Deux Sevres* service, champagne on ice, while fresh flowers adorned the rooms of *Avalene*. She showered and came down to organise the food in the kitchen, wearing a satin wrap, her moist hair coiled in a towel.

While the scallops were cooking gently in the white wine and herbs, she hummed and expected to hear her darling's footsteps any minute as he turned the key in the lock. There he would stand, with his jacket slung over his shoulder, briefcase in one hand and the side of wild Irish smoked salmon in the other, which he had promised her.

But the minutes dragged into half hours and then into hours and soon it was almost ten o'clock and there was no sign of Pierre. Nor was there any reply from his mobile. If his flight had been delayed he would surely have phoned her as he was always meticulous about such matters.

She called the airport but the number rang and rang. Finally somebody answered and confirmed that the flight had been on time. But unfortunately they would not confirm if Pierre had been on it. Who could she call? Then the phone rang. She ran to it expecting to hear Pierre's voice at the other end. Maybe he had been diverted to Brussels or Paris, but it was Olivia.

'Hi, Sis, how are things?'

'Oh fine. I mean, they are and they're not,' Rose-Ellen said concernedly.

'What do you mean? Are you OK?'

'I don't know. I was expecting Pierre back from Ireland this evening on the flight from Dublin, and the flight's arrived in La Rochelle and he's not on it. It's just so unlike him not to call, and there's no reply from his mobile; it's as if he's just vanished!'

'I'm sure that there is a very simple reason. Look, he's probably on another flight at the moment and he can't call you. I bet that's what has happened,' Olivia said, trying to placate her sister.

But Rose-Ellen looked at the clock over the fridge and it was nearly ten-fifteen pm. She sensed that something had happened. 'I'll hang up, Olivia in case Pierre is trying to contact me.'

'Sure, I understand. Ring me later if you haven't heard anything. I'd hate to think of you there on your own worried to death.'

'I will, I promise,' Rose-Ellen said, and put the receiver back.

Slowly Rose-Ellen made her way up to bed. She would try to sleep; maybe tomorrow there would be better news. She drifted off to sleep, but it was a brief restless one. She could hear the rumble of thunder in the distance to the west and wondered if this were heralding bleak news. She had a strange sense of unease. She awoke suddenly as her mobile by the bedside rang jarring her out of her unquiet dreams. It was just after midnight. She grabbed the phone and heard a voice at the other end.

'Hello. Is that Ms Rose-Ellen Power?'

'Yes, yes,' she answered fearfully.

'I'm Dr Kavanagh, a doctor in casualty in the Dublin City Hospital. Do you know a Dr Pierre O'Hegarty? We were asked to phone you by a relative.'

'Yes, yes, he's my *fiancé*. I was expecting him this evening. Has anything happened?'

Rose-Ellen was frantic.

The doctor's voice continued in a cool, clinical tone, developed over the years from having to impart the gravest of news to patients' relatives. 'I'm afraid that there's been an accident. I'm sorry to be the bearer of such bad news. Is there somebody with you?'

She had a premonition that something terrible had happened. She had to find out the truth. She sat up in bed, waiting for the worst. 'Yes, there's somebody here,' she said hurriedly.

'I'm afraid that Dr Pierre O'Hegarty was hit by a bus this evening while cycling. He was taken to the casualty department here in the late afternoon and we worked on him all evening until now.' There was a pause. 'But his injuries were very serious. He had lost too much blood and went into shock. I'm very sorry but I have to tell you that Dr O'Hegarty passed away about a half an hour ago.'

Rose-Ellen let out a scream. She did not know what was happening; she felt as if she were still dreaming. 'I can't believe this. Are you sure that he's gone. I mean, I mean is there any hope? There must be some mistake, not Pierre, no, please no, no, it can't be him, this can't be true!'

'I'm terribly sorry.'

'Oh my God, my God,' she screamed into the phone.

'Have you somebody with you there in France as this has been a terrible shock.' The voice at the other end of the phone sounded distant and faint.

'Yes. Did he have anybody with him when he passed away, any friend, family member?' she could barely get the words out, as she was choking with sadness.

'Yes, we called his aunt as her name was on his passport in the case of an emergency. She is with him right now and it was she who asked us to contact you. We found your number on his mobile.'

Although Rose-Ellen had never met Pierre's Aunt Grace each woman would have been aware of the other's existence as Pierre had talked of each to the other. At least Grace was with him when he died and would tell the immediate family, Rose-Ellen thought. After hanging up, she wrapped her dressing gown around her and ran out of the house. She was delirious and did not know where to go following wherever a path led her. She needed to be with somebody, needed to be hugged and listened to right now, but all was silent and black in the village behind closed shutters.

Rose-Ellen walked through the silent streets sobbing to herself, eventually coming to the bend in the river where she lay down on the river's embankment beside a large oak tree, and cried her eyes out. She could not believe that she would never see Pierre again, never hear his distinctive voice, witness his broad smile, or feel his arm stealing around her waist. He, who had given everything he had for the betterment of the terminally ill, to be snuffed out of life by a bus in such a ridiculous, mindless way, seemed to her the cruellest of ironies. He, who had defied death with two bullets, was now lying on a marble slab in a Dublin hospital as a result of multiple injuries from being hit by a bus. She looked up at the pale crescent moon in the sky.

'God, if you are there, where is the justice? If you exist at all? He bloody well didn't deserve to die! He was needed by so many. Why couldn't it have been somebody else hit by that stupid bus?' Exhausted from trying to understand this freak accident she dragged herself up, returned to the house and poured herself a tumbler of brandy and fell asleep on the couch.

The next day Rose-Ellen awoke and for a brief transient time comforted herself into believing that it had all been a bad dream and that everything would be fine, but it was not to be. The next few days were passed in a trance while she made preparations for her journey home to attend Pierre's funeral. She did things automatically and had to take tranquillisers to help get her through each day. Her heart was aching inside with the numbness and the sense of loss and the awful dreadful fact that she would never, ever see Pierre or hear his lovely velvet voice again.

Delphine, Charlotte and Jean-Francois were wonderfully supportive and agreed to take care of everything while she was away. Rose-Ellen had few recollections of the journey to the airport or of landing in Dublin. It was all just a blur. At the funeral, people gripped her hand firmly with kind words.

"He was the best", "Only for the doctor, the wife would be six foot down under", " a man in a million", "a cruel act of fate", "it shouldn't have happened", "I'm sorry for your troubles", just muffled voices, echoes, mumblings, comforting words and sounds, but Rose-Ellen was numb to the core in her heart. Someone propelled her to a waiting car, as she could barely focus on immediate matters, as her heart was heavy with grief. Before stepping in to the car, Finn came over to her.

'God almighty, you didn't deserve this, Rose-Ellen. I'm truly, truly sorry.'

'Oh, Finn, I wish I had been there with him.'

'Ah, it's just one of those freak things in life, most unfortunate.'

'Of all the reasons to die,' she muttered, but it was no use. Nothing would bring Pierre back. He was gone for ever and she was going to have to come to terms with this devastating loss.

Pierre was to be buried at sea off Dun Laoghaire and Rose-Ellen accompanied the many who turned up to pay their last respects at the pier there. It was a dull day, grey and overcast, with the colour and consistency of gloomy mushroom soup. A small crowd of close friends and relatives had already assembled when the hearse purred silently up the pier.

Rose-Ellen thought of the few times she had sailed with Pierre out from this harbour. His body was to be buried at sea as he would have wished. She turned to barrister Joe, who gazed out to sea with all its hidden mysteries and secrets, as the boat left the harbour. 'It's hard to believe that this is the final journey for him,' she said, looking out at the horizon.

'Yes indeed. It almost makes a mockery of life, someone as precious as him dying so absurdly and so many of the bloody wasters of life remaining making no contribution whatsoever,' he said morosely. He then turned to Rose-Ellen. 'In life some are cheated of money and that is unfortunate. But there are others who are cheated of time and that is the greatest tragedy of all. We'll never understand this kind of reasoning; it is beyond me,' he said gravely, and they both watched the heaving tide where Pierre would soon be laid to rest within its silent depths, off into some kind of infinity unknown. Rose-Ellen rarely had thought of death and its finality, but now this moment had brought with it some poignancy and reminded her of the fleeting fragility of life. She felt oppressed by the enormity of Pierre's loss as she cast a white rose into the great depths as the coffin slid under the furling tide.

Finn accompanied Rose-Ellen and Olivia to the airport. 'I don't want to go back without him, but I must. My life is there now; so much depending on me,' Rose-Ellen said, sniffling into a tissue.

Finn gave her a big hug. 'Rose-Ellen, what can I say? I thought I had said everything to you when we parted. There is nothing that will compensate you for this tragic loss except that if things get tough then give me a call; it's always good to talk to somebody.'

'Thanks, Finn, it's good to know that.' She dried her eyes.

He seemed to relax a little. 'If you need any help, let me know. Running one's own business has its advantages too.'

'What do you mean?'

'I'm in the security business now; set up on my own and I can work from anywhere with my laptop. Oh yes, lots of changes since I saw you last. I'm also engaged to a nice girl called Cliodhna.' He sounded confident and positive; gone was the old cautious Finn. She looked at him now. Strange how he had changed with an air of authority she had not noticed before.

'Thanks, Finn, you're very kind.'

'Forgive me for saying this, Rose-Ellen, and maybe it doesn't seem appropriate under the circumstances, but here I am again with a girl I have never quite forgotten. I won't say any more because my heart and thoughts would run away with me so I'll leave it at that. Go safely, pet, and mind yourself,' he said, kissing her on the forehead, and he watched as she walked over to the security line.

As Rose-Ellen slowly made her way down the lonely corridor of the airport to the departure gate to take the plane to La Rochelle, she sobbed continuously with an unbearable grief and held Olivia's hand. She could hardly stand on the moving walkway, and at one stage had to hold on to the rails, such was her sense of loss. She almost turned back rather than face the future in France, but demurred as Olivia held her close. She sat down on a chair at the departure gate and pulled out one of the few photos she carried of Pierre and cried her heart out.

'Oh, Olivia, I keep thinking it's all only a dream.'

As Olivia held Rose-Ellen's hand, she wondered how her sister would get through the next few months on her own.

Chapter 61

Time passed and Rose-Ellen struggled to cope with *Chez-Ellen* and *Avalene*. Little things reminded her of Pierre; the photograph of both of them taken on the pier in La Rochelle, healthy young things having spent a day sailing, his scent and the gentle way he came behind like a cat and kissed her on the cheek as she prepared supper. Pierre left few possessions which went to the local charity shop and with them the memories. She wept inconsolably into his perfectly ironed, crisp shirts hanging in the wardrobe before parting with them. His great-grandmother's beautiful engagement ring, his telescope and selection of cufflinks she gave to his sister Catherine. Rose-Ellen could not bear to change the sheets in the bed where she and Pierre had last slept together, and kept one of his cashmere jumpers in bed close to her chest, hugging and weeping in to it. She wanted to savour his smell, his shape and mostly to remember their tender moments together in this bed which held memories of all their spent energy, their tiredness and mostly the love and hope they shared.

Getting through that winter was difficult, but after spring she felt more energetic. Olivia and Brendan were married at Easter and that at least had been something which had kept Rose-Ellen's spirits up. Olivia looked lovely and radiant on her wedding day, dressed in a simple cream silk dress and Kitty's laced veil. Rose-Ellen cried when she turned round and saw Olivia walk up the aisle on Maurice's arm in the small local church. That evening Rose-Ellen took her beautiful young sister aside. 'Dear Olivia, I'm so happy for you. Brendan's the salt of the earth. Mam would be very proud today.'

Olivia reached over and touched Rose-Ellen's gloved hand. 'I know she would. She would have loved all of the banter and wedding stuff. I'd love if she could have been here, but at least we have each other and that's important.'

'Yes of course.' Rose-Ellen looked at her sister through a coil of gold net covering the top part of her face, giving her a strange sense of allure. She wished she could have been wearing that veil and dress instead of her baby sister and that the day could have been hers. But it was not to be.

Later that night as she had a glass of whiskey with Maurice, she felt an overwhelming desire to settle down and raise a family. This thought seized her like a vice grip and she could barely stir the lemon in her father's hot whiskey.

'Are ye all right, pet?' Maurice asked leaning forward stiffly on the heavy armchair.

'I am, Dad. I just wish Mam were here to witness the day.'

'Ah, she would have loved it all. Well here's to Olivia and Brendan.' She supposed he did not really understand her mood or sadness as he moved into his own silent world of the past.

Back in France, Rose-Ellen tried not to think of what should have been as the business took up all her energy. People everywhere were kind and considerate and did not intrude into her privacy but at times the loneliness in France was overwhelming. She cried herself to sleep most nights while reflecting on the type of life which would now elude her because of a freak bus accident. 'If only he had kept to the kerb; if only that bus conductor had been more careful,' Rose-Ellen said, over and over to herself like a mantra. These permutations and possibilities circled her head until she could take no more.

One night, after a few drinks, she called Finn. 'Hello, Finn, it's me. I'm just so bloody lonely. I hope you don't mind me calling, but I had to talk to somebody. I miss Pierre terribly. I feel awful phoning you and loading all of my cares and woes on you like this, but I need to talk to somebody.'

There was a slight pause at the other end and she wondered if he wanted to hear from her at all. 'Of course, Rose-Ellen. I can imagine how difficult it must be now without Pierre. I don't know how you did it. I mean going back out to France after losing him. You're a great girl!'

She started to cry. 'Oh, Finn, I'm thinking I'll come home. I just can't go on like this. It's just too damn hard.'

'Now, pet, take it easy. Don't do anything rash. You've been through a terrible ordeal, but your life is out in France now; that is where you have put your stake so to speak. Rose-Ellen, what can I say? I mean, I can't alter the terrible past and what's happened. God knows, you've had a rough time of it.'

She briefly regretted having phoned him. 'Is it convenient to talk?' she asked him tentatively.

'I'd always find time to talk to you, Rose-Ellen. You know that.' She relaxed upon hearing his soothing words.

'I, I just find it hard to concentrate and be nice and polite and smile all the time when my heart is breaking underneath.'

'Jesus, I wish I were beside you now so that I could give you a big hug and tell you to hang in there and not to despair. Time is a great leveller and healer.' He spoke slowly and authoritatively. 'I'm sorry, pet. I feel ridiculous now saying this kind of stock remark, but it's hard to think of anything else to say, but I genuinely do feel for you right now.'

'If you ever want to come out and stay you are more than welcome,' her voice was quaking with emotion.

'Well that's very nice of you and we might take you up on the offer,' he said.

She had forgotten. Finn, her link with the past, was going to be married.

'I know you'd like Cliodhna. She's a great girl, strong and feisty, a bit like yourself.'

'Bring Cliodhna along. After all, it's a lovely part of France and more so in summer. You know you're always welcome here.'

'It'd be nice to see what changes you've done to the place.'

'Oh, Finn, if you do come, you'll see all the changes.'

Chapter 62

Finn fixed dodgy shutters and loose bolts around *Chez-Ellen* and painted the dirty green and grey wall over by the dovecote a sparkling white. Rose-Ellen went over and gave him a big hug. 'Finn, it hasn't been much of a break for you.'

'I just couldn't bear the thought of you here struggling on your own.'

That night after dinner in *Avalene*, a group of Italians sat around the fire in the large room over coffees. One of them thrummed a doleful tune on a guitar. Finn soon got chatting to them and before long Rose-Ellen could hear his familiar voice singing the beautiful song *Carrickfergus* as he delicately picked on the guitar strings.

The other guests were spellbound. She stole in to the room and sat listening to him. She wondered why she had never really taken any notice before of his musicality and supposed that she had been just too busy and bound up in her own selfish world. She watched Finn as he adjusted the various keys on the instrument. Finally he stood up and burst into a hearty rendition of *Santa Lucia* to the amazement of all. The Italians cheered and clapped him. When he had finished and was about to leave, Rose-Ellen came over to him and whispered, 'That was lovely Finn. I never really appreciated how musical you were.'

He winked and said, 'I'm a man full of hidden talents, Rose-Ellen and if I'd the time…ah,' and he stopped.

'Well go on,' she said impatiently.

'It doesn't really matter now, does it?'

The day before he was due to leave for Ireland, Finn and Rose-Ellen were working in the garden and Rose-Ellen moved away some grass grown over the stone that Finn had bought for her.

'So, Finn, when's the big day?' she asked.

'We haven't decided on a date yet, but it'll be soon, please God.'

'Do you miss them, the fags? I noticed you hadn't smoked all weekend.'

'It was terrible at the beginning. Jesus, the cravings in the middle of the night drove me mad. Cliodhna said she wasn't marrying a smoker, and that was that!'

'I couldn't get you to give them up,' Rose-Ellen said, pruning one of the many roses in *Avalene*.

'No you couldn't. I smoked twice as much when I was with you. Rose-Ellen Power, you'd put anybody's blood pressure up!'

'I don't know what you mean,' she said smirking.

'You bloody well do know what I mean,' he said, and his eyes followed her while she made her way through the rose bed. She put away the *secateurs* into the large pocket in her apron and picked up the clippings. He put out his hand. 'I'm sorry, Rose, I shouldn't have said that, but you know how you affect me.'

'Not any more!'

'I don't know about that.'

'Ah, Finn, stop playing with my emotions,' she said, tapping him gently with one of the cut rose stems.

'The man who gets you will be mighty lucky,' he called, as he wheeled the wheelbarrow to the shed at the side of the house.

Before Finn left to return home he took her in his arms and kissed her. 'For old time's sake.'

She warmed to his kiss, and he pulled her closer to him. 'We shouldn't be doing this.'

She pushed him away. 'Don't Finn! You're going to be married and it's not right, and besides I can't get used to any other kisses but Pierre's.'

'I've never forgotten you, Rose. Do you know that?' She turned away from him and leaned against the large walnut tree. He put his hand through her hair which caught the light in the evening sun. 'Darling, don't cry like this. I hate to see you upset,' he said, taking a stray lock from her face.

She looked up at the soaring branches of the great tree. 'I know, Finn, but if only. Oh what's the point?'

He took her hand. 'If only you and I could be together. Is that what you are thinking?' He looked at her intensely.

'It doesn't really matter what I am thinking,' she said, picking off a dead twig from the mighty tree.

Later that night before Finn went to back to his *auberge*, he said to her, 'Look, I hope you don't mind me asking and maybe you think I'm being a bit cheeky, but would you mind if we dropped in on our way down south to the Spanish border? I promised Cliodhna I'd take her to France by car.'

'Do you think it's a good idea?'

'It'll just be a quick stop to say hello.'

'Why not,' she said, shrugging her shoulders as if indifferent. Finn had his own world now with his fiancée Cliodhna, and Rose-Ellen realised that she had to distance herself from any kind of involvement, however remote, otherwise she was just going to be hurt.

The summer at *Avalene* was hectic as the rooms were packed every night with guests from Malaga to northern Sweden. The silences of Rose-Ellen's life were filled with the sound of eager and delighted tourists, strangers mostly.

Winter came and went and *Avalene* continued to prosper under the careful eye of Rose-Ellen. On Easter Sunday she called Olivia who was now expecting her first baby.

'How are things?' Rose-Ellen said.

'Great, I am starting to feel tiny kicks.'

Rose-Ellen wondered if she would ever share the joy of having a child, but at nearly thirty years of age she began to wonder. 'Ah, I'm thrilled, it's a great healthy sign. It means life is there. And how's the morning sickness?'

'Oh, that seems to have gone, but now I have terrible cravings for Chinese food. Poor Brendan has to go out late at night and bring me takeaways.'

Chapter 63

Some months later one evening, a car purred up the avenue of *Avalene*. Rose-Ellen went outside and wondered who it was as nobody else had made reservations for the night. Now she would have to get another room ready as she hated turning people away. She was about to move back into the house when she heard someone shout her name, and turned around.

Finn took off the shades, stepped out of the car and approached Rose-Ellen with open arms. He looked well in a crisp white shirt and smartly cut grey denims, and designer sunglasses. 'Great to see you, Rose,' he said, giving her a big hug.

'Finn, what on earth are you doing here?'

'Let's go inside and I'll tell you all.'

They chatted together as they linked arms and she showed him the new herb garden which she was building to the side of *Avalene*. After a while, as the sun went down, they sat out on the sunny patio at the back as both caught up on the news over a glass of champagne. Inevitably the conversation came round to why he was here.

'Well, it's like this, pet. I broke off my engagement.'

'What? But I thought…Oh, Finn, I'm so sorry, I really am,' she said, reaching out and holding his hand. She could hardly make sense of what he was saying.

'Now I didn't come here to talk about myself. I want to know how you are and how you are coping.'

'Ah, just getting by. I try to keep busy as otherwise my mind would start to think of another life – a life with Pierre. I keep wondering what things would be like now if he were here. I mean, if only that bus had veered another half a foot out of the kerb. I know it's pointless, but I can't come to terms with how a life, especially one as important as his, can be just snuffed out like that.'

'Who knows, Rose-Ellen, why these things happen? You can't keep going over what life would be like if A had happened and B hadn't. You're only torturing yourself and it's a terrible waste of energy. Look, I know this sounds cold, but what happened, happened, and you cannot change anything. You have to move on.'

'And to think that McAdam is at large out there somewhere!' she said, banging her fist on the small table.

'There's an extradition warrant out for that bastard for another link with a murder so it's only a matter of time before he is behind bars. He was up to his neck in every possible vice from murder and fraud to selling fake drugs on the internet.' He looked out on to the beautifully manicured garden at *Avalene*. 'It's hard to be on the run for ever. Something will slip; he'll get slack. That's the way these scumbags like McAdam end up. It's their undoing in the end. He should have been locked up years ago and the key thrown away,' Finn said.

Rose-Ellen felt like crying and wondered at the justification of such happenings. But she knew that she had to move on and not dwell on the past and all its shadows.

That night she cooked dinner for both of them in the large kitchen in *Avalene* after the guests had finished. 'It's like old times, Finn. I know I shouldn't say this to you, agh......it doesn't matter,' and she got up and turned to leave the room. He followed her out.

'What were you going to say?' he asked.

'Ah, nothing really. I remember the fights and quarrels with Danny before we broke up. Oh, I'm sorry, Finn for all you've been through and the break up of your engagement. You must be really upset. It's a difficult time for you and I can understand that you want some space,' Rose-Ellen said.

'Thanks, love. It's hard to talk about it as it's so intimate and only involves the two people.'

'I know what it was like after I lost Pierre; it was very, very difficult. Oh, people were kind and they meant well, but it's you, just you, who has to get on with your own life,' she said, bringing out the desserts. She started to cry and Finn came round and stroked the back of her neck.

'It's hard, I know it is, love, but that's life and its unpredictability.'

They sat back and finished their desserts. 'Sometimes I can't believe he's gone, Finn, gone forever. It just seems so unreal; the whole frightening accident,' Rose-Ellen said, spooning up the last of the ruby-red pomegranate dessert from its tall glass. She was glad that she had added a few tablespoons of rosewater to it as she could still savour the aftermath scent of roses on her lips. 'But I have to move on and that's the hardest bit; letting go of the past and thinking of what my life and his would have been like had he lived. My mind was haunted by memories since his death, but I've reached the stage of acceptance that he will never be coming back.'

They stayed up together and talked for hours in to the morning over a few brandies. Rose-Ellen had not really spoken to anybody so intimately since Pierre's death and found herself opening up to Finn in ways she had not dreamt. He was kind and listened to her and she liked the way he put her at ease.

'By letting go of the past, letting go of your memories of Pierre, you will have a new lease of life, a new kind of freedom. Whether we like it or not, irrespective of our circumstances, life moves on and passes us by and we are left in a state of the unknown. The old tried and tested is gone and we are in a world of uncertainties, and I suppose that is where you are at the moment Rose-Ellen and it possibly scares you a little bit. God almighty, stop me if I'm ranting on. I probably sound like a priest.'

'Oh, Finn, you are so right. It's the only way. I mean letting go, otherwise I'll never take a risk or face the new challenges that running a business here and indeed surviving is all about. But it is so hard at times and the most difficult thing to come to terms with is the fact that he died in such a ridiculous way and was so young. He wasn't even thirty-five!' She reached out and touched his hand. 'But thanks for being so understanding, Finn. It means a lot to me.' That was something she had always liked about Finn O'Donnell, and was glad that they had time together to reminisce about old times.

The next day they managed to snatch time for a walk together by the river, but that evening Rose-Ellen had to give her full attention to a group of wine *connoisseurs* from Bergerac who were staying at *Avalene*. She had promised that she would reserve the following few days for Finn who was only here for a short break.

On Saturday they took a picnic down by the river, Chantal having insisted that she would look after the wine group that afternoon. Rose-Ellen linked Finn who carried the picnic basket. When they arrived at the bridge Rose-Ellen leaned over it and looked at the slowly meandering water that curled and gurgled underneath. 'You know, Finn, I simply love this river. I can't explain it. It's so beautiful. Always the same, loving, restful, free-flowing water. When I look down from here I wonder what secrets it holds. It has seen me sad and happy, in all my various moods,' she said, recalling the night she heard of Pierre's death.

'We all have our secrets, some we even take to the grave with us. Rose-Ellen you look so lovely there. Just watching you lean over the bridge; you're as pretty as a picture.'

'You're an awful flatterer, Finn!' she said, laughing and then turning on her back to look up at the sky. At that moment Finn put down the picnic basket, leaned across and gently kissed her on the lips. It seemed the most natural thing to do.

'I've wanted to do that for months,' he said, and kissed her again.

'That brought back all the warmth I felt for you and could feel for you again,' she said, and put her arms around him.

He lifted her up on to the bridge and said, 'Now make a wish.'

She closed her eyes and said, 'Done. I've made a wish. What about you?'

'Oh, I've made mine. I've only one wish, Rose-Ellen.'

'And what's that, Finn?'

'Now come on down there, and let's go further along the river to have a bite to eat.' They walked on together hand in hand, wherever the footpaths trailed under the trees. 'Take it easy, Rose. You don't have to decide anything. Just follow me from now on,' he said, and curled his arm around her.

They had a quiet restful weekend together during which Finn helped out in *Avalene* as much as possible. Several times during the weekend Rose-Ellen thought about the kiss on the bridge and how secure she felt in Finn's arms, and wanted to re-live that sweet, tender, moment in her mind again. After all it was a long time since she had been kissed.

Finn and Rose-Ellen were to have supper together on the Monday night. He arrived early bearing an enormous bunch of beautiful flowers and a bottle of excellent red wine. He was due to fly back home tomorrow.

The big, heavy side door to *Avalene* was already open so he let himself in and made for the kitchen.

'Hi, darling. Em, smells delicious,' he murmured.

Tasting the sauce on a wooden spoon, Rose-Ellen turned with a look of surprise.

'Finn, I wasn't expecting you so soon!'

He was smiling, came over and drew her to him, and kissed her. He then reached behind her and turned off the gas. 'Some things can wait,' he whispered, and taking her by the wrist led her to the other room where the fire was blazing. Finn stood by the mantelpiece, his elbow resting on the ledge. Rose-Ellen sat on the sofa and looked at him.

'To be perfectly honest, I came out here with one thing on my mind and that was to tell you how I feel about you.'

Rose-Ellen wondered what he was going to say. 'Finn, you've only just broken off your engagement and you're on the rebound. Isn't that likely?' she said.

'Not really. I broke off the engagement because I didn't feel that deeply about the person; that's it! I couldn't imagine spending the rest of my life with her. Is that such a crime? The same old feelings for you just won't go away, Rose-Ellen. Maybe I shouldn't have come out here again, but it's like this. I had to.' He moved away from the mantelpiece and started to pace the room. 'Oh, my friends thought me mad, foolish, naïve, coming out here seeking disaster.' He stopped and stared at her. 'And maybe I am. But love is strange and dark and unpredictable.' He scrutinised her as she sat there gazing into the fire. 'You know you look lovelier than ever sitting there. That same slightly wistful expression I've seen before,' he said. He came over and sat beside her, and took her hands in his. 'What I'm saying is that I still have those old feelings for you. They are always there.'

She put her head in her hands. 'Oh, Finn, stop it. This is ridiculous and you know it.' But he was on his knees in front of her.

'I don't care about anything else right now. I'll ask you one more time, Rose-Ellen. If you'll marry me, I'll make you the happiest woman on this earth, and if you say no, then that's it, I will never, ever see you again.'

She looked at him, his face eager with expectation. She realised that she did care deeply for Finn and had always had a special place in her heart for him. Calmly and deliberately she said, 'I've been unkind to you, Finn and sometimes I was blinded by my own selfish desires to succeed and to suit myself, but I have always had a special corner for you in my heart.' She took a deep breath. 'I realise that when you were here with me I did love you, if that is possible to believe. Oh, I know it sounds crazy, but please believe me. When you left and went out of my life, I was devastated. There were days when I wanted to ring you, to hear your voice, your assurance, but my pride, my stupid pride wouldn't allow me. And then there was the business always getting in the way of emotions and love. When I went home for Olivia's wedding I felt sad and isolated and I began to think of my own life and where it was heading. I wondered if I would end up forlorn and alone in my old age, and then as the months went by I became slowly resigned to this fate. I suppose that's what weddings do to us single girls; make us broody and hanker after commitment and bonding.'

'That's perfectly understandable and natural,' he whispered, bending down to kiss her hand.

'Oh, Finn, I don't know what to say. It's all so sudden and...'

His expression softened and he took her hands in his, turned them up and kissed the palms. She wanted to put her hands through his soft silvery hair and tell him how she longed for him to take her in his arms and to make love to her like in the past.

Finn held her close and she felt a deep sense of contentment, something she had not felt for some time. 'My love, my own lovely Rose. I have loved you from the day I set eyes on you, and there would never have been anybody else, even if Pierre had lived and I had married someone else. It sounds selfish, and maybe you don't believe me, but that's how I feel.'

'You can't begin to believe how lonely I've been. Nothing to live for or hope for, and nowhere to go. Every day the same ding-dong; the relentless demands of running my own business.' She was crying now, crying and laughing with joy and happiness.

'So, Rose-Ellen, what's your answer?'

She stopped laughing and looked seriously at him. 'Yes, oh yes, Finn,' she said, barely able to take a breath.

He was kissing her now, madly and passionately. 'There, there, my love. I can't tell you how happy you make me. I'm overjoyed with happiness,' and he got up and took her in his arms and kissed her long and hard until the fire's great flames became mere embers.

As Rose-Ellen closed the shutters of *Avalene* that night and mounted the stairs to bed with Finn, the church bells struck the hour and watching the night owls fly and perch silently among the soaring pines, she thought about their future, a future full of hope and promise.

She lay beside Finn in bed after he had spent himself declaring his love over and over to her, kissing, touching and tenderly loving her and assuring her how he had never wanted anybody else. They had stayed talking till the early hours, Finn reminiscing about his life, Rose-Ellen intrigued by each minute detail which became more alive with the telling. She looked at him now in the dim light of morning, lying on his back and pondered on their future.

Sitting up at the first spear of light, she lifted her head and kissed him gently on his half-open mouth. She who had come close to losing almost everything was now back again with Finn O'Donnell, her trusted friend and lover. As she kissed him once more she lay back and fell asleep in his arms. A sleep that dipped into dreams of fears and longings, until she woke to a new dawn of hope and renewal.

Acknowledgements

I would like to thank the following people for their help in getting the book to final stage: Keith Dixon for a first draft edit; Ali Reynolds and Mark Comisini of SilverWood Books for a thorough and professional final draft polish and proofread; Dorothy Podmore for her keen eye, observant and critical appraisal; Pippa Meehan who came up with the apt title *Cross-Currents*; Avril Price Gallagher, artist, for original watercolours from which the jacket design was developed.